Frozen
Past

Frozen Past

By

Richard C Hale

This book is a work of fiction. Names, characters, places and incidents are either the product of the author's imagination or are used fictitiously. Any resemblance to actual persons, living or dead, or to actual events or locales is entirely coincidental.

For Lynn, Who Has Always Been My Hero

Please Visit the Author's Website at:

http://www.richardchaleauthor.com

Richard always answers e-mails. Drop by the website and say 'Hello!'

ACKNOWLEDGMENTS

First, I'd like to thank my wonderful wife and family. If not for their support, I may never have had the courage to continue on the journey. They inspire me in everything they do and my life would be incomplete without them. Thank you.

Special thanks to my readers: Kin Daniels, Amanda Hale, Dianne Hale, Tanya Christensen, Doug Blair, Mark Brown, and Chuck Barrett. Your wisdom and insight helped shape the story and keep me on the path.

Those who know me have heard me tell the tale of the frozen pool. Though the event was real in my childhood, what follows is a work of fiction and this author has taken it beyond anything that has happened in real life. For that I am thankful. I would not wish this tale upon anyone. If you would like to read the inspiration for the story, visit my website at www.richardchaleauthor.com.

Books by Richard C Hale

Near Death

Near Sighted

Frozen Past

Cache 72

Father Figure

Blank

Blank 2

Blank 3

Blank 4

Blank 5

Blank 6

Short Stories

The Camera

Flash Mob

The Sandbar

Part 1

Richard C Hale

PROLOGUE

Stewy Littleton had stayed out too late.

He didn't know what happened or why he'd lost track of time, he just knew his mother was going to kill him. That was a certainty. In the whole of his twelve year old life, he'd never been this late.

His costume was torn at one shoulder and the bag of candy he carried was much too small for all the time he'd been out, so he knew his mother would know what he'd been up to. He would have some serious explaining to do.

This was his last Halloween, the last time he would be allowed to roam the neighborhoods scaring the little kids and loading up on free candy. He was getting too old. He had wanted to make it the best Halloween ever. Now he'd had too much fun and was going to pay for it.

He grinned to himself even though he knew he was in trouble. It had been worth it. His black outfit and white mask had made him almost impossible to see on the moonless night, at least until he'd wanted to be seen. The best part had been when he'd jumped out from behind a tree and made the little five year old kid dressed up as Spiderman pee his pants. A grown man probably would have screamed.

The eggs he'd stolen out of the fridge hadn't lasted very long, but Old Lady Whitney had gotten splattered by one when Stewy plastered her door as she opened it. The little kids waiting for her to give them candy had screamed and sprinted off. He laughed so hard he thought for sure she had heard him.

Now, as he made his way through the dark empty streets, he tried to come up with an excuse. Everything his little mind thought of would not stand up to his mother's questions and he began to realize he'd just have to live with whatever happened. He'd probably get put on restriction for a couple of weeks with no TV and no friends. Hopefully she would let him keep the candy.

"Help me…"

Stewy froze.

The sound came from the bushes to his right. He waited and listened. It was so quiet. Nothing moved or made a sound. Maybe he had imagined it. As he took another step toward home, the voice came again, a little louder.

"Help me…"

Stewy knew he wasn't imagining it now. Somebody was definitely there, but it was so faint. The voice was weird and he couldn't tell if it was a girl or a boy. It was like a whispered croak. A whispered croak of pain.

"Who are you?" Stewy said softly, bent over, trying to see into the gloom of the hedge.

"Help me…"

The voice rasped the two words together like dry paper.

Stewy shivered as a cold finger of fear ran up his spine. The voice was directly in front of him, but he could see nothing. He looked left, right, and then licked his lips not sure what to do. He waited a whole minute frozen there but nothing happened. His whole body listened, trying to hear the faintest sound, straining against the darkness and silence that pressed up against him.

He finally said, "I can't see you. Where are you?"

The voice didn't answer. Nothing moved, nothing made a sound. Stewy stood up straight, looked left and right again, and was about to take a step when the voice came again.

"Help me…please."

Now the voice sounded different. Not so much in pain, but maybe a little like it was making fun of him. Stewy did not like it. In fact, he wanted to run.

"Please…help."

"I can't help you if I can't see you," Stewy said, his voice shaking. "Where are you?"

"Right here." the voice said, louder, a little titter of laughter trailing off at the end.

Stewy frowned in puzzlement and he leaned in closer to the hedge, taking a step toward it. An arm shot out from inside the bushes and grabbed him by the hair. It yanked him hard into the hedge as a searing pain shot through Stewy's scalp. He opened his mouth to scream but a large sweaty hand clamped over it, smashing his lips against his teeth, his scream a muffled gag as he was pinned to the ground.

The hand came away and was immediately replaced with a rag that covered his mouth and nose. It smelled like some chemical. He didn't want to breathe, but he couldn't help it. The world he knew began to spin and then Stewy's last Halloween blinked out like a switch.

CHAPTER 1

Luke Harrison knelt and packed the rectangular block of snow tightly against the previous block, making the wall he was building about six feet long.

"That's enough, isn't it?" Luke said.

"Yeah. That should do it," Jimmy Besner said. Jimmy was the oldest of the three teenage boys and it usually fell to him to make the decisions.

Jimmy's brother, John, looked it over and said, "I don't know? Looks lopsided over here."

"It's fine," Jimmy said.

"I can't make any more anyway," Luke said. "My hands are freezing."

"Start making snowballs, then," John said. "We didn't have near enough last time."

"Why do I always have to make the snowballs? You guys never make 'em."

"You're the youngest. You make the snowballs," Jimmy stated matter-of-factly.

Luke cursed under his breath, but did what he was told. He also knew he was the best at it and this was why he always got the job.

He could barely feel his fingers, even with the mittens on, and he blew into his hands trying to get some feeling back. It had been an unusually cold winter for Annandale, Virginia, but the plus had been lots of snow, and lots of snow days from school. Ninth grade was a pain and Luke hated it, so any chance to get out of it was the best thing that could happen.

John came and knelt next to Luke and began making snowballs with him. Jimmy stood watch. The attack would be coming soon. They needed to be ready.

The three of them had been in a constant war with the kids from Willow Branch Court, two blocks to the north. It was their turn to defend and so far the contest was tied. Two battles apiece. The problem was the kids from Willow Branch outnumbered them five to three. Luke didn't care, he was better at throwing than all five of the attackers put together. They never even considered it unfair; it was just the way it was.

The pile of snowballs grew to a decent number, but Luke knew they needed more. He hurried to make as many as he could, but then Jimmy yelled, "Here they come!" and jumped down behind the wall. He began forming snowballs and adding them to the pile as quickly as he could.

Peering over the top of the wall, Luke got a good look at their opposition. He cursed.

"Crap! They have a wagon full. We're gonna get killed."

"Just 'cause they have more doesn't mean they're any better than last time," Jimmy said. "Now get down and make more."

Luke started forming snowballs as fast as his frozen hands would let him.

"Do we make the special ones?" John asked.

Jimmy paused for a second and said, "No. Paul got stitches last time. We fight fair."

The 'special ones' were snowballs with ice in the middle. They were very fast and highly accurate, but could put a serious hurt on someone. Namely, Paul Bannon.

Paul started it by getting the Willow Branch kids to make a few and Jimmy was hit in his throwing arm, causing it to go numb. Luke, Jimmy, and John lost that battle.

To get back at them, Jimmy made some for the next battle, and the three targeted Paul with the special snowballs. One nailed him right in the face. Paul ran home screaming with blood running down his chin and had to go to the emergency room where he received seven stitches. It was agreed upon after that, no one would use ice balls any more. This was supposed to be fun, after all.

Luke peeked over the wall again. "They're splitting up."

Jimmy stood and watched for a second. "All right. Enough. We don't have time for more. The wagon and three of them are moving toward our left, so John, you cover the right side, and me and Luke will cover the left. Make 'em count."

The rules were simple, the team with the most hits won. If you were defending, you were not allowed out from behind your barrier. If you were attacking, you could basically do anything you wanted. There were no referees, so the teams had to agree upon the winner after the battle, and this sometimes resulted in a shouting match over who the victor was. The honor system worked for the most part, but kids will be kids.

If you made a kid cry, the battle was over automatically, and the team with the crybaby lost. Because of this rule, both teams worked hard at making somebody bawl.

Two premature snowballs sailed over their heads and Luke grinned at Jimmy.

"They suck!"

Jimmy laughed as he hefted two snowballs in his hands. "Ready?"

Luke nodded. "Yep," John said.

"Now!"

All three stood as one and picked their targets. Luke saw Patrick Pemberton struggling with the wagon in the drifts of snow and aimed for his face. The first shot went wide right, but his second caught him in the neck. Patrick abandoned the wagon and ran for cover behind a tree a couple of feet away.

"One!" Luke yelled.

A snowball whizzed over his head, and he ducked down and grabbed two more. Jimmy knelt down and was hit in the top of his head as he grabbed for more.

The other team yelled, "One!"

John yelled, "Two!" and then a second later, "Three!" and started laughing.

Snowballs were flying in all directions and it was hard for Luke to stay up for more than a second or two. Jimmy was whipping his arm in a frenzy, and John couldn't stop laughing. Luke caught a slushy one in the chin. His face stung but he didn't care. He pegged Patrick twice more and he and Jimmy hit Alan Grimes at the same time. They both yelled "Twelve!" together, then Luke grinned and yelled "Thirteen!"

The pile of snowballs was shrinking and Jimmy told Luke to make more. The wagon the other team had was still half full but lay in the open, stuck in the drifts. The other team had to break cover to get to their hoard, and every time they did someone would get pelted. Luke's team was leading thirteen to seven.

Luke started scraping the ground. Dirt was showing in places and Luke couldn't leave the cover of the wall for more snow. He shifted over to the right to dig deeper and began frantically scraping snow into a pile.

"I'm out!" John yelled.

"Take some of mine," Jimmy yelled, tossing his brother a few. "Come on Luke!"

"There's hardly any snow left!" Luke said. "I'm trying!"

A snowball bounced off the top of the wall and skipped into Luke's hair. He didn't even notice. He was forming snow into balls as fast as he could and when his pile was gone he knelt next to John and started digging near the right side of the wall. The Willow Branch boys were gaining on them and he heard them shout out 'Eleven!' as Jimmy cursed and spat snow from his mouth.

"Damn that hurt!"

Luke reached out beyond the wall and scooped snow into his side. A snowball whizzed past his head. He scraped another armful and something caught his eye. It looked like tan carpet or somebody's discarded dirty coat buried in the snow. He scraped another armful toward him, uncovering more of the buried object, which now looked like fur and what Luke thought might be a red collar.

He stopped and stared, not sure what to do. The battle seemed to fade into the background as his arm took on a life of its own, reaching toward the matted, dirty fur. He carefully scraped away some more and then stood, horrified. A snowball smacked into the side of his face and then he vomited all over the white snow as Patrick Pemberton yelled, "Twelve!"

CHAPTER 2

Eliana Pemberton cried into her pillow wondering when the ache in her chest would stop.

Bentley, her two year old poodle mix and best friend in the world, was missing, and no one in the neighborhood had seen him. She put flyers up on every lamp post, knocked on every door, and searched relentlessly in all the places she knew he loved. He had disappeared, and she blamed herself.

Two years ago, it had taken quite a bit of begging and pleading for her mom to finally give in and let her have the dog. She promised no one else would have to take care of him, swearing she'd be the one to housebreak him, cleaning up after his messes. Her mother actually said she was proud of how Eliana stuck to her promise, even when Bentley was sick and having diarrhea, even when he cried at night the first week, and especially when her brother threatened to drown the dog after he chewed up his favorite shoes.

Eliana paid for new ones herself with her babysitting money. Two weeks of cleaning up after the Harris' twins had been a nightmare, but Bentley had been worth it.

And now, one little lapse in attention, one moment of laziness, and everything she'd done in the past meant nothing. All the devotion and attention wasted and tossed away because she hadn't wanted her feet to get cold. She hated herself and sobbed even harder as she thought of the last time she had seen him.

The snow had just fallen new and white, and Bentley needed to go. She had just gotten her PJs on when he whined at the back door.

"Bent, no. You just went. It's cold now," she said, and he cocked his head the way he always did at the sound of her voice, but then scratched at the door and whined again. She sighed and walked over as he wagged his tail and yipped at her, seeming to smile. He was so cute it was hard for her to stay irritated at him.

"All right, but I'm staying in. It's too cold and I don't have any shoes."

He cocked his head again, his ears perking up as she unlocked the back door and held it open. He took a few steps into the icy night and then stopped, waiting for her. He never went out by himself.

"No—you go. I'll wait right here. Now hurry up."

She shooed at him with her hand and he got the point. She watched him make his way through the snow and ice, sniffing here and there, but taking his time.

"Bentley, come on! Hurry up! It's freezing!"

He looked up once as she hugged herself against the cold and shivered, then he trotted off around the corner of the house into the dark as if on a mission.

"Bentley, no! Stay in the back yard! Bentley!"

That was the last time she ever saw him.

They searched for over an hour with flashlights, but found nothing. It was as if he just up and vanished. They followed his footsteps in the new fallen snow to the front of the house where they disappeared into a row of bushes and never emerged again.

Her mom couldn't figure it out. It was as if someone picked him up and flew off with him. She waited all night by the back door so that when he found his way home, she would be there for him, but he never came back and she eventually dozed off sitting up against the door.

Now, as she cried harder, she hated herself for abandoning him. If only she'd put her shoes on and gone out with him on the leash, she'd be hugging him to her right now while he licked her face and rolled over to get his tummy scratched. She missed him so much.

She heard the front door slam shut and then her loser brother, Patrick, yelled up from the bottom of the stairs, "Ellie! I found your stupid dog!"

She couldn't believe her ears.

"Bentley!" she shouted as she jumped up from her bed and bounded down the steps. Her brother stood at the base of the stairs with a wicked grin on his face, but she was too excited to question it.

"Bentley! Where is he?"

Her mom came into the hall from the kitchen, drying her hands on a towel. "You found the dog?" she said to Patrick.

He nodded, still grinning.

"Where is he?" Ellie asked, almost pleading.

"He's over on Cotton Court," Patrick said.

Ellie made a move for the door, but her mother grabbed her arm. "Hold on a sec', hon. Why didn't you bring him home?"

Patrick's grin grew and he glanced at Ellie and then his mother.

"I couldn't move him," he said.

"What do you mean?" his mother said warily.

Ellie felt something in her stomach lurch. She grabbed her brother's arm tight and said with a voice that sounded far away, "What's wrong with him?"

Her brother continued to grin but said nothing.

Ellie bolted for the door, bursting out into the morning cold and snow in just her PJs and socks. She ran as fast as she could, her feet numb from the snow and tears streaming back into her hair as she fought back the panic rising in her throat. Her mother's voice chased her down the street, but Ellie was too fast and nothing would have stopped her anyway. Cotton Court was up ahead.

* * *

Jimmy and John stood staring at what was left of the dog while Luke scraped snow over the vomit with his shoe. He didn't want to look at the headless dog any more even though he had little left to throw up. He'd seen worse in his short life and it wasn't that he couldn't handle some cut up animal, but he knew this dog and knew its owner. In fact, Ellie Pemberton was someone very special to him. And Bentley had been pretty cool, too.

"Crap," Luke said. "Why did someone do this to Bentley?"

Jimmy and John knew the dog, too, and shook their heads slowly in unison, like they were watching some demented tennis match.

"I want to know WHO did this," Jimmy said. "'Cause when I find out..." His voice trailed off as his fists clenched and unclenched in his gloves. It was so quiet, the leather squeaked as his fingers squeezed.

The other boys had left and Patrick Pemberton had gone home to tell his sister. Luke had seen the glint in his eye and knew he would not be gentle with the news. Had Luke known exactly what Patrick was going to do, he would have never let him go alone. Luke couldn't understand the huge difference between Patrick and his sister, Ellie. It was like night and day.

Luke caught movement out of the corner of his eye and turned to see a harried and distraught Ellie lurching through the snow toward them.

"Oh crap!" he said, and hurried to cut her off. John and Jimmy moved in front of the frozen Bentley to block her view.

"Ellie! No!" Luke said grabbing her shoulders and stopping her from getting any closer.

Her face was pale except for two red spots high on her cheeks. Her breath came in gasps and she was trembling beneath his hands.

"Lucas Harrison, you get out of my way!" she said, trying to look past him.

"No," Luke said, and he shook her shoulders once. "Look at me."

She wouldn't at first and struggled a bit in his grasp, then her lip trembled and her eyes went to his. As she saw what was in them, she dropped her head to his shoulder, clutched at his coat and sobbed, "No!"

He held her that way until her mother came up and took her into her arms.

CHAPTER 3

A week passed since the discovery of Bentley's frozen and decapitated body, and Luke finally stopped having nightmares.

School re-opened and he trudged through each class as the day dragged. Ellie shared two classes with him and he tried talking to her but she was withdrawn and quiet. He understood, he just missed his happy go lucky friend.

On the fourth day after they found the dog, Luke put a small, white, stuffed bear on her locker and watched from a distance as she finally smiled for the first time. She looked around finding him, and she raised it in a salute as her eyes found his, a small glimmer of a smile sneaking across her lips. He knew then she would be all right.

Ellie's mother had called the police and they came out and looked around, inspecting the dog's carcass and hauling it away. They promised they would follow up but they told the Pembertons it had probably been some kids. The one detective had eyed Luke's little group of boys as he said this, but didn't question any of them. Luke had been pissed that he would silently accuse them just because they were conveniently there. At least Ellie hadn't seen the detective look at him that way. He didn't know if he could handle Ellie blaming him for Bentley.

On Friday, snow started to fall again and they were expecting a blizzard. Hopefully it would snow all weekend and school would be canceled again on Monday. Luke was walking home from the bus stop with Jimmy and John when he saw Ellie sitting on her front step. She hadn't been at school.

"I'll catch up with you guys later," he said, and wandered over to her.

When he got closer he could see she was crying. He stopped short of her porch thinking he should just leave her alone, but then she wiped her face and looked up at him.

"Hey," she said.

"Hey. Missed you in class today. You sick?"

She shook her head. "No, I didn't want to go."

"Me neither. Maybe school will be canceled again on Monday because of the snow."

"Uh huh. I hope it snows hard."

Luke didn't know what to say so he just stood there for a minute as the silence dragged out.

Finally he said, "Whatcha doing?"

"Just watching the snow."

He nodded and the silence went on for a few more seconds. "Are your parents gonna let you get another dog?"

He watched her face fall and realized, too late, what an idiot he was. He tried to backtrack. "I mean, when you're ready. Jeez—I'm sorry Ellie. I didn't mean…"

"I know. It's ok. Come sit by me." She patted the spot next to her and he walked over and sat. "I just don't know right now," she said. "I can't even think of looking at another dog. Maybe it sounds stupid to people, but he was like my best friend. I could never replace him."

Luke nodded. "He was pretty cool."

She was silent for a moment and Luke could actually hear the snow falling. Just a hint of a whisper as the snowflakes fell past his eyes. Ellie had a few flakes stuck to the bangs around her face and he thought she looked like an angel.

"I'm glad you stopped me the other day. I was a little out of my head."

"No problem," he said. "He was…uh, kind of messed up."

She looked about to cry again. "Was he really that bad?"

Luke nodded. "I got sick."

"Oh God—maybe I shouldn't have asked you."

"I'm sorry. I won't say anymore."

"Ok—I don't want to know. They took him away and I won't ever see, so that's good, right?"

"Yeah."

"I'll just remember him the way he was."

Luke looked at the ground thinking he wasn't helping her at all. He didn't know how to talk to her without upsetting her. He felt like a jerk.

She was staring off into the falling snow and a single tear ran down her cheek. He wanted to reach up and brush it away, but was scared, so he just sat and shuffled his feet, not knowing what to do.

"You know," she said, "I blame myself. I let him out all alone and I never do that. It was just cold and I…"

"Ellie, it's not your fault. Somebody else did this to him. You would never hurt Bentley."

"I know, but if I had gone out with him, he wouldn't have run off like that."

"I think whoever did this, would have gotten to him no matter what. I think they were waiting for the right moment."

She turned to him. "Why do you say that?"

"I don't know. Just a feeling, I guess. You said it was like he just disappeared. Somebody had to make it look like he vanished without a trace."

She didn't look convinced.

"So some dog stalker is out there stealing dogs and—and doing stuff to them?"

He shrugged. "I don't know—maybe. Some sicko is out there. Why else would his head be missing?"

Her mouth dropped open and then she made a small cry as her hand went to her lips. She stood abruptly and ran into the house. Luke tried to think of something to say to stop her but he just sat there kicking himself and wondering why he was so stupid. He went to the door and knocked, but no one answered. He was turning to go when the door opened and Mrs. Pemberton said, "Hello, Lucas."

"Hello Mrs. Pemberton. I think I upset Ellie. I wanted to tell her sorry."

She looked back behind her and up the stairs. "I'll tell her for you. I'm sure she'll be ok in a bit."

"Sorry about Bentley," he offered. She nodded once and shut the door.

* * *

Luke climbed the steep driveway to his three story house and concentrated on keeping his footing in the new fallen snow. In the short walk from Ellie's house, the snowfall had intensified and a few inches had already accumulated on everything. The older, brown, dirty snow was covered completely and the world had a new, white, clean sheen that made Luke feel better despite the fact he had botched it with Ellie.

He pushed the front door open just as his older sister Deana pulled from the inside. He stumbled off balance and fell into her.

"Watch it, loser!" she grinned, and pushed her way past out into the whiteness. Apparently she was in a hurry. Her boyfriend's beat up Ford F-150 was just pulling up. Luke's mom yelled from the kitchen, "You tell that boy to drive careful in this," but Deana was already gone.

"She didn't hear you, Mom," Luke said.

She peered around the kitchen door and said, "Where have you been? It's already 4 o'clock."

"I stopped and talked to Ellie."

"How is she?"

"Worse now. I'm an idiot."

His mom smiled and shook her head.

"I'm sure that's not true. You two have been friends for a long time. What did you say?"

Luke and his mom were close. He was still at an age where he would let her help him if he needed it and right now he needed it. He relayed the conversation to her and she laughed.

"You men really have a way with words," she said.

"Thanks Mom—I feel so much better now. I told you I was an idiot."

"She'll be fine. She would have found out eventually anyway. I think you just shocked her. Apologize when you see her again and give her one of these."

She held up one of her famous chocolate chip cookies and Luke knew Ellie would smile at that. All the kids in the neighborhood knew of his mom's chocolate chip cookies.

Luke smiled. "Could you put some in one of those awesome girlie bags you have?"

"Of course." She turned and started sorting through a drawer looking for the bags. "So, how was school?"

"Stupid."

She stopped and stood up straight.

"Are you talking about the school system itself or maybe the student."

"Both."

"I know the student, and he is definitely not stupid."

"I just hate school. Ninth grade seems like such a waste."

"We've had this conversation before and you know what I'm going to say."

"I know. I can't see the forest for the trees right now, blah, blah, blah…"

She put her hands on her hips and pursed her lips.

"Do I need to be worrying about you?"

"No. I'll be fine." He grabbed a cookie and took a bite. The warm chocolate was heaven.

"Don't spoil your appetite. We'll be eating in an hour. Any homework?"

"No," Luke lied. "I did it at lunch."

"All right, I know you don't want to hear this but you're going to be a wonderful man some day."

Luke blushed but said nothing.

"Until that time, though, your father wants you to shovel the walk."

He felt duped. Sometimes he wished his mother would stop being his mother for five minutes. He shook his head, said "All right," and headed for his room.

As he climbed the stairs, he could hear his little brother Christopher and his younger sister Katy laughing at something in Katy's room. He stopped at her doorway and looked inside. Katy, a year younger than himself, held six year old Christopher hanging by his feet and was tickling him while he laughed hysterically. Luke couldn't help but smile at the two.

"You're going to make him puke," Luke said.

As if on cue, Christopher threw up all over the floor. She almost dropped him. Christopher looked shocked for a second and then started laughing again. She put him down and said, "Aw Christopher! Gross!"

"I'm not cleaning that up," Luke said and shuffled down the hall to his room. Katy was yelling for their mom as he closed the door.

Luke turned his computer and cell phone on and waited for both to boot up. He carried the cell with him but wasn't allowed to have it on at school. Sometimes he forgot to turn it on until he got home. His mother reminded him periodically that she wasn't paying for the phone for his enjoyment. It was supposed to be for security and a way to get in touch with him. If he didn't answer it or turn it on, then that was defeating its purpose. This usually came after she had been trying to get a hold of him and couldn't.

The cell phone didn't have any messages, but when he logged onto Facebook, he had a new friend request. He didn't recognize the name and the avatar was just some cartoonish dog, but he figured it was someone from school, so he hit 'accept.'

A message sat waiting from the new friend whose name was William Smith. He navigated to the message page and clicked on it bringing up the note 'Hi!' with a link embedded in the page. He clicked on it and the web browser went blank for a second, navigating to another page.

When the page came up he froze and a small squeak came from his mouth.

Right in front of him, bigger than life, was a picture of Bentley's head. His tongue hung out, whitish and stiff, and his open eyes were gray and glazed over. Matted, dried blood dotted his fur and Luke could see raw flesh where his head had been separated from the body. He gagged a little but kept everything down.

He tried to look away, but the picture was so obscene his eyes stayed glued to it despite his effort. The caption read, 'This is what happens when you get lazy.' The emoticon for a frown followed the word 'lazy.'

After the shock wore off, the only thing he could think of was what if Ellie was looking at this too? He dialed her number in a panic. Her mom answered on the third ring.

"Hello."

"Mrs. Pemberton? This is Lucas Harrison. Can I speak with Ellie?"

"She's lying down right now, Lucas. I'll tell her you called."

"It's pretty important, can I please talk with her. I promise I'll be quick."

"Lucas, you already upset her earlier. I gave her your message, now I think it's best if you let her be for a while. Don't you?"

Luke didn't know what to do. If Ellie saw the same picture, she would freak out.

"All right. Just tell her to call me as soon as she can. And tell her not to get on Facebook until she talks to me."

"What's going on Lucas?"

"Just tell her that for me, please."

She was quiet for a moment.

"I hope you kids aren't doing anything to upset her. I told her I didn't like that website, but she begged me to let her on it. I'm not going to regret that decision am I Lucas?"

He paused. "No ma'am." He hoped he hadn't just lied to her.

"All right. I'll give her the message." She hung up.

Luke put the phone down and looked at the picture again. He shivered. He clicked the link taking him to his new *friend's* page and looked it over. There was no Bio info and the person only had one friend. Him. That didn't mean he hadn't requested other friends it just meant that no one else had responded.

He didn't know any William Smith, or Bill Smith, or Will Smith, or any Smith at all for that matter. At this point he had no way of finding out the identity of the unknown photographer.

He was about to un-friend this person and delete everything about him when he hesitated. Maybe he needed to keep it. He might be able to find out more about who it was if he went along, keeping the contact open. If he deleted and un-friended the person everything would be lost for good. He moved the mouse cursor away from the delete button and moved it over his own home page button and clicked it.

John was online and Luke sent him a message to meet him out front. John and Jimmy lived next door.

CHAPTER 4

Luke leaned into the shovel and scooped more snow off of the sidewalk.

John stood by and watched while Luke sweated in the cold. John offered to help but Luke told him he could handle it. He knew John had his own shoveling to do later.

His cell phone rang. He pulled it out and saw it was Ellie.

"Hey."

"Who is doing this!" she cried. She was almost hysterical and Luke knew she either hadn't listened to him or never got the message.

"Are you ok?"

"No I'm not! What is happening here? Who is William Smith and why would he send me that picture?"

"I don't know. I got it too. I tried to keep you from seeing it. Did your mother give you my message?"

Ellie didn't say anything for a minute and Luke could hear her crying. Finally she said, "Mom gave me the message. But I looked anyway. I know I shouldn't have but I couldn't help it. I wish you had tried to talk to me."

"I did. Your mom wouldn't let me. She said I upset you enough already and now it looks like I've done it again."

"It's not your fault. I was warned and I did it anyway."

More silence as she cried.

"Me and John are out in front of my house," Luke said. "Do you want to come over and talk about it?"

"Ok. I'll be over there in a minute," and she hung up.

"Ellie got the picture too?" John asked after Luke put the phone away.

"Yeah. She's pretty upset. She's on her way over."

Luke bent with his shovel and worked on the sidewalk a little more while John watched and kept silent. When Luke rested on the handle for a minute John asked, "I can understand some sick bastard sending the picture to her, since it was her dog, but why did he send it to you?"

Luke shrugged. "You didn't get a friend request right?"

"No," John said, "and I asked Jimmy too. Nothing."

"It's weird isn't it? Just me and Ellie. I wonder if her brother got one."

"Here she comes. Ask her."

Luke watched Ellie make her way up the street. She trudged through the snow with her hands shoved in the pockets of her coat and her head bent staring at her feet. Her short blonde hair peeked out from beneath the hood of her coat and her jeans were carefully tucked into her boots. Luke couldn't help thinking she looked cute no matter what she was doing or wearing.

She looked up as she got closer and her face was red from crying, but her eyes were dry.

"Hey," she said. "Shoveling snow?"

"Yeah. Dad never does it anymore. Are you ok?"

She nodded but kept quiet.

"We were wondering if Patrick got a friend request too?" John asked.

"I don't know," she said. "I didn't think to ask him, and I really didn't have time. I called Luke right away and then came straight here. Mom doesn't even know I'm here."

"I know this is upsetting for you but what was in your picture?" Luke asked.

"It was Bentley's head."

Her eyes looked shiny and wet again and her voice was a whisper, but she held it together.

"Was there a caption on it?"

She nodded, clearly upset. "It said, 'Tell no one, or you're next.'"

"Are you sure? Nothing else?" Luke asked.

22

"Yes. Why?"

He looked at John and John shrugged. Luke said, "That's not what mine said."

"What did yours say?"

"Are you sure you want to hear?"

Her head nodded up and down but he could tell she wasn't sure.

"It said, 'This is what happens when you get lazy' and it had a frown emoticon at the end."

Her face went white and her mouth formed a little 'oh' as she took this in.

"Who is doing this to me? Why are they doing this? It's like they know everything about me." A tear fell down one cheek and Luke dropped his shovel and went to her.

"It'll be ok, Ellie." He touched her sleeve and she looked down at the ground.

"I'm scared," she said.

"We won't let anything happen to you."

"How will you stop it? We're just kids."

Luke looked at John for help. John said, "We stick together. Watch out for each other. We make sure we all know what's going on. No secrets."

Luke nodded. "No secrets."

"But he said tell no one. He could be watching us right now and we wouldn't even know it," she said.

Luke unconsciously scanned the court and then focused back on Ellie.

"Even if he is, he can't do anything to us when we're together."

She didn't look as convinced. "Maybe I should talk to my mom. Tell the police."

Luke shook his head. "I don't think so. Not yet."

"Why not?"

"That would definitely provoke whoever it is. If it's just us, he might leave us alone."

"I guess," she said. "This is a nightmare."

"I agree," John said. "But right now, he's only done something to a dog. I know the dog meant a lot to you, Ellie, but he hasn't actually done anything to a person."

She looked mad.

"Killing Bentley was like hurting me," she snapped. "If he could do this to an animal, it's a small step away from doing it to a person."

"You're right," Luke said, "but what John means is he hasn't done anything to a human yet and maybe we can keep it that way. Everybody liked Bentley and we're all mad about what happened. We're not trying to make it anything less than what it is, ok?"

She nodded, slowly, looking a little better. "I know you guys liked him too. I'm just upset."

"You have every right to be," Luke said softly. "I had nightmares for three nights after finding him." He could feel his face redden but kept his eyes locked on hers. Her face softened and then she looked at him funny as she reached up and grabbed his arm.

"Thanks for being my friend," she said, looking at Luke intensely and then shifting her gaze to John. "Both of you."

Luke smiled. "It wouldn't be so hard if you weren't such a Goofy Goober."

She smiled at that. It was the nickname they called each other in third grade.

When they met for the first time back when Luke first moved into the neighborhood, she told him he was a Goofy Goober and he'd gotten mad until he realized she'd been joking with him. They hadn't called each other that for a while now and it brought back good memories.

"You're the Goofy Goober," she said, poking him in the shoulder.

"You are!" he said.

"What's this Goofy Goober crap?" John asked.

Luke and Ellie smiled at each other, but Ellie said, "Nothing. Just a joke between us."

"Do I need to leave you two alone?" he asked, grinning.

Luke felt his face redden again and Ellie looked away quickly.

"No," Luke said.

"I gotta get back home," she said. "I didn't tell my mom I was leaving."

"We'll walk you," Luke said.

"I can walk myself."

"Remember," Luke said, "we stick together."

She smiled. "Ok."

They walked her home and at her doorstep Luke said, "No secrets. Let me know if anything comes up. Call me at anytime and I mean anytime. Day or night."

She nodded once.

24

John said, "Ask your brother if he got the same thing."

"All right," she said. "Thanks guys."

They said bye and Luke and John headed home. Luke hoped they could keep her safe.

* * *

Ellie locked the door behind her and headed up the stairs to her room.

She felt a little better after talking to Luke and John, but she was still frightened out of her mind. It took everything just to keep climbing the stairs. All she could think about was turning around and telling her mother the whole story. She even stopped midway and started to turn around, but Luke's words rang in her ears. *We stick together. No secrets.* She still wasn't convinced they were doing the right thing.

Walking down the hall she passed her brother Patrick's closed door and remembered John and Luke wanted to know if Patrick got the same friend request. She started to knock, then heard a noise.

Her brother was two years older than she was, and at sixteen, was insanely private. He had warned her not to bother him when his door was shut and she knew he could be mean and cruel. She hoped one day he would grow out of his mean streak, but she knew it wouldn't be any time soon. The way he chose to tell her about Bentley proved that. He was an ass and at times she hated him with all her heart.

She decided she didn't care if he got mad, she needed to know. She knocked softly and waited. Usually he would yell through the door at the person who had the nerve to bother him in his domain, but the only thing she heard was the strange noise. She tried the doorknob and it turned so she pushed the door open slowly and peered in.

He was facing away from her seated at his desk and she gasped as she saw what he was watching on his computer screen. Two naked women engaged in something she'd heard about but never in her life had she imagined. He had headphones on and the noise was coming from them.

He seemed to sense something behind him because he turned quickly, ripping the headphones off and pressing the power button on the monitor all at the same time. The look on his face showed shock and anger, and then he grinned.

"Enjoying the view?" he asked.

Her mouth hung open and she forced it shut, backing out of the doorway. She was too embarrassed to even remember what she had wanted and there was no way she was sticking around anyway. She shut the door, heard him laughing behind it, and headed for her room where she closed her door softly and sat on the edge of her bed. It had been a hard week.

CHAPTER 5

Two weeks passed and Luke almost forgot about Bentley and the Facebook link.

Almost.

Ellie, of course, hadn't, and she brought it up periodically, but Luke thought at least it wasn't on her mind 24/7.

No other messages had been sent and nobody received any new friend requests. It was as if the person dropped off the face of the earth.

It had snowed and melted twice over the last two weeks and now they were expecting another blizzard today. Virginia hadn't seen this much snow in over a century. Everything was icy and slippery, and the roads were covered in dirty, brown slush. All the parents were grumbling about the cold, and the heating bills, and the driving, and, especially the school closings.

Luke couldn't understand how anybody could be upset about the school closings. His dad pointed out that even though they didn't have to go to school now, they would have to make it up at the end of the year, which meant their summer break would be shorter. Luke didn't care. He just wanted out of school now, at this exact moment, and it didn't matter what had to be repaid later.

Luke, John, Jimmy, and Ralph, the kid who lived three doors down from Luke, were walking home from the bus stop when Patrick, Alan, and Paul ran past and pelted Jimmy with slush balls they had made from snow in the gutters. Ice, dirt, and oil ran down the inside of Jimmy's shirt. Jimmy froze with his shoulders hunched, and Patrick ran up and shoved another one down the back of his shirt. Jimmy lost it.

"Hey you dickheads!" Jimmy cursed, and grabbed Patrick by the collar as he turned to run. Jimmy yanked Patrick backwards and he came off of his feet, landing on his butt in the street with an audible thud. Patrick, who was three inches taller than Jimmy and a year older, looked stunned, then pissed. Alan and Paul laughed at him as he slipped and fell again trying to stand in the icy road. Jimmy stood over him with his fists balled up at his side.

"Get up!" Jimmy yelled.

Patrick finally got his footing and stood over Jimmy glaring down at him. "I'm up."

"What the hell was that?"

"Just having a little fun, man," Patrick said and shoved Jimmy in the chest.

Jimmy stood his ground. "It wasn't fun for me!" and shoved back.

John moved closer and Luke could see the anger growing in him. Paul and Alan sensed it and starting walking toward the group again. They were no longer laughing.

Patrick, looking uncertain, glanced around quickly. He seemed to shrink a little as Jimmy refused to back down.

"Easy, Besner. We were just having fun."

"I don't care. It was wrong, man!" Jimmy pushed his face into Patrick's. "Tell me why I shouldn't pound you into the ground right now!"

Patrick seemed to regain a little of his courage. "Because you'd lose," Patrick said coldly.

"Bullshit!" But Jimmy made no further move.

"Hey!" Luke said, "Patrick, back off! You'd be pissed too if we had done the same thing to you."

"Shut up, Harrison!" Patrick said. "You stay out of this."

"No," Luke said. "None of us are staying out of this. You back off."

Patrick looked at John who nodded and never took his eyes off of him, then at Jimmy, and finally at Luke. Paul and Alan kept their distance and it looked to Luke like they wanted no part of it, though they didn't leave.

Patrick put his hands up and smiled. "Hey, no problem. I'll be the man. This is me backing off." He took two steps back. Jimmy wasn't so easily swayed. He took two steps toward Patrick and started to say something but Luke yelled at him, "Jimmy! Enough!"

Jimmy stopped and turned to look at Luke as if to say 'you're just a ninth grader,' but then his brother grabbed his arm and said, "Come on, Jim. It was just a joke. Let it go."

Jimmy stood for a minute and then seemed to relax a bit, letting John pull him away.

"Don't do that again," Jimmy said finally, and turned, walking off.

Patrick shrugged, joined his buddies and they left in the opposite direction. Nobody looked back. Luke knew the next snowball fight, if there was ever going to be one, would be bad.

* * *

That evening at dusk, they all played kick the can in the snow storm.

The game was something their parents had taught them, and though it was old and dated, they all loved it. Most of the kids from Cotton Court were there including Luke's sisters Katy and Deana. Ralph (the kid from three doors down) and his little sister, Marsha, were there too. She was twelve and he was thirteen.

Ellie came over from Willow Branch Court along with Paul and Alan, but Patrick didn't show. Ellie said he was locked in his room, and though she didn't tell Luke why, she refused to knock on his door. Finally, the three new kids at the end of the court showed up and Luke learned their names were Cece, Ashley, and Chad. Cece was the oldest at fifteen, Ashley was fourteen, and Chad, eleven. They seemed all right but couldn't play kick the can for crap.

The game had been an almost nightly ritual ever since Luke moved here in the third grade. No one ever seemed to tire of it and it was especially good at night. With the snow falling, it was even better.

John had just kicked the can (which in this case was a red rubber ball) and freed all the prisoners. Jimmy, who was 'it,' chased it down and hurried back to base hoping to catch some slow runners. Everybody made it into a hiding spot in time. Luke and Ellie were currently hunched down in a hedge at the side of Luke's house and they smiled at each other in the dark.

"I like your new haircut," she whispered.

"It's stupid," he said and fiddled with it.

She reached up, pushed his hand out of the way and combed the hair over to one side with her fingers. Little electric shocks ran up and down his spine as she played with his hair. He didn't want her to stop.

"There," she said. "That's better."

He grinned and said, "Thanks." He could feel himself blushing and was glad she couldn't see it in the dark.

He looked up and found her staring at him with a little smile on her lips. He couldn't help it. He smiled, too, and said, "What?"

She leaned in and kissed him on the lips.

It startled him and he almost pulled away, but then her soft, warm lips held him and he kissed her back. She pulled away a bit and whispered, "I know you've been wanting to do that, and I knew you never would, so…"

It was like he was floating in a pool of warm water. Sounds grew muffled and distant, his breath was quick and shallow, and all his senses tingled, feeling electric. He reached up, holding her face in his hands, and pulled her to him. He kissed her and felt everything else disappear.

Nothing existed but her. The feel of her face in his hands; the smell of the soap she used; the heat from her body radiating out to him; her soft, moist, lips pressed against his; all those things and so much more. It was just him and her in the world and no one else.

Then he heard the voice.

"Help me…"

She jerked away, and now he saw fear in her eyes. "What was that?"

"I don't know," he said, thinking John or Jimmy must have seen him kissing her and was messing with him. "You heard it too?"

She nodded quickly and kept looking around in the dark. He started to say something but she put her finger to his lips and shushed him. They both listened to the silence drag out and Luke could actually hear his heart beating. Nothing happened for a bit and he was about to say something when the voice whispered again.

"Help me…"

It came from behind. He heard her take a sharp breath in surprise and look up over his shoulder. He was afraid to see. A palpable presence felt like it was pressing up against his spine and he shivered as he slowly turned.

He could see nothing in the gloom as his eyes tried to penetrate the dense growth of bushes. He heard a faint sound, almost like laughter, but it was so soft and seemed so distant he wasn't sure if he was imagining things.

Ellie whispered in his ear. "I heard a laugh."

He nodded but stared into the darkness where they heard the voice.

"It sounded creepy," she whispered and shuddered.

He suddenly grabbed her hand and said, "Come on!"

He crawled from the bushes with her following behind and stood up.

"Time!" he yelled and it sounded huge and booming in the silence. "Jimmy! John! Get over here! Quick!"

A grunt of anger came from the direction of the voice and then a crashing noise as someone, or something, broke through the hedge and ran off down the path through Luke's backyard.

Ellie and Luke jumped at the sound, and Luke had a hard time holding his ground. He wanted to bolt and run in the other direction, but he couldn't leave Ellie there. He squinted into the darkness as he tried to follow the noise, but he could see nothing. John ran over and then Jimmy was there too.

"What's up?" John said. "You guys quitting?"

"Someone was here," Luke said.

"What do you mean?" Jimmy asked.

"Someone was in the bushes with us," Luke said.

"So," John said, not understanding. "You can hide wherever you want. Everybody could hide in the bushes at the same time if they wanted. It would be stupid, but they could do it."

"No," Ellie said. "Somebody else was here. Someone not in the game." Her face looked haunted and she held on to Luke's arm with a vice-like grip.

Jimmy's mouth was set in a tight line and he looked at John, who stared back at him.

"Was it him?" John asked quietly.

"I think so," Luke said. "It was creepy. This voice whispered 'Help me' twice, and then we heard a laugh. Not a funny laugh, but a mean laugh. That's when I yelled 'Time' and called for you guys."

"Is he still there?" Jimmy whispered.

"I don't think so," Luke said. "We heard a grunt and then someone ran off through my backyard."

Just then Paul and Alan came running around the corner and they all jumped in surprise.

"What's happening?" Paul asked. "We quittin'?"

"Yeah," Jimmy said. "We're done."

"Why?" Alan asked. "It's still early."

"We're just done." And Jimmy yelled, "All-e-all-e-all-come-free!" Jimmy led the way back to the center of the court.

"Hey! What the heck?" Paul said. "What's wrong with you guys?"

"Nothing," Jimmy said. "I said we're done and that means we're done."

"Man—ever since you guys found that dumb dog you've been acting weird," Alan said.

"Hey!" Luke yelled. "That dog was our friend!"

"Yeah! That so called 'dumb dog' was mine," Ellie shouted, her voice breaking.

"Jeez! It's just a dog!" Alan said.

Luke got in his face. "Tell her you're sorry!"

Alan was taken aback. "What?"

Luke grabbed Alan's jacket sleeve and repeated himself, poking him in the chest with every word. "Tell—her—you're—sorry!"

Ellie had tears in her eyes even though she was angry. She stood waiting for the apology. Alan looked around. Jimmy and John were staring at him intensely. Paul looked at the ground shuffling his feet.

"I'm sorry," Alan said.

Luke let go of his sleeve. "All right."

All the other kids were coming out of hiding now and as Ralph walked up he asked, "What's up?"

"They're quitting," Paul said. "Game's over."

"What happened?" Ralph asked.

"Nothing," Jimmy said. "We're just done."

"But it's early," Ralph whined.

"I don't care," Jimmy said. "I'm telling you, go home. We're done."

"I don't want to go home," Ralph said. "You're not the boss of me."

Jimmy strode over and pointed a finger into Ralph's face. Ralph's eyes grew big and he flinched a little.

"If you know what's good for you, you'll go home," Jimmy said, and then looked around. "All of you. Game's over."

"Fine," Ralph said and grabbed his sister and started home. All the others mumbled something and headed off down the street.

Luke could tell the three new kids didn't know what to make of it all. They stood around for a minute and then Cece said, "Well, it was fun for a while. Nice meeting you guys." They waved goodbye and walked home.

Luke, Ellie, John, and Jimmy were left standing in the middle of the street. They stared at each other for a moment and then John said, "Do we go look?"

"For what?" Luke asked.

"Footprints."

"Why?"

"To see if someone was really there," Jimmy said.

"Someone was there all right," Luke said. "Ellie heard it too."

"I did. It was creepy," she said, wrapping her arms around herself.

"I think we should wait until it's light out," Jimmy said. "No use traipsing around in the dark."

"I agree," Luke said. "Besides, what if he has a gun or knife or something?"

Nobody said anything for a minute as they all thought about that. Finally, Ellie said, "Sorry you had to be the bad guy Jimmy. Everybody seemed pissed."

"I don't care about that," Jimmy said. "They'll get over it."

Ellie smiled at him. "Still—it was big of you to take the heat." He waved it off.

"You guys do know that if this gets worse, we're going to have to tell them all," John said. "For their own safety."

Everybody nodded, but Luke didn't want to think about it getting worse. That voice he heard was going to keep him awake tonight as it was.

"We should walk Ellie home," Luke said.

"Thanks, guys," she said. The four of them headed off toward Ellie's house.

The snow was falling hard now and Luke could hardly see ten feet in front him. They talked about mundane stuff as they walked and their voices had an odd quality to them; muddled and stale, like they were trapped in a vacuum. Ellie said only a few words here and there, then suddenly yelled at the top of her lungs. "Whoo hoo!"

They stopped and looked at her as she smiled, sheepishly.

"Did you hear that?" She said. "No echo at all. It was like my voice was sucked away."

"You are weird," Jimmy said, but was smiling. Luke laughed and John just stared at her.

"You scared the crap out of me," John said.

"Whoo Hooooooo!" Luke yelled, and then laughed.

"Aaaaeeeeeee!" Jimmy piped.

Pretty soon they were all yelling at the top of their lungs and laughing at the stupidity of it. As they stopped, the giggling quieting down, they heard a distant "Whoo hoo!" mocking them and they all froze. Ellie shifted next to Luke and grabbed his arm. Luke felt suddenly colder and wished he were home in his warm house.

"Come on," John said, and started walking faster.

They got to Ellie's house and stood at her door.

"It could have been anybody, you know," Jimmy said.

"Yeah," Luke mumbled. "But it could have been him, too."

"Thanks for walking me home," Ellie said. They were all quiet for a minute, then Ellie added, "You guys are my best friends."

Luke didn't know what to say and apparently neither did Jimmy or John, because they all stood there shuffling their feet.

"Bye," she said reaching for the handle, but then stopped. She turned, quickly took a step toward Luke, and kissed him softly on the lips. She smiled coyly and Luke felt himself turning red. She opened her door and disappeared inside.

"What was that?" John asked, grinning.

Luke couldn't help the big grin on his face, but he said nothing. He could still smell her hair and feel her lips on his. He looked away, embarrassed, and led the way home.

CHAPTER 6

Luke couldn't sleep.

The evening's events had his head in a spin and he couldn't shut it down. The voice kept replaying in his head and that laugh chilled him to the bone. He could not seem to get warm. Several times over the last few hours he thought he heard it again, outside his window, a whisper, like sandpaper against the glass, or a little titter of laughter. He thought he was imagining it, but he couldn't be sure. It did little to help his restlessness.

Then there was Ellie. Every time he thought of her, the voice would slip from his thoughts. He relived the kisses over and over again and felt silly at how good she made him feel. The smell of her was still on his jacket so he lay with it next to him.

Jimmy and John would think he was stupid, but he didn't care. She was the most beautiful thing in his life right now and he clung to that ferociously. He could hear her voice in his head saying to him, "I know you've been wanting to do that, but I knew you wouldn't, so…" and he thought it very cool she was so bold. She was right. He would've never kissed her first.

His cell phone vibrating on his bedside table startled him. He looked at the clock. It was 3:32 am. He picked up the phone looking at the caller I.D. and smiled.

"Hey," he whispered.

"I can't sleep," Ellie said.

"Me neither."

"Is the voice keeping you awake?"

"Yeah," he said, pausing. "Along with you."

"I'll hang up then," she teased.

"No—I mean—not now. Thinking of you was keeping me awake."

"I know, silly. I was teasing you. You're keeping me awake too." And he could tell she was smiling even though he couldn't see her.

Silence for a moment and then he could hear her rustling in her bed. Imagining her laying there was making him feel funny.

"Are you ok?" he asked.

"Yeah. Just scared. I've been wanting to call you for the last three hours but I was afraid I'd wake you."

"You can call me any time, remember? I told you, for any reason. Any time."

"I know, I just…"

"Any time."

"Ok. I'm glad you were awake."

"I'm glad you called."

She giggled. "Now we know we're happy about that. Why can't we sleep?"

"That creepy voice won't leave my head. I keep thinking I hear it again outside my house."

"So do I," she whispered. "But that can't be, could it? Not at both our houses."

"Yeah. No way. I know it's my imagination, but I still hear it."

She was quiet for a long moment and then said, "What are we going to do?"

"I'm not sure, but you could kiss me some more tomorrow." He couldn't believe he had said it.

She laughed. "Ok. It's a date."

"I'm glad you did it first. You were right. I probably never would have gotten up the nerve."

"I figured, but what I can't figure is why? Do I scare you that bad?"

"How long have we known each other now?" he asked.

"Oh…let's see…third grade…about five years. Why?"

"We've gotten to be pretty close friends, right?"

"The best."

"I guess I was scared to mess it up. What if you got mad at me? I couldn't stand the thought of you hating me."

"How long have you felt this way Lucas Harrison?" she asked.

"Since you called me a 'Goofy Goober.'"

She laughed at him and he realized if he couldn't hear that laugh all the time, he would feel lost.

"I could never hate you," she said quietly.

"Ok. Promise?"

"Promise."

"I feel better," he said. "Don't you?"

"Yes. I think I can sleep now."

"Me too."

"See you tomorrow?" she said.

"I can't wait."

They both hung up and he was asleep before he could count to ten.

* * *

All four were in the backyard of Luke's house looking at the ground. The white snow made everything new and clean, and it was hard to feel threatened in the crisp, white world that now surrounded them. The sun was out, shining bright, and everything sparkled and twinkled.

"The snow has covered any tracks he made," Jimmy said, more to himself than anybody specific.

"There's nothing in the bushes," Luke yelled from the side of his house where the hedge they hid in stood covered in snow.

"Let's check by the pool," Ellie said and they all trekked down the hill in Luke's backyard toward the hole in the fence that led to the sports complex.

Luke's fence backed up to the tennis courts and pool complex that belonged to the neighborhood. The homeowners would pay a yearly fee and have use of all the amenities for everyone in the family. There were tennis teams, swim teams, diving classes, water aerobics, a kiddie pool, and swimming classes. Just about anything you could think of.

Cotton Court's entrance was all the way on the other side of the main street into the neighborhood and was a pretty good walk to the pool area, but Luke's backyard lay right up against it. There was a path that ran down the side of his house and through the backyard to a hole in the fence. Everyone in the court cut through it to get to the pool.

Luke's Dad was upset about this at first, but now he didn't seem to care. Nobody hurt any of his shrubs or grass and it was convenient for him also. Just a quick jog down the short path, slip through the hole between the fence and the giant hedge of honeysuckle, and you were right there.

Ellie peeked through the hole in the fence and then slipped through. The rest of them followed and they squished through the snow toward the pool about a hundred yards away. The empty and quiet tennis courts were to their left, and not a single footstep, or animal track, marred the new snow as far as the eye could see. The heavy snowfall had wiped everything clean.

They came up to the fence that encircled the pool and peered through the chinks at the iced over water.

Ellie suddenly smiled and said, "Let's try to walk on the ice."

"I don't know," Jimmy said. "Could be too thin."

"Let's see," she said and started climbing the fence.

Luke shrugged at John and Jimmy, and then followed her over the fence onto the deck. All the pool furniture was covered in snow and the ice in the pool had a ghostly layer over top of it.

Ellie stood at the edge and said, "Hold me."

Luke grabbed her arm and John held onto her coat. She put one foot on the snow covered ice and slowly put more weight down. Luke kept expecting to hear a loud crack and watch as Ellie slipped from his grasp, sinking into the freezing water. She had all her weight on one foot now and she lifted the other leg off the ground, standing solely on the ice. She looked up and grinned.

That's when the ice broke and her leg slid into the water.

She let out a little cry as Luke and John held her tight, but not before her right leg went into the icy water up to her thigh. They quickly pulled her up and onto the pool deck. She was laughing as she fell onto Luke who had tripped trying to pull her out. He didn't think it was so funny.

"That didn't work," she said.

"No crap," Jimmy said.

"If you had fallen in, I don't know if we could have even seen you," Luke said.

"You wouldn't jump in after me?" she teased.

"You know I would," Luke said. "I wouldn't like it, but I'd jump in."

She leaned over and gave him a peck on the cheek. "Thanks for saving me."

"Hey!" John said. "What about me?"

"Thank you, John," and she kissed him on the cheek too. Luke felt a little twinge of jealousy, and it bothered him that he would feel that way toward his best friend.

Jimmy was studying the pool, lost in thought, when he said, "You know, if somebody fell in this thing, I don't think anybody would find them 'til spring."

"Nah—somebody would see," John said.

"Wanna bet?"

"How're you going to prove it?" John asked.

"I got an idea." And Jimmy explained his plan. They all grinned.

* * *

That evening, at dusk, they met together at the side of Luke's house with the items they had collected.

Jimmy had his dad's giant MagLite flashlight, and John had an ice pick along with some old clothes. Luke and Ellie had brought old clothes too. They sat in the snow and put together a stuffed dummy with the clothes and rags. The only things missing were shoes and hands. Luke didn't think it would matter.

Ellie held the stuffed dummy up and said, "He needs a name."

"How 'bout George," John said.

"George it is," Ellie said. "Come on George, let's go swimming."

It was full dark now, no moon, and Jimmy led the way through the wooded backyard with the flashlight shining the way. It was very quiet and Luke kept thinking he would hear the voice again, but nothing made a sound.

When they got to the pool fence, they tossed 'George' over and climbed after him. Jimmy doused the flashlight and they worked in the dark. John took the ice pick and chipped the ice around the hole Ellie had made earlier until it was big enough for 'George' to fit through.

"Get the lifeguard pole, John," Jimmy whispered.

John grabbed the pole that was hanging by brackets on the fence and brought it over. Jimmy used it to stuff the dummy up under the ice and push it out deeper into the pool. He then took the hook end and pushed the snow around on top of the ice, clearing an area so they could see the dummy through the murky thin ice. From their point of view, 'George' looked exactly like a body that was trapped under the ice.

"Come on," Luke said and giggled at the sight. "Let's go!"

They all quickly climbed back over the fence, laughing nervously and trying not to make too much noise. Luke got stuck at the top of the fence for a minute, his coat snagging on the chain link. He panicked and pulled it hard, ripping it as it tore free. He almost fell when it came loose.

They ran back to the hole in the fence, worked their way back up through Luke's backyard, and stood in his driveway, proud of themselves.

"Now we wait and see how long it takes for someone to find him," Jimmy said. "I give it 'til spring."

"I say two weeks," John said.

"Three weeks," Luke said.

"A month," Ellie said.

They were all wrong.

CHAPTER 7

After they made bets with Jimmy and John on when 'George' would be found, Luke and Ellie said goodnight to the brothers and then went to his house.

"Mom? Ellie's here."

"Ok," Luke's mom yelled back. "What happened to kick the can?"

"It's too cold."

"All right, don't keep her here too late. Her mom will be worried."

"I'll call her, Mrs. Harrison," Ellie yelled.

Luke's mom came to the door of the kitchen and looked them both over. "Ok, Honey. That would probably be good. Are you doing ok? We haven't seen you here in a while. So sorry about Bentley."

"Thank you, ma'am. And yes I'm doing better." She looked at Luke and smiled.

"That's good. You guys gonna watch some TV? I could bring you some cookies and milk."

"Thanks, Mom. That would be great. Come on, Ellie."

Luke led her down into the basement where the Harrisons' had a game room of sorts. Luke found the TV remote while Ellie called her mom. He grabbed a blanket, since it was a little chilly in the basement, and waited until she finished with her mom.

"I have to be home at 9:00," Ellie said.

"Ok, that's cool." He turned the TV on and found an old movie to watch. Luke's mom came down with the cookies and two glasses of milk on a tray and set it on the coffee table in front of them.

"It's freezing," she said. "Are you sure you guys want to stay down here? You can watch upstairs in the living room."

"We'll be fine, Mom. We have a blanket. Thanks for the cookies."

"Thank you Mrs. Harrison," Ellie said, grabbing a cookie and taking a big bite.

"You're welcome, Sweetheart. Ok. If you guys change your mind..." and she turned and went back upstairs.

They ate a few cookies in silence and then she snuggled up next to him, pulling the blanket over them both. Her head was resting on his shoulder with his arm around her and he could smell the shampoo she used. He put his hand on her head and gently stroked her blonde hair, feeling the fine softness of it as his fingers ran through it.

She hummed softly and said, "That feels so good. Is that weird?"

"Not to me," he said. "I've wanted to do this for a long time now. Is that weird?"

"You should have done it sooner."

"I told you, I was too scared."

"You don't seem scared now."

"You promised not to hate me."

She looked up at him. "I did, didn't I?" She kissed him shyly and then more confidently. He felt he could get lost in those lips.

She broke the kiss and touched his face. "So, are we boyfriend and girlfriend now?"

He hadn't thought about it. "Well, I'm a boy and you're a girl, so..."

"Really?" and she punched him playfully. "I suppose you're going to say 'And we're friends...so...'"

"We are, aren't we?"

"The best."

"Ok then. We're boyfriend and girlfriend." He smiled at her and she kissed him again.

As he got lost in the softness of her lips, a faint 'tap, tap, tap' invaded his senses. She pulled away and looked toward the back sliding glass door a few feet away.

It came again. Three quick, light taps, as if someone was using their fingernail against the glass. Luke tensed and he felt her shrink into him.

"What is it?" she said.

"Wait," he said softly, and she waited.

Tap, tap, tap.

"Shit," he said and got up.

She followed him to the door and he tried peering through the glass into the darkness. He could see nothing. He flipped on the outside light and brightness flared into the backyard illuminating the white snow.

He could see nothing out there.

She held onto his arm, leaning into him, as he took another step closer to the glass. Suddenly an object crashed into the door and she screamed as they both jumped back.

It was small, black, and fluttered around on the ground for a second outside the door, then grew still. Luke knew what it was.

"A bird," he said. He stepped up to the glass and looked closer. "A crow. That's weird." And that's when they heard the sirens.

CHAPTER 8

The whole neighborhood, it seemed, had turned out to watch the spectacle.

Luke, Ellie, and his mom and sisters, all stood at the edge of the crowd surrounding the pool and watched as the firemen and policemen rescued 'George.' His dad and little brother had stayed at home.

John, Jimmy and their dad came up and stood with them, joining the growing crowd.

"What's going on," Mr. Besner said to Luke's mom.

"I don't know. I think someone fell in the pool."

Luke tried not to look at John and Jimmy, but he could sense their nervousness. Ellie held his hand tight and pressed up against him. He could feel her trembling beside him.

"Are you gonna be ok?" he whispered in her ear.

She nodded quickly but said nothing. Her eyes were shining in the flashing lights and her mouth was set in a tight line. He felt surreal and wondered what they had got themselves into. He looked around at the crowd and thought for sure everyone was staring at them though he knew he was probably imagining things. *How could anybody know?* No one had seen them he was sure.

The rescue workers grew a little more active and the crowd murmured louder seeing that something was happening. Luke watched as they pulled 'George' out of the pool and then quickly lay him on the ground. The paramedics seemed frantic.

Something wasn't right.

Luke craned his neck to look and saw the paramedics urgently hooking up I.Vs to 'George' and one was pressing on his chest doing CPR. Luke's knees suddenly felt weak and he turned to John next to him, but John stared dumbfounded at the scene, his mouth hanging open.

Luke looked harder, straining to see through the crowd and as he heard Ellie gasp, he saw a small, white hand poke through the sleeve of the clothing they used to make the dummy. Then, as someone shifted in the crowd, he saw a paramedic bend to a white face and press his lips to the cold blue lips of the boy they pulled out of the pool. The paramedic was giving mouth to mouth to a real person.

Luke grabbed Ellie as she swooned and sank to her knees.

* * *

Detective Jaxon Jennings, homicide investigator for the Fairfax County Police Department, looked down at the boy the paramedics were frantically working on and shook his head. He turned and scanned the crowd, looking for anything. All he saw were scared parents and children of a quiet neighborhood suddenly turned upside down. He knew this place. He had been here a couple of weeks ago on a call about a mutilated dog. No big deal, right, but the department had a policy of investigating all acts of cruelty toward animals. The FBI training they had received dictated it. Too many people who tortured animals graduated to humans later in their demented lives.

"Is he gonna make it?" Sally Winston, his partner, asked over his shoulder.

One of the paramedics working on the boy thought she was talking to him. "Don't think so. He's been gone too long. We don't even have any electrical activity in his heart."

She looked at Jaxon and her eyes conveyed a sadness he no longer felt at his age. At forty seven, he'd seen too much to feel anymore.

"How long are you guys gonna work on him?" Jaxon asked.

"As long as it takes," the paramedic snapped.

Jaxon took it in stride, nodded his head and wandered over to the fence, looking out at the crowd.

"What do you think?" Sally said to his back.

He turned and looked at the boy again. "Hard to say right now. Looks like a simple drowning. There are no marks on him I can see at the moment, but that doesn't mean he doesn't have any."

He looked around the pool deck and something caught his eye. He wandered over to the southern side of the deck and stared at multiple footprints near the fence. On the other side, they led off into the parking lot and the crowd.

Sally came over and bent down to look.

"Have any of our people been over here?" Jaxon asked.

"No. The area hasn't been contaminated. Didn't know if it was a crime scene yet."

She stood, and he watched her follow the footprints with her eyes as they meandered over to the edge of the pool, where they blended with the footprints the paramedics and cops had made.

Jaxon bent down and looked at the imprint of one shoe. "Kids?" he asked.

She joined him. "Looks to be about the right size."

"We better get some imprints of these," he said.

"Sure," and she left to get the kit.

Jaxon continued to look around and noticed something brightly colored, caught on the top of the fence, fluttering in the breeze. He walked over, careful not to disturb any of the other tracks, stood on his tip toes and pulled the piece of fabric off. He studied it, and then stared out into the crowd again not sure what he was looking for. He pulled an evidence bag out of his jacket pocket and slipped the fabric inside. He was beginning to think there was more to this than met the eye.

* * *

Luke's mom knelt in front of Ellie and ran her hand across Ellie's face. She looked up at Luke. "Lucas, you should get her home. She shouldn't be seeing all this. It's upsetting her."

"I'm all right, Mrs. Harrison. Really," Ellie said and stood.

"Are you sure?"

Ellie nodded and grasped Luke's hand. "I'm sure."

"All right."

Ellie gripped Luke's arm tightly and leaned up against him. "Sorry," she whispered in his ear.

"It's ok. It shocked me too."

"What is going on?"

"I have no clue. Let's talk about it later, ok?"

She nodded and stared at the ground. Luke turned to John who gave him a worried look and then proceeded to ignore him. Jimmy looked stoic as he watched everything happening in the pool area.

Luke scanned the faces, worried the person behind *The Voice* was mingling with the crowd. *Didn't they say the person always returned to the scene of the crime?* All the faces seemed normal, and he could see no one acting weird or suspicious. He wondered how he looked to everyone else.

He turned back to the pool and saw the cop who had come out to investigate Ellie's dog, Bentley. He tensed and then shifted a little so he was hidden behind the man in front of him as he watched the cop scan the crowd. Peeking around the shoulders of the man, he stared as the cop talked to another woman and then they walked over to the fence and looked at something on the ground.

Ellie nudged him. "What are they doing?" she whispered.

"I think they're looking at our footprints. Crap!"

"Maybe we should go."

"No, not yet. Let's see what happens."

They watched for a while longer, and then the paramedics loaded the body onto a stretcher and attached a machine which continued the CPR compressions with a piston like arm. They loaded him up in the ambulance and drove off with the siren wailing. Shortly, a uniformed police officer announced there was nothing more to see and asked if everyone would kindly return to their homes.

People shuffled off, talking about what they had seen.

Luke and Ellie joined his family and the rest of the neighbors from his court as they all headed back home. He glanced back as they left and saw the woman cop fiddling with some equipment by the fence. He couldn't tell what she was doing, but he knew it had something to do with them.

CHAPTER 9

Jaxon hated this part of the job.

He was tempted to pass this on to Sally, but he was the lead and the job was supposed to fall to him. Contacting the family of a deceased relative was never easy, but when it involved a child it was even more difficult.

The boy from the pool was now in a refrigerator at the county morgue awaiting an autopsy, if the family so desired, or if the evidence dictated a crime had taken place.

In the boy's back pocket, a school paper had been found with the name of the boy at the top left. It had been blurry and faint on the soggy paper, but with a little work they had been able to determine who it had belonged to. It had then been a simple act of pulling school records on the child to get the address and phone number of the parents. He wouldn't need the phone number. He would do this in person.

Sally decided to go with him and he was glad about that. She handled civilians much better than he did. They arrived at the house at 9:00 in the morning and knocked on the door. His hands were sweating and he was irritated with himself for how he was feeling. He had been quiet all morning and Sally kept turning to look at him as if something was wrong.

"Are you getting a little case of conscience?" Sally finally asked as they waited at the door.

"Why?" he said.

"You look a little nervous and upset."

He paused, then said, "I'm just pissed I have to be here on a Sunday."

She shook her head, but said nothing else.

The door was answered by a woman in her mid thirties, brown hair and eyes, pink robe and slippers, holding a spatula, smiling as if the world was good and her life was perfect. He knew he was going to ruin that perception in a few seconds.

Jaxon had his I.D. out and he held it out to the woman.

"Morning ma'am, I'm Detective Jennings and this is Detective Winston. We're with the Fairfax County PD and we'd like to have a word with you regarding your son."

"My son?" She said, the smile slipping from her face as she glanced at the badge.

"Yes. May we come in?"

She hesitated, and then opened the door wide. "Yes, please do."

He let Sally go first and followed, entering a foyer with a staircase to his left leading to the upper floor, and a small half bath on his right, painted in a dark red color that reminded him of blood. The entrance to the kitchen was directly in front of him. She led them to the living room, which fell to the right of the kitchen just past the half bath. She gestured to the couch and said, "Let me get my husband."

They nodded and sat.

She disappeared up the stairs and silence permeated the room as they waited. Jaxon glanced around, noting the loveseat to his right, large flat screen TV on a dark wood stand in front of them, and various tables and cabinets spaced throughout the rest of the room. A small dining room joined the living room and what must be the kitchen through an entrance to the right of the TV.

They heard footsteps on the stairs and then the woman returned, followed by a short, stocky man of about the same age. He had light, sandy, blond hair, blue eyes set wide, and a goatee, neatly trimmed.

"Morning officers," he said. "What's this about my son?"

Jaxon cleared his throat. "This is never easy so I'll get right to it. Your son was found dead early last night."

The woman's hand flew to her mouth as a gasp escaped her and the husband, though clearly shocked, turned and supported his wife as her legs gave out and she held on to him trying to remain standing.

"No!" The woman wailed. "It can't be. He was just with me last night."

The husband appeared angry, and said, "Where?"

"He was pulled from your neighborhood pool about 8:30 p.m. last night," Sally said in a soft voice. "We are truly sorry."

The woman looked at her husband and then began to laugh hysterically.

Jaxon had seen a lot of different reactions from people, including screaming, fainting, vomiting, crying, wailing and shocked giggling, but he had never seen the kind of laughter he was watching. He questioned his tactic now, and wondered if he had caused the woman to lose her mind completely.

The woman stopped laughing and turned to him, "You're wrong officers. My son is not dead."

As if on cue, a boy of about fourteen entered the room, sleep still in his eyes, a rumpled Washington Redskins t-shirt twisted around his torso. He looked at Jaxon and shock registered for a brief second on the boy's face and then he seemed to recover.

"What's going on, Mom?" the boy asked.

Jaxon looked at Sally and had a sinking feeling in his gut as he watched her face. She had come to the same conclusion he had. He turned back to the boy.

"Are you Lucas Neal Harrison?" Jaxon asked.

The boy looked at his parents and then back at Jaxon and said, simply, "That's me."

Jaxon cursed quietly under his breath.

* * *

Ellie lay in her bed, her head resting on her hands, looking out the window at the bright sunshine streaming in.

The vision of the boy being pulled from the pool dressed in the clothes they had used for 'George' the dummy had haunted her all night. She hadn't slept well and had only just dozed off an hour ago when her noisy brother had startled her awake by slamming the toilet seat in the bathroom next to her room.

Jimmy's idea of putting the dummy in the pool had seemed innocent enough at the time, but even before the revelation of the real body, she had questioned their act when she saw all the activity it had attracted. With the shocking discovery of the real boy in the pool, she had this terrible feeling of sinking in quicksand with no way out and nobody to help her.

She sat up and brushed her short hair, the simple act reminding her of Luke's finger's doing the same thing last night before all the weird stuff started happening. She smiled to herself as she remembered how good he felt. Why couldn't these good feelings stay? Every time something went right, it was followed by something going bad. It made her feel cursed.

She had called Luke in the middle of the night again and found he was wide awake. They had talked for a while, but the comfort she found with him the previous night escaped her last night. She could tell he was tense and worried about what might happen. He wasn't his usual happy go lucky self and she had been a little disappointed he hadn't been able to alleviate her fears. She had finally said goodnight to him at about four in the morning.

Two nights in a row with little sleep left her feeling anxious and sluggish all at the same time. She went into the bathroom and splashed cold water on her face and then brushed her teeth. The dark circles under her eyes stood out against her pale face like small bruises.

She went back to her room and logged onto the computer wanting to see if there was anything about the incident from last night in the news. She saw she had an e-mail notifying her of a message on Facebook. She logged onto her Facebook account and froze.

The message was from William Smith.

She was afraid to look, but she was also curious. Clicking on the link showed one word: "Surprise!"

"Yeah—it sure was, you sicko!" she said aloud to herself.

There was nothing else. She was relieved there were no pictures. She wondered if Luke got the same message. She didn't want to call this early since he might be asleep, but then again he had said call anytime.

She reached for the phone and held it in her hand, not sure if she should call him. It vibrated in her palm and she jumped. It was Luke.

"Hey, I was just thinking about calling you," she said.

"The police just left my house," he said.

"Why? What did they want?"

"They thought the body was me. They told my parents I was dead and then I walked into the room. The one cop seemed pissed."

"Why did they think it was you?"

"That's the weird part. The cop said they found a school paper with my name on it in the back pants pocket of the kid. I made sure those pockets were empty when we made the dummy. Where did our friend get a school paper of mine?"

"Could he have put your name on a piece of paper and stuck it in the pocket? Did you see the paper?"

"Yeah, the cop showed it to us. It was our homework from last week in Mrs. Litchfield's class. The crap on nouns and stuff. Remember?"

"That is weird," she said. "I wonder how he got it."

"Beats me. My dad went berserk. Really laid into them about scaring the crap out of him and Mom without being sure whose body it was and stuff like that. The two cops kept apologizing, but my dad wouldn't let it go. I thought he was going to hit the guy cop. I think his name was Jaxon."

"That's the one who came to my house about Bentley."

"Uh huh. The woman who was at the pool was the other one."

"It must have scared the crap out of you when you saw them in your house."

"It was a shock," he said.

"I just got a message on Facebook. Have you checked yours yet?"

"No. What was the message?"

"It was from him," she said. "No pictures, just the word 'Surprise!'"

He was silent for a moment and she thought he hung up.

"Still there?" she asked.

"Yeah, sorry. I was just thinking what a bastard this guy is. I'm logging on to my computer now. Let's see if he sent me something."

A few minutes passed as she listened to computer keys clicking and then Luke said, "Same message. No pictures. Wait…oh crap!"

"What? What happened?"

"He's logged in right now. He just sent me a chat request."

"Are you serious? Don't accept!" she almost shouted.

"Too late. He says, *So, how did you like my surprise?*"

"Don't answer him! He's just messing with us!"

"I want to see what he has to say."

"Please, Luke. He's dangerous."

"I know. I'll end it if it gets bad. I'll tell you everything he says and you can be like my safety gauge, ok?"

She didn't know what to say. Every fiber of her being was shouting at her to make Luke stop but how could she from her own room? Luke was stubborn sometimes and he would do whatever he wanted.

"I don't like this," she told him. "But I'll stay with you."

"What should I type back?" he asked.

"Be honest with him," she said. "Tell him we didn't like it." She heard his fingers on the keyboard and she waited.

"He typed, *Figures. I make your prank more exciting and you don't even appreciate it.*"

She heard him typing again. "What are you typing?" she said.

"I'm telling him 'At least we didn't kill anyone.'"

"Don't provoke him!"

"Let's see what he says."

She waited for what seemed like forever but it was probably more like a minute. She realized she was holding her breath and she let it out. Luke must have heard.

"Are you ok?" he asked.

"No! I don't like this. The only reason I'm still here is because I care about you and I'm scared."

"How much?"

"I'm terrified!"

She heard him chuckle and she couldn't believe it.

"No," he said. "How much do you care about me?"

"Oh..." She felt a little foolish, and then, still a little angry. Now was not the time to be talking about this kind of stuff.

"Lucas, you're my best friend, but you drive me nuts sometimes."

"That's not a very good answer."

"What is he typing?"

"He hasn't answered yet. So...I'm just your best friend?"

She could hear the playfulness in his voice and she realized he was just trying to get her to relax a little.

"How can you be so calm when this killer is harassing us?"

"I'm not calm. But I feel stronger with you here."

"Luke, I..." She started to cry and she knew he could hear her.

"Hey," he said. "This has been the best and worst week of my life. The best part is you. The worst part is this jerk. I don't want him ruining what we have and I'll do anything to keep that from happening."

"We're just kids. How can we do that?"

He was silent for a minute and then he said, "I don't know yet, but I'm not going to sit here and let him hurt you or anyone else."

"This has been the best week for me too. All this other bad stuff makes me so confused."

"Me too...wait...he's typing...he said, *You have a message. See you around.*"

"A message?"

"Hold on..."

She heard clicking as his mouse navigated the screens.

"Shit..."

"What is it?" she said.

"It's a picture."

"Oh no...what's it of? Is it bad?"

"I don't know how he did this...it's me...well, at least my face...it's me they're pulling out of the pool last night. I'm dressed in the dummy's clothes and I'm dead."

CHAPTER 10

Jaxon felt like an idiot.

He had made a horrible, rookie mistake and was kicking himself for it. Kicking over and over again. How could he have been so stupid? In his twenty five years as a policeman he had never screwed up so badly.

He downed his twelfth Bud, crushed the can in one hand with a vengeance, and grabbed another one out of the cooler he had sitting by his chair.

His doorbell rang.

He didn't want any visitors so he stayed where he was and ignored it. It rang again and then knuckles rapped on the wood of the door.

"Come on, Jaxon. It's me. I know you're in there."

Sally. He was surprised. She never came to his place. He got up, opened the front door and was greeted with a twelve pack of Bud held out to him by his partner.

"Thought you could use this, but I see you've already started."

He looked at the beer he held in his hand, shrugged, and then held the door wide, gesturing for her to come in. She handed him the twelve pack and walked past him into the small apartment he shared with his dog, Reverb. He closed the door and followed her into the living room. She sat and grabbed a cold beer from the open cooler.

"What brings you to my lovely abode?" he said. "Surely not the company."

"I thought you might like to hear the latest on the kid." He didn't answer so she went on. "And I thought you could use my company."

"I don't need you trying to boost me up. I'm fine," he said.

"Yeah, you look fine. How many have you had already?"

He ignored the question and said, "So, what's the latest on the kid?"

She took a drink of the beer and set it down.

"Preliminary cause of death is asphyxiation," she said. "But not from drowning. The ME wants to wait on the autopsy to confirm it until the family is notified."

"So, the body was moved?"

"That's what it's looking like. He died somewhere else and was put in the pool. Now, as far as notifying the family, they haven't been able to positively identify the body. We've run fingerprints and come up with a big goose egg."

"What about the FBI fingerprint database, IAFIS?"

"We haven't hit it yet. That's next."

"Dental records?"

"Yes, but nothing has popped up yet. And no one has reported a missing child. At least not within the local and surrounding states."

"So he's still a John Doe?"

"Yes."

"We need to widen the search. If he was killed elsewhere and dropped in the pool, he could have come from anywhere. Let's start working national databases and see if we get any hits."

"Already started it boss. I submitted the query in the computer system before I came over." She smiled, took another drink, and waited as silence took over the conversation. "You know, it was an honest mistake."

He shrugged.

"How else were we going to find someone to positively I.D. the body?" she asked. "It's normal procedure. Do your best to I.D. the body on your own, contact the family and have them do the positive I.D. You know it's the fastest way."

He popped another beer and took a long pull on it as she sat and waited. "But I went about it all wrong," he finally said. "I could see it on your face, as soon as I made the abrupt announcement their son was dead."

"It's your way. Not my place to question."

He gave her an exasperated look and she turned away. When she turned back her expression was one of patience, as if with a small child who needed a lesson.

"Look, I wouldn't have done it that way, no, but that's me."

"You should have stopped me."

"What? How was I supposed to do that?"

"You should have been the one doing the talking."

"You're the lead. You lead. I follow. If you wanted me to do the talking, you should have told me. Now you're trying to blame me?"

"No—you're not understanding. I'm saying I agree with you. I should have let you do the talking. I'm not blaming you for something you didn't do. Am I that much of an asshole?"

She smiled at him. "No, boss. You're just a little rough around the edges." She took a long drink of her beer and looked around the room as if for the first time. "Nice place. Where's Reverb?"

"Probably hiding from you. He's not very social."

"Great watchdog."

He shrugged. "I trained him well."

She stood, walked over to the bookshelf and looked at the pictures. She grabbed the one of his dead son, looked it over and then set it down again in its spot. She knew about Michael, but thankfully never brought it up with him. Everyone knew about Michael.

She wandered around the rest of the room, glancing at his limited knick-knacks and furniture and he watched her in a way he had never seen before. She had great legs and the skirt she was wearing showed them off. He figured the alcohol was contributing to this new perspective, but he didn't care. She turned and noticed him noticing her. A tiny, little smile formed on her lips, but she said nothing. He quickly looked away.

"What about the footprints in the snow? Anything on that?" he asked.

She nodded. "All consistent with children or teenagers, unless the perp is a very small man or woman, which can't be ruled out, of course. No other footprints were in the vicinity except for the rescue crew and ours."

"What's your gut feeling?"

"I think some kids were there. I don't know what they were doing, but I bet they know something. If we can find out who, we can probably learn something about what actually happened."

"What about the accidental death scenario?"

"Explain," she said.

"A group of kids kill their buddy by mistake, panic, and try to ditch the body. I've heard about it happening before."

"The only thing about that scenario that doesn't make sense is the lack of a reported missing person. If the kid is local and had some horrible accident that's being covered up, why hasn't some distraught mother called us looking for her baby?"

He saluted her with his beer. "Good point. Unless it's some parent that doesn't care or isn't expecting their kid to be home. Maybe he was away at a sleepover or party and he wasn't due back home until today. Could be overlooked for a day or two."

"Yeah. I guess we'll see in the next twenty four hours. Should we check out the neighborhood kids tomorrow?"

"That's my plan."

"What about the Harrison kid? Think he knows anything?"

He paused. "My gut feeling is yes, but I'm going to leave that can of worms alone for a while, don't you think?"

She nodded, drained her beer, crushed it and then added it to the pile of destroyed empties he had already accumulated.

He laughed. "Have another," he said, holding up the beer to her. She grinned and took it from him.

CHAPTER 11

School on Monday was abuzz with the story of the boy pulled from the pool.

It hadn't made the news, not even a blurb in the paper, but that didn't keep it from spreading like wildfire around the campus as the day went on.

Luke kept out of the conversations, but kept his ears open hoping to catch some clue about who the kid was. By the end of the day, the rumors flying around about his identity amounted to nothing more than gossip and couldn't be judged reliable. *Could anything a teenager said be held truthful,* Luke thought to himself? He wasn't above criticizing his generation, which he knew to be fickle and irresponsible, himself included.

At lunch he sat with Ellie, joked with her about everyday nothingness and held her hand as the rest of the kids noticed the new closeness between them. He spotted, more than once, whispers and giggles among their friends and even a few evil looks from some of the other girls, but for the most part, his eyes were only on her.

She had slept a little better on Sunday night and so had he. She looked beautiful with her short hair pulled back in a red band and her blue eyes clear and bright. He whispered to her that he really wanted to kiss her here in front of everyone and she smiled and turned red.

"Well, why don't you, Mr. Harrison?"

"I think I will, Miss Pemberton," and he plopped one on her right there in the cafeteria. It was cool.

Luke, Jimmy, and John walked her home from the bus stop, keeping to the plan of sticking together. Patrick, who still looked pissed asked, "What the hell are you guys doing with my sister?"

"I'm walking her home," Luke said, "and they're with me."

"What are you guys? Stupid or something?"

"Shut up, Patrick," Ellie said.

He laughed at them but didn't push it.

They dropped Ellie off, and as they turned in to their court, they saw the cop, Jaxon, and the woman, talking to Ralph and his sister. They were showing him a picture. They looked up at Luke and seemed to dismiss Ralph while they turned and walked to their car. They got in and drove off without a second glance.

"Hey Ralph!" Luke yelled. "Wait up!"

Luke, John, and Jimmy jogged up to Ralph and his sister and Luke asked, "What were they doing?"

"Asking us a bunch of questions," Ralph said.

"Like what?" John asked.

"Did we notice anything weird or any weird people around lately, and did we see anything at the pool that was strange or suspicious?"

"What else?"

"They showed us a picture of a boy and asked if we knew him or recognized him, but we didn't."

"Did they ask anything about us?" Luke asked.

"No. Why?"

"Nothing," John said. "See ya'."

Ralph looked at them funny but didn't say anything more.

They walked the rest of the way home, slogging through the slush in the road and Luke said goodbye as Jimmy and John turned in to their house. Luke's dad was waiting for him at the top of the drive and he looked angry.

Oh crap, Luke thought. *Now what?*

Luke and his dad had an ordered relationship at best. His dad ordered him around and he did whatever he was told. He learned a long time ago not to question his father. It didn't go well when he did.

"Hey, Dad," Luke offered as he made his way up the icy drive.

"What kind of crap have you boys been up to?" his dad asked.

"We've been at school."

He gave Luke a look that said, 'Don't take me for an idiot.' "I've been watching those two cops for the last hour and they stopped every kid coming home except you four. As a matter of fact, they almost ran off when they saw you. What the hell is going on?"

Luke hesitated for a second, then said, "I don't know, Dad. Maybe they got the information they needed."

"What do you know about this boy in the pool?"

"Nothing."

"Who was he?"

"I don't know. Nobody at school knows."

His father eyeballed him and he tried to keep eye contact but finally had to look away.

"You seemed awfully nervous when you saw the cops at our house."

"Everybody gets nervous around cops," Luke said.

"But how did you know they were cops? They could've been anybody visiting your mother and me."

"I recognized the one from Ellie's dog and the pool. The woman was at the pool too."

His dad frowned, and then said, "You had better not be lying to me. This is serious stuff and you could get yourself into big trouble. Now, get on in and get your homework done."

Luke nodded and went into the house relieved the confrontation was over. His dad could usually see right through him. Maybe he was getting better at lying or his dad was willing to let it go for now.

* * *

The next day Luke was at Ellie's house watching TV in her basement.

They were huddled up under a nice warm blanket and he was enjoying the feeling of being close to her. Plus he got to feel those lips against his as much as he wanted. At least until her stupid brother showed up.

"Ellie, you got a phone call," Patrick said, handing her the cordless phone and disappearing up the stairs, but not before he gave Luke an evil look.

"I never heard the phone ring," she said to Luke as she covered the mouthpiece. "Hello?"

"Help me…"

Luke could hear the voice faintly and watched her face go white and her mouth fall open. Then she freaked out.

61

"Leave me alone!" she shouted into the phone and threw it across the room.

Luke could hear laughter coming from the speaker as it lay against the wall. He went over and picked it up.

"Who is this?" he said, but the line was dead. He hung up and went over to Ellie who had her face in her hands.

"He's gone," he said softly. "Are you ok?"

She shook her head. "Every time I think everything's going to be fine, something else happens. How did he get my number?"

"He knows our names and your number is in the phone book. It's just that easy."

Luke's cell phone started ringing and they both froze, staring at each other. He pulled it out of his pocket and looked at the caller ID. It read 'Unavailable.' He showed it to her.

"Don't answer it," she said.

"I want to," he said.

"Why?"

"I don't want him to know I'm afraid."

She shrugged and he pressed 'send' and said, "Hello."

He couldn't figure out why, but the voice that came across the cell phone made his teeth hurt and seemed to vibrate directly down his spine. It was so abrasive, yet so quiet, it hurt more than someone shouting into his ear. He actually pulled the phone away from his head a little.

"Help me…"

"What do you want?" he said, trying to sound tough but it came out thin and shaky.

"For you to help me…" and then a thin laugh.

"Help you with what?"

"To kill your girlfriend. What else?" More laughter, almost like a child giggling.

"I'd never do that."

"You already are."

The line went dead in his hand. He looked at the phone and saw it shaking in his hand. Ellie saw it too.

"What did he say?" she asked.

He turned away from her, paced to the opposite wall and then turned back to face her.

He couldn't tell her. He wasn't supposed to keep secrets, that was part of their pact, but he couldn't find it in him to tell her. Not this.

"He was just messing with me. He said 'Help me…' and then laughed. The voice was horrible. It made my teeth hurt."

"You said you'd never do that. What did he want you to do?"

Luke paused. "To help him."

"Do what?"

"Whatever it is he does. He didn't say. Kill someone I guess."

Luke hated lying to her. It was the worst feeling in the world. Apparently he didn't do it very well.

"Luke," she said softly, "what are you not telling me? Please don't lie to me. No matter how much you think I can't stand to hear, we promised not to keep secrets. Please."

His felt his shoulders slump and he sat down next to her. He couldn't look at her.

"He asked me to help him kill you."

"Oh, God!"

He turned to her quickly and said, "I won't let him hurt you! Ever! I'll stay outside your window every night if I have to. I'll go everywhere with you. I'll get a gun. I promise I won't let him touch you!"

"You can't do all that. You're not superman. We have to tell someone. We need help."

"But he told you not to tell anyone."

"It doesn't seem to matter. Apparently he's out to get me anyway."

Luke's cell phone beeped showing he had a new text message. He held it up so they could both see. It read *Tell a soul, and you both die.*

He looked at her and she started to cry.

CHAPTER 12

The killer was thirsty. The dog had not been enough.

His hunger had taken over and it was like a living thing. No cat, or raccoon, or lost dog was going to satisfy his urge and he knew the time had come. He had been under control for a very long time now, and he thought his routines had left nothing to be desired. He knew now that it had all been just a ruse. He had been fooling himself and delaying the inevitable. He may have even made it worse.

He lay in wait at his chosen place, like he had done numerous times in the past. Fortunately, he had not followed through then, forcing himself to see things as they were and letting the urge pass. Tonight, that was not going to happen. His lust for this release was going to win and he could feel himself on the verge of total bliss. He lay in wait.

The boy approached. Alone, distracted, not a care in the world.

The blood rushed through the killer's veins and he could hear it sing, the notes a cacophony of tension and anticipation. As the boy drew closer, he imagined the blood of his victim and the notes it would play as the pulse slowed and the pressure waned. He'd heard it before and thirsted to hear it again.

As the boy passed, he spoke the words and knew there was no turning back.

"Help me…"

The boy stopped.

CHAPTER 13

Jaxon felt déjà vu.

He was standing over another boy who had just been pulled from the same pool and the paramedics were working hopelessly trying to revive him. It wasn't going to happen. He knew it, the paramedics knew it, and Sally knew it. The kid was gone.

The crowd stood quietly in the cold night air in utter disbelief that this could be happening in their quiet suburban lives.

Jaxon knew they believed they had chosen a place to live and raise their families free from the activities and discretions of the less desirable among the human race. He knew they were questioning their skewed perceptions and asking themselves *What now? We were supposed to be immune to this kind of thing.*'

Immunity was a fragile thing. If you let a bad germ in, it could corrupt the whole system. Jaxon had seen it many times before.

"There are no footprints this time," Sally said. "At least none we can see. We've contaminated this part of the scene and that's probably where he was brought in and dumped."

He nodded and turned away, scanning the crowd. "You're out there. I can feel it," he whispered.

"What did you say, boss?" Sally asked.

He shook his head. "This is going to get bad. You know what this could be, right?"

She hesitated and he could tell she wasn't sure. He knew she was a good cop and a hell of an investigator, but she had little experience with this kind of thing.

"It's definitely not an accident," she said lamely.

"The FBI is probably going to pay attention now. We may have someone who is going to keep doing this."

"Serial?"

He nodded.

"Shit."

"Yes—shit," he said. "This will get complicated."

"Are we even sure it's the same guy?"

"What's your gut feeling on it?" he asked, the teacher now.

"It's the same guy."

He nodded. "All right, let's get the Crime Scene techs here and go over this place with a fine tooth comb. I want some uniforms working the crowd right now to see if anybody saw anything. The first kid gets his autopsy now. We need to know what killed him and who the hell he is."

"On it," she said, and walked away to start everything rolling.

"And find out if anybody is missing another kid!" he yelled.

* * *

It had been two days since they had pulled Paul Bannon from the pool and Luke was still in shock.

Not only had William Smith, or whatever his real name was, killed one of his friends, he had put him out in plain sight. The guy wasn't even trying to hide it. At least he hadn't tried to communicate with either him or Ellie yet, but Luke knew something would be coming. He could feel it.

Paul's Mother had reported him missing the morning they had found him. She told the police he hadn't come home the night before and she had stayed up all night worrying. This story and more were making it around campus faster than the speed of light and Luke had heard more than his fair share of it. He had watched them pull Paul from the pool, just like the first kid, and felt a pain deep inside he never knew existed. He couldn't help thinking he had somehow contributed to his friend's death.

Ellie apparently felt the same way and was distant and depressed at lunch.

He couldn't seem to get through to her and he knew she was blaming herself. They had filled Jimmy and John in on everything and the two were feeling some of the burden also. He could see the stress on John's face. Paul had been a jerk sometimes but he didn't deserve to die and they all felt somehow responsible.

"What if we had gone to the police?" Ellie asked all of them. "Maybe we could have saved Paul."

Nobody had an answer. They all felt as she did and the burden of guessing what could have been laid heavy on all of them.

At the bus stop, Patrick seemed edgy and Alan hadn't even shown up at school. Paul had been his best friend. Many of the parents picked their kids up at the bus stop or even went as far as to provide their own transportation to and from school. Fear was weighing heavily on the community.

Luke's little group had assured their parents they would stick together so they were some of the only ones walking from the stop. They dropped Ellie off at her house and then strode the short distance to their houses. Luke wasn't worried. He knew the killer wouldn't touch them in the open. He seemed to be someone who liked remaining hidden, yet put the results of his actions out there to taunt everyone.

As he reached for the front door, his cell phone beeped and he stopped, pulling it from his pocket. *You're off the hook…for now!* Luke could hear the voice in his mind as he read the text message. He shivered in the afternoon cold.

He dialed Ellie's number and she answered on the second ring. "You just left. Are you ok?"

"He just sent me a text message," Luke said.

"I didn't get one." Just then her phone beeped and Luke could hear it through the speaker. "Wait! I just got a text. Hold on…"

Luke prayed her message was the same and that the jerk hadn't decided to mess with her more.

"It says, *You're off the hook…for now!*"

"That's what mine said too." Luke let out the breath he was holding and leaned up against the door.

"Do you think we should believe him?" she asked.

"I don't see why. I'm planning on keeping my eyes and ears open. You should too."

"Ok."

Luke could hear the disappointment in her voice and he wondered if maybe he should have told her to relax. Everything will be ok now. She was so tense he could feel it through the connection.

"Hey, at least we should be ok for a while," he said, changing his mind. "He's probably had his fill of things and will leave us alone for now. Maybe for good. We did what he told us to. We haven't told anyone."

"I hope so. I can't take much more."

"I know. Call me if you need to talk. Do you want to come over later? I could come and get you."

"Ok! That would be good. You always make me feel better."

He could feel her smiling and he smiled too. "All right. I'll call in a bit and come get you."

"See ya'."

"Bye," and he hung up and went inside.

He only hoped William Smith would keep his promise.

CHAPTER 14

Jaxon had just gotten off the phone with the Medical Examiner and was doodling on his napkin as he thought through what he'd just learned.

They still had no name for the first kid in the pool and the autopsy had shown very little. He had died of asphyxiation caused by the inhalation of a chemical. Diethyl Ether. The ME thought a rag had been held over the victim's mouth and nose until he passed out and then the killer continued to hold the chemically soaked rag on his face until the kid died. Mild bruising had been found on the face around the mouth and nose consistent with this theory.

Paul Bannon had died the same way. Asphyxiation. Same chemical traces in his bloodstream. Same bruising of the face.

What was bothering Jaxon more than anything was the peculiar state of the first kid's body. The ME had told him some of the boy's internal organs were frozen.

"Are your refrigerators set too cold?" Jaxon had asked.

"I checked. They're fine. The rest of him was not frozen but he had some patches on his skin that resembled freezer burn. I think this boy has been frozen solid and recently thawed."

"How long?"

"I haven't been able to determine that yet. I'm checking with a colleague in North Dakota. He has some experience with this kind of thing. I should know something within a day or two."

Freezer burn? What the hell? Jaxon thought.

This kid may have been missing longer then they originally thought. He'd have to start looking back months and see if anything came up. In the mean time, it was probably worth it to take a trip back out to the neighborhood and see if any of these kids had anything to tell him.

* * *

Luke had just picked up Ellie from her house and they were heading back to his place through the frozen streets when a car pulled up next to them and rolled down its window.

"Lucas Harrison, Eliana Pemberton. Can we talk to you a moment."

It was the two cops who had been to Luke's house that Sunday morning when they thought his was the body in the pool.

Luke looked at Ellie and then back at the cops and shrugged. "I guess," he said.

"Was Paul Bannon a friend of yours?" the one named Jaxon asked.

They both nodded. "He lived a couple of houses down from me," Ellie said.

"Had Paul said anything to you two about being frightened or worried?"

They both shook their heads. "No," Luke said. "He seemed normal to me."

"Had he been absent from school more than normal lately?" The woman cop asked.

"No," Luke said. "He was always there. He never missed a day unless school was canceled."

"Did you guys get along?" Jaxon asked looking hard into Luke's eyes.

He hesitated. "Yeah...I mean we were friends and stuff. He was mad at me for a little while when he had his stitches."

"What stitches?"

"We would have these snowball fights and he had the bright idea to put ice inside of the snowballs. He hit my friend Jimmy in the arm with one and made his arm numb. The next battle we got him back, only he got hit in the face and had to have stitches. It was stupid, I know. We don't use ice balls anymore."

Jaxon turned and looked at the woman. She raised her eyebrows but said nothing.

He held up a picture and asked, "Do either of you know this boy?"

Luke and Ellie leaned in to get a better look. It was a shot of a face. A kid about Luke's age. His skin was pasty white and his lips looked slack and lifeless. His eyes were mostly closed, but not because he was sleeping. One of his irises could barely be seen through the cracked left eyelid. It made Luke shudder involuntarily. He leaned back, looking away quickly.

"No," Luke said and Ellie shook her head, a frown now on her face.

Jaxon put the picture away and Luke asked, "Was that the kid from the pool? The first one?"

Jaxon looked at Luke's shoes, ignoring the question, and asked, "What size shoe do you wear?"

"Uh…I don't remember. You'd have to ask my mom. I don't pay attention to that kind of stuff. Why?"

"What happened to your coat?" the detective asked next, pointing to the rip in his sleeve.

"I'm not sure," Luke said. "I think I ripped it on a branch while we were playing kick the can the other night."

"On a branch, huh?"

Luke nodded and looked at Ellie who nodded too.

Jaxon reached into his coat pocket and pulled out a baggie. Inside was the piece that had been torn from Luke's coat. Luke swallowed and his knees felt a little watery.

"I don't think it was a branch," Jaxon said. "I think you ripped it climbing the fence to the pool. This is the torn piece I have in this bag and I took it from the top of the chain link fence. Are you gonna stick with the 'branch' story?"

Luke decided to remain silent.

Jaxon opened the door and stepped out of his car. The woman did the same on the other side and walked around the front of the car to stand next to Jaxon.

"All right," Jaxon said, "I know you guys were in the pool area. We have footprints that we can match up and we have this torn piece of your coat. What I want to know is what did you see? You don't have to be afraid of anything happening, we just need to know what's going on. How about helping us?"

Luke looked at Ellie and then down at his feet which he shuffled in the snow. "We were in the pool but we didn't see anything."

"What were you doing in there in the dead of winter?" asked the woman.

"We were trying to skate on the ice but it was too thin. She almost slipped in but I grabbed her. Then we left."

"That right?" Jaxon asked Ellie.

"Yes, Sir," she said.

"And you didn't see a thing? No body in the pool? No footprints in the snow? Anybody else hanging around the area?"

Luke and Ellie shook their heads, no.

"Just you two?"

Luke and Ellie nodded, yes.

Luke watched Jaxon look at the woman in exasperation and she shrugged her shoulders. He knew they weren't buying it but he didn't know why they weren't arresting them or something. He was pretty scared but he wasn't going to admit anything he didn't have to. Ellie was looking like she was going to throw up and he hoped she could hold it together.

Jaxon turned back to Luke and said, "I don't believe you two." He pointed his finger at both of them, one at a time. "Something is going on and I'm going to find out what it is whether you tell me or not. A murder investigation is a serious thing and obstructing justice can get you both thrown in jail. Do you understand what obstruction of justice is?"

Luke nodded, as did Ellie.

He waited. Finally he said, "You have nothing else to add?"

Luke shook his head no and he could see Ellie out of the corner of his eye doing the same thing.

"Fine. If you think of anything else to say call me at this number." He handed them both a business card. "Don't be surprised if we pay a visit to your parents soon."

They both got back in the car and drove away. When they were gone, Ellie started to cry.

* * *

Luke and Ellie were back in his basement, the TV was on but neither one was watching it.

He was holding her as she sobbed into his shoulder. They had made it into his house and down the stairs without anyone seeing them. Ellie had been crying non-stop since the detectives had driven away. He couldn't seem to console her. She mumbled things he couldn't understand so he just held her and stroked her hair as she sobbed.

She finally got herself under control, lifting her head off of his shoulder and looking into his eyes.

"What are we going to do?" she asked. "My mom is going to kill me."

"I don't think they know everything," Luke said. "If they did, they would've asked us more stuff."

"They knew we were in there. I bet they know John and Jimmy were there too."

"Maybe. Their footprints were all over the snow, like ours, but they probably don't know who they belong to. I think they're just trying to find out who killed Paul and the other boy."

"But they acted like we did it. He looked at me like I was a killer. We haven't done anything."

"Yeah—that bothers me too. I felt like they were blaming us or trying to get us to confess something. I wonder if they know who that other kid is."

"You're not going to ask them are you?"

"No—I'm not going to call them for anything. We need to just leave stuff alone and this will all go away."

"I hope so," she said. "Just when William Smith backs off, the cops show up and start harassing us. I can't take too much more of this."

"Me neither."

They were quiet for a moment and she rubbed her face drying her eyes. He reached up and brushed a tear from her cheek and she grabbed his hand, pressing it to her face. "Will you keep me safe?" she said.

"Always."

She smiled finally, and then kissed his fingers. That smile could brighten his world no matter how bad things were. She was everything to him and at that moment, he would die for her if he had to. He just hoped it wouldn't come to that.

* * *

Jaxon turned to Sally and said, "Do you believe them?"

"They're keeping something from us," she said.

"I agree. With kids though, who knows if it's important or not. They could have been in there smoking his mom's cigarettes and afraid to tell us about it. Could be absolutely nothing."

"Could be everything, too."

He nodded, quietly navigating the streets back to the station.

"They did look scared," he finally said.

"Wouldn't you if someone like us came up and started grilling you about a murder?"

"True, but they looked a little more intense than just being intimidated. I thought the girl was going to puke all over her shoes."

"She was the one with the dog, right?"

"Yep."

"Any chance it could be related?"

"I don't know. We picked the dog's carcass up with the intent of disposing of it. Let's see if it's still in cold storage, and if so, we'll have forensics look it over."

Sally pulled out her cell phone and made the call. "Billy says they still have it. He's pulling it out of storage now and will go over it with a fine tooth comb."

"Maybe we'll get lucky."

"We need something. Right now, we have absolutely zip."

He nodded absently and sighed. They definitely needed something to break.

* * *

A day later, Jaxon and Sally were down in the forensics lab with Billy Halson, huddled over the decapitated corpse of the dog. Billy pointed to a section of the neck as he spoke.

"Lacerations here and here are consistent with a serrated knife used to make the initial incision on the neck. This incision continues deep into the tissue until reaching bone, then a larger non-serrated edge, probably consistent with a small axe or hatchet, was used to hack through the bone and tendons separating the head from the torso. The mostly clean initial cuts indicate the animal was most likely dead or incapacitated at the time of the beheading."

"So, a steak knife and a hatchet?" Jaxon said.

"Pretty much," Billy said. "Now the interesting thing about this whole situation deals with how the dog was subdued."

"What do you mean?" Sally asked.

"He was put to sleep. Like anesthesia. A chemical very similar to Chloroform, but one that isn't used much medically anymore."

Jaxon looked at Sally and she smiled. "Don't tell me," Jaxon said. "Diethyl Ether."

Billy looked disappointed. "How did you know?"

"The two boys in the pool. Same thing," Jaxon said.

"Damn," Billy said, "then you'll definitely find this useful."

He walked over to a counter opposite the dog and pulled a small vial from a tray holding multiple vials and test tubes. He held it up for them to see.

"What is it?" Sally asked.

"It's a fingernail," Jaxon said looking closer.

"Pulled it from a small laceration on the dog's abdomen," Billy said. "If you get a suspect, we can rule out the owner and family with simple saliva tests for DNA and hopefully get a match on the perp. I know it doesn't help you find the guy, but…"

"Have you looked at where our boy is getting his hands on Diethyl Ether?" Jaxon asked.

"It's still pretty common. Though it's not used medically any longer, the agent is used quite a bit, commercially, in certain chemical formulations and fuels."

"Fuels?"

"Yes. Alcohol based fuels used in radio control aircraft and high performance racing type engines. They call it 'Glow fuel.'"

Jaxon smiled. "Who's working on the Bannon kid?"

"Chris," Billy said, "but he's off today."

"You make sure you guys talk to each other on this. It looks almost certain our guy did the dog too."

"You got it."

CHAPTER 15

The next day Jaxon and Sally were in the Medical Examiner's Wing of St. Catherine's Hospital in Reston.

The morgue was set aside in the eastern section of the hospital farthest from the main entrance. To get to it you had to park in the E.R. garage and trek through the steam and heat of the laundry facility. The Nuns who ran the hospital were serious about keeping the undesirable aspects of death and dying away from the public eye. Jaxon couldn't help but wonder how the laundry workers liked having so many of the county's dead wheeled through their work station on the way to the morgue. Maybe they got used to it.

They walked into the outer office where a male receptionist dressed in faded green scrubs and too many gold bracelets ignored them as he read through the latest Cosmopolitan. The name on the counter read Boris. It was difficult to associate the name with the effeminate person seated on the other side of the desk. Surely, he must be a temp or something. Jaxon wondered how many people in this world were actually named Boris.

Jaxon cleared his throat. 'Boris' looked up from the magazine and smacked his gum.

"Can I help you?"

He definitely didn't sound like a Boris, Jaxon thought. He held out his badge and Sally did the same. "Detectives Jennings and Winston, Fairfax County PD. We're here to see Dr. Barstow."

"Oh yeah, I think he's expecting you. Hold on."

He picked up the phone and punched in some numbers with the end of a pencil. He stabbed the keypad of the phone like he was spearing shrimp on the end of a sharp stick. Quick little jabbing motions. Sally rolled her eyes at Jaxon.

'Boris' carried on a conversation with whomever answered at the other end and then quickly hung up. "Go right on back. He's in Bay C. Have you been back there before?"

"Yeah," Jaxon said. "Bay C. Got it."

They passed through a set of double doors and followed a long hallway which emptied into another reception like area. This is where the families waited as their loved ones were placed on cold stainless steel tables pending positive I.D. so their deaths could be confirmed and recorded.

A long time ago Jaxon had been one of those family members and whenever he came back here, it was like he was suffocating all over again. The room seemed way too small and cold. Sally glanced at him sideways and he realized he was taking quick shallow breaths, almost panting. He got himself under control. He was not going to lose it in here.

Pushing quickly through the waiting area, they entered Bay C through a single swinging door that had a small window in it about head high. They didn't knock. This room was even colder than the waiting area and Jaxon shivered despite his jacket.

Dr. Barstow was in his green scrubs and gloves standing next to a stainless steel table with the body of an older woman laid out naked. He turned when they entered.

"Detectives, glad you could make it."

"No problem, Doc," Jaxon said. "What have you got for us?"

"Something I think will surprise you. I hope it will help I.D. our John Doe."

Dr. Barstow walked over to the group of refrigerators along the far wall and pulled a drawer open, sliding a body out for them to see. It was the first boy from the pool. He slid some plastic sheeting out of the way exposing his midsection and chest, the sutures from the Y incision clearly visible.

Jaxon took an involuntary step back and felt his chest tighten at the sight of the boy lying on the slide. This was all too familiar and he couldn't keep the vision of his son out of his mind. Twelve years ago he had been in this exact spot, watching them pull his dead son out of the refrigerator so he could I.D. him.

He placed a hand on the counter and took a couple of deep breaths. Sally was watching him, but remained silent. Dr. Barstow didn't seem to notice.

The doc picked up the boy's right arm.

"He has a few broken fingernails from what looks like a struggle and we were able to get some skin cells from underneath the remaining nails. We've sent them off for DNA and when we get the results back we'll run it through the database and see if we get any hits. It's not very promising and I'll explain why in a minute."

He put the boys hand down and circled to the other side of his body. Sally had to move out of the way to let him pass.

"Here's one of the freezer burn patches I told you about."

He pointed to an area just below the right ribcage. It looked roughened and white compared to the surrounding skin. "Here and here, also," he said pointing to an area just above his groin. "I sampled a section of skin from here and performed a few tests my colleague up in North Dakota told me to try and I came up with some very interesting findings."

He turned and walked over to a counter behind them and moved in front of a microscope set up there. "Come take a look."

Jaxon and Sally moved to the microscope and Jaxon bent over and peered into the instrument. "What am I looking at, Doc?" He seemed to do better when he didn't have to look at the boy's body.

"Do you see the jagged edges around the cell wall structure? It looks ruptured in various places correct?"

"Yeah, I see that."

"This indicates the cells have been frozen at a very cold temperature and for a very long time."

The Doc paused letting that sink in. Jaxon stood up and let Sally look.

"How long is a very long time, Doc?"

"More than ten years, maybe even twenty. I can't tell exactly. I can just give you a vague range."

"Damn. Somebody kept this kid in deep freeze for more than ten years?"

Dr. Barstow nodded slowly. "That's what it looks like."

"Is it possible to get a more accurate date?" Sally asked.

"At this point I don't know of any way. I'm looking into it."

"How about Carbon 14 dating? Can we use that on him?"

"Not unless he's been dead for more than two hundred years," the Doc said. "It's not accurate enough on substances that are within two hundred or so years old. There are other testing methods and I'm looking into them."

"But you estimate between ten and twenty years," Jaxon said.

"That's my estimate, yes."

"That's quite a big time frame to search, but at least we know we're not looking for something recent," Jaxon said.

"No wonder nobody is looking for him or reported him missing," Sally said. "He's been dead twenty years."

"Doc, Billy Halson in Forensics has found something interesting on a decapitated dog we got a call on a number of weeks back. Apparently the dog has traces of Diethyl Ether in its bloodstream, just like John Doe here and Paul Bannon. We think it's the same guy. But in a twenty year span? It's hard to get around that."

"With the exceptions of the frozen organs and freezer burn, the two boys have very similar traits. I would have bet my life that it was the same guy, but this huge space in time really puts serious doubts into my mind. It's not impossible, but it is somewhat unlikely."

"Has any other evidence turned up? What about residues or fingerprints on the bodies?" Jaxon asked.

"The pool water washed most of that kind of thing away. Did you guys drain the pool and filter the water?"

"No, not yet. We haven't been able to get in touch with the sports complex manager to get permission to drain it. He's in Miami at the moment. That's definitely on the agenda."

"Well, John Doe will stay here for a while longer anyway," Dr. Barstow said, "but I'm going to release Paul Bannon to his parents so they can bury him. Any problems with that?"

"Do they plan on cremating him or burying him?" Sally asked.

"Burial, at least that was the desire expressed to me. If it's important to you, you should contact them."

"No, if you feel you've retrieved all the evidence he has to offer that's good enough for us," Jaxon said. "Thanks Doc. Let us know if you find anything more definitive on a date for John Doe."

"I will."

"Let's go, Sally. We've got some digging to do."

Jaxon left Bay C quickly, glad to leave the coldness and the memories behind. He hated coming here, but he knew it was something unavoidable in his line of work. He couldn't count the number of times he had visited the facility. All he knew was he expected it to get easier. It didn't.

'Boris' was still reading his magazine as they pushed through the double doors and he looked up and smiled as they left. "Have a nice day," he said, flapping a hand at them that jangled.

"Yeah. You too," Jaxon said, but thought, *Too late for that.*

Part 2

CHAPTER 16

Five Months Later

Luke dived into the pool and started his practice laps.

The swim team was halfway through its season and Luke, John, Jimmy, and Ellie were all in the pool stroking away while the coach pushed them harder. The team consisted of about thirty five kids from the neighborhood and had done fairly well winning six of the eight meets already concluded. There were seven more to go.

Ellie was the star, placing first in all her heats, and rumors were spreading she was to be selected for the state team in her event, the women's one hundred meter butterfly. Luke wasn't nearly as competitive, finishing second in two of his heats and third in all the others. He still had fun and wouldn't miss it for the world. If Ellie got to go to state, he would be without her for a week. Even though he was proud she was so good, he didn't want her to leave. Maybe he'd get to go anyway and cheer her on.

Jimmy crossed the lane divider and bumped into Luke. He stopped and then pushed Luke down deeper into the pool. Luke came up sputtering, his rhythm broken. Jimmy grinned at him looking goofy in his swim goggles and Luke jumped at him trying to dunk him. The two laughed and wrestled until John came up and pushed them both under. John then cut straight across the pool through all the lanes as Luke and Jimmy swam after him. All the other swimmers doing laps had to move out of the way or stop as the boys disrupted the pool.

"Harrison! Besner! Will you three cut it out!" Will Francis, their swim coach, yelled. "You're messing up the whole team!"

Ellie swam into Luke and came up looking frustrated until she saw it was him. "Hey cutie! What the heck are you doing?" she said, her nose clip making her sound all stuffy.

"Waiting for you to pay attention to me."

"What? You don't get enough of me the rest of the day?" She smiled at him, breathing a little hard from the exertion.

"I could never get enough of you," he said seriously, but then splashed her in the face.

"Hey!"

He dived away and swam hard for the far end but she caught him mid-pool and they came up in each other's arms laughing. She tickled him as the other swimmers passed around them.

He squirmed, laughing out loud and reached to tickle her back but she slipped from his grasp and swam away. He caught her and said, "Oh, you're not getting away that easily."

"Dammit Harrison! Now you're messing with my star. Will you let her swim please?" Coach Francis stood there with his hands on his hips and the whistle dangling from his lips. "Twenty more laps for you today, Luke. Now get moving."

"You got me in trouble," Luke said to Ellie, but grinned. "Now you owe me."

She pushed him away and laughed. "We'll see, you Goofy Goober." She dived under the water and resumed her training. He followed after her.

After practice, they were walking home when John said, "Hey! Let's go check out the creek. It rained a bunch last night and I bet it's full."

Instead of going through Luke's fence at the back of the tennis courts, they turned right and followed a path into the woods. The trail gave access to the pool and tennis courts for the neighborhood which existed on the other side of the creek.

They passed a couple and their two children loaded down with towels and floats, all headed for the pool. The little kids kept running ahead of the parents and the dad would yell at them to 'Wait up!' Ellie reached out and grabbed the little girl, tickling her as she squirmed in her arms. She squealed with delight.

"Ellie! Stop!" the little girl yelled as she laughed.

"Thanks, Ellie," the dad said.

"No problem Mr. Stinson." To the little girl she said, "Mel, you listen to your Daddy, now. He's smart." And she smiled at the little girl.

"Ok, Ellie. I will. I'm a good girl."

"I know you are sweetie," Ellie said putting her down and giving her a big hug. "I'll come play with you soon, ok?"

Mel's face lit up and she yelled, "Yea! Ellie's gonna play with me! Ellie's gonna play with me!" She did a little dance in her swimmies and started to take off again, but then seemed to remember she wasn't supposed to. She stopped and looked at her dad and then walked up to him taking his hand. "Sorry, Daddy."

"It's ok, Mel. Just stay close to me, all right?"

She nodded her little head and waved at Ellie as they continued on their way to the pool.

"You haven't babysat for them in a while," Luke said.

"I know. I think he lost his job or something. They haven't been going out much. I love Mel and Robby. I like to just go and see them every once in awhile for the fun of it."

"I hate babysitting," Jimmy said. "What a waste of time."

"Who've you ever babysat?" John asked.

"Nobody. I just think it's a waste of time and I know I would hate it."

"My little brother's ok sometimes," Luke said. "He used to crap his pants and I hated cleaning that up."

"See," Jimmy said. "I'd hate that. Baby crap, what a load of shit."

Luke noticed Ellie wasn't saying anything. He turned around and found her stopped in front of a tree looking at a sign hanging on it.

"What is it, El?" Luke yelled back.

"Come and look at this!" she said.

They went back and Ellie pointed at it.

"It's a lost dog," Jimmy said. "Do you know it?"

"No," she said, "but I've seen like five lost pet signs in the last two weeks."

"So," Jimmy said.

"Maybe they're not lost," she said seriously.

Jimmy wasn't getting it and said, "What? Somebody's scamming people, hoping someone finds a real dog and calls them."

"No, Jim," Luke said. "It's not a scam. These people really don't know where their dogs are."

"Do you think it's him?" Ellie said quietly.

"I don't think so, El," Luke said moving next to her. "He's probably gone now. We haven't heard anything from him in months."

"I know—it's just weird. All of a sudden, these cats and dogs go missing."

"It could be a coincidence," John said. "It's summer. People let their dogs outside more and they just run off because no one is paying attention to them."

"Just like Bentley?" she said, a little anger edging into her voice. "What are you saying? I didn't pay attention to my dog?"

"No," John said quickly, "I'm not even talking about you."

"But you make it sound like these people don't care about their animals. They just got lazy and the dog ran off, right? Well, I wasn't lazy. I was cold and somebody took Bentley and then cut his head off!" She was shouting now and on the verge of tears.

"All right—all right! I didn't mean anything Ellie."

Luke touched her arm. "Hey," he said softly. "We get it, ok? Nobody would ever say you were bad to Bentley."

"But you guys aren't taking this seriously," she said, pointing to the sign.

"We just don't want you to get all worked up about it. It doesn't mean we don't get what you're saying," Jimmy said.

"Well I am worked up about it."

"We know," John said, sarcastically.

"Shut up, John," Luke said.

"Jeez!" John said. "All right, Ellie. I'm sorry."

She looked at all three of them and then said, "You know, sometimes it's hard hanging out with just boys."

"We know," Luke said, smiling. "We can be pretty stupid."

"Speak for yourself, dumbass," Jimmy said, a grin spreading across his face.

She finally smiled and said to Luke, "Well—you're not stupid." And she leaned up against him resting her head on his shoulder.

"What?" John said. "Does that mean I am?"

They ignored him and started walking again, Ellie and Luke with their arms around each other and her head leaning on his shoulder.

"You know," Jimmy said, "you two are so cute sometimes it makes me want to barf."

"Me?" Luke asked.

Jimmy just gave him a look. "Come on. Let's go see the creek."

They went deeper into the woods and Luke could hear water rushing in the distance.

"Do you hear that?" John asked. "Come on!" and he started to run.

They all chased after him and as they came up to a foot bridge they could see the creek filled to the top of its banks. The water was rushing past under the bridge just a few inches below their feet.

"Man!" John said. "It's rockin'!"

Luke watched Ellie pick a stick up and throw it upstream into the creek. It zoomed past them under the bridge in a matter of seconds.

"It's pretty strong," she said. "Better not fall in."

Luke sat down on the edge of the bridge and stuck his feet in. The current was quick and powerful. He had to grip the wood to keep from being pulled off.

"Be careful," Ellie said.

"Come on," Luke said. "Stick your feet in!"

They all sat and put their feet in the rushing water.

"Damn! That's cold!" John said.

"It feels like it's gonna pull me in," Ellie said, yanking her feet out of the torrent and standing back up.

Suddenly, two kids on bikes came barreling down the path straight on to the foot bridge.

They were side by side and taking up the whole trail. As they sped across the bridge, one of the kids stuck his foot out and knocked Ellie backwards. She was apparently in the way. She stumbled, falling against John who was just barely hanging on, the strong current pulling at his feet. He went over into the water and disappeared under. Luke was able to hold on to Ellie and keep her from following John in.

"John!" Jimmy shouted and ran off the bridge to the shore of the creek, chasing after his brother. Luke pulled Ellie up and they followed after him. John still had not come up.

"Where is he?" Jimmy yelled, panicking. "I can't see him!"

Luke searched the water trying to find any sign of John in the foaming liquid. Suddenly, fifty yards downstream, his head popped up and his arms flailed air as he tried to grab hold of something.

"There!" Luke pointed.

Jimmy saw him and chased after his brother who was racing away in the current.

"Hold on John! We're coming!"

Luke ran after them and watched as John was able to catch hold of a branch hanging low over the creek. The branch was straining against his weight but holding fast. Jimmy got to him and frantically looked around for something he could extend out to his brother. Luke tripped and fell. Grabbing his shin in pain, he looked at what he tripped over. It was a long branch. He grabbed it and dragged it over to Jimmy.

"Here! Use this!"

"Oh man! That's good! Got it! Help me."

"I'll try," Luke said, limping.

"I'll help," Ellie said, and grabbed hold of the branch too.

John was holding on but he looked tired and he kept choking on the water when it lapped into his face as it rushed by. They extended the branch out to him, but it kept getting pushed away by the current.

"We need to move a little more upstream," Jimmy said, and they moved up the shore a few feet. They tried again and the branch hit John in the head.

"Grab it, John!" Jimmy yelled. "We'll pull you in!"

"I can't! It will pull me under!"

"We won't let go! Come on man, it's gonna pull you under in a minute anyway!"

John thought about it for a second and then made up his mind. He let one hand go, grabbed the branch they were holding out to him, and then let his other hand go. He floundered for a second and Luke thought he was going to get swept away, but he managed to get his other hand on the branch and they all pulled him quickly to shore.

He stumbled climbing up the bank and then collapsed from exhaustion as his brother held on to his arm like he would never let go. After a few seconds John said, "You can let go now Jim, I'm ok."

"I know," Jimmy said, letting go of John's arm. "I know." And he grinned at his brother who, despite his exhaustion, grinned back at him.

"Thanks," John said.

Ellie hugged him around the neck saying, "I'm sorry, John! I didn't mean to make you fall in. I'm so sorry!"

"It's ok, Ellie," John said. "I know it wasn't your fault."

"Who were those kids anyway?" Luke asked.

"One of them was Jason Margot," Ellie said. "I don't know the other one. Jason was the one who stuck his foot out."

"Sounds like Jason deserves a little payback," Jimmy said.

"Let's just let it go," Ellie said. "John's ok and nobody got seriously hurt."

"Bullshit!" John said. "I'm not letting this go. They almost killed me!"

Ellie let go of John and sat back on her knees looking distraught. Luke wasn't sure how to feel about this. He wasn't one who liked revenge, but John was right. They almost killed him.

"I got a cool idea and nobody will get hurt," Jimmy said, "but it should scare the crap out of them. Come on."

John got up slowly and they all followed Jimmy back to Cotton Court.

CHAPTER 17

After five long months with nothing breaking in the case, Jaxon received a call that got his blood going.

He grabbed Sally from the break room saying, "Come on! We've got a lead on the pool kids. Let's go!"

They drove into the familiar neighborhood and made their way to a house which sat directly across from the pool complex. It was a two story, brick affair with a perfectly manicured yard and fresh paint on the eaves.

A man stood in the yard watering a patch of flowers planted around his matching brick mailbox. They parked in the driveway and stepped out into the bright morning sun.

Jaxon could see what looked like a swim team practicing at the pool. A man who appeared to be the coach was blowing his whistle and gesturing at something in the water Jaxon could not see.

"What are we doing here?" Sally asked as they watched the man put his hose down and make his way toward them.

"You'll see," Jaxon said and grinned.

As the man walked up, Jaxon produced his I.D. and asked, "Are you Mr. Lolly?"

"Yes sir," the man said. "Glad you two could get here so quick. But please, call me Burt." And he stuck out his hand to shake. His grip was like shaking a stone statue. Only one that gripped back. It took everything for Jaxon not to flinch.

"Detective Jennings, FCPD and this is Detective Winston."

"Nice to meet you two," Burt said. "Come on in and I'll show you what I got."

They followed the short stocky man of about seventy through the garage, entering the house through the kitchen. An older woman with bright red hair stood at the sink washing what looked like the breakfast dishes. She turned as they stepped in behind Burt.

"This is my wife Marie. Honey, this is Detective Jennings and Detective Winston."

"Nice to see you," she said as she wiped her hands on a dish towel. "Can I get you some coffee or something to eat?"

"Coffee would be great," Jaxon said.

"And you young lady?"

"A cup of coffee would be spectacular," Sally said with a smile. "What a lovely kitchen you have."

Marie beamed, said "Thank you," and grabbed two coffee mugs from the cupboard behind her.

"We'll be in the den, sweetie," Burt said. "Could you bring the mugs in there?"

She smiled and nodded.

Jaxon followed Burt through the house to a room which was in the rear of the spacious first floor. It was lined with books and had a dark wood desk on the wall opposite the door. Small and tidy, it was a man's space and Burt had it decorated with small models of military jets along with pictures of a younger Burt in uniform standing next to various aircraft and servicemen. Framed medals hung on the wall behind the desk and Jaxon recognized the Distinguished Flying Cross in a frame all by itself.

Burt saw him looking the medal over and said, "Were you in the service?"

Jaxon nodded. "Army. Major in the M.P.'s. Ten years, but I never saw battle. Got out before Desert Storm and was too young for Vietnam."

Burt nodded. "Doesn't mean you're anything less than you are. It shaped all of us that have been in. One way or another. Good or bad."

"What was the DFC for?" Jaxon asked.

"Chu Lai, Vietnam. Hill 488. I helped one of the war's greatest heroes make it off that hell hole alive. His name was Gunnery Sergeant Jimmie Howard. He was Staff Sergeant at the time. He was awarded the Congressional Medal of Honor for that battle. He deserved a medal more than I."

"What did you fly?" Jaxon asked, guessing at his occupation.

"A-4 Skyhawk. Best damn attack aircraft McDonell Douglas ever built. Tough too. Brought my ugly ass home every time, even when she had holes in her."

He looked dead serious and Jaxon believed every word. He looked at a picture of two A-4's in formation over an aircraft carrier at sea. He assumed one of them was Burt.

"I didn't bring you back here to reminisce about the past," Burt said, getting down to business, "but if you want to come by another time, I'll tell you the whole story. Deal?"

"Deal," Jaxon said.

"All right, let me show you what I found," Burt said, sitting at his desk and logging on to his computer. "I have a motion sensing surveillance system in the front yard, and as I was reviewing the recordings from Christmas, so I could clean up disc space, I saw this…"

He hit play and they watched as a nighttime shot from a camera high up looked over the front yard toward the street. His mailbox was in plain view and Jaxon recognized the pool across the street. From the right came what Jaxon could only assume was an adult male, about six feet four inches tall, huge, wearing black and moving in a crouch around the cars in the driveway, past the mailbox, and into the neighbor's yard where he stepped behind a hedge and crouched down out of sight. He turned toward the camera as he hid and they caught a brief glimpse of a bright white face.

"An albino?" Jaxon asked no one.

"A mask," Sally said. "It looked like a Halloween mask."

"That's what I thought too," Burt said. "Now, here is the interesting part. If you look at the time stamp," he pointed to the upper right of the computer screen where the time was displayed and a few other numbers Jaxon could not decipher, "you'll see thirty three minutes have elapsed." He paused the video and pointed to the time. "The system is set only to record when it senses movement and it will continue recording as long as an object is moving in front of the sensor. It stops after five minutes of inactivity."

Jaxon nodded understanding. He had seen many systems use this feature, especially ones which recorded to computer hard drives. It saved precious space and allowed for much longer monitoring times if it wasn't running the whole time the system was armed.

Burt hit play again and they watched as the camera caught a young male walking down the sidewalk coming from the same direction as the masked man in the bushes. As he got closer, Jaxon recognized the clothing, even in the greenish glow of the night vision.

"Oh shit," Jaxon said unaware he had cursed.

"Yes," Burt said. "Now watch."

"Is that Paul Bannon?" Sally asked.

Jaxon nodded his head, but didn't reply.

Even though there was no sound with the recordings, he seemed to think he would miss something if he spoke or made a sound. He realized he was holding his breath and he exhaled trying to relieve some of the tension.

Paul casually walked past the mailbox and seemed to be talking or singing to himself. As he approached the boundary of Burt's yard, the boy suddenly stopped and cocked his head. As they watched, he turned toward the hedge and seemed to be listening to something. He took a step into the yard and then stopped again as if unsure what to do.

He stayed that way for a moment and then looked in both directions. He made a move to continue on his way and then jerked back toward the bushes as if surprised. He waited, and then took some steps toward the hedge again. He was bent over at the waist as if trying to hear something very faint. He kept edging closer to the bushes and when he was about a foot away, he was yanked into the hedge by some unseen force and disappeared from view. The recording continued but nothing else moved. Burt stopped the playback.

"I called you right away," Burt said.

"Damn," Jaxon murmured, his face tense at what he'd just witnessed.

"Is there more?" Sally asked.

"I don't know," Burt said. "I didn't watch any more. I didn't want to risk doing something stupid like erasing it by mistake. This is the boy they found in the pool, isn't it?"

Sally nodded her head. "We've been at a standstill on the case for months. Not a clue as to who would do this."

"Until now," Jaxon said. "What do you need to do to see if it caught any more?"

"Just hit play," Burt said. "But it's approaching the end of the disc space." He pointed at a number which read 98. "It's 98% full now. That's why I was going through stuff and deleting things. It will record over the oldest stuff first once it reaches max capacity, but sometimes it messes up. I lost some stuff for you guys last year when the kids vandalized my lights."

"Lights?" Sally asked.

"Yeah. I run a pretty large animated Christmas Light show and I bought the surveillance system because kids were vandalizing some of the display. I put signs up too, warning them about the cameras, but sometimes they still ignore them. Maybe they're just stupid."

He looked a little embarrassed but Jaxon thought it sounded pretty cool.

"I'll trust you," Jaxon said. "We need to see if there's more."

Burt nodded and pressed a key on the computer. He pointed at the time stamp and they saw it had advanced twenty minutes. The man emerged from the hedge in a crouch carrying Paul Bannon over his shoulders like a sack of potatoes. He walked straight to the street and then stopped. He turned toward the camera and seemed to look directly at it. His head was tilted up and he stood motionless for about twenty seconds.

"He's mocking us," Sally said. "He knows the cameras are there."

"I'll be damned…" Burt said.

They watched as the white masked man turned toward the street and crossed it heading for the pool. He stopped at the fence and pushed Paul Bannon up and over the top, letting him crash to the ground on the other side. The man then started climbing the fence, but before he reached the top the recording ended.

"That's it," Burt said.

CHAPTER 18

They waited in the woods for Jason and his friend to return from the pool.

John was the lookout and would make some kind of animal noise as a signal. Laughable, Luke knew, but it was their only way of pulling the prank off without Jason and his friend being tipped off. By the time they figured it was some kid making the animal call, it would be too late.

Jimmy, Luke, and Ellie were upstream from the bridge, just behind a tree at a bend in the creek. Sitting in front of Jimmy was an Estes rocket launching system primed and ready for firing.

They had taken some of Luke's dad's wire fishing line and strung it from the tree they were hiding behind to the base of the foot bridge, right at the midway point. A 'D' sized rocket engine was hanging from the line by a piece of soda straw super-glued to the engine's body. When fired, the rocket engine would shoot toward the bridge, guided by the wire, and impact the large support beam the line was tied to. The rocket engine had a small charge that would ignite at the end of its firing run. This charge was supposed to expel the parachute most rockets carried. It was basically a firecracker that would explode with a loud bang right at the feet of whoever was crossing the bridge at the time.

Sometimes Luke couldn't believe the stuff Jimmy came up with. He was trying hard not to laugh out loud as he imagined what would happen to the two kids when this loud whooshing noise came straight at them followed by a large bang.

"What are you giggling at?" Ellie whispered, her face betraying the anxiety she felt. She hadn't wanted any part of this, but she was here in support of her friends.

"Nothing—just thinking about what's going to happen when that rocket engine hits the bridge."

"I hope nobody gets hurt," she said.

"It's not going to hit them, El," Luke said. "It'll just scare the crap out of them and then we'll jump out and give 'em hell about making John fall in the creek."

"I hope that's all it does," she said.

"Will you two be quiet. I can't hear John if he signals," Jimmy said, adjusting his position behind the tree.

"Sorry," Luke whispered.

They had tested the system once with a smaller sized rocket engine that didn't have the explosive charge. They didn't want the bang attracting attention until they were ready, but they needed to get the timing down. When John signaled, Jimmy would pull the firing pin. And wait.

The system had a failsafe of three seconds before the firing button could be pushed, but once pressed, the engine would fire immediately. It had worked flawlessly and they had all hooted and hollered at the brilliance of it. Now they would see if John could get the timing right for riders approaching rapidly on bikes.

The creek had calmed down quite a bit, but it still carried more water than normal. The level had dropped considerably and now stood a good two feet below the bottom of the bridge

Jimmy set the firing unit down for a second to get a piece of gum out of his pocket, just as John made the bird call they all recognized as the signal.

"Crap!" Jimmy cursed under his breath and snatched up the firing mechanism. His gum fell to the ground, forgotten. Luke watched Jimmy pull the pin and wait the three seconds for the ready light to come on. Ellie leaned against him, anxiously holding him around the shoulders. He could feel her breath in his ear and reached up to hold her hand. They waited for the light.

* * *

John cramped up as he knelt in the bushes just up from the bridge.

The soreness he felt from the swim in the creek still lingered and his lungs hurt every time he took a deep breath. He had never been that scared in his short life and never wanted to feel that way again, but he didn't mind making someone else feel it. Especially if that someone was Jason Margot and his friend. What pricks. He would be the first one laughing in their faces after the rocket engine scared the crap out of them.

John heard a noise and peered around the bush. Jason and his friend were slowly riding up the path and he tensed in anticipation. He knew he had to get the timing right or the two boys would either be past the bridge or not yet to it when the rocket engine was fired. He figured he would count to three after they passed his position and that should be about perfect.

Suddenly, little Mel Stinson and her brother Robbie came running up the path behind the two bikes. John hesitated not sure what to do. He didn't want the two little kids anywhere near the action, yet if he didn't signal shortly, the opportunity would pass. He waited and watched. Just as he was about to nix the whole plan, Mr. Stinson came running up behind his kids and grabbed them both, scooping them up in his arms as they squealed.

"You two need to wait for your mother," John heard him say, and watched him turn toward the pool carrying the two little ones back around the bend, disappearing. Just then, Jason and his pal passed his hiding place at a leisurely pace, chatting about dunking some little girl and laughing when she came up crying. Assholes.

He gave the signal.

* * *

The light came on and Jimmy pressed the button, looking up. Luke could see the two kids riding up onto the bridge as the engine fired. It made a loud 'whooshing' sound, streaking away from them toward the two riders.

They both turned toward the sudden noise and Luke watched as their mouths fell open in shock. The rocket engine impacted the beam just as the front tire of Jason's bike reached that exact point. The loud bang echoed through the woods. John's timing couldn't have been better.

Jason reacted by reflexively veering away from the loud concussion and steering his bike into his friend's who kept pace to the left of him. Luke watched in horror as both bikes and riders drove off the side of the bridge into the creek. Jason actually let out a little scream.

"Oh damn!" Jimmy yelled as he jumped up and ran toward the bridge. Luke and Ellie followed right behind him.

"I told you guys!" Ellie yelled. "I knew something bad would happen."

All Luke could think about was what happened when John went into the creek. They were barely able to get him out in time. How would they rescue two kids who also might be hurt from falling in on their bikes?

It took them a few seconds to get through the dense woods and Luke could see John approaching from his hiding place. John had a huge smile on his face and looked to be laughing as he whooped and hollered. Jimmy got to the bridge first and stood at the edge looking down. When Luke arrived next to him he was shocked at what he saw. Ellie sank to her knees next to him and said, "Thank God!"

The two boys were sitting in the mud on the other side of the creek. Their bikes lay to the side with one halfway in the water, its back tire spinning as the current rushed through the spokes. They were covered in mud, but appeared to be unhurt.

John stopped next to Jimmy and bent over with his hands on his knees trying to catch his breath. He was laughing between gasps. Jimmy started laughing too and then Luke joined them in relief. Ellie, apparently, did not think it was funny.

Mr. Stinson ran up behind them with Mel and her brother in tow.

"What was that noise?" He said. "Are you kids ok? It sounded like a gunshot!"

It was then he saw the two boys below and began to put two and two together. He rushed over the bridge and down the embankment, helping Jason and his friend up the slope with their bikes. Jimmy and Luke followed to help. Ellie stood there as Mel came up to her and grabbed her hand. John didn't move.

"You two ok?" Mr. Stinson asked Jason and his friend when they made it back up to the path. They nodded, but said nothing. Mr. Stinson walked on to the bridge and looked down at the wire that was still attached to the support beam. A small charred area blackened the wood at the point of attachment. He looked up at Luke and his group of friends.

"What did you guys do?" he asked.

"We just wanted to scare them," Jimmy said. "We didn't know they would drive over the side of the bridge."

"You kids could have killed them," he yelled angrily. "You know that, right?"

"They almost killed me this morning!" John said, just as angry. Luke couldn't believe he was talking to an adult like that. "They came barreling over the bridge while we were sitting on it and Jason kicked Ellie out of the way. She fell into me and I fell off into the fast water. You saw how strong it was this morning right? I almost drowned and they didn't even stop."

"That still doesn't give you the right to endanger their lives." He looked at Ellie who was holding his daughter's hand as she hid behind her leg. "And Ellie, I can't believe you'd be a part of this. Does your mother know what kind of people you hang out with? Maybe I need to call her." He noticed his little girl and said, "Mel, come here."

The little girl didn't move and she shyly shook her head.

"Now!" her father demanded and she reluctantly left Ellie's side and went to her father.

"We're sorry Mr. Stinson," Ellie said, as tears began running down her cheeks. "We didn't mean for this to happen."

"You should be telling these boys you're sorry, not me," he said.

"I won't," John said defiantly. "They owe *us* an apology."

"What is your name young man?" Mr. Stinson demanded.

"John Besner. Do you want my phone number too? I'm sure my dad would love to talk to you, especially after you take up with the two boys who tried to kill me."

"Who tried to kill who?"

The voice made them all turn and Luke's heart sank when he saw Detective Jennings and his partner standing with Mrs. Stinson.

"Just what the heck is going on here?" Jaxon said. "We heard a gunshot."

CHAPTER 19

Jaxon and Sally had spent the rest of the morning with the forensics team at the Lolly residence collecting the video data and scouring the yard and bushes next door for any clues.

They had been able to preserve the video surveillance data but had pretty much struck out on any evidence left by the killer around the surrounding environment. Burt looked very anxious as the crew trampled through his and his neighbor's yards. Jaxon kept reassuring him they would damage as little as possible.

When it was all said and done, the grass looked a little beaten down and the neighbor's hedge had some leaves misplaced, but the majority of the yards looked unscathed. The neighbor had not been home.

They were just about to leave the scene, saying their goodbyes to the Lollys, when they heard what sounded like a gunshot. Jogging off toward the sound, Jaxon radioed in as he ran that possible shots had been fired and they needed back-up. That order was quickly canceled when they discovered the scene at the foot bridge. Jaxon was highly amused.

After the eldest of the teenagers explained what had happened and what they had done, Sally smiled at Jaxon and he almost chuckled as he turned away from the kids and the Stinson family. *Kids! What next?* He thought.

Turning back to address the small group, he tried to put on as stern a face as he could.

"You kids do know this could be considered assault, right? Maybe even assault with a deadly—uh—rocket engine." He heard Sally snort behind him and struggled to keep it together. "This is serious stuff."

"Yes sir," they all chimed in. All except the one kid who fumed off to the side. John was his name if he remembered correctly. Jaxon sent his best glaring stare John's way and the kid eventually looked down at his feet.

"And you two," Jaxon pointed to the kids with the bikes, "kicking someone off of a bridge into a flooded creek could also be considered assault. You have to learn to share the road—uh path—with other pedestrians. They have the right of way. You hear me?"

They both nodded but said nothing. One of the kids, the one covered from head to toe in mud, looked about to cry. He was doing his best to hold it together.

"All right, I want to hear apologies from all of you and then sweep this thing under the rug. Let's go."

Mumbled 'sorries' worked their way around the group and Jaxon was glad to see the John kid even joining in.

"Good. Let's all try to get along now. Don't make me have to pay a visit to your parents." Jaxon pointed to Jimmy and then John. "You two, dismantle this little project you have attached to the bridge and carry it back to your house. Harrison and Pemberton, I need to talk to you."

The girl and boy looked at each other and then walked over to where Jaxon and Sally were standing off to the side. Stinson walked up and said, "That's it? You aren't going to do anything to these kids? Maybe I should talk to their parents if you aren't. They almost got someone killed!"

"It was a prank gone wrong," Jaxon said. "I'm not going to make this more than it was and create more hardship for these kids than already exists. They seem to be genuinely sorry for what happened and it doesn't appear they meant any serious harm. It's your prerogative if you want to seek out their parents. I can't stop you. I just think it's best to let it go."

"Fine," Stinson said, and turned to leave. "Come on kids. We need to get home. Who knows who else will rig some bomb or trap and get someone else hurt."

"Daddy! I want to stay with Ellie!" Mel said.

"No!" Stinson said, pulling her by the hand, "Ellie is not coming over again, ever!"

The little girl started crying as her parents led her home. Ellie Pemberton watched her walk off and started to cry herself. Jaxon actually felt a twinge of pity for the girl.

* * *

Luke watched Jimmy and John dismantle the rocket launcher and thought to himself, *How in the world could it have come to this?* He couldn't believe how quickly things had taken a turn for the worse and he never would have predicted the outcome.

Jaxon was saying something to his partner, who Luke now knew as Sally, but he couldn't hear the conversation. He knew they were talking about him and Ellie, but he hoped they were going to let them go. Luke looked over at Ellie who had fresh tears running down her cheeks and reached out and grabbed her hand.

"Are you gonna be ok?" Luke asked.

She nodded but didn't speak. He couldn't tell what was going through her head, but he knew she was angry at him for getting her into all this. Hell, she was probably angry at all three of them. Now, she had lost a babysitting job and embarrassed herself in front of a family she really liked. Luke felt she would probably never be able to gain her respect back from them. She probably wouldn't even try.

Jaxon turned back toward them and scowled as he looked them over.

"You two keep showing up in all the action in this neighborhood. Do I need to be concerned?"

"No, sir," Luke said. Ellie just shook her head. She had dropped his hand when Jaxon started talking.

"I like you two," he said, "but that doesn't mean I enjoy our little get-togethers. The less I see of you two, the better. Do you understand?"

"Yes, sir," Luke said. This time Ellie spoke too.

"Good. Now what really happened here? Is there more to this than I'm seeing?"

"No," Ellie said. "Not really. It's just like Jimmy said. We didn't mean for anything bad to happen. I realize now how stupid we were."

"Me too," Luke said. "The two kids on the bikes just made us mad and we wanted to get them back. It was dumb."

"This friend of yours, John," Jaxon said, pointing, "do I need to be worried about him? He seemed pretty angry."

Luke shook his head. "No. He's probably more scared than angry. I think his close call in the creek shook him up pretty good."

"He's lucky to have friends like you guys," Jaxon said. "You saved his life. He could've died in there."

Luke shrugged, not sure what to say. He knew John had been lucky.

"Do you guys remember our little conversation a couple of months back?" Jaxon asked.

Luke could see Ellie nodding and he said, "Yes."

"Anything jog your memories since then?"

"No, sir," Luke said.

Jaxon looked at Sally.

"It's important guys," Sally said. "Even the smallest thing might help us. You didn't see anything?"

Luke and Ellie remained silent.

"We've been given some new evidence," Jaxon said, "and we know you two had nothing to do with the murders, just so you know. You aren't suspects. We just need a little help filling in the blanks."

Luke watched Ellie open her mouth, look at him and then shut it again. Jaxon shook his head.

"All right, let us know if you think of something. Here is our number again in case you lost the other one." He handed them each a business card, then turned and left, heading back toward the pool area.

CHAPTER 20

Jaxon and Sally were at the station going over pictures from the missing person's files.

They had been searching through the files since late December without a single hit. They had even expanded to the surrounding counties and were currently going through Prince George's County in Maryland.

Looking at pictures of thousands of missing persons was a tedious and time consuming task and Jaxon was about to go blind from it. He put down the shot he was holding and rubbed his eyes. He had a headache spreading from the back of his neck into the crown of his scalp. He needed a Coke.

"I'm getting a drink," he said. "You want anything?"

"A Diet Pepsi," Sally said. "Here..." she grabbed a dollar and stuck her hand out to him.

"I got it." He waved her hand away and walked around his desk.

"Thanks!" she yelled after him.

The John Doe had been a thorn in their sides. He had never had this much trouble identifying an individual before. He couldn't understand why they were having such bad luck. The fingerprints came back negative and this led to a suspicion Jaxon had in regards to the age of the boy. Nowadays every mother out there had their kids fingerprinted, photographed, and even DNA typed, anything they could think of in the unlikely event they would have to report their child missing or even provide some kind of identification should the worst happen. He'd even heard of some parents having chips implanted underneath the kid's skin so they could be scanned into a computer system like a dog or a cat.

This trend was only about fifteen to twenty years old though, and this made Jaxon sure they were searching for a name that had been in the database for over twenty years. Somebody had kept the kid frozen for a hell of a long time.

The decapitated dog had provided little usable evidence. The fingernails they had pulled from the skin of the dog had in fact belonged to the John Doe. After running DNA on the skin found underneath the kid's fingernails, the lab called and told Doc Barstow it was animal DNA. Specifically that of a dog. A poodle mix. It only took a few minutes afterward to match up the missing fingernails of the kid to the ones they pulled from the dog. The problem was the kid had been dead for quite a while and the dog was recent.

Dead end. This asshole was smart. He was throwing all kinds of empty leads at them to slow them down and it was working. Jaxon felt like he was spinning his wheels for naught.

Doc Barstow had been frustrated too. He was used to seeing things that most people considered appalling, but when he explained what the perp had to go through just to get the John Doe's fingernails embedded in the dog's skin, it set him off.

That had been five months ago and they had little reason to visit the morgue since then. John Doe was still on ice there and would remain in the morgue until they either identified him or they no longer needed the body.

Jaxon walked back into the investigations department and put Sally's Diet Pepsi on her desk.

"Thanks," she said.

"Don't mention it," he said and grinned.

Sitting back down at his desk, he grabbed another stack of photos and started leafing through them.

"I'm getting a headache," she said.

"Can't be worse than mine."

His phone rang. "Jaxon."

"It's Halson. Found something interesting on the fibers in the Doe/Bannon case."

"Shoot," Jaxon said.

"Some of the fibers pulled from the filtered pool water match the clothing on the Doe boy and then some do not."

"So…"

"I'm getting there," Halson said. "The fabric from the Doe clothing is manufactured using a very new and modern technique. The textile mills in India began developing a type of nanotechnology to enhance their fabrics. Basically they were looking for ways to improve softness, durability, inflammability—that kind of thing. It's almost like genetic engineering for cloth."

"What are you saying? The clothing is special?"

"Sort of. It's only sold through one chain in the U.S. Old Navy stores, of which there are three in Fairfax county. Jaxon—these are modern clothes on a kid who has been dead for a long time."

"Ok—so he dressed him in new duds for the swim."

"Wait, I'm not finished. We found a few other fibers which were also unusual. Two small samples of a Dacron/cotton mixture which are no longer manufactured and a rubber type compound that is also obsolete. Both of these types of materials were found to be toxic in some form or another and the production of them was halted in 1985."

"But if the…"

"Hold on. Both the rubber and the cloth were new to the market back then and were only made for a short time before they were pulled. Specifically, the production of the cloth began in March of 1984 and the rubber in April of that same year. They were both shut down in September of 1985."

"How confident are you these fibers are from our John Doe?" Jaxon asked, a grin forming on his face.

"Pretty damn sure. The management company says they drain the pool yearly for maintenance. I mean you could have some old 'has been' with his rejects from the 80s hanging out by the pool looking for babes, but that's highly unlikely. I'd say about 80% sure."

"Halson, you are my hero as of this moment."

"Don't get too excited. You still have some work to do to find out who the kid is."

"We're on it."

* * *

Luke and Ellie were at her house sitting in a swing in her backyard.

They both had a glass of lemonade in their hands and were leaning shoulder to shoulder against each other sipping the drinks. It was hot.

He could tell she was still upset at him about the rocket episode, but at least she was talking.

"I'm sure after this cools off a bit," Luke said, "Mr. Stinson will be a lot more forgiving. He's just upset at us right now."

"I doubt it," Ellie said. "He looked pretty angry. Adults seem to hold on to grudges almost as long as girls." She smiled.

At least she could joke about it. "We'll see. I'll bet you're babysitting for Mel and Robby again before the summer's over."

"I'm not counting on it, but it would be nice. I like those two a lot."

She was quiet for a minute, then said, "Are you worried about the missing pets?"

"No—not really. It might just be coincidence. I know you're worried."

"Do you really think five missing dogs and cats is a coincidence?"

"Is it that many?"

She nodded. "Three from your court, one from mine, and one from Oak Street."

"Three from my court? Damn—I guess I wasn't paying attention. Does sound like a lot. Have any of them been found?"

"I don't know. I didn't go around asking anybody. They would think I was weird."

"True."

"What? I'm weird?" she asked.

"Totally. The weirdest person I know. I mean, look at the company you keep."

She punched him in the arm and he spilled his drink in his lap.

"Hey!" he yelled, laughing. He threw the rest of the lemonade at her and it hit her right in the face. She sat there with her mouth open in shock.

"Oh crap! I'm sorry, El! I didn't mean to."

She laughed and dumped her lemonade over the top of his head. It ran down his face and back and he cringed from the cold. "That's it weirdo! You're in for it now!"

He reached for her but she jumped up and ran. He caught up to her near a big maple tree in her backyard and she squealed as he tackled her to the ground. She rolled over on top of him and he let her pin his arms to the ground. The sticky lemonade made grass and dirt cling to their faces and clothes.

"Who's a weirdo?" she teased.

"You!"

She tickled him in the ribs and he squirmed uncontrollably underneath her. "No! Not tickling! I can't control myself!"

"Who's the weirdo?" she repeated.

"I am! I am!"

"Damn right you…!" She stopped.

He squirmed for a second longer and then realized something was wrong. He looked up at her above him and saw her staring at something behind his head.

"What?" he said, breathless. "What is it?"

Silent, she got off of him and stood staring. He rose up and looked behind him. He didn't know what he was looking for at first, but then he saw it.

Sticking up about two inches above the ground, just under the maple tree, was an animal's paw. The brown fur and black nails clearly visible above the dirt. A single fly buzzed around it and then landed on a toenail.

He stood up next to her and then walked over to the tree. It was a dog's paw. Pretty good sized dog from what he could judge. The soil he was standing on was loose and squishy and he stepped back away from the area, uncomfortable with the way it felt beneath his bare feet. Ellie stood next to him and stared.

"Do you have a shovel?" he whispered, his voice sounding funny in the shade of the tree.

She looked at him. "In the garage, but…"

"Go get it."

She looked at the dog's paw again, her lip trembling, and then she left to get the shovel.

He looked at the area around the paw and could tell it had been disturbed. The grass looked funny. He reached out and pulled a piece and it shifted easily in the soil. It had been dug up and then put back. He would never have noticed it unless he was standing right on top of it. Another fly buzzed around the protruding paw and then a third. Luke could now smell a whiff of decay and he backed away, unsure if he wanted to dig up the rest.

Ellie came back with the shovel and she handed it to Luke.

"Are you sure?" she said.

Luke grabbed the shovel and started to dig. It only took a minute for him to realize the dog was not the only thing buried here.

* * *

"Bingo!" Sally shouted. "We got him!"

Jaxon rushed over and peered at the picture she was holding in her hand. Dead Ringer. Their John Doe now had a real name.

"Stewart Alan Littleton," Sally said. "He's been missing since October 31, 1984. Last seen by his Mother, June Littleton, before he went out Trick-or-Treating."

Jaxon scanned the statistics on the sheet. "He lived right here in Fairfax. Reston. Last address Southgate Square."

"Twenty seven years ago," Sally said.

"Yeah," Jaxon said. "Unbelievable huh? Let's see if we can get a contact. Parents, brothers, sisters, anything."

"Last known phone number and address are current as of September," Sally said. "They kept it updated every year. The number listed is for June Littleton."

"This time we do it the right way," he said. "You contact her and we'll bring her in to identify the body."

"Thanks, boss. I find him and you make me do the dirty work."

"You're better at it than I am. Remember what happened?"

"I'll handle it." She smiled.

His cell phone rang. "Jaxon."

"Mr. Jennings?" A kid's voice.

"This is Detective Jennings. Who is this?"

The kid paused for a second and Jaxon thought they hung up.

"You told us to call you if we had any more information on the pool kids."

"Harrison?"

"Yes, sir. This is Luke Harrison. Ellie's with me too. Can you come to Ellie's house? Something bad has happened."

"We're very busy right now, Harrison. Can you just tell me what's going on?"

"We found more decapitated animals."

"You say animals? Plural?"

"Yeah. Five of 'em. Three dogs and two cats. They were buried in Ellie's yard."

"Don't touch anything else. I'll send some people over there now."

"You're not coming?"

"I can't at the moment. We have something very important to do."

"What?"

"I can't talk about that with you."

"Did you find out who the other kid is? Because there's something buried with the animals you need to see."

"What is it?"

"It's a picture. A school picture, but it's old. I think it's the kid from the pool. I'm not sure though. That picture you showed us a while back? The one you asked if we knew? Is that him?"

"Yes."

"You need to come out here. There's a name on the picture, but it's all covered in—uh—dead gunk and guts. The one name I can read is Little."

"Littleton?" Jaxon asked.

"That could be it, yes. How did you know?"

"We'll be right there. Don't touch a thing."

CHAPTER 21

Jaxon stared into the hole and felt Sally move next to him. "The heads are all missing," he said.

"I see that," Sally said. "Three dogs and two cats?"

"I believe so. The little one looks like a dog. The fur is right. It's hard to tell without the head. Maybe a Chihuahua?"

He held up the picture. It was in a Ziploc baggie and he was holding it with gloved hands. "Stewart Littleton," she said. "Dogwood Elementary, 1984. Good likeness. I wonder why our guy decided to give us a little help?"

"Down deep, they all want to be caught. They can't stop themselves unless they are locked up, so they subconsciously help the investigation. He just doesn't realize it."

"Is that what your FBI training taught you?"

"That and Michael."

She nodded.

Apparently, she didn't want to go there, and that was fine with him. Michael's murder was something he thought about every day, or maybe he should say, tried *not* to think about, and though the case had been solved, he lived with his own failure in everything he did. He couldn't save him.

The Crime Scene team arrived and he let them move in. It was going to be messy and he was glad he wasn't the one going through it. It had been tough enough pulling the picture out of all the rotting flesh.

He glanced over at the small crowd gathered in the backyard and saw Luke Harrison and Ellie Pemberton. Her mother was there too along with a boy he didn't recognize. He had the features of the Pembertons and figured he must be related. They all looked anxious.

He turned to Sally and said, "Let's find out what they know." She walked with him up to the group.

"Mrs. Pemberton, remember us? I'm Detective Jennings and this is Detective Winston."

"Yes, Detectives, I remember you. I'm a little disappointed I'm seeing you again. I would have expected all this to be resolved by now."

"Yes ma'am. I agree. We seem to be having some difficulty. Maybe you can help."

"I don't see how."

Jaxon tried to plaster a smile on his face, but it felt strained. "Who found the gravesite?" he asked.

"We did," Luke said.

"You and Ellie?" Sally asked.

Luke nodded. "We were goofing around and she saw a dog's paw sticking up out of the ground."

"What else?" Jaxon asked and Luke told them the rest of the story.

"Why would you dig it up?" Sally asked. "Pretty gross."

"We noticed a bunch of signs all over the neighborhood," Luke said. "Actually, Ellie noticed them first. Missing pet signs."

"Five different signs," Ellie said. "We kind of thought maybe this was one of them. I never would have guessed it would be all of them."

"So these are all neighborhood pets?" Jaxon asked.

"I think so," Ellie said. "I recognized one of the cats. It's Jinxy. The Eldridge's cat on Cotton Court."

"Have you seen anyone back here?" Sally asked.

They all shook their heads.

"Have there been any strange things happening?" Jaxon asked.

"You mean like dead children showing up in frozen pools? That kind of thing?" Mrs. Pemberton said.

Jaxon just stared at her.

"I'd like to ask you two a few questions," she said. "What's being done to protect this neighborhood? When will my children and I feel safe? It started with our dog and now more decapitated animals are buried in my yard. It sure looks like someone is targeting my family and I want some protection."

Jaxon looked at Sally who seemed to sympathize with Mrs. Pemberton, but she remained silent.

"Mrs. Pemberton, I'm sure that…"

"I don't believe you're sure of anything Detective and I want something done. You and your department seem to be ignoring the whole problem. I haven't seen a single police car or heard of any police action inside this neighborhood in over four months."

"I assure you ma'am, we are doing everything we can…"

"I don't believe you."

She stood there with her hands on her hips staring at him. He couldn't blame her. She was technically correct. The department had not gone out of its way to provide any added security or surveillance in the area, relying mainly on evidence already collected to further the investigation along. Hell, they'd been at a standstill until just yesterday.

"I don't blame you, ma'am," Sally said, calmly. "A police investigation can leave many unanswered questions lingering for the civilians. Unfortunately, it's what has to be done. Certain information needs to be kept from the press so we can weed out every Tom, Dick, and Harry volunteering useless information. As far as security in the neighborhood, we will step up patrols and place a squad car in front of your house. That should help you feel safer until this investigation closes."

Jaxon looked at Sally, impressed. She avoided eye contact with him and remained focused on Mrs. Pemberton.

"Well—ok," Mrs. Pemberton said. "That will make me feel a little better. I just wish this nightmare was over."

"So do we, ma'am," Sally said. "So do we."

* * *

Luke and Ellie were in front of Luke's house hanging out with Jimmy and John.

Luke told them about the discovery of the dead animals and John apologized to Ellie again, saying he was sorry he criticized her about the signs yesterday.

"You were right," he said.

"It's ok. I know what you were trying to do. I seem to have a short fuse when it comes to Bentley. It's probably because I do blame myself for what happened."

"Why did you guys call those cops?" Jimmy asked. "I thought we were supposed to keep this stuff to ourselves."

"My mom came out and saw what we were doing," Ellie said, "and she made us call them. Sorry."

Jimmy looked concerned. "So he's back?"

"It looks like it," Luke said. "But we haven't heard anything from him. He's been quiet."

"What do you think we should do?" John asked. "Do you think it's time to tell someone what we know?"

Ellie was nodding her head, but Luke was still not so sure.

"I don't think so," he said. "He's left us alone this long because we've been quiet. I think we should keep it to ourselves."

"What about the other kids? Maybe we should tell them to watch out," Ellie said.

"Like who?" Luke said. "I don't trust any of them to keep it quiet."

"But we said we would warn them if it got bad," Ellie said.

"It's not bad yet."

"I think five dead animals buried in my backyard's pretty bad."

Luke saw her face flush and he could tell she was getting angry. They had never had a fight and he didn't like where this talk was leading. Still, he didn't want to endanger her life by breaking their silence.

"It's just animals. He hasn't killed anybody else yet."

He knew as soon as he said it he had stepped over the line.

"But that doesn't mean he won't!" Ellie shouted. "What if someone else dies and we could have stopped it? I can't live with that. Can you?"

"El, don't get mad at me. I don't like it either, but if we start talking, he may come after you and I can't let that happen."

"That's not up to you to decide!" she yelled. "I won't let him hurt anybody else."

"I don't want him to hurt anyone else either," he said, "but he's already threatened us. If we start talking and something happened to you, I couldn't live with myself. I can't lose you! I love you!"

She stared at him.

"What did you say?" she whispered, the anger gone now, a look of wonder on her face as she took it all in.

"I said, I love you."

She searched his face, a single tear trickling down her cheek, then she reached for him and pulled him to her.

"I love you too," she whispered. "I'm sorry I yelled at you."

"This is awkward," Jimmy said, smiling.

"I think I'm gonna barf," John said.

Luke and Ellie ignored them. She pulled back and looked into his eyes and he smiled at her.

"How long have you felt this way?" she said.

"I already told you that."

"You did?"

"You don't remember?"

She shook her head, then stopped and smiled. "Oh—you did tell me."

"You had me at Goofy Goober."

She laughed. "I did, huh? You're easy."

"We're still here," John said. "And I'm getting more nauseous."

Jimmy said, "Should we leave you two alone?"

Luke and Ellie let each other go, but she grabbed his hand and held tight.

"All right," Luke said. "I don't want to be the one making all the decisions so let's vote. Do we tell the neighborhood kids?"

"Yes," John said.

"Yep," Jimmy said.

"I think we need to," Ellie said. "Don't you?"

"You guys are probably right. Ok, we tell everybody we hang out with. Let them know what's going on. Let's call a kick the can game tonight and spread the word."

Ellie smiled and leaned against him. He hoped they weren't making a huge mistake.

* * *

Jaxon and Sally arrived at June Littleton's house in Reston late that afternoon.

She was expecting them. Sally had called and asked if they could come by and talk to her about her son's case. Sally said she seemed somewhat distant, but agreed to see them.

Knocking on the door, Jaxon said, "You got this, right?"

Sally nodded.

The door opened and a woman in her late fifties scowled at them from behind a screened door. She wore a cheap flower print dress with a mismatched belt cinched around her waist, tight, so that her belly hung over it. Her feet were bare and she held a dishrag in her right hand.

"You the police officers?" she said.

"Yes ma'am," Sally said. "I'm Detective Winston and this is Detective Jennings. May we come in?"

"I'd rather you didn't. My Mister is napping and I don't want you wakin' him. What do you want?"

"Is your 'Mister,' Stewart's Father?"

She seemed to flinch a little at the mention of her son's name. She wrung her hands in the dishrag and said, "No. That man is long gone. Hell, he wasn't around much anyway when he was here. Why?"

Sally nodded. "Things like this are never easy, ma'am and I know you've been waiting a long time for something to surface in regards to your son. I think we've found him, but we need you to come with us and identify him. Could you do that?"

Her face did not change, but her hands stopped the constant wringing of the rag and she sagged against the doorframe. "Is he...?"

Sally nodded. "I'm sorry Mrs. Littleton. I know you must be upset, but it is very important you identify him for us. To be sure. Can you do that?"

She nodded her head slowly, eyes transfixed on some distant object. Then, she seemed to remember they were there.

"I'll get my things," she whispered, and disappeared back inside. She returned a moment later with her purse and a pair of flat white shoes that clashed with the off-white patterned dress. She shuffled along next to them as they escorted her to the car.

At the morgue, Boris alerted Dr. Barstow and he got Stewart ready for them as they helped her back to Bay C.

Before they entered she said, "Will I be able to tell it's him?"

"I believe so, Mrs. Littleton," Sally said.

"June. Call me June."

Sally smiled. "Yes, June. I think you'll be able to tell us if he's your son or not."

She nodded and seemed to shrink a little as they pushed through the door. Dr. Barstow waited for them next to the sliding tray and introduced himself to her before pulling back the plastic sheet.

She gasped.

She reached out to touch his face and then recoiled ever so slightly at the feel of him. Then, she began softly crying. Jaxon felt that was as good a confirmation as anyone could give.

"He's still so young," she said. "Have you had him here this whole time?"

"No ma'am," Sally said. "He was found in a neighborhood swimming pool five months ago. We weren't able to identify him until today."

"But how can he look the same? Shouldn't he have…uh…"

"We think his murderer kept him frozen all this time," Jaxon said, and she flinched at his voice. It was the first time he had spoken since they met.

"Frozen?"

"Yes, ma'am."

"Why would anyone do that?"

"I don't know, June," Sally said. "Whoever did this to your son is a very demented individual."

"You don't know who did this?"

"Not yet," Sally said, "but we've made some progress and we will catch him."

June turned back to her son. "Twenty seven years. He would be thirty nine now."

A single tear tracked down her face and then she began to sob. Sally went to her and put an arm around her. Jaxon knew exactly how she felt.

CHAPTER 22

That evening, everyone was there, even Patrick.

Luke wasn't sure if Patrick was still sore at them and he guessed it didn't matter. This was more important than any petty differences they may have had.

All the kids knew about most of the stuff, but the Facebook friend William Smith, and the text messages and phone calls Luke and Ellie had gotten were all new to them. 'George,' the pool dummy, drew a few laughs but most were shocked at how the dummy had been traded for a real dead boy.

"That must have been a shocker for you guys," Ralph said.

"I about crapped my pants," John said.

Luke's older sister, Deana, looked mad. "I think you guys are stupid," she said. "The police need to know about this and you idiots are keeping it from them."

"Didn't you hear a single word I said?" Luke asked. "He threatened Ellie and me, and said that if we told anyone, he would kill us. Don't you think we would have done something by now if we didn't have that hanging over our heads?"

"The police can protect you," Deana said.

"Like they protected Paul?" Alan shot back.

"Paul was out all by himself. No one could have helped him," Deana said.

"That's right," Luke said. "Paul was out all by himself and that's what we need to make sure doesn't happen to the rest of us. We stick together. Nobody goes anywhere alone. Nobody talks about what we know unless it's with each other. Nobody keeps any secrets from the rest of the group. Something happens, you tell us."

"I still don't like it," Deana said.

"Deana, we're trusting you," Ellie said. "Luke didn't want to tell you all because he thought the group couldn't keep it to themselves. Please don't prove him right. We need help, and we wanted to make sure everybody else was safe. I convinced him to break the silence, but if you involve any adults at this point, you could be hurting your brother. And me."

Deana was quiet for a minute, then finally said, "All right, I'll keep quiet for now. But if I feel like you guys are being dumber than normal, I'll involve the police."

"Come to us first," Luke said. "If we go to the police, it will be a group decision. Ok?"

Everybody agreed, even Deana.

"Now that's out of the way," Jimmy said, "let's play."

Luke thought it had been the best game they had played in a long time.

CHAPTER 23

Luke, Ellie, Jimmy, and John were always the first at the pool in the morning.

It was their job to open up. Jimmy pulled the keys from his gym bag and unlocked the gate. They split up with Luke and John opening the locker rooms, while Jimmy checked the pump house and Ellie started working on the lane dividers.

Luke was singing in the locker room, the echo creating a cool sound, when he heard Ellie scream.

"Ellie!" he shouted, and ran out of the locker room onto the deck.

She was standing at the edge of the pool, one hand holding a lane divider and the other clasped over her mouth. In the pool was a boy. He was resting on the bottom at the six foot mark and the water was tinged pink around him. As Luke walked closer, he could see the body was missing its head. It was floating a few feet out, face up. The eyes were half open and the mouth was set in a gasp with water sloshing in and out of it.

"Ah crap" Jimmy said, kneeling at the edge of the pool.

Luke stood next to Ellie who turned and buried her face in his shoulder, crying.

"I think it's Jason Margot," Luke said.

"Damn," John whispered, coming up behind them.

Jimmy turned and threw up all over the deck.

* * *

Jaxon turned to the swim coach, Will Francis, and asked, "So the kids open up every morning?"

"Yes. They get everything ready for practice," Will said.

"Does anyone else have a key?"

"Yes, several people do, including the head lifeguard, snack shop manager, and the management company."

"What time do the kids usually show up?"

"Probably around 7:15. Practice starts at 7:30."

"Right. Thank you Mr. Francis. Please help keep all the kids out of the area for a while. The pool will be closed for a couple of days while we gather evidence."

Jaxon walked over to where Harrison and his little group were sitting.

"You guys keep showing up whenever something happens. If I didn't have in my possession proof you didn't do anything, I'd swear you were involved. You're lucky I have that proof."

He knelt in front of Ellie. "Are you all right?"

She nodded. He could tell she wasn't, but couldn't do anything about it. Sally hadn't arrived yet, but when she did, he'd have her talk to the girl.

"Think you guys can talk about it?" he asked them all.

He watched them all nod.

"Who wants to go first?"

"I found him, so I guess I will," Ellie said.

He listened as she went through the trauma of finding the decapitated boy. The story was pretty consistent with what the coach had described and then what the boys told him next. He felt bad for them. They seemed to be getting caught up in a lot of stuff kids their age shouldn't see. His cell phone rang and he looked at the number expecting it to be Sally. It read 'unavailable' and the number showed up as 000-000-0000.

He answered it. "Jaxon."

"Hello Detective." The voice was grating and high pitched. It had a metallic quality to it and he could tell it was being electronically altered. It drew out the word 'Detective,' mocking him.

"Who is this?" Jaxon asked.

"Did my little gift help?"

"What gift would that be?"

"The picture, of course. You really didn't think the animals were meant for you, did you?"

"Not really. But we had already identified the boy yesterday morning."

"So you say. I was becoming worried you would never honor him. Five months is a long time to find someone, isn't it Detective?"

The voice was hurting his ear. The way he liked to drag out his title caused a kind of feedback through the speaker of the phone and he had to pull it away from his head. He saw Sally walk up and he frantically signaled for her. She walked over briskly.

He put his hand over the phone. "Call downtown," he whispered to Sally, "Have them set up a trace on my cell. Hurry!"

She took out her phone and moved away.

"Still there Detective?"

"Yes. Who are you?"

"Come now, Jaxon. We don't have much time. Can't you think of something more useful to ask me?"

For some reason, Jaxon could think of only one thing. "Why?"

"That's better. That wasn't too hard was it?"

Jaxon remained silent.

"Because I can, Detective."

"Why are you calling me?"

"It's obvious, isn't it?"

"Help me."

"There you go. You just answered that question yourself."

"Where are you?"

"Tell Winston I like her yellow blouse."

Jaxon's eyes snapped up as his heart leapt into his throat.

He's here!

The line went dead.

* * *

They searched the area and finally found a battery powered web cam mounted to a lamp post at the southern end of the pool complex. It was the kind of video camera hunters used in the woods to track game.

Jaxon found out an hour later the image was uploaded to a server run by the manufacturer of the web cam and the video was accessed through a log-in page for each individual user. No personal information was kept on the users. All you needed was the serial number for the hunting cam to access the website. He would have his I.T. guys see if they could pull any information on where he was accessing the server.

"Any luck with the cell phone?" Jaxon asked Sally.

"Nothing useful," she said. "The call was placed using an internet based phone service. Basically you can call from anywhere in the world and pick your number you want displayed on the caller I.D. The internet company is based out of Moscow. Good luck trying to get any information out of the Russian Mob."

"I think we may need to get the FBI involved. They may be able to get some information we can't access. I'll call Holt in Washington today."

Emory Holt was a FBI agent out of D.C. who handled the District of Columbia and the surrounding counties. Jaxon hated involving the FBI, but he felt he had no choice at this point. Things were getting out of hand and they needed some help.

"Your call, Boss. I know we need help, but they will come in here and take over."

"I'll try and approach it from an informational stand point first. See if he'll stay out of it for now," Jaxon said.

"Knowing Holt, he'll want in," she said.

Jaxon shrugged. What could he do? Kids were dying.

A commotion at the entrance of the pool caught their attention.

"I don't care sir," a patrolmen was saying, loudly, "this is a crime scene and I can't let you pass."

"I know that. Just get a message to Detectives Jennings and Winston that Burt Lolly needs to see them. I have some more video. They'll definitely want to see it."

Jaxon walked up with Sally and said, "Mr. Lolly. What have you got?"

"Everything," Mr. Lolly said, his face pale and troubled. He had the look of someone with information he really didn't want to possess. "And you won't believe it."

CHAPTER 24

Luke and Ellie were at her house up in her room.

She was quietly crying into his neck, her hot, wet tears slipping down his shoulder as he held her tight. He felt on the verge of some emotional breakdown himself, but was doing his best to hold it together for her.

They had left Jimmy and John at their house, saying they would meet up later and talk to everyone else. So far, nobody was panicking and Luke attributed this to the fact Jason Margot was not in their little group. Selfish, maybe, but they couldn't protect everyone, could they?

He was beginning to have doubts about their lack of involvement with the police and though their pact among one another only went so far, Jason Margot still did not deserve to die.

Could they have prevented his death had they gone to Jaxon and Winston? Probably not, but maybe he wouldn't feel so bad right now if they had.

Ellie lifted her head up off his shoulder and looked into his eyes. The pain he saw there bore right into his heart and his breath caught in his throat as he felt her hand touch his face. *I'm not going to lose it*, he said to himself. *I'm not going to lose it.*

He had to look away as he felt his eyes well up. Apparently she wasn't going to let him off the hook that easily. She turned his face back toward her.

"Look at me," she said. A single tear slipped down her cheek, but her voice was strong. "We have to stop this, now. I can't live with another death hanging over my head. We go to the group today and then we go to the police."

He couldn't find his voice. If he opened his mouth to speak, she would hear the weakness in it and he couldn't let that happen. He needed to be strong. He nodded his head, trying to buy a little more time to get himself under control.

"You're agreeing with me?" she asked, pulling back a bit and searching his face.

He waited a beat. "We need to have the group vote," he finally said, his voice sounding stronger than he expected. "We all need to decide."

"Why? It's our problem. He hasn't threatened them, only us."

"We made an agreement with them. And besides, maybe someone will have some better advice."

"You're going to try and convince them to keep silent, aren't you?" Another tear trickled down her cheek and her lip trembled ever so slightly. "You're going to fight me on this?"

He didn't answer. He couldn't risk anything going wrong and her, somehow, ending up on the wrong side of all this.

Her face fell again and she looked away.

He stared at her, his heart breaking in his chest. He felt as though he was betraying her, but so much more was at stake. He loved her with every fiber in his body and he didn't care who else got hurt, as long as it wasn't her.

She stood.

"You're being selfish," she said, angrily wiping away her tears. "You're thinking only of yourself."

"How can you say that?" he asked, but feared her answer.

"I know you. You're thinking only of saving me," she said, her voice cracking, tears streaming down her face, "not of anybody else who could get hurt. Well, I can't let you. You'll destroy us, don't you see? I can't live with him taking someone else's life to save mine and I'll hate you for letting it happen. Do you understand? I'll hate you if you let it happen!"

He stood and went to her, grabbing and holding her tight. She resisted and softly beat on his chest, then succumbed and fell against him sobbing. A single tear fell from his face as his world came apart.

* * *

Burt Lolly loaded up the video while his wife, Marie, brought them all some coffee.

"Honey," Burt said. "I don't think you should see this. It's pretty upsetting."

She nodded at him and said, "Let me know if you need anything else." And she left the room.

"I pulled last night's video and watched as soon as I saw all the commotion this morning. You two may want to sit down."

"We're all right, Mr. Lolly. Go ahead and show us what you have."

"Burt," he said. "Please call me Burt." He hit play.

The screen showed the front yard again just as the masked individual entered the area from the left carrying what Jaxon presumed was the boy. He paused in front of the yard, turned and looked, facing the camera. He actually waved.

"Bastard," Burt whispered.

He was wearing the same clothing and had on the white mask they had seen in the earlier surveillance video, but no other distinguishing marks or clothing could be made out. The boy was over his shoulder, his head hanging down his back, limp and still. Jaxon could not tell if he was alive or dead.

The masked individual approached the fence and wrestled the boy over it, following after him, up and over the chain link. He dragged the body toward the pool and left him, disappearing from view for a moment. He returned a few minutes later with something in his hand. It looked to be long and metallic.

The video jumped. It now showed the masked man back on this side of the fence jumping up and down in the road waving his arms. He stopped suddenly and then climbed back over the fence.

"He was triggering the camera again," Burt said, quietly. "It timed out and the sensor doesn't reach all the way inside the pool." Burt turned and looked at them. "He wanted us to see this part, so he climbed back over the fence and jumped up and down to get the camera going again."

Jaxon and Sally remained silent. He had a feeling what was coming.

The masked individual approached the body again and turned toward the camera. It was a little difficult to see from the distance and the chain link fence was making it even harder, but when he brought his arm up, a glint of light shining off of the metallic object Jaxon now knew to be a machete, there was no mistaking what was going to happen.

Burt looked away and Sally gasped as the machete was brought down again and again until it finished its evil purpose. He then picked up the boy's head and held it high above him, shaking it at the camera. The frame jumped again and the scene was empty, the killer finished with his show, the night still and silent in the aftermath. Jaxon shook with anger as Sally hung her head.

"We have to get this son-of-a-bitch," she said. "Today."

* * *

Ellie's cell phone rang and she pulled away from Luke reaching for it. She looked at the caller I.D. and her face tightened.

She angrily punched the button with her finger and yelled, "What do you want, you sick bastard!"

The eerie voice came out of the speakerphone, laughing.

"I thought you would be thanking me," he said. "I did you a favor, right? Your little friend will never hurt or bother you again. Ever."

"Why?" Ellie said. "Why would you do this? He never did a thing to you."

"Oh—but he did, my dear. He did. He should have known better than to damage my ultimate treasure." The voice turned angry now. "Nobody will damage you but me. And only when it's time."

"Leave us alone, you sicko!" she yelled.

More laughter and then silence.

She was breathing heavily, her face red and tight and her fist bunched in a ball. Luke thought she was going to throw the phone through the window.

Suddenly the voice said, "Remember, tell no one or I make it look like your friend John did it. No one will be able to help him then. Ask your cop buddies what they found on the body. You'll see." He hung up.

She looked shocked. "He knows," she said and sagged onto her bed.

Luke could not figure out how this asshole knew every move they made. It was like he had some supernatural powers or something.

How could he have known they talked to the police? If he knew that, then he must know they hadn't really told the cops anything.

"We have to be careful," Luke said. "He seems to know everything."

She looked into his eyes again, frowned and slowly turned away. "There must be some way…" she said.

"I'll think of something," Luke said, but felt little confidence he would.

Suddenly, she grabbed his face, searched his eyes and then kissed him hard. He reached out and held her against him, but then she pulled away.

"Whatever happens," she said. "I love you."

"El, what are you saying?"

"Everything," she said. "Everything that matters to me anyway. I love you and that's all there is." She smiled and he felt better.

* * *

After getting a copy of the video from Burt Lolly, Jaxon and Sally paid a visit to the J. Edgar Hoover building on Pennsylvania Ave. in downtown Washington D.C.

Having been there many times in the past, Jaxon still hated the building, not only for its Brutalist style of architecture, the huge concrete structure taking up an entire city block, but for the memories it wrung from his much maligned brain regarding his son's murder and the subsequent investigation.

As a victim of another notorious serial killer, Michael had been the catalyst for the FBI's involvement and Emory Holt's rapid advancement to section chief. The then twelve year old Michael, had suffered at the hands of Malcom Switzer, and with the public outcry at the brutal slaying, the FBI felt they needed to get involved. Jaxon's Department had gotten nowhere on the case and Holt had come in and broken it wide open.

Of course, Jaxon had remained outside the investigation of his own son. At least officially, but when they arrested Switzer at his sleazy Herndon trailer, Jaxon had been there and it had taken the entire force to keep him at bay. Jaxon had still managed to shoot the killer in the leg.

He survived and was now on death row, awaiting his execution for the murders of Michael and five other victims of his sick and demented mind. Jaxon would be there, front row and center, when the time came, to help him on his way. If only they would let him pull the switch.

Jaxon's ex-wife was another problem.

She had been a police officer in Fairfax with him, but after their son's murder, she could not hide the blame she felt Jaxon deserved and had terminated their relationship along with her employment with the Fairfax County Police Department. She had then enlisted Holt's help in securing her a position with the Bureau. After that it had only been a matter of time before she and Holt became a couple. Victoria Elliot was here, and the hatred he believed she felt toward him was something he could feel oozing from the walls as they entered the main floor.

"Detectives Jennings and Winston to see special agent Holt," Jaxon told the receptionist.

"Is he expecting you?" she asked.

"No."

She nodded and picked up the phone.

The main lobby was decorated in early 1970s government. The furniture looked new, just not new in design. Framed pictures of the President and Vice President loomed over the reception desk while previous Bureau Directors trailed off in either direction. Silence permeated the area with the exception of a keyboard clicking somewhere and Sally sniffling as they waited.

"Agent Holt will be with you shortly," the receptionist said, and indicated they were to sit until he arrived. Jaxon stood and stared at the pictures. Sally sat in a pale green, plastic, upholstered chair that looked far from comfortable. She fidgeted around in it for a few minutes, then stood up again.

"Maybe if you turned it upside-down with its little stubby legs sticking up," Jaxon said, "you might be able to relax in it."

She smiled at him. "This place rocks!"

"It does, doesn't it?" Emory Holt said from behind Jaxon's back.

Jaxon turned around and took in his old friend's appearance. Taller than Jaxon, Holt's graying hair was neatly trimmed tight around his ears and his gold, wire rimmed glasses sat down on the edge of his nose. His gray eyes conveyed a warmth Jaxon had a hard time appreciating. Holt smiled and extended his hand. Jaxon took it.

"Jaxon, good to see you. Detective Winston," Holt grabbed Sally's hand and pumped it once.

"Special Agent Holt. How are you?" Sally asked.

"Fine, fine. I hear you two are having a little trouble down there. Finally decided to bring in the experts, huh?" He laughed, but his humor failed to elicit the correct response from Jaxon. Sally smiled.

"Not yet, Holt," Jaxon said. "We're just looking for information and hoping you could give us a hand with it."

"Whatever you need. Come on. Let's go up to my office."

They entered the elevator by the reception desk and rode up three floors to Holt's office. He sat behind his desk and gestured to two chairs across from him. As they sat, Jaxon glanced around, his eyes settling on the framed picture of his ex-wife in a formal dress beside a tuxedoed Holt. Holt saw him looking and then pretended to miss it.

"So, what can the FBI do for Fairfax County's finest?" Holt asked.

Jaxon pulled out a printout and handed it across the desk to Holt.

"We need to see if you can track where this call originated. It was routed through a Voice Over Internet Protocol, VoIP, phone service called Cobra Call based in Moscow."

Holt was shaking his head.

"Tough one my friend," Holt said. "We've only been able to get information out of them once or twice. It's the Russian mob and they are not too friendly with us."

"I figured," Jaxon said, "but I'd like for you to try. Can you give it a shot? It's important."

"I suspected as much or you wouldn't be here." He stared at Jaxon for a moment. "Is this related to the pool murders?"

"Yes," Jaxon said.

Holt nodded, sat up straight and looked over the printout. "Who was the call made to?"

"My cell."

Holt's eyes looked up at him over the printout. "Who was the caller?"

Jaxon fidgeted for a second. "We're pretty sure it was the perp. His voice was electronically altered, but he had knowledge of the case that has not been publically released."

"What did he say?"

"He was basically taunting us."

"Yes, I would suspect so, but what was the exact conversation?"

Jaxon sighed and pulled out his notebook. He read from his notes and Holt listened carefully with his fingers tented over his desk and his eyes focused on the ceiling.

"He's a brazen bastard isn't he?" Holt said when Jaxon was finished. "Any luck finding traces of him after the call? I'm assuming you combed the area."

"That's the other favor we need," Jaxon said, pulling out another printout. "He installed a kind of web-cam on a light pole and accessed the feed through a server belonging to a company here in the U.S." He handed the information to Holt. "We could subpoena the company for its records, but I thought you might be able to do it faster."

"This one will be easier," Holt said. "Though it may not be what you expect. Usually these companies allow access to the server with just a user name, password, and the serial number from the device itself. They do not have to collect any personal information such as addresses or phone numbers."

"I'm aware of that," Jaxon said. "I was hoping to find out where he is accessing the server."

"We can usually get an I.P. address from the server records, but if it ends up being a public internet café or some wi-fi hotspot, it may not prove useful."

"Anything will be helpful at this point," Jaxon said.

"I'll see what I can find out. When do you want this?"

"As soon as you can. He's killing kids and it doesn't look like he's going to stop."

"Has he started helping you yet?"

Jaxon was surprised.

"As a matter of fact, yes. That was part of the phone conversation. He provided us with a means to identify his first victim. It was a class photograph from the boy's school."

"You were unable to identify the first victim? Was he badly mutilated?"

"He was frozen. For twenty seven years."

Holt's eyebrows went up and he sat forward.

"Where?"

"We don't know. He could have kept him in a freezer anywhere."

"No," Holt said. "Where was the boy from?"

"Reston."

Holt sat back in his chair, his finger resting on the side of his temple.

"So this was 1984?"

"Stewart Littleton disappeared Halloween night, 1984. Yes."

"Any animals turn up frozen?" Holt asked.

Jaxon looked at Sally who was staring at Holt with a face he couldn't read.

"Not frozen. Decapitated. Why?"

"We had a case turn up twelve years ago. Very similar. Indiana. About the time of Michael's murder. A boy of twelve surfaced in a pond and they had trouble identifying him. Nobody had reported a missing child and the usual dental records and fingerprints were coming up negative. They contacted the local FBI office for assistance and we discovered he had been frozen for sixteen years and had gone missing from Hobart, Indiana in 1985. The case remains unsolved. Everything dried up and the only other associated incidents in the area involved frozen animals. At least they had once been frozen."

"Let me ask you something," Sally said. She had been quiet the whole time and it startled Jaxon when she spoke. "Was anything found in the bloodstream?"

"Yes. As a matter of fact that's how we linked the animals to the boy. Diethyl Ether."

"Shit," Jaxon said, and stared at Sally who was grinning.

CHAPTER 25

Luke and Ellie had called everyone during the day and they met that evening under the guise of a kick-the-can game.

It was dark outside as they all gathered in the street. The conversation was somewhat heated. Luke hadn't expected anything less.

After a few minutes of hot debate, most wanted to go to the police.

Luke stood up. "We have an issue you should know." The group grew quiet. Ellie lowered her head.

"Apparently he knows quite a bit about what we do and he seems to be able to track our every move."

"How?" Patrick interrupted.

"If I knew that, we probably wouldn't be having this discussion. He's smart," Luke said.

"What does he know?" Ralph asked.

"Just about everything. He called Ellie's cell phone today and made some threats. He also knows we have talked some to the cops, Jaxon and Winston."

"What was the threat?" John asked. "Anything new?"

"As a matter of fact, it was toward you, John. He said there is some evidence he planted on Jason's body that would point to you if he wanted it to. Ellie and I don't know what it is, but he said if we talked to anyone else, he would somehow frame John for Jason's murder."

"It's bullshit!" John said. "There's no way he could pin this on me. I haven't done anything."

"We know that, John," Ellie said. "I don't know what he's done, but I can't imagine what it would be that would make the police believe you did it. We need help. I think we should call Jaxon and Winston right now."

Luke felt he was losing the battle. There was a lot of talk amongst themselves for a minute and he could hear them all agreeing with Ellie. How could he stop this? He needed to find a way to keep her safe until he could figure out what to do.

"I think we should tell the police everything we know," Katy said, "and then stay in hiding until they catch this guy."

"That could be a long time, Kat," Luke said. "We have no idea if what we know will even help them. It could be months and I don't know about you, but I can't stay cooped up in our house for that long. Sooner or later, we're going to get lazy, or tired, and then he'll make his move. We stay safe and keep quiet like he wants, and no one will get hurt."

Suddenly cell phones started going off. Anyone in the group who had their cell phone was getting a message. Luke's heart rose in his throat as he pulled out his phone and looked at the text message.

Nice town meeting. Hope you're discussing how to keep quiet. I'd hate to see someone get hurt in your little club. W.S.

Deana squealed and dropped her phone like it was diseased. "How does he know! How does he know! How does he know!"

Katy grabbed her sister and hugged her tight.

"Damn!" Jimmy said.

"Oh no," Ralph whined. "How did he get my number?" He pointed at Luke. "Now you've done it. He knows who we are!"

Ellie's face looked pained and she stared up at him with eyes that broke his heart. She didn't say a thing. Luke knelt down and took her in his arms.

"We can't stop this, can we?" she whispered.

"I don't know," he said. "But I'm going to try."

* * *

Jaxon and Sally were leaving the Hoover building when he heard his name being called.

He would recognize Victoria's voice anywhere and it bothered him she still evoked some kind of deep emotional response that made him have to stop and turn around.

She walked up smiling. Her long, dark hair was down, but held back behind her ears with a black band that matched her gray skirt and black blouse. She still had great legs and at age forty five, carried herself as if she were in a body twice as young.

"Hey, Sally," Victoria said, casually, then to Jaxon. "What, Jaxon? You weren't going to stop and say hello?"

"We didn't have much time and I knew you were busy."

"I wasn't so busy I couldn't say 'Hi' to an old friend."

"Vick, we haven't been old friends in a long time."

Her smile faltered just a fraction, but she recovered quickly. "Still, I thought you'd at least stop in. I called you a couple of months ago and you never returned my call."

"I must have forgotten." In fact, he had looked at the phone for three days, but could never make himself pick it up.

"Uh huh. I found some old stuff of Michael's and I wanted you to have it."

He didn't know what to say so he remained silent. She stared at him for a second and then brushed it aside like she always did.

"So, what are you guys up to?"

"We came to see Holt about a case. He's going to do some digging for us," Jaxon said.

"What's the case?"

"Couple of murders."

"I hadn't heard."

"Three kids actually," Sally said, and Jaxon shot her a look.

Victoria frowned. "How old?"

Jaxon fidgeted. "Twelve to thirteen."

"Oh no, Jaxon. Is it happening again?"

"This is different, Vick."

"Are you sure? Because you know there were some unknowns in the case."

"Switzer's behind bars. Case closed. This is different."

"How?"

"I don't have time right now. It's our case and if I wanted to involve you I would have. Besides, Holt is in on it."

She looked hurt and angry. A difficult look to pull off, but she did it well.

"All right. Be careful."

"Sure." She locked eyes with him and stayed that way for what seemed an eternity. Finally, Sally cleared her throat and Victoria looked away.

"Ok," she said. "I'll get back to work. If you need anything, call."

"Yep," he said.

"Actually, call me anyway, so I can get that stuff to you."

"All right."

"Promise?"

He crossed his heart and she smiled. He knew he'd break it.

CHAPTER 26

Jaxon and Sally were riding back from DC when she asked, "What were the unknowns?"

"In what?"

"The murder of your son. Victoria said there were some unknowns."

He drove for a bit without saying a thing and he finally glanced over at her. "You really want to drag this up?"

"I just want to know."

He sighed. "With Michael, the timeframe had some holes in it."

"Like what?"

"The time of death didn't match up with Switzer's activity."

"Ok…"

The silence dragged out as the memories flooded back in.

"What? Was he doing laundry at the time? Baking bread? Come on. How did it differ?"

He stared straight ahead driving in silence for a minute as she waited patiently. He really didn't want to go back there.

"Most people don't know this," he said, "but Switzer was taunting me. We were getting close to him and he started making threats against my family. I ignored them and it got Michael killed."

"You've told me some of this," she said, "and I know it's tough for you to talk about, but what if it helps us with this case? Maybe we're overlooking something. We seem to have a lot of unknowns."

"Yes we do."

"So, why didn't the time of death match up?"

He sighed. "You know time of death is not exact."

She nodded.

"The M.E. determined Michael's time of death as 11:00 p.m. Unfortunately, Malcom Switzer was under surveillance close to that time."

"Who was watching him?"

"Me."

Her face showed surprise at this. "I've never heard this before. How were they able to get the conviction?"

"He was tried on multiple counts and Michael's murder was just one of them. Because of the inexactness of the Time of Death Certainty Principal, the D.A. was able to convince the jury Switzer could have done it in that timeframe."

"How?"

"Remember the Certainty Principle states that if the subject was certain to be alive at a known time, and you know with certainty when they were found dead, then we are 100% certain the death took place within that interval. Then the M.E. uses other techniques to narrow that down further. Lividity, rigor, vitreous humor, etc. It can still be off an hour or two based on how long the person has been dead."

"What was the interval?"

"Five hours."

"That's pretty good. How did they know?"

"I know when I left him and I know when I found him."

"Tell me."

He drove in silence a little more and then it spilled out of him like water.

"Victoria was out on her own case with Stansfield. I was at home with Michael. He was in bed at 9:00 when I got the call about Switzer. We'd been trying to track him down, but he had been missing for over a week. He showed up at his trailer and they called me. He only stopped for a few minutes inside the run down piece of shit he lived in and then was on the move. They figured he was on the hunt again. I needed to go, but I couldn't leave Michael alone. I called the babysitter and I apparently woke her up. She said she was sick, but would be right over. Michael was only going to be alone for a few minutes, or that's what I thought. I had to go, so I left him asleep and locked up. The sitter had her own key."

"What happened to the sitter?"

"She never made it over. She told us later, she had taken some cold medicine earlier, before I called, and fell back asleep immediately after. She didn't even remember me phoning. Switzer killed him while I was out supposedly watching his every move."

"Oh Jaxon—I'm sorry. I'd heard things about Michael, but I never knew all this. Jesus, I'm sorry."

He nodded without looking at her and they drove in silence for a few minutes.

"How did Switzer do it?" she asked.

"We lost sight of him for forty five minutes at 10:45 p.m. We picked him up again coming out of the bar we lost him in. He headed straight to his trailer and never left it until we arrested him two days later. He must have gone out the back of the bar and done the deed, then high tailed it back to the bar and walked out the front like nothing happened."

"Wasn't Switzer fond of ears? He was known to keep the left ear of his victims as a souvenir, right?"

"That's another one of the unknowns. He cut the left ear off of the first four victims. We found them in his trailer folded up in newspaper and sealed inside a Ziploc bag in the freezer. Michael had both ears missing and they have never been found."

CHAPTER 27

"Q, it's Luke Harrison."

"Yo! Luke! What's up?"

Luke smiled into the phone as he heard Quentin Jenson's Jersey accent. Even though the kid was from Atlanta, Georgia, you would never know it unless he told you. Luke guessed it was cooler being from Jersey than Atlanta.

"How good are you?" Luke asked.

"Depends on what it is you need," Quentin said.

Everybody knew Q was the local hacker and could penetrate just about any electronic device known to man. Maybe even gadgets that were not of this world. Too bad there weren't any to test this theory.

"I need you to hack my phone."

"Damn, I thought you needed something that was challenging. Bring it over and we'll crack it open."

Luke yelled to his mom he'd be back in a while, hopped on his bike before she could object, and rode over to Q's house.

He lived in the neighborhood just behind Luke's in a beat up 1950s era cinder block home. Three large dogs roamed the chain link fenced in yard and Luke had to whistle to get Q to call them off.

It was amazing to watch the transformation from vicious attack beasts with their teeth bared and saliva drooling from their mouths, to panting and wagging, happy go lucky pets that wouldn't harm a fly. Q said their names were Wynkin', Blynkin' and Nod. Luke guessed the one with the missing eye was Wynkin'.

Q led him through a house which was littered with trash, boxes, and clothes, and they entered another world which Q said was his 'Cave.'

Everything in the room either lit up, blinked, or hummed. It was an amazing assortment of computers, iPads, Smartphones, video monitors and web-cams. His desk contained three, twenty-four inch monitors lined up in a row and some program was displayed, running on each screen.

"Dude, this is awesome!" Luke said.

"Nothing but net," Q said. "I paid for everything but the iPad. That was a Christmas gift from my uncle Bodey."

Luke walked up to the desk and watched a video running on the screen to the left. A cat was playing a piano while a dog licked himself. He wasn't sure what it was supposed to represent but it was funny as hell.

"Let's see the phone," Q said, his hand held out waiting.

"Will this ruin it?" Luke asked.

"This will make it better," Q said with a grin. "What exactly do you want out of it?"

"I need you to find out where a text message came from."

"Ouch!" Q said.

"Problem?"

"We'll see. A lot of that kind of stuff is encrypted, but I just downloaded this new hack my uncle came up with and it might do the trick. I haven't even got to use it yet."

"Is it legal?"

"Define legal."

"Uh—never mind. I don't care. I need to know."

Q took the phone, hooked a USB cable to it and plugged the cable into one of the many computers he had arrayed around the desk.

"Is your uncle a hacker too?" Luke asked.

"No. Better. Bodey's a systems engineer for CRAY computers. He writes this stuff."

Luke smiled. "Cool."

Q loaded up a program and Luke watched as he typed in some commands and a list of calls and phone numbers came up on the screen. He could see Ellie's number and John's, along with his own house and various others. Q clicked something and all the text messages came up. Most were from Ellie and, as he saw them, Q turned and grinned at him.

"You and Ellie gettin' hot and heavy, huh?"

"Just ignore that stuff," Luke said. "This is the one I need to know about."

He pointed to the message he had received during the group's little get together last night. Q read the message and asked, "What town meeting?"

"It's not important. Can you tell me where this came from. The number shows up only as zeros."

Q clicked another screen and said, "Yeah, I see that. Whoever made this message didn't want you to find out who they were, that's for sure. It's routed through a special server that people like me use so we can't be traced."

"Damn! I thought you'd be able to get it. Oh well."

"You're kind of impatient aren't you?" Q said and then grinned. "I didn't say I couldn't get it."

He clicked through a few more screens so fast Luke couldn't tell what they were and arrived at a screen that held a series of ones and zeros all lined up throughout the whole page.

"This is the binary code the server is using to scramble the cell phone numbers that make the incoming calls." He clicked through another page and a list of numbers showed up.

"Awesome! I'm going to have to tell Bodey this program rocks. The phone number you're looking for is right here." He pointed to a ten digit number about halfway down the screen. The area code was not familiar to Luke.

"Can you tell where it's texting from?"

"I can even do better. I can track where the cell phone is right now."

He opened another program on another screen and typed in the cell number. The screen changed to a busy hourglass and then a map popped up with a blinking icon in the center. Luke bent over his shoulder to look. Nothing on the map looked familiar.

"How can I tell where that is?" Luke asked.

Q zoomed out and Luke could see it was in the state of Indiana. Northern section in a town called Hobart. The blinking icon was not moving.

"It's stationary," Q said. "He's currently staying put. If he was in a car, or walking or something, you would see it move. Does this help?"

"Yeah, at least now I know the number."

"What's your e-mail?"

He told him. "Why?"

"I'm going to mail you this program and you can track the phone whenever you want."

"Sweet!"

* * *

Jaxon woke with a killer hangover.

After yesterday's visits with Emory Holt and Victoria, along with reliving the night Michael died, his mind had had enough for one day and he elected to numb it. With Crown Royal. It worked like a charm, but now he was paying for it. His phone rang and he held his head as he looked at the clock. It was 10:00 a.m.

"Shit." he said, reaching for the phone. "What?"

"Are you up?" Sally asked, a little pity in her voice.

"Yeah. Sorry. I'll be there in a few."

"Good. The chief's looking for us. He wants an update. Holt called him."

Shit. That's all he needed. "I'll be there in fifteen."

He threw on a tie and grabbed his jacket as he tossed a cup of food in Reverb's bowl. The dog looked mournfully at him.

"What?" he said. The dog did not have an answer.

Swinging through Starbucks for a quick jolt of caffeine, he made it into the bullpen in twenty minutes. Sally was waiting impatiently.

"I thought you said fifteen minutes," she said as they walked to the chief's office.

"Fifteen—twenty—somewhere in there. I made it."

"Oh God—you need a breath mint. Here. And it's been twenty five."

She handed him a stick of gum and his stomach revolted as he stuck it in his mouth. He hoped he could keep things down until the meeting was over.

"Nice of you to find time in your busy morning to see me," Chief Horace Benton said, as they walked in.

"Sorry, Chief," Jaxon said.

"Sit."

Sally and Jaxon grabbed chairs and sat in front of the desk.

Benton was five years his senior and someone Jaxon actually respected. The man had not brown-nosed his way to the position. He had earned it in the trenches, and that meant a lot to Jaxon. The Chief didn't seem to be sharing the love this morning, though.

"Why didn't you discuss the FBI with me? I had to hear from Emory Holt this morning that my two lead investigators visited the J. Edgar Hoover building soliciting the help of the FBI and I was in the dark. Thanks."

"Sorry Chief, we got a lead and we followed up on it," Jaxon said.

"Do you want to fill me in or do I need to ask Holt to do that?"

He let Sally do most of the talking since his head and stomach ached. The sunlight streaming in through the window felt like molten gunshots to his head and at one point he had thought the bile in his throat was going to make an appearance that would probably earn him a day without pay. He forced it down, only barely. The Chief was saying something and he had missed some of it.

"The FBI wants to be involved. Holt informs me they have a case that is quite old, but he feels could be the same guy, and if that's so, the investigation crosses state lines and they want to jump in. I'm inclined to grant them access since we seem to have run into a brick wall in this thing."

"I don't want Holt in on it," Jaxon said.

"Why?"

"We've got this thing covered and I told him yesterday we weren't ready to bring them in. We just needed a little information and they were the best source for it."

"This doesn't have anything to do with Victoria, does it? I would be highly disappointed if you put your own personal difficulties before the welfare of the people and children of this county. That's not happening is it Jaxon?"

"I can't work with him," Jaxon said.

"Dammit Jaxon! You're going to have to. Do I need to pull you two off of this thing? Because I'll do it in a heartbeat. Holt's in and you two are going to have to learn to love it. Got me?"

"Fine," Jaxon said and stood. "I'll break out the welcome mat."

144

CHAPTER 28

Luke hesitated with his finger poised over the send button.

He wanted to send the text message, but something was keeping him from doing it. Maybe he was having second thoughts about the logic of harassing their tormentor. His phone vibrated in his hand and he jumped. It was Ellie.

"Hey."

"Hi," she said.

"What are you doing?"

"Waiting for you to call me, but I guess that was never going to happen. What are you doing?"

"Sorry, I was over at Q's house."

"Quentin Jenson?"

"Yep."

She sounded serious now and asked, "What were you doing over there?"

"You won't believe it. You need to see this. Can I come over and get you? I need to show you something."

"Ok," but he could hear a little apprehension in her voice.

"Be right there."

When he got her back to his house, they went up to his room and he booted up the computer.

"What's this all about?" Ellie asked.

"Just watch."

He loaded up the tracking program Q emailed him and typed in the phone number. After a minute, the map came up and the blip was moving east. He turned to her and watched her study the computer screen. Her face showed confusion for a moment and then she looked scared.

"Is this—him?" She said.

He nodded his head, grinning.

"How?" She asked.

"I got Q to hack my cell phone and he used a special program his uncle wrote to find the phone number that sent the text message we all got last night. This is it." He pointed to the number in a box at the top of the screen. "Then Q gave me this program that can track the cell phone anywhere in the country."

"So, we can tell where he is?" She smiled.

He nodded.

"Where is this, now?" she asked pointing to the blip.

"Q said if the blip was moving then he was in a car or something. Hold on…" Luke played with the program and zoomed out so they could see he was in Pennsylvania. He zoomed back in and the map displayed roads and highways. "It looks like he's on I-70 near Somerset Pennsylvania, heading this way."

"What's he doing?"

"I don't know, but he was in Indiana earlier. Seems like a long way to drive. I wonder if he lives there."

"Do you think he's coming here to hurt somebody else?"

Luke shrugged. "Could be. I can't even imagine what would be going on inside that psycho's head."

She stepped to him and hugged him. "We can go to the police now. We can show them where he is and they can take him away. We need to call Jaxon."

"We will. As soon as we're sure it's him."

"But you said it was his number."

"How well do you trust a hacker?"

She turned away, thinking. "What are we going to do?"

"I was going to text a message to him and see if he responds like we expect. If he does, then we know it's him."

"Won't that let him know we're on to him?"

Luke frowned. "I was kind of worried about that too. I was about to text him before you called but I hesitated for some reason.

Something was telling me to wait." He smiled. "I guess I needed my smart girlfriend to see how stupid I am."

She finally smiled at him. "Let's figure this out together. There's got to be a way we can tell if it's him or not."

* * *

Jaxon's desk phone rang and he picked it up. "Jaxon."

"It's Holt." Jaxon rolled his eyes and Sally chuckled. Apparently she could hear his voice from her desk. "I've got some interesting information for you."

"Shoot. I'm going to put you on speaker so Sally can hear."

"The Russians were not very forthcoming on our request for information. I wouldn't count on anything coming out of Moscow, but we'll sit for a few days and see if they bite on our offer."

"What offer?" Jaxon asked.

"We promised them we'd back off of an investigation into their activities associated with a scam coming out of Western Iran through Dayton, Ohio. Nothing political, it's all about money. They've been silent so far."

"How can you promise that?"

"We lie."

"All right. That doesn't help me."

"The other thing you asked about has proven more lucrative. I'm optimistic this will help in the cold case in Indiana as well as your cases in Fairfax."

Jaxon looked up at Sally who raised an eyebrow.

"Sounds promising. What have you got?"

"An I.P. address and a physical address."

"You're serious."

"As a heart attack. We're going to Indiana in two hours. Benton's agreed already and has cleared you. You two need to get your butts to Dulles and you'll fly out on a company plane."

Jaxon was grinning and Sally joined him. "Where do we meet you?"

"It won't be me. As section Chief I get to coordinate, not participate. The agent I've assigned will meet you at the Custom's office in two hours."

"Who is it?" There was a pause and Jaxon thought he hung up.

"It's Victoria. She's worked on the cold case and is the most up to date on it. Problem?"

Jaxon swore under his breath. Sally smiled.

"Still there, Jaxon?"

"Yeah, I'm still here. All right. Two hours." And he punched off.

* * *

After a couple hours of racking their brains, William Smith actually made it easy for them. He texted Ellie.

Eliana Pemberton is not your real name.

She began to cry.

"He's just messing with you," Luke said, holding her against him. "You know that, right?"

She nodded against his chest, but then raised her eyes to his. "He's right, though."

He searched her eyes and saw something in them that confused him.

"What do you mean? Eliana's not your real name?"

"No, Eliana's my name but I was born Eliana Ann Worthington. My mom's maiden name is Pemberton and when my father left her, she had it legally changed back along with her children's."

"Why would she do that? I mean I guess I could understand her changing her name, but why yours?"

"She hated him. She told us she didn't want any part of him left in our lives. He abused her, left her for dead, then took every bit of savings they had and left her penniless."

"I've never heard this before."

"I usually don't make a habit of telling people. It just doesn't occur to me. I've been Eliana Pemberton as long as I can remember."

"When did she tell you?"

"When I was nine."

"We were in third grade."

She nodded. "Do you remember the week I missed school because I had the mumps?"

"Yes."

"I wasn't sick. I was upset. She had just told me."

"I remember. You were sad for like a month after that. Why didn't you tell me?"

"I was embarrassed. My family was messed up and I felt small. All I wanted to do was hide."

"You must have been young when he did all this," Luke said.

She nodded. "I don't remember him. I've only ever seen one picture of him. Patrick remembers him a little. He doesn't talk about him much though. He was four when our father left. I was two."

"I'm sorry Ellie. That sucks. All this time I thought he was dead or something."

"He might as well be."

"Who knows all this?"

"My family, my grandma I guess, probably my aunt and uncle. Not many."

"Then how did William Smith know it?"

"I don't know. That's why I'm so upset. I could care less about my father. This asshole seems to know everything about me and I want to know how."

Luke smiled.

"Why are you smiling?"

"Let's ask him how he knows." And he explained what he wanted to do.

CHAPTER 29

The private jet touched down in Valparaiso, Indiana, four hours later and a car picked them up at the ramp.

Victoria had remained mostly silent on the short flight, but did fill them in on the old cold case. When she described the bruising around the mouth and the Diethyl Ether, Jaxon interrupted and asked where the body had been found.

"In a small pond. It had frozen over and some kids had seen something beneath the ice. They got their parents and in turn the parents contacted the local sheriff's office."

"How did you find the boy's parents after so much time?" Sally asked.

"Very similar to yours," Victoria said. "The local Police Department called the FBI after a few months. We were able to narrow the time of death down to within a year and we found him using missing person's files from the surrounding counties and states. Of course, I wasn't involved then. I was still with the FCPD. This was 2001."

The year was not a good one for Jaxon. Victoria either.

Just the mention of it brought the temperature down in the cabin a few degrees. Nobody said a word for the rest of the flight.

They arrived at the local sheriff's office and met with the detective who had handled the case back in 2001. His name was Vernon Scoggins.

Jaxon disliked him immediately. He was bald, overweight, and wore sneakers with his suit. He chewed tobacco and chose to spit the juice into an empty Zephyrhills water bottle he carried around with him. Jaxon swore if the son-of-a-bitch spilled one drop on him, he would break his leg. Victoria seemed to like him.

Holt had discussed the information they had obtained through the web-cam's manufacturer with Scoggins and his chief, so they knew what the three of them were there for. Scoggins told them the address associated with the computer I.P. address was in a section of town known for its extracurricular activity, mainly prostitution. The house was currently under surveillance, and per the FBI's instructions, no one was to interfere with anyone entering or leaving the premises. So far the place had been quiet as a tomb.

Public records showed a deed recorded under the name of Walter Peacock. Contacting the owner had been relatively easy, but the information he provided on his renter proved useless. The tenant, William Smith, paid in cash every six months through the mail and the only contact information he had provided listed a name and address which did not exist. William Smith apparently did not want to be bothered. Mr. Peacock could not remember ever meeting the tenant. Scoggins said the man sounded drunk on the phone.

Scoggins told them the neighbors had very little information about the man except to say he usually showed up late at night and was very white.

"White?" Victoria asked.

"Yes," Scoggins said. "You know—pale—albino—I don't know. One guy told me he's only ever seen him from a distance and his face was very white."

Jaxon and Sally shared a look.

"What?" Victoria said looking back and forth between the two.

"Our perp looks to be wearing a white Halloween mask on the two surveillance videos we have of him," Jaxon said. "At first I thought he was albino, but Sally said it was probably a mask. I think she's right."

"Could be our guy, right?" Scoggins said.

No one answered.

"The plan is to wait until he shows up," Victoria said, "and then move in. If he doesn't show, we get the warrant to search the place. Right now, we sit tight and wait."

"Great," Jaxon said. "Can we at least join the surveillance team?"

"No," she said. "I don't want anybody spooking this guy. We wait for the call."

* * *

Three hours had passed and everyone was on edge.

Jaxon noticed Sally was on her third cup of coffee and Victoria was sucking down Diet Pepsis like they were going out of style. Jaxon kept busy with a crossword puzzle.

Victoria walked over and sat next to Jaxon.

"You know, you haven't said more than five words to me the last six hours."

"Actually, I said seventeen."

She smiled. "That bad, huh?"

"Torture," but he didn't smile. He was in no mood for playful banter with his ex-wife.

"So, how is Reverb?" She asked.

"Old and nearly dead."

"I miss him."

He looked up from the puzzle and searched her face. She hadn't so much as asked about the dog in ten years. Reverb had only been two years old at the time of Michael's death and he distinctly remembered a time before that when she said the dog had to go. The only reason he eventually stayed was because Michael adored him. She couldn't break his heart, but she was angry at Jaxon for weeks because he went behind her back and brought the dog home without consulting her.

She was smiling and he wondered if she genuinely meant what she said. Probably not.

"I thought you hated him," he said, turning back to the puzzle. "You've never come to see him."

"It's not for lack of trying. I can't even get you to return my calls much less answer the door."

"You've knocked on the door?"

"Three times."

"Wow—three times in ten years. You must have wanted to see him pretty bad."

"I've wanted to see you," she said.

He looked her in the eye, expecting her to look away, but she held his gaze with a strange look on her face. One he hadn't seen in a long time. It brought back a flood of memories; times that had been good, but now seemed bitter in the light of the florescent lamps. He didn't know what to make of this conversation and hoped it would end soon.

"Me. The dog. We've both been there. I've never heard you knock."

"Maybe you weren't listening," she said, cocking her head slightly and giving him the little grin that used to drive him crazy. Now, it was just pissing him off.

"What? Is there supposed to be some deep meaning in there? Because I've missed it. What is it, Vick? What do you want?" His voice had grown louder and he saw Sally look up and Scoggins staring.

"Apparently you're still deaf," she said, getting up. "I'll try pounding on the door next time."

"You do that."

And she walked away.

The radio crackled to life.

"We've got a visitor."

Time to move.

* * *

Luke and John were hunched over his desk watching the blip creep up the street behind Luke's house.

Ellie was sitting on the bed and Jimmy was standing looking out the window. Luke's room faced the rear of the house and even though there were quite a few trees in the backyard, you could still see headlights if a car drove into the cul-de-sac behind them.

"I got lights!" Jimmy said.

"That's him," Luke said. "Is he stopped?"

"Yeah—the lights just went out." Jimmy stepped back away from the window and looked at the computer. Luke pointed to the blip that was now stationary on the map.

"All right, remember," Luke said, "this is just for verification. We don't want him to see us. John, set up the three way call with me and Jimmy. When we're in position, Ellie, you send the Facebook message and we'll see what he does. Come on Jimmy."

Luke and Jimmy left the room and Luke's phone vibrated first. He had the earpiece in and he said, "Got ya' John."

"Roger," John said, and put Luke on hold.

When the three way was set up, they were all linked, and Luke and Jimmy went out the back door, splitting up. Luke went to the back of his fence slipping through the hole between it and the hedge, and snuck around the tennis courts to a spot he could easily see the car, yet remain hidden. The night was moonless, and the darkness, oppressive. Luke shivered in his spot despite the warm, humid air.

Jimmy went in the opposite direction, hid in the neighbor's backyard and watched from around their fence. When he was in place he said, "I can see the car. He's still inside."

"Yep, he hasn't moved," John said.

"I got him too," Luke said. "I can't make out his face but I see his silhouette. Tell Ellie to send the message."

What Luke hoped for was that the killer owned a smart phone. When Ellie sent him the message on Facebook, he should get some kind of notification. At least if he was as meticulous as Luke thought he was. Then they would watch and see if he would use the phone while they observed him. Visual confirmation was their only option at this point. They did not want to alert him to the fact they knew his cell phone number.

A few minutes went by, and Luke asked, "Did she send it?"

"Yeah," John said. "Give it a minute."

Luke's legs were starting to cramp from the position he was in, and he shifted a little trying to get comfortable. A soft glow of light showed inside the car and Luke could see him bring what must be a phone up to his face.

Luke was shocked at what he saw. The man was completely white. His face, hair, and lips looked to be the shade of vanilla yogurt. He wasn't even sure if he had any hair.

"I can see his cell phone!" Jimmy said, excitedly. "He's doing something."

Luke then heard Ellie's phone ringing through the connection with John.

"Her phone is ringing," John said.

Luke watched as the man put the glowing phone to his ear, then the light went out and all he could see was his silhouette. He listened carefully but could only hear the sound of Ellie's voice, but not the conversation. At least at first.

Her voice rose and she started yelling. "I don't want that!" she shouted. "You leave them alone! Please don't hurt anyone else! Hello? Hello?" and then Luke heard the sound of her crying.

"You guys better get back in here," John said.

* * *

They were down from the house about a hundred yards, crammed in an unmarked van with two other detectives.

A small SWAT team was set up and waiting behind the house next to their guy's shack. That's exactly what came to Jaxon's mind when he saw the place. Run down, piece of shit, shack. The roof sagged in the middle and what was once a porch now resembled a listing or sinking boat. One lone rusted chair stood on its side in the section that remained intact. The windows were mostly glass, but one just to the right of the main entrance was covered in plywood. The yard was overgrown and weeds poked up through cracks in the broken driveway. No vehicle was visible.

The night was quiet except for a lone dog barking somewhere in the distance. Movement caught his eye and a drunken man weaved down the street approaching the van from their right. He moved past and they could hear him mumbling to himself. Something about *Layla wantin' to blow Henry, but Henry don't know no Joe.*

"He's been in there how long now?" Victoria asked one of the detectives.

"Twenty minutes."

There were no lights on in the house and no movement had been seen since the detectives observed a darkly dressed individual enter the residence from the rear. He had crept along the street near the front of the houses as he made his way to the shack. They said he looked like a man not wanting to be seen.

"All right, we move in two minutes," Victoria said, and opened the van door exiting to the street. Jaxon, Scoggins, and Sally followed.

They each had an earpiece and radio, and wore Kevlar vests and FBI Jackets. The SWAT team would move in first, then Jaxon and Sally would follow with Victoria and Scoggins. They remained hidden from view behind the van, but Jaxon peered around the rear of the vehicle and watched as the SWAT team moved silently into place at the front and rear of the shack. It was like watching shadows as they crept around the plants and trees in the yard.

Jaxon's cell phone vibrated. Victoria glared at him, but he pulled it out and read the text message. His knees suddenly felt like jelly. The text message was from him.

I know where his ears are. You'll have them soon. My gift.

* * *

Jimmy caught up with Luke in the backyard and they went up to his room where John was doing his best to console Ellie.

She leapt into Luke's arms when he stepped into the room. He held her tight and stroked her hair softly trying to calm her. She finally looked up at him and said, "He's going to kill somebody tonight."

"What did he say?" Luke asked.

"I asked him how he knew so much about me and he ignored the question, but told me with that creepy voice he has that one of my friends would be gone tonight."

"Who?"

"He didn't say." She looked around at all of them. "We can't let him. We have to call Jaxon now. We know this guy," she pointed out the window, "is him."

"Let's do it," Luke said and pulled out his cell phone and the business card Jaxon gave them.

He walked over to his desk and glanced at the computer program showing them the position of the killer. His phone was still in the same spot. Luke hoped that meant William Smith was there too. Just then a little window popped up on the computer screen showing some text.

201106172012 OUTGOING MESSAGE SENT TO 555-432-2020
MESSAGE COMPOSITION AS MMS
BODY OF TEXT:
I KNOW WHERE HIS EARS ARE. YOU'LL HAVE THEM
SOON. MY GIFT.
END OF MESSAGE.

"What the hell is this?" Luke asked no one in particular.

"Oh," John said. "That same kind of thing popped up when he called Ellie's phone. Her phone number showed up along with all these numbers and then went away when the call ended."

"He just sent this text message to this phone," Luke said pointing to the screen. The telephone number bothered him. He knew he'd seen it before and wondered if the killer was playing games with other kids. He looked down at the business card and saw his mistake.

"What the hell?" he said.

"What's wrong?" Ellie said.

"He just sent that message to Jaxon's phone." He held up the card so they could see.

"What?" Ellie came up and looked at the card, then the computer screen, then back at the card in disbelief. "Why would he be texting Jaxon?"

"Apparently to send this message," Jimmy said.

"I wonder what the hell it means," John said looking over their shoulders. "Whose ears is he talking about?"

"We need to call Jaxon now!" Ellie said.

"Right," and Luke dialed the number. It went straight to voice mail. "Crap! It went to voice mail! What do I say?"

"Tell him to call us right away," Ellie said.

Luke did just that. "Now what?"

"We wait and watch, I guess," John said.

* * *

"Dammit! Turn that thing off, Jaxon!" Victoria chided. "I thought you knew better."

Jaxon stood there staring at the message. He looked up at Victoria and his face must have betrayed what he felt because she came over to him and said gently, "What? What is it?"

He showed her the message. She looked like she had been slapped.

"Is this from him?" she said.

He nodded. He was afraid to speak. Not because he felt like he couldn't. He was scared to hear what his own voice would sound like right now.

"They're about to move in," Scoggins said. "What's the deal, here. You two gonna stand there gawking at each other or do your jobs! Let's go!"

Their earpieces came alive. "Moving in...Now! Now! Now!" Jaxon finally spoke. "He may know we're here."

"Shit!" Victoria said. "Come on!" She turned and ran across the street with Jaxon, Sally, and Scoggins in tow. "And turn that thing off!"

* * *

Luke sat and watched the blip on the screen waiting for Jaxon to call back.

It had only been a few minutes but it felt like hours. Jimmy was using the bathroom and John was talking to Ellie while they waited and watched.

Another window popped up on the screen and Luke said, "He's doing something on the phone again."

John and Ellie walked up and looked over his shoulder. The window filled with letters and numbers they couldn't understand.

201106172017 OUTGOING MESSAGE SENT 015552319000
MESSAGE TYPE MMS
BODY OF TEXT: EXECUTE *##*
END OF MESSAGE

"Where did that one go to?" John asked

"I have no idea," Luke said. "I wonder what 'EXECUTE' means?"

"Maybe he's getting ready to kill his next victim," Ellie said.

"But he hasn't moved," Luke said.

"I don't get it," Ellie said.

Neither did Luke. "Come on Jaxon! Where the hell are you?"

* * *

The swat team had just entered the structure as Jaxon was crossing the street at a run.

He trailed behind Victoria, Sally, and Scoggins, in that order. Victoria was almost to the front door when the house self destructed and a giant fireball filled Jaxon's world as he was tossed backwards into the street. The concussion knocked the wind out of him, his ears ringing from the blast.

Jaxon lay on his back, dazed.

Things swam in his peripheral vision, but the world around him remained eerily silent. The stars above winked down at him as an orange glow began to wash them out. Suddenly a face was above him, the lips moved, but no sound escaped them. Another face appeared next to the first and Jaxon recognized the two detectives from the van. One was gesturing frantically at something beyond Jaxon's vision while the first continued to shout something at Jaxon which he could not hear.

A low roaring began to rise in his ears and faint voices bled through the noise. Jaxon tried to sit up, but pain in his back forced him back down again. He realized he hadn't taken a breath in a long while and opened his mouth, breathing in. He choked on something and spasms racked his body as he coughed uncontrollably. He rolled over on his side, gasping for air and saw the destruction laid out before him.

The shack was nothing but a burning pile of rubble on the ground. Fire shot up in a plume thirty or forty feet in the air and Jaxon's mind was having a hard time wrapping itself around what it was seeing. Maybe a ruptured gas line? One of the detectives from the van shouted in his face and Jaxon barely made out "...all right?"

Jaxon nodded and tried to sit up again taking it slow. Pain shot up his back but it was bearable. Something was laying across Jaxon's legs and when he realized it was a severed arm clad in black with the words 'SWAT' stenciled on it, he kicked at it frantically, ignoring the pain that shot in spasms up his back. He saw blood dripping on his shirt and realized it was coming from somewhere on his head. Reaching up, he felt warm liquid ebbing from his nose, though he could not feel his fingers touching it. His face felt numb. He went to a kneeling position and tried to stand.

"Don't think you should try that, Detective," a voice said, faintly, through the roaring that continued in his ears.

He tried his voice. "Victoria?"

"What?" the detective yelled, but to Jaxon it sounded like he was whispering through cotton.

"Where's Victoria?"

"I don't know. I haven't found her yet. It's chaos. Are you ok?"

He nodded and stepped toward the burning wreckage. He had to find Victoria. The detective grabbed his arm, trying to hold him back.

"No Sir! It's too dangerous!" Jaxon shook him off and stumbled through the debris toward the fire.

"Vick!" he shouted, but his voice sounded so far away. "Victoria!" He tripped over something and saw a leg protruding from under a piece of siding. Ignoring the searing pain in his back, he bent and flung the siding off to find Sally staring face up at him, her eyes open and vacant. Her face was calm and unharmed. No dirt, or soot, or even a scratch could be found, but the lower half of her body was a mangled mess. Jaxon knelt and retched to the side. She was gone.

"Oh shit! Sally! Dammit!"

Scoggins was just to the left of where he and Sally were, or at least what Jaxon thought was Scoggins. He looked back down on Sally's face and a feeling of emptiness swept through him. He could not believe how wrong this had all gone.

This son-of-a-bitch had set them up and led them right into the lion's den and now Sally lay dead in front of him, the SWAT Team more than likely suffering the same fate, and Scoggins in pieces scattered across the yard. He had to find Victoria, though he was terrified at what he might discover.

One of the detectives came up next to him.

"Oh Damn!," he said. "I'm sorry Detective. Shit!" He then saw Scoggins and took a step toward him, but stopped. He turned and vomited all over his shoes.

Jaxon stood, pain shooting down his legs now, and scanned the area. A small swatch of white caught his eye in all the destruction and he shambled toward it. Victoria had been wearing a white blouse that evening but had covered it with the blue FBI jacket. He hoped he was not seeing part of her in the wreckage.

Stepping over a piece of burning door, he saw an arm and hand sticking out from underneath it. He lifted the door and pushed it over out of the way exposing Victoria laying face down in the weeds. She was bleeding from her head and her FBI jacket was torn half off. He knelt and placed a shaking hand on her back. She was breathing.

"Hey! You! Detective! Help me. She's alive!"

His voice still sounded far away, but he could see the detective react to his voice and step quickly through the debris toward him.

"The ambulances should be here soon," he shouted. "We called them as soon as the blast went off."

"Help me carry her away from here," Jaxon said.

They picked her up carefully and lay her by the street. Her hair was matted with blood and she had small spots of it soaking through her clothing scattered all along her back, but Jaxon could see no other injuries. He was relieved. She had been the one closest to the front door, yet had survived while Sally and Scoggins had not.

She came to and rolled onto her back, moaning. Jaxon knelt down next to her and smiled at her when she looked at him. "Hey there," he said.

"Are we dead?" she asked, and though Jaxon's hearing was starting to come back, he still could not hear what she said, but could read her lips.

"I was worried there for a minute you were," he said.

"You were worried?"

He nodded.

"About me?"

"Scared shitless," he said and she finally smiled, but then winced in pain.

"What the hell happened?"

Jaxon looked up at the destruction and shook his head.

"He must have rigged it to blow. He must have some surveillance cams around here somewhere. He knew exactly when we were going in."

"Sally?"

Jaxon shook his head and looked away. "Scoggins too. I don't know about the SWAT team. I haven't seen anybody else come out of there but me and you."

"Aw shit, Jaxon." She looked angry, even with all the blood streaked on her face.

He saw flashing red lights and watched as the ambulance pulled up followed by a fire truck and two squad cars.

"You look like shit," she said.

"Thanks. So do you." But he smiled at her and reached for her hand. She clasped it in hers and held it tight to her chest.

"Stay here with me?" she asked.

"Sure."

CHAPTER 30

"He's moving," John said suddenly, startling the others out of their own thoughts.

It had been an hour since Luke first called Jaxon and he had tried every fifteen minutes since, but Jaxon had not called them back. Luke was starting to get worried and Ellie kept looking at him with her sad eyes, as if asking him to come up with something. He was just about to try Jaxon again when John spoke up.

Luke went to the computer and watched the blip slowly move across the map. He was heading past the tennis courts in the direction of the pool complex.

"Do you think he's on his way to do it?" Ellie asked.

"I have no idea," Luke said, but was worried she was right.

"We need to call somebody," Ellie said.

"Nobody will believe us," Jimmy said. "We're just a bunch of punks to them."

"It's their job," Ellie said. "They're supposed to believe us."

"Come on, El," Jimmy said. "If somebody called you with this crazy story, would you believe them?"

"Jaxon's the only one who knows what's going on," Luke said. "Jimmy's right. Nobody will take us seriously."

"We have to do something!" she said. "We can't just sit here and watch."

"I know," Luke said, frustrated, "but what can we do?"

"Call 911," Ellie said.

"What do I tell them?" Luke said.

"I don't know," she sounded frustrated. "Tell them we think somebody is going to be killed."

Luke shrugged and dialed 911.

"911. What is the nature of your emergency," the operator said.

"Uh…yes. I'd like to report a killing," Luke said.

"You want to report a murder?"

"Well…not yet. I mean it hasn't happened yet. But we think it's going to."

"What is your name and how old are you?"

"My name is Lucas Harrison and what does it matter how old I am?"

"How do you know there's going to be a murder, sir?"

"We don't know for sure. He told us he was going to kill someone tonight."

"Who told you?"

"The killer. He calls himself William Smith, but I don't think it's his real name. We're wasting time. He's moving now!"

"I'm not following you sir. Where is this so called William Smith moving to?" Luke could tell the operator wasn't believing anything he was telling her.

"We're not sure, but we can track him."

"Uh huh," she said. "How are you tracking him?"

"By his cell phone."

"Right. You know it's a felony to prank call 911 don't you?"

"This isn't a prank! He said he was going to kill someone tonight. One of our friends."

"Who?"

"He wouldn't tell us that."

"Tell her he's the swimming pool killer," Ellie said.

"He's the one who's been killing the kids and putting them in the pool at The Woods," Luke said.

Silence on the other end for a second.

"Detective Jennings told us to call if we had any information, but he won't answer his phone," Luke said.

"All right," the operator said. "Jaxon is out of town, but I'll have the officer in charge look at it. Where is this going to happen?"

"He's currently…" Luke looked at the monitor. "He's moving through the neighborhood of The Woods toward the pool area. Aren't you supposed to have some officers in this area?"

"How do you know that?"

"Jaxon and Winston promised my girlfriend's mother there would be."

"We'll send someone to check it out."

"Thank you," and Luke hung up. "They're going to send someone to check it out."

They all looked relieved. Ellie sat on the edge of the bed and sighed.

"They're not going to know where he is," John said, looking at the computer screen.

Luke walked over and looked. "Where is he?"

"It looks like he's in this house," John pointed, "but I can't tell."

They were all standing around the computer now.

"Should we call the police back?" Ellie asked.

"No," Jimmy said. "I think we should follow him and see where he goes."

"We're the only ones who can see what he's doing," Luke said.

"This is stupid," John said. "We should call them back."

"We don't have anything to tell them. We could follow him and see where he is and then you could call the police and let them know." Luke pointed at John. "You'll stay here, like before and stay in touch with us over the phones. Me and Jimmy will find out where he is."

"I'm going too," Ellie said. "I'm not sitting here, waiting for all of you."

"No," Luke said. "It's too dangerous. He talks to you the most. If he gets the chance, he might hurt you."

"I'm going and you can't stop me."

She was right. What was he going to do? Tie her up or knock her out? Luke could think of nothing that would change her mind so he just went along with her.

"All right," he said, "but you're with me."

"What if he does something?" John asked. "What are you guys gonna do?"

"I don't know," Luke said, slowly. "I guess we'll think of something."

They all looked at each other, and Luke could see the fear in their eyes. He wondered if they saw it in his.

"Let's move," Luke said and stood.

The three of them made their way down stairs and were opening the door when Luke's mother called to them from the kitchen.

"Who's going out this late?"

"It's me Mom."

She peaked around the corner and then stepped into the foyer. "Why? It's kind of late to be playing outside."

Luke glanced at Jimmy who was staring off into the distance shifting from one foot to the other.

"We're going over to Jimmy's for a minute to grab something," Luke said quickly. "John's still upstairs on my computer. He's gonna wait for us."

He must have sounded funny because she stepped toward him with that look only she could produce. The look that said, *You're trying to pull the wool over my eyes and I'm not buying it.*

"What's at Jimmy's?" she said.

"It's a…" Luke stammered.

"…game." Jimmy finished for him.

Luke looked at Jimmy and nodded. "Yeah—it's a game. We're bored and Jimmy's got this new game we were going to try." Luke smiled, trying to look sincere.

Ellie shifted closer to him. He could feel the tension in her body. It was like an electrical field around her and it made him feel jumpy. His mom glanced at Ellie and wrinkled her brow.

"Eliana, are you all right?" she asked.

Ellie's head snapped up and she nodded quickly. "Yes—uh—yes ma'am."

Luke's mom stepped to Ellie, reached her hand up and felt her face. "You look feverish," his mom said. "Are you sure you're feeling ok? These boys aren't getting you into any trouble are they?" and she glared at Luke.

"No, Mrs. Harrison—no. I'm fine, just a little hot."

Luke's mom let her hand fall to her side and she glanced at Ellie again, quickly, seeming to come to some conclusion in her mind that everything was ok. Her face relaxed a bit and she seemed to lose interest in the three. She turned back to the kitchen and said, "You three stick together. Don't make me come look for you." And she disappeared through the doorway.

Luke let out a big breath, not realizing he had been holding it. Ellie grabbed his hand and they went outside.

"That doesn't give us much time," Jimmy said. "Your mom will be looking for us soon."

"I don't think so," Luke said. "She's probably already forgotten about it."

"I hope so," Jimmy said.

John broke in on the earpiece, "What are you guys doing?"

"We're outside," Luke said. "What is he up to?"

"He's stopped at that house on the other side of the pool. I can't tell if he went into it or not. He's just sitting there."

"We're gonna take a look," Luke said. "Let us know if he moves."

"Got it."

The three made their way down through Luke's backyard and out the hole in the fence. They stayed to the left of the tennis courts and followed a path past the pool and then stopped, staying hidden from the street the front of the pool house faced.

"Jimmy," Luke whispered, "see if you can cross the street and hide in those bushes." Luke pointed to a house across the street from them with a large hedge that ran perpendicular to the street, separating its yard from the one next to it.

Jimmy nodded and ran at a crouch to the bushes Luke had indicated.

"John, can you still hear me?" Luke said.

"Yeah," John said. "He hasn't moved. Where are you guys?"

"We're right next to the pool along the side fence. Jimmy is across the street from me in the bushes."

"You guys are really close to him then. I wouldn't move any more. He's right across the street and up a little bit. Can you see the house that's right across from the pool house?"

"Yep," Luke said.

"I think he's hanging out at the house right next to that one."

Luke stood slowly and stretched his neck up looking for the killer.

"I don't see anything. The street and yard are deserted." He crouched back down. "Jimmy, can you see anything?"

"Nothing," Jimmy said. "It's quiet."

"All right," Luke said, "we'll wait a little bit and see what he does."

"What's that red light on top of that house?" Ellie asked.

Luke peered through the dark, straining his eyes and could just make out what looked like a camera mounted to the roof of the house directly across from the pool. "Looks like a security cam. I wonder if it's one of those dummy ones or it's real?"

"A dummy one?" she said.

"Yeah—they make fake ones with lights on them to keep people out of the yard. It doesn't really work, just lights up."

"I bet it's real," she said. "Mr. Lolly has problems with people messing with his lights at Christmas. I wonder if William Smith knows it's there?"

Luke shrugged. If they got him on tape, then that would be a good thing. Out of the corner of his eye Luke caught movement. Two kids were walking down the street toward them. Luke didn't recognize them. "Do you know who that is?" he whispered to Ellie.

Ellie raised up a bit and then knelt back down. "I think it's Jenny Hipps and Ames Bledsoe. They've been together for a while."

"I wonder what they're doing over here," Luke said. "Don't they live in Hollowbrook?"

"He does. I don't know where Jenny lives."

"Should we warn them?"

Jimmy could hear the conversation over the phone and he said, "No. We don't want to alert him we're here unless he does something. Let's see what happens."

"Where are the police?" Ellie asked frustrated.

Luke shrugged his shoulders.

The couple passed in front of them talking softly and holding hands. Luke could see Jenny's face now and recognized the slump of Ames' shoulders. They called him Quasimodo because he had such a bad hunchback. The other kids called them the grenade-face ugly couple.

Luke watched them pass by and continue on up the street where they eventually faded from view. William Smith had not moved.

"What's happening?" John said through the earphone.

"Nothing," Luke said. "The grenade-face ugly couple walked by and he didn't do anything." He could hear John chuckling. "They're gone now."

Ellie tugged at his shirt and pointed up the street.

A kid about their age was slowly making his way down the street on his bike. He was weaving back and forth across the width of the street making long arcing turns from one side of the street to the other. As he got closer he could hear the kid humming to himself.

"Hold up, John," Luke said. "Somebody else is coming."

The kid passed in front of them, oblivious to anything around him. Luke thought it strange that someone his age would be out on the street all by himself this late, especially with all that had been happening lately. The biker weaved his way past the pool house and then suddenly stopped. He turned toward the house John had been talking about, the one next to the Lolly's, and Ellie took a quick breath in, digging her fingers into his arm as she tensed.

"Oh no," she whispered.

Movement caught Luke's eye and he looked at Jimmy who was frantically waving his arms. Luke moved his hand up and down, trying to tell Jimmy to stay put. Jimmy reluctantly squatted back down but peered out around the hedge and watched.

The biker kid was just standing there straddling his bike. His head kept looking left and right, and his feet shifted uncertainly. He laid the bike down, moving slowly toward the house, bent over as if straining to see or hear something. He stopped again halfway through the yard and stood up straight.

"We have to do something," Ellie whispered. "He's going to kill him!"

Luke hesitated.

He wasn't sure what the kid was doing, though it was looking like he was being drawn toward the house by something or someone they could not see.

"John, has he moved?" Luke said turning away from the street trying to keep his voice from carrying.

"Still there," John said. Just then Ellie screamed, jumped up and ran toward the house.

"Crap!" Luke said. "Ellie! Stop!" The biker kid had disappeared and Luke watched, frozen, as Ellie ran full speed toward the house. She was screaming at the top of her lungs.

"You leave him alone!" She shouted frantically. "Don't you dare hurt him! You leave him alone!"

Luke found his legs and started running after her. He shouted into his earpiece. "John! Call 911, now! Send them here. Hurry!"

Jimmy was streaking across the yards of the houses on Luke's left, legs pumping, arms swinging, and Luke put on a burst of speed so they would get to Ellie at the same time.

Luke saw the biker kid burst out of the bushes up against the house and stumble toward his bike. His eyes were huge and terrified as his head swiveled toward Ellie who was sprinting toward him.

Suddenly, the killer erupted from the same bushes and sped toward the kid as he knelt to pick up his bike. Ellie was only a few feet away and Luke was surprised she didn't even slow down. She threw herself at the killer's running body, slamming into it and knocking him off balance. She bounced off of him and fell at his feet.

The killer looked stunned for a moment and then roared in anger as he bent over and picked her up with one hand. She kicked and screamed, swinging her fists at his arms, but they had little effect on the man. He was huge, like an Ultimate Cage Fighter. Nothing seemed to faze him.

Luke and Jimmy got to him at the same time and Luke didn't even think. He tackled the man as Jimmy did the same. Ellie fell from his grasp as they drove him onto his back. Luke pummeled the man's face and neck while Jimmy stood and started kicking him in the side.

The killer's face was so white it shone in the dark. Every time Luke's fist struck his face, it felt like his skin was stretching and he couldn't even make a scratch. It was then Luke realized he was wearing a rubber mask.

The killer grunted and grabbed Luke by the hair, flinging him to the side as if he weighed nothing. The pain was nothing like he had ever felt before. It was like having a thousand angry wasps sting you on your scalp all at the same time.

He hit the ground with a jarring thud and couldn't catch his breath.

He watched, lying on his side, air trying to move in and out of his lungs, but it felt like he was breathing through a straw. He could do nothing as the killer swung his feet around in an arc and cut Jimmy's legs out from under him. The killer stood and pulled an object from his pocket and Luke saw the glint of metal in the light of the streetlamp and knew it was a knife.

Ellie screamed. "No! You bastard! Leave them alone!"

She flung herself at him again and began pounding on his chest and arms, but he didn't even flinch. He bent over, grabbed Jimmy by the hair and pulled him up. He raised the knife toward Jimmy's face and that's when the gun fired.

The killer's head jerked up and he dropped Jimmy to the ground. He didn't even hesitate. William Smith turned, ran faster than Luke would have imagined, and disappeared around the pool house, heading for his car. Mr. Lolly ran up holding a pistol in his hand.

"You kids all right?"

Just then a siren could be heard.

CHAPTER 31

Victoria was in the back of the ambulance and Jaxon was feeling a little better after they had given him a muscle relaxant for his back spasms.

Apparently the blast had pulled some muscles in his back as he was thrown from the scene.

The place was crawling with local cops and federal agents, and the media circus had arrived, though they had not been allowed access to the site, or given any information.

The FBI was running the show and the Chicago office was currently in charge. Jaxon had been on the phone with Holt back in Washington and Victoria had even spoken to him briefly, but she was in no condition to take charge. An agent named Sal Wilmer was heading up the task force at the moment.

Holt had been somewhat cordial with Jaxon, even after being informed his girlfriend had sustained some injuries in the blast. He only touched briefly on her condition and then moved on with the business at hand. Jaxon couldn't help but think Holt was putting on a show for him and he could tell Victoria was somewhat hurt by her lover's lack of concern.

"Are you all right?" Jaxon asked her after the paramedic stepped out for some air.

She nodded but remained silent. Her hair was still matted with blood, but her face had been cleaned and a bandage plastered to her forehead, blood seeping into it, showing through the whiteness. She reached up and gingerly touched it, wincing. She squirmed.

"Any word on the SWAT team?" she finally asked.

"No survivors, if that's what you mean. Just you and me."

She looked somber at the news but held it together. Jaxon knew how she felt. She was in charge and would take the brunt of the accusations and questions when the investigation into the incident began. Jaxon felt responsible, not only for Sally's death, but for all the players in tonight's debacle. He had underestimated this guy and hadn't reacted quickly enough to the clues he had given them. He should have called it off as soon as he received the text message.

She read his mind. "Stop beating yourself up," she said. "We both missed it."

"She was my partner."

Victoria looked into his eyes and he saw something there he hadn't realized still existed. She reached out her hand, turned it palm up and wiggled her fingers. It was a gesture so familiar, yet so far gone from his mind all these years that it took him by surprise.

She used to do that to him when he'd had a particularly bad day and she used to do it to Michael when he needed a pick me up. He couldn't help it. He smiled, reached for her hand and clasped her fingers in his. She closed her eyes and put her head back.

One of the FBI agents stuck his head in the door.

"Detective Jennings? I think you should see this."

Jaxon stood, let her hand go and followed the young agent toward the wreckage. The fires had all been put out and the gas line that had shot flames into the night sky had been closed off making the area reasonably safe.

The house had pretty much disintegrated leaving the rooms and layout of the structure indistinguishable from the rest of the refuse and scraps strewn throughout the area. A large rectangular box was the only thing left standing mostly intact, and the agent was guiding Jaxon toward it.

As he got closer he could see there was a door into the box, which stood eight feet square and was built of some kind of thin aluminum sheeting. A few agents were coming in and out of the box carrying various items wrapped in plastic. Jaxon realized it was a freezer.

The inside of the freezer must be thawing because the items the men were carrying from the box dripped water. He stopped one of the agents and asked what was in the plastic.

"Parts," he said.

Jaxon must have had a funny look on his face because the man explained.

"This is a dog's head. That's another dog's head, and Sheila there has a cat's head."

"How many?" Jaxon asked.

"At least thirty animals."

"Anything else?"

The man nodded. "Are you Jaxon?"

"Yes." Jaxon felt like his voice was coming from somewhere else.

"There's something in there for you."

The agent turned and carried his package to a waiting evidence van and Jaxon approached the entrance of the freezer and stepped in.

On the right were five shelves stacked up from floor to ceiling. A man and a woman were going through the various 'packages' and they looked up when he stepped in. Neither one said a word.

On the back wall was a small table with a single plastic baggy laying on it. Jaxon moved through the cold air as if in slow motion. He couldn't feel his feet touching the surface of the freezer but he knew his legs were moving him forward because the table was growing larger. A hand came into his view and he realized it was his own. He didn't want that hand anywhere near the bag, but it seemed to be operating on its own.

He watched as if from some far off place as the fingers gripped the bag and picked it up, bringing it closer to his face. There was a piece of freezer tape across the plastic with black lettering spelling some words that Jaxon's brain could not decipher at first. Snapping himself out of his fog, he concentrated on the lettering.

As he read, his body seemed to throb from the force of the words. They were like a physical thing and he couldn't wrench his eyes away from the small package.

Jaxon. These are not Malcom Switzer's. They are mine. I return them to you now.

His hands still took on a life of their own as they worked the Ziploc on the baggy, though his mind screamed from some distant place for him to stop. His fingers spread the plastic open and inside were two perfectly preserved ears. A right and a left. Small ears, like those of a child. He heard a gasp behind him and turned to find Victoria with her hand over her mouth and her eyes boring into what he held in his hand.

She whispered, "Michael," and sank to the floor.

CHAPTER 32

Luke sat with Jimmy and Ellie on the curb sipping a Gatorade and watching as the police and rescue personnel moved about the area.

John and his mom were standing next to them. She looked to be in worse shape than any of the kids. A cop named Stansfield was in charge and he was currently on the phone talking to someone. The conversation looked strained and Luke could hear Stansfield cursing into the cell phone.

"I don't give a shit! You get Jaxon on the phone," Stansfield yelled. "I know he's in Indiana, but he has a cell phone, right? Just do it!" He closed the phone and stared at Luke and his group.

Mr. Lolly was talking to another officer but Luke couldn't make out anything being said. Stansfield walked over and paced in front of the group.

"So, let me get this straight," he said. "You kids tracked this William Smith guy here using his cell phone GPS position and then called us? That about right?"

Luke nodded.

"How do you know it's the killer?"

"It's a long story," Luke said.

"I have all night," Stansfield said, but the way he was pacing made Luke feel that was not the case.

Luke explained the best he could and twenty minutes later Stansfield knew all they knew. He had a few questions.

"Why didn't you tell anyone this?"

"He said he would kill us," Ellie said.

Stansfield nodded. "How did you get his cell phone number?"

Luke paused. "I'd rather not say."

"Well, I'd rather you did say. This is important."

"I don't want my friend in trouble. You can use the software he gave me, but I'm not telling who gave it to me."

Luke looked at Ellie and Jimmy and he could see they agreed with him.

Stansfield ran his hands through his hair exasperated and then his phone rang. He held up his finger to them and answered the phone.

Luke turned to Ellie and said, "I don't want Q in on this. If the killer finds out, he'll be after him."

"I know," she said. "I won't say anything. They can torture me and I won't talk."

He smiled at her and she grabbed his hand. "We saved that boy."

"We almost got killed," he said.

"But you rescued me from him."

"Only because I wasn't thinking."

"Are you guys gonna kiss and stuff," Jimmy said. "Because I'm gonna puke if you do."

Ellie leaned over and kissed Jimmy on the cheek. He stared at her for a second and then grinned from ear to ear.

"All right, you can love on him if you want," Jimmy said.

She leaned up against Luke and he stroked her soft hair, thinking how close he had been to losing her. He didn't like thinking about that.

Stansfield hung up and said, "All right, Officer Hinton's gonna drive all of you to your houses. I want you to stay in them. Do not leave for any reason unless you are accompanied by your parents or a police officer. Detective Jennings will be over to see you when he gets back tomorrow." He pointed at Luke. "I'm coming to your house and you're going to show me this software. If we can get him tonight, I'll feel much better about everything."

* * *

Luke was in his room with Stansfield and the computer program was up and running, but Smith's cell phone must have been off, because nothing was showing on the map. Luke was worried the killer may have figured things out.

"I need a copy of this program," Stansfield said. "I bet the FBI doesn't have anything this good. You sure you don't want to tell me who gave you this?"

Luke shook his head. "The best I can say is I'll talk to him and see if he wants to talk to you guys."

"And he has another program that lets you decode the cell number the perp was calling you from?"

"Yep."

"That would be worth a million bucks to us. You need to convince your buddy to cough it up. Might save some lives."

"I'll see what he says."

Stansfield nodded and turned to go.

"Remember, stay inside until we nab this guy. He's gotta' be pretty pissed at all of you right now. Squad car will be parked out front to watch the house. You'll be safe here."

Luke wasn't so sure about that, but he didn't say anything. Stansfield went downstairs and he could hear murmurs through the floor as the cop talked to his parents. Luke wondered how Ellie was doing.

* * *

The Citation 500 cruised at thirty three thousand feet and barely a ripple coursed through the aluminum skin as the jet made its way back to Virginia.

Jaxon sat, tense, as the smooth air cradled Victoria in her seat and she snored from the effects of the pain killers she had been given back in Indiana. He stared at her, unable to sleep himself, the events of the night too fresh in his mind.

Vick's hair was fanned out over her arm and the dark strands stood out starkly against her pale skin. He remembered a vision from his marriage with her sleeping just as she was, a wispy smile on her lips, hair spread out around her and her bare skin glowing in the soft candle light. It had been one of those rare evenings when Michael was out of the house at his grandparents' and they had an evening to themselves. He had too much to drink and she took advantage of him. Not that he had complained or anything. He had watched her sleep afterwards and felt his life could not get any better. He had been right. It had gotten worse. A lot worse.

He turned and looked out the small window into the night and thought of his dead son.

Malcom Switzer had professed his innocence to Jaxon over and over again. Pleaded with him as he pointed the gun at the killer's head, two of his buddies trying to keep Jaxon from shooting Switzer the night they took him down. It hadn't mattered to Jaxon. He didn't hear him. Wouldn't hear him. He pulled the trigger just the same and as his friends and workmates wrestled Jaxon to the ground, only one of the bullets found its mark. In Switzer's thigh. He had screamed like a woman and it had made Jaxon smile.

Now, he had to wrap his mind around the reality that Malcom Switzer had been right. Or at least it appeared he was right. The two frozen ears were on this very plane, along with the various animal parts, kept in the hold, under ice, awaiting the FBI's forensic lab to analyze them and determine who they belonged to. Jaxon didn't need the FBI to tell him that. He knew they belonged to Michael.

His anger and guilt had been aimed at the wrong man for so many years and apparently his aim was as bad as the night he shot Switzer. Switzer was a cold and brutal killer, Jaxon knew, but he wasn't Michael's cold and brutal killer.

This new man...no...man wasn't a word he could put next to him...this new beast was killing kids and stalking Jaxon's mind. He had to be stopped. There would be none of Jaxon's 'friends' around this time. No one to influence his aim. He would make sure of that. This asshole was going to die a slow and painful death in front of Jaxon's eyes and nobody would be able to help him.

"What are you thinking?" Victoria's voice startled him out of his thoughts.

He turned toward her. "Just imagining this guy dying slowly in front of me as I wrap my fingers around his neck and squeeze."

She searched his face and yet he couldn't read her reaction one way or the other. She sighed and finally said, "I'll hold him down."

CHAPTER 33

The funeral for Sally was three days later.

Jaxon, Victoria, Holt, and the chief were up front along with the entire force. Some of the FBI guys on the case were in attendance too. The news crews had shown up and there had been an uncomfortable compromise reached after a few of the cops made their feelings known concerning the appearance of the local reporters. The crews elected to keep their distance until the proceedings were over.

Victoria's face looked better, but she still had a small bandage just above her left eye. A sickly, yellow, brown color could be seen peeking out from underneath it. Jaxon's back was still sore but he was able to function. He had even been a pall bearer.

As the priest intoned his words over the audience, Sally's father sat stoically next to her mother who leaked tears the entire time. Though she was crying, she remained eerily silent.

Her father periodically looked up at Jaxon. The man seemed to be questioning him with his eyes or maybe it was just his imagination. Jaxon didn't blame the man. Hell, he was questioning himself ever since the explosion.

Jaxon's phone vibrated in his pocket and he chose to ignore it. The whole force was here and if they needed him, someone would tell him. Jaxon's eyes wandered the grounds. He couldn't seem to bring himself to look at Sally's casket. Every time his eyes passed over the flag draped aluminum box, he would jerk them away as if he were staring into the sun. He knew there was probably some psychological term or condition for what he was doing, but he didn't care about that now. He just wanted to be away from here. And soon.

A few groundskeepers were busy tending the flowers and hedges in the distance and he could hear the purr of a leaf blower bleeding through the priest's voice. A few coughs into fists and quiet sniffles made their way to his ears as he scanned the headstones and flowers.

Something caught his eye.

Just a brief flash of black in the distance. He wasn't even sure if he actually saw something, but his subconscious held his eyes on the spot. From behind a tree an arm clad in black appeared followed by the torso of a person. The face remained obscured behind the tree.

His cell phone began vibrating again and for some reason the urgency in the vibration seemed more pronounced than the last call. He was imagining this, he knew, but the urge to pull it out of his pocket was overwhelming. The black flash disappeared behind the tree again. The phone buzzed and buzzed in his pocket.

The priest was rambling on about life after death, and the leaf blower was growing louder, but the buzzing in his pocket stopped. At least for a moment. The phone began vibrating again and Jaxon's eyes were drawn to the tree. The black clad arm was in view again only it was raised to a head as if someone was holding a cell phone to their ear. Jaxon started, and then frantically reached into his pocket for his phone. Victoria turned to him and the chief cleared his throat as Jaxon struggled to gain access to the buzzing gadget trapped in his pants.

People were starting to look at him as he finally freed the phone and brought it to his face. The caller I.D. display sent a jolt through his body. He showed it to Victoria who took a quick breath. It was all zeroes.

He looked up finding the tree again and watched as the flash of black stepped back behind it. Jaxon pointed to the tree and then turned around and began gesturing to the uniformed men around him. Victoria turned to the chief and whispered something in his ear and Jaxon watched the man scowl.

Jaxon moved quickly to the edge of the crowd, Victoria and Holt on his heels, and murmurs began traveling through the crowd as Jaxon's actions disrupted the proceedings. The phone continued to vibrate in his hand while Jaxon kept an eye on the distant tree.

It was difficult to make anything out as the people attending the service kept getting between him and his view of the tree. He answered the phone on the move.

"Jaxon."

"Hello, Detective," the electronically altered voice drew out his title just like before, the mocking tone finding its way through the eerily irritating voice. Jaxon cringed but his anger boiled through.

"What the fuck do you want?" Jaxon tried gesturing toward the distant tree but Victoria wasn't quite getting it. He put his hand over the phone and whispered, "He's behind that tree over there. Get some men to it." She nodded and moved away.

"Now, now, Detective, no reason to be so angry. I'd thought you'd be a little more appreciative of me by now. I did give you a gift."

"You're going down."

"Probably—eventually. But not before we have our little fun. I'm not finished yet."

Jaxon could see cops fitted in their dress blues making their way out of the crowd. Many were already drawing their weapons. A murmur was building in the crowd as people began to realize something was happening.

"What do you want?" Jaxon asked.

"We've been through this Detective. I thought I made myself clear the last time we had this discussion."

"Enlighten me."

Victoria was directing the action and as she moved men into position, Jaxon saw the flash of black appear again from behind the tree. He pointed and she finally saw.

"I want to help. We're helping each other."

"Why don't I make it easy for you," Jaxon said. "I'm here waiting. Come help me."

The laugh that came through the speakers made Jaxon pull the phone away from his ear. The metallic quality of the voice vibrated nerves in his head he didn't know existed. Jaxon watched as the police officers approached the tree from both sides and then he could hear shouts as they ordered the man down on the ground. He put the phone to his ear and listened. More laughter echoed in his head and then the voice said, "Did you really think it would be that easy?"

Jaxon could see the officers holding up something black that moved in the breeze. It looked to be a coat, or jacket, on a hanger. One of the maintenance men was walking over to them, gesturing. The laughter grew louder in his ear and then it abruptly stopped.

"The girl is next," and the line went dead.

CHAPTER 34

Ellie lay on her bed, bored.

Three days cooped up in her house was getting to her. The swim team was on hold, the pool closed, Luke was trapped in his own house, and her mom was being a total bitch. She really didn't blame her, she just wished her mother could see things through her eyes.

All her mother wanted to do was lecture her about how irresponsible she'd been keeping all this to herself. She tried arguing with her that if she hadn't, her mother might be attending her own daughter's funeral, but it hadn't seemed to phase her. She rambled on and on until Ellie couldn't take it anymore and got up in the middle of one of the speeches and left the room. Her mother yelled at her, but Ellie turned her back and stomped up to her room. That had been yesterday. Her mother hadn't talked to her since.

She sat up and went to her desk. Maybe Luke was online and he would tell her he loved her again. Even if he was just typing it into a computer screen it was still pretty epic. She knew they were young and it didn't matter what other people said, her mother included, she felt what she felt, and no one could take that away from her. Up until last year she hadn't even known she could feel this way. When Luke held her or stroked her hair, the world and all its stupid crap would disappear and everything else didn't matter. She only prayed it would last.

Luke wasn't online so she checked her Facebook page and saw she had a message.

It used to be so cool, the messages exciting and fun, but lately the feeling that washed over her when she saw the notification, was panic. What if it was from him? Would there be some awful picture embedded in it? Would he tell her something else she didn't want to know? She hesitated, the cursor hovering over the link. She pressed it.

It was from him.

Her heart leapt into her throat and her hand recoiled as if shocked. She didn't want to open it, didn't want to see it, yet she couldn't help herself. She had to know what he wanted. Had to see the horrible picture. Had to know the new lie he needed to tell her. If the fear she felt equaled her sick curiosity, the computer would probably have found its way through her upstairs window, crashing into a million pieces on the ground outside, but her curiosity won and she opened the message.

I know your father.

She sat back, deflated.

To her, her father was dead. She had never met the man, never hugged him or felt his rough beard scrape her soft skin as he kissed her goodnight, never felt him pick her up to play or lay her down to sleep. He was a mystery to her.

She had only ever seen one picture of him and she had been very little, almost too little to even remember. The picture was old and worn, a Polaroid stuffed in her mother's drawer under some old coloring books, and the memory of it even more worn than the tattered shot.

If someone asked her to describe her father, all she could come up with was tall. Big and tall. He had towered over her mother in the photo.

So why did she feel like her world was crushing her under its weight? If she cared so little about the stranger known to her only as Leonard Worthington, the father she never knew, why did it matter if the killer knew him? Why was she letting this madman push her buttons?

Because if he knows my father, he knows me, and I don't want to know him.

She felt violated. Dirty. Everything about her was unclean.

She shivered and rubbed her hands unconsciously on her pants. If he even knew a little bit about the man who fathered her, then he knew intimate things about her that she couldn't stand thinking. What had her father said to him? What did he show him? Did he have pictures of her or some other mementos she couldn't even fathom? If Smith knew her father, then he knew her and this terrified her beyond all other things he had done so far.

The psycho knew her.

She suddenly felt very sick. She ran to the bathroom and gave up her lunch.

CHAPTER 35

Another web cam had been found mounted in a tree at the cemetery and when the FBI contacted the company administering the relay service for the camera, the IP address they gave led Jaxon to an internet café in downtown Washington D.C.

The security cameras in the café gave them very little information despite having the timing down to the second. The killer kept his face hidden the whole time though they got a good indication of his body type. He was big, but it had only confirmed what the kids had told them the night of the attack in The Woods neighborhood. The man knew how to avoid detection.

The remainder of Sally's funeral service had been a fiasco. Her parents had not appreciated the gravity of the situation and vocalized their disappointment at the outcome in as few words as possible. Most of them starting with the letter 'F.'

The news crews had a field day with the coverage and the department looked incompetent. The story had been broadcast on every station for two days. Jaxon watched himself deflate on TV as the black coat, hung on a branch by a gardener, fluttered in the wind, the officer holding it frowning into the camera.

Jaxon was frustrated.

The computer program he got from Luke Harrison gave them nothing. They had designated one officer the sole task of monitoring the cell phone's signal, but the damn thing hadn't even been turned on since the software had been copied to the IT department's computers.

The phone Smith had called from during the funeral was a new number and they had no way of decoding it. The dead ends were like alleyways with thirty foot walls and Dobermans trapping him inside. He felt like he was clawing his fingertips off trying to scale the massive barriers. He'd give Harrison one more try.

He called Victoria at home first.

"You actually know my number," she said, without saying hello. "It's a true miracle. Are you bringing Reverb over?"

He smiled to himself for the first time in three days. "Should I? He's mean and grouchy, but he might remember you."

"Thanks. I thought dogs always remembered their owners."

"He has a drinking problem. He can't even remember where to pee."

"Sounds like someone I know."

"Like owner, like mutt."

"Uh huh."

"How is the head?" he asked.

"Sore, but I don't have the bandage anymore. Looks worse than it feels. It's got that sick yellow tinge to it old bruises get after a few days. Looks like a bird crapped on my head."

"Well, I was going to ask you to come with me so your beauty and wonderful personality would offset my anger and bad manners, but maybe the bride of Frankenstein will make things worse."

She laughed and the sound was good in his ear. "I could throw some sheet or bag over my head."

"Worse."

"What's the plan, anyway?"

"I wanted to see if we could sweet talk the Harrison kid into giving up his hacker."

"Smith's cell phone hasn't been turned on?" she asked.

"No. Not even for a second. He's moved on to a new one and I doubt he'll go back. This is a smart asshole."

"When do you want to go?"

"Now."

"I'll be ready in fifteen minutes. Think you can find your way?"

"Sure."

"You've never been here."

Embarrassed he paused. "I know where it is."

"You have been here," she said, and he could hear the grin in her voice. "Why didn't you knock?"

"I just know where it is, ok?"

"Uh-huh. See you in a bit."

Jaxon put the phone in the cradle, slowly, and kicked himself for looking like a fool. She was not going to get to him this time. He swore to himself it wouldn't happen. He needed a partner is all and she was the only one on top of everything. Just a partner. Besides, she was seeing Holt now. Their relationship was over and probably irreparably damaged.

The death of a child had a tendency to do that.

It was a known fact, a lot of marriages failed after the loss of a child. It was just too much to handle. Blame worked its way into the fabric of the love and weakened the threads. Slowly, the material began to unravel and the ragged pieces would give little shelter and warmth.

In Jaxon's case, the blame had been huge. Still was.

He carried a massive amount of guilt around, the burden rendering him ineffectual at times. The alcohol helped, but never pushed it completely out of his mind. He had to live with it every day and he could see it in her eyes, even now, though they were getting along better than they had in years. He imagined her blame as a inferno of resentment and the smoke and embers on the surface reflected in her eyes.

Then why was she being so nice? Why was she flirting with him? Or was he imagining that too?

This kind of thinking drove him nuts, so he just shut it off. No time for the bullshit. He needed to find and kill this son-of-a-bitch and do it soon.

He made his way to Reston, where she and Holt held residence, and parked on the street in front of the condo. He knocked on the door and she opened it, smiling. She was beautiful and his mouth must have been hanging open because he forcibly shut it. She smiled even bigger.

"I dressed to impress. Even a teenage boy. They're the easiest."

"The way you talked, I expected to have to shelter you from the neighbors so they wouldn't run screaming in terror." He paused. "You look good."

"Thanks," she said as she pulled the door shut and locked it behind her. Her hair was down and shiny black, the makeup she had applied only let a hint of the bruise through and the bright red lipstick drew enough attention away from her injury that you had to be looking for it to even notice it. The blouse she wore was cream colored and low cut, her cleavage impressive enough to draw any idiot's eyes away from her face. The bruise would never be seen by most. The tight skirt and heels finished the ensemble, making her radiant in the late afternoon sun.

"I had a thought," she said.

"Just one?"

"One for now. Do you want to hear it or what?"

"Shoot." He opened the car door for her and she looked surprised. She slipped into the seat and waited.

"I think it would be good if we picked up the girl too and brought her with us to the Harrison kid's house. Those two are an item and maybe we can use that to our advantage. She looks so much more open to suggestion than the boy."

"How do you know this?" but he grinned. "You haven't even met them."

"I read Sally's report as well as yours. She always touches on the more personal aspects of a case where you just stick to the facts. She made reference to the fact they were a couple and the girl, more emotional, as would be expected. The personal stuff can make or break a case you know."

"Whatever. I like it. Call her mother while we drive. Play the big FBI agent so we can borrow her for a while."

"That's me, United States Government employee. Pension plan and all."

He gave her the number and she made it look easy.

Jaxon remembered Madison Pemberton and was glad it was Victoria dealing with her and not him. The woman could be a total bitch.

They picked Ellie up and made a little small talk on the short one minute drive to the Harrisons'. The girl seemed distracted. Jaxon could tell something had happened and he would press it with her when the boy and girl were together. Jaxon hated to think he would be interrogating these two, but there was a lot on the line, including their lives. Especially the girl's. Smith had said she was next.

As they knocked on the door, Jaxon looked around the court and it occurred to him there just may be hidden web cams somewhere around here. The kids did say it seemed like the killer knew every move they made and a lot of personal information about them. He'd have to check the area when they were done here. The web cam seemed to be the asshole's tool of choice.

The door was answered by the father who glared at Jaxon but then softened when he saw Victoria. This was going to work like a charm. They were led into the house to the same room he and Sally had been in when they came to give the horrible, but inaccurate, news of their son's death. The room felt chilly.

The Harrison kid was sitting on the couch waiting for them and when he saw the girl, his eyes lit up and he jumped up and stepped quickly to her, taking her in his arms.

This was going to be easier than he thought. Even though he felt confident about getting the information they needed, he couldn't help but feel a little twinge of happiness at the cuteness of the young couple. Apparently, three days apart was just too much.

Victoria turned to him and smiled, giving him a look he was having a hard time reading. Her eyes were shining and he thought she might actually cry, but it didn't happen. She may not be as useful as he originally thought.

The father left them alone and Jaxon cleared his throat. The kids reluctantly separated but sat next to each other holding hands. They looked happy, but terrified.

"How are you guys holding up?" Jaxon said, taking a seat in a wing back chair whose back rest was so vertical he felt he was almost leaning forward as he sat.

One 'ok' from the girl and one 'crappy' from the boy.

"We're tired of being cooped up," Luke said. "How long before you get this guy?"

"That's what we're here for, of course," Jaxon said. "This is Special Agent Jenn—uh—Elliot, from the FBI. She's helping in the case now."

Victoria took the cue and ran with it.

"Hi. I know you guys are going nuts trapped in your houses, unable to see each other. Maybe we can find a way to give you a little time together every day until we catch the guy. Would that be good?"

Their faces both lit up and they looked at each other and smiled, Ellie bouncing up and down on the couch a little.

"That would be epic!" Ellie said.

Jaxon watch Victoria smile and he appreciated the way she became the pair's best friend right off the bat. He relaxed. Victoria was great at this kind of stuff and he had forgotten how caring she could be. He knew she did what she did not only out of a desire to get them on her side, but because she could tell these kids needed to be together. They were falling apart without each other's support. It was the least she could do.

"Ok," she said, "but you have to do it by our rules, all right?"

They nodded vigorously.

"We'll figure it out after we talk, ok?"

More nodding.

Jaxon looked at Ellie and said, "Miss Pemberton, is everything ok? Has something else happened?"

Her lip trembled immediately and she started to cry. So much for getting them on their side, he thought.

"It's all right, sweetheart," Victoria said. "Just tell us what happened."

Ellie looked at Luke and then said softly, "He sent me a message on Facebook."

"El, why didn't you tell me?" Luke said. "When did this happen?"

"Just a little while ago."

"What did he say?"

"He said, 'I know your father.'"

"Oh, El. How could that be? He's making stuff up now, to get to you."

"Why would he be bringing your father into this, Eliana?" Victoria asked.

"He sent me another message the other day saying 'Your real name is not Eliana Pemberton.' Now, I know how he knows that."

"Is that true?" Victoria asked.

Ellie nodded.

"What is your real name?"

"Eliana Worthington."

And she told them the story of her divorced parents and her mother's desire to separate the children and herself from their father's legacy. Victoria shared a look with Jaxon.

"What is your father's name?" Jaxon asked.

"Leonard Worthington."

"Do you know anything about him? Where he lives? What he does for a living? What he looks like?"

She was shaking her head no.

"I never knew him. He left when I was very little and my mother kept only one picture of him I found by mistake. She hates him."

"Do you think she knows where he is?"

"I don't know," Ellie said. "You'd have to ask her."

"Anything else bothering you?" Victoria asked.

Ellie sat quiet for a moment holding her boyfriends hand tightly in hers. Finally she said, "Why?"

Victoria looked at Jaxon again and then turned back to face the kids.

"Why did he pick you?"

Ellie nodded.

"We don't know," Victoria said. "If we did, we might have a lead that would help us get him. Can you think of any reason someone would want to do this to you? Someone you angered or someone who doesn't like you?"

"Everybody likes Ellie," Luke said. "Except her stupid brother, but he's an asshole. Sorry."

"Aren't all brothers jerks?" Victoria asked and Ellie smiled again.

"Yeah."

"At least when they're young. They grow up and are a lot better. For the most part," Victoria said. "What we really came to talk to you two about is the computer program your friend used to decode the cell phone number Smith was using."

"You guys can't track him with the software I gave you?" Luke asked.

"He hasn't turned that cell phone on again," Jaxon said. "We think he's ditched it. He called me two days ago from an untraceable cell number and it wasn't the one you gave us. We've been monitoring it 24/7/365 and he hasn't used it."

"I don't have the program my friend used to decode it. He didn't give me that one."

"Can we talk to your friend? It's very important," Jaxon said.

Luke looked down at the floor, uncomfortably. Then he looked at Ellie. She stared at him with a look that said, 'Tell them.'

"I don't want to give you his name without him saying it's ok," Luke said. "I promised."

"Do you understand what's at stake here, Lucas?" Victoria asked very seriously. "Ellie's life is at stake. Do you think your friend's feelings are more important than Ellie's life?"

Jaxon watched the kid crumble. Victoria had been brutally honest with him. She stayed silent now, letting him work it out.

"His name is Q," Luke said. "Quentin. I need to call him first if we're going to see him. His family may not like a bunch of cops just showing up."

"Do you want to use my phone?" Jaxon said.

He shook his head. "No. I'll do it from mine. He knows my number."

"Can you try now? The clock is ticking," Jaxon said, "and we need to find this guy. Before it's too late."

Luke nodded and left the room. He returned a moment later with a cell phone against his ear. Jaxon could hear it ringing. After twenty rings or so, Luke hung up.

"He always answers his phone. Maybe he knows what's going on. It's been in the news. He could be hiding," Luke said.

"Can we go to his house?" Victoria asked.

"His family won't like it," Luke said uneasily. "They have big dogs and I know his dad has guns. I don't think they're legit."

"Legit?" Jaxon asked.

"Luke means his parents have both been to jail," Ellie said. "They sell drugs."

"We just want to talk. We don't want to arrest them," Victoria said. "Can you take us there?"

Luke looked at Ellie and she nodded slightly. "All right," he said. "It's not far."

* * *

They arrived at Q's house and Jaxon was not impressed.

The house was a shack. The last shack they had been to exploded on them and Jaxon looked apprehensively over this beat up 1950s era block home. A chain link fence encircled the whole front yard and abandoned motorcycles, toys, washers, chests, and coolers littered it making it look deserted.

Luke said, "Where are his dogs?"

"How many are there?" Jaxon asked.

"Three. Mean ones. I'm surprised they're not here, snarling and frothing at the mouth."

Jaxon looked at Victoria. She shrugged.

"You kids stay here. If anything happens, get on your cell phones and call 911. Don't go near the house."

"What's wrong?" Ellie asked.

"Probably nothing," Victoria said. "Just let us check it out."

The two kids nodded their heads and stood close to each other.

"Wait in the car," Jaxon said. "And lock the doors."

Jaxon walked to the gate and then stopped. He looked up at the trees and light poles, trying to see if any cameras or something unusual stood out against the trashy and run down neighborhood. He could see nothing that looked out of place. Victoria joined him in the search.

"Do you think he has it rigged?" she said.

"I don't think he's had time. I don't know how he would even know about this kid."

"He's been one step ahead of us this whole time."

He nodded. "We take it slow."

"Do you want to call back up?"

"No. Do you?"

She grinned and shook her head.

He turned toward the house and whistled. "Here boy! Kujo! Fifi! Here girl!"

She said, "That's great. Will you just open the gate?"

"Just making sure," he said. "That book was creepy."

He reached over and lifted the latch. The gate swung open slowly on rusty hinges. No dogs attacked. They approached the front door and knocked. Nothing. He motioned to the side of the house and she nodded. Weaving through the trash, they stepped over a rather large dirty bathtub and came up on the rear yard. A window was to his left. He looked inside, but the grime coating the glass made it impenetrable. Nothing inside made a sound.

The backyard was worse than the front and an ancient above ground pool sagged onto the back porch, the remaining water black with algae and whatever else had accumulated over the years. As he scanned the backyard, brown fur caught his eye. Victoria saw it too. She motioned to the right and they worked their way around the pool.

Three dogs lay next to each other just outside their doghouse. Jaxon could not tell the breeds. Their heads were missing. He drew his weapon and Victoria did the same.

He noticed the back sliding glass door was broken. He motioned toward it and they worked their way through the yard to the back door.

Dirty, gray, sheer curtains blew in and out of the broken glass, but nothing inside made a sound. Jaxon pushed the curtains out of the way and entered the house. The smell assaulted him instantly.

Victoria followed and said under her breath, "Ah, Jesus."

Jaxon didn't expect to find anyone dangerous still in the house but he kept his weapon out just the same. They stepped into the kitchen and found dirty dishes and trash littered throughout the room.

As they pushed the door open into the living room the smell grew stronger and as Jaxon's eyes adjusted to the gloom, he found the origin.

Two men and a woman were seated on a couch, bullet holes in their heads, flies buzzing around them. They looked to have been dead at least three days. Jaxon imagined the terror they must have felt as their killer lined them up and shot them one by one.

Victoria had moved to a hallway and he followed her down the short dark space.

A door to the right yielded to a room full of junk. It was stacked to the ceiling in places with crap Jaxon remembered fondly growing up. Toy G.I. Joes, Atari game consoles, tricycles, big wheels, hundreds of board games, clothing. Jaxon could not believe these people had amassed so much useless crap over their pathetic lifetimes. And why had they kept it all?

The next room was locked.

Jaxon felt along the top of the sill and found a key. He slipped it into the lock and it turned. They opened the door into another world.

A hacker's dream realm laid out before them, computers and monitors and Ipads and PS3s and Xbox360s. Everything a computer geek could want.

This computer geek was sitting in his chair in front of the three huge computer monitors arrayed across the littered desk. A video of a cat was playing on the screens, but the boy was not watching it. His head was missing.

CHAPTER 36

The killer's rage was now a living thing.

It boiled inside of him, the heat building to such a degree that he felt his intestines would burst from his soft belly, a boiling mass of shit and blood exploding from within him. He paced back and forth across the small motel room in Herndon, the pain inside him unable to let him rest. He had emptied his stomach contents completely over the last hour and though he had little left, he felt full of acid and bile. He needed a release.

They were keeping the girl close to their chests, holding and coddling her like a baby. She hadn't left her house except to visit the boy, who he now knew to be behind the discovery of his cell phone number.

The boy and the hacker.

The hacker and the boy.

The hacker was not a problem any longer, but he still needed to be careful. He had to dispose of the boy. Lucas Neal Harrison had hung on long enough, and since he no longer needed him to entertain the girl and keep her distracted, the time had come, and his boiling rage would cool to a simmer once the boy was eliminated.

But first, he needed to send her a gift. She would be so happy to get it.

He could see her face smiling as she held it and he would be in her life. He would know her even more. He moved the hacker's head to the side of the freezer and grabbed the gift. It would only take a moment to wrap. The busy work cooled his insides and his roiling stomach calmed and grew silent. He sighed and thought only of her.

CHAPTER 37

Jaxon stood outside the hacker's home which he now knew belonged to one Bartholomew Jenson.

The headless teen was more than likely Quentin Jenson, but since the head was not in the house, they would have to wait for fingerprint ID or DNA. The mother, Jeanette, had been the woman on the couch and the other male, Quentin's older brother, John. All of them had rap sheets, including the hacker. Jaxon was confident it would only be a matter of minutes before they confirmed the headless kid's identity.

Victoria was working with the Crime Scene Lab, trying to extract anything they could from the boy's computer, but they had to collect any evidence from the room and the body before they could move the boy out and concentrate on the computers in the room.

Initially, Victoria hadn't been able to manipulate the main system to display anything other than the cat video where the feline tickled the ivories of a pink piano while a large mutt licked his balls in the background. Funny, but pretty much useless and annoying at this point. At least they could turn the sound off.

Jaxon had called the Harrison father and given him instructions so he could come and retrieve the two kids. They were a wreck and even the boy leaked a few tears when Victoria told him his friend and his friend's family were dead. She didn't provide specifics.

The girl buried her face in Luke's shoulder and sobbed until the father came and took them home. Jaxon gave explicit instructions to the man not to stop for anything. Take the kids straight to the house and do not leave until instructed. The girl was to remain at the Harrisons' until Jaxon came by to get her. The police officers stationed in the neighborhood would double their presence in front of both their houses.

The father didn't look impressed. "I have a gun," he had said.

Normally, Jaxon would scold the man or tell him to let the police do their job, but this time he didn't.

"Do you know how to use it?" Jaxon asked.

Surprised, the father nodded his head. "I go to the range once a month."

"A range is different than pointing it at a man. If you point it at a man, are you prepared to see it through?"

Mr. Harrison hesitated, but then nodded.

"Keep it close," Jaxon said and looked the man hard in the eye. Mr. Harrison frowned but nodded once and got in his car. Jaxon watched him drive away.

If anything happens to those two… but he didn't let himself finish the thought.

Jaxon's phone rang. It was him.

"You're a busy Son-of-a-bitch, aren't you?" Jaxon said.

"Hello, Detective. We're getting to know each other now, aren't we?" Same numbers—all zeroes—same altered voice.

"Oh, I know you well, asshole. You're becoming predictable."

"So you say, Detective. How is my girl? I see you've been spending a little time with her today. Did she enjoy her outing?"

Jaxon looked around again, trying to find a camera, but nothing was in plain sight. He had to have something around the area.

"Why her? I thought this was between you and me. You take my son and I find you and screw you up beyond belief."

"Your son was nothing to me…"

"Don't you do that!" Jaxon shouted, people turning and staring at him. "Don't you knock him down to some discarded toy you got tired of. He was everything!"

"No. She is everything. And she will be mine. I've changed the plan. See if you can guess what it is, Detective."

"I'm coming for you!"

Suddenly the voice changed. The man must have turned off the filter device. What came across was a deep, gravelly, rumble of rage and anger that shook Jaxon to the core.

"That's what I told Michael. But you never came!"

* * *

Ellie held on to Luke tightly.

She was done crying and Luke had shed a few tears of his own with her although he had tried not to. It had just been too much. The roller coaster they were riding was taking its toll on them both.

"I don't want to go to my house," she said. "I want to stay with you."

"Maybe you can."

She looked up at him. "Are you serious?"

"I think it would be cool. My parents won't, but this is a messed up situation. If you're over here, Smith won't know that and you'll be safer. I bet Jaxon and Victoria would think it was a good idea."

"My mom will never go for it. She'll think it is an excuse for us just to be together."

"A bonus," he said and grinned.

She smiled for the first time all afternoon and it warmed him. "It can't hurt to ask, right?" she said.

"Right. Let me talk to my parents first and if they agree, it will be easier to have them convince your mom."

She nodded and then kissed him.

"Go ask," she whispered.

Luke and Ellie approached his parents and at first his dad was against it but his mom saw the wisdom of it. She had some rules, though.

"Ellie will sleep in your brother's room and your brother will sleep with you," Luke's mom said.

Luke didn't like it, but he knew it would be the only way they would allow her to stay.

"I don't want to put anybody out, Mrs. Harrison," Ellie said. "I could sleep on a couch or even the floor."

"Nonsense, it will be no trouble. There's a spare bed in the room anyway and Christopher's car bed is easy to move. This is not a party, you two. If your mom agrees, then you're welcome for as long as she will let you stay. But if she wants you to come home, we'll take you right away. She'll probably be worried. And no funny business."

"We promise, Mom," Luke said and smiled at Ellie who nodded vigorously.

Luke's mom grinned back at them and gave Ellie a hug. "You'll be safe here, sweetheart."

Luke's dad made the call and after a little convincing, Ellie's mom agreed to let her stay. She would gather some things for her and bring them over a little later. Luke's dad pointed to him and said, "You, come with me for a minute. We need to talk."

The conversation that followed was not what Luke expected. His dad was very worried about Ellie and he told Luke that if something happened, the gun would be in his sock drawer.

"Dad, I don't…"

"Luke, I love you son. You may have to grow up a little quicker than you want. I know this is scary for you, hell, it's scary for me, but you'll do what you have to do, when you have to do it."

"I've only fired it a couple of times with you at the range. Will you show me how to load it again?"

"Tonight, when your mother has gone to bed."

Luke looked at his dad. He couldn't remember a time when he seemed so tired.

"Dad, we're gonna be ok, right?"

His dad smiled weakly. "Yeah, we're gonna be ok. The police are keeping an eye on things and I'll watch over us too."

"Ok." Luke felt exhausted. He hoped the police would do what they said they could do. It just seemed like he and the other kids were doing better when it was only them dealing with the killer.

"Now, I don't want you disrespecting that girl while she's here. You get my meaning?" His dad grinned and Luke nodded, his face feeling hot all of a sudden. His dad did something that surprised him, then. He hugged him and said, "I'm proud of you son. I know you'll keep her safe. Go on. Go be with her and make her feel better."

The doorbell rang and his dad got up to answer it. It was Jaxon and Victoria to pick up Ellie. Luke heard his dad explaining the plan to them and they seemed to believe it was a good idea. Jaxon looked in and saw Luke watching and he turned back to his dad and said something Luke couldn't hear. His dad closed the door and talked with them outside for a few minutes and then came back in looking pale.

"What is it, Dad?" Luke asked.

"Nothing."

But Luke could tell he was lying. It was something all right, and it looked like something big. His mother could see it too and she joined him in the kitchen where they murmured in low voices Luke and Ellie couldn't hear.

Luke sat with Ellie who leaned in to him and he closed his arms around her and stroked her soft, blonde hair.

"Thanks," she said. "I couldn't stand being alone in my house."

"Your mom and your brother were there."

"But I felt alone. My mom just wanted to yell at me."

"I'm glad you're here," he said.

She kissed him softly on the lips, and then stared into his eyes.

"You know, my dad told me I wasn't to 'disrespect you' while you're here."

She giggled. "Are you going to?"

"Depends on what you consider disrespectful, I guess," and he smiled.

"Nothing you could do would make me love you less," she said, a little smile on her lips, but her eyes were serious.

"I know," he said in a whisper.

He searched her face and was overcome by a desire to grab her and hold her as tight as he could. Never let her go. The feeling was so strong and so intense, it almost brought tears to his eyes. She must have seen it, because she grabbed him and pulled him close, holding on to him as if she would never see him again. They clung to each other like that for quite a while.

CHAPTER 38

On the ride back into the station, Jaxon remained quiet.

Victoria had heard about the phone call, but when she asked him about it, he said the killer was just taunting him. He could tell she knew something else had happened, but she didn't press him.

The fingerprints they had scanned into her cell phone of the boy had confirmed what they already knew. Quentin Jenson would never hack another computer. Ever. The boy's head had yet to be found. The dogs' too.

When they were able to move the body and actually work on his computer systems, the FBI boys could do little with what they found. The Jenson kid had rigged the system to lock down if it was tampered with. Smart kid. Too damn smart.

They had loaded everything up and taken it to Quantico to see if they were able to get anything useful out of it. It would take weeks and Jaxon did not have weeks.

Stopping by the Harrison house to pick up the Pemberton girl, they discovered the folks were thinking for themselves and Jaxon liked what he heard. If they could keep the killer guessing as to the whereabouts of the girl, it would buy them a little more time to track him down.

The new message Jaxon got from the killer on the phone bothered him though, and he didn't understand what was going on in the asshole's head. The plan had changed. He was supposed to guess what that new plan was. Prick.

If he could think like a killer, then Smith would already be dead. Jaxon's mind was not quite up to the task of sedating kids and then mutilating corpses, but he thought the killer might be gunning for the Harrison boy. It was just a gut feeling, and at this point, it was all he had.

"Are you going to let me in on the phone conversation?" Victoria said after they had been in the car for a while.

He told her.

"Is that all he said?"

He hesitated.

"Come on, Jaxon. What are you not telling me? I thought we were working on this together."

He sighed and then coughed in his hand. "I got a little unprofessional with him."

"And…"

"I told him I was coming for him."

"So—I would probably have said the same thing."

He paused again. "He told me Michael was nothing to him and I lost it. I started screaming at him and that's when I told him I was coming for him."

"Ah, Jaxon. I'm sorry."

"That's not all."

She waited, staring at him.

"He turned off his voice altering device and let me hear his real voice. He said he told Michael I was coming to rescue him and I never showed up."

She turned away and stared out the front windshield, silent. After a moment, he saw a single tear trace a line down her cheek.

"I don't blame you, you know," she said quietly.

"What?"

"I don't blame you for what happened to Michael. I know you think I do, but I don't."

The air became like a dead thing in the car. Jaxon was having a hard time sucking it into his lungs.

"What are you talking about?" he said. "You left me. You said you hated me and you left."

"I don't think you remember things as clearly as you would like. I was out of my head with grief. I said things to lash out at anything and anyone around me. You did the same, but you decided to take all the blame and turn it into something you could hold onto.

Something that numbed the pain, something that pushed me away. You drove me away."

"You told me I killed Michael. You said that to my face."

"I said *we* killed Michael." Her voice broke. "We killed our son and I hated you for it. I hated you because I hated myself! We couldn't stop it! We let him die and I hated myself."

He pulled to the side of the road, angry drivers honking at them. He ignored them.

"You wouldn't look at me," he said. "For days you wouldn't even glance at me. Then when you did, I wished you would go back to ignoring me. I could see it in your eyes. Your baby—our baby was gone, and it was my fault. And the truth of the matter was, I knew you were right. I had let that monster have our son, let him take him away from me. I thought I was protecting him by going after the wrong madman, but in the end it was my mistake, my anger, my pride that killed Michael. And I hated myself." He slammed his fist into the dash. "I still hate myself!"

Silence followed for a moment as he tried to get control of himself. He looked at her and saw silent tears streaming down her face.

"I would have done the same thing," she said. "I would have gone after the bastard like you did. I've thought about that night every day. Thought about what we could have done differently, what I didn't do, what we missed. I've tortured myself and cried until I thought I would disappear. I wanted to disappear. I wanted to join him. It didn't make a difference. It didn't change a thing. I'm still here and Michael is gone and no matter what, I can't bring him back. Michael's gone and so were you. I needed you, and you abandoned me."

She turned toward him and looked into his eyes.

"I know how much you hurt," she said. "I know because I hurt just as much. I feel everything you feel. You didn't believe that, but it's true. I didn't know how to help you then, because I couldn't help myself. But I need you. I need you to be there for me. I can't take another day of this. I can't live through this nightmare we're still in without you beside me. I forgive you."

He couldn't look at her. His mind was whirling and everything seemed out of focus.

"Look at me," she said and reached up and touched his face. He turned to her and saw in her eyes everything that had meant something to him in the past. Everything that had been missing since the day his son was taken from them. He could see Michael in her eyes and something snapped inside of him. He could hear it break. A sharp, quick, SNAP! and then a release. Something eased inside and he could breath. At least a little.

"I need you," she whispered. "I love you."

He watched his hand move up to her face and touch her skin. The face he had loved so long ago, the face he could still trace in his mind if he closed his eyes. It was like touching an angel. A thing so beautiful and so forgiving, he gasped at the feel of her. Deep inside, buried beneath all the self hatred and loathing, he had longed to feel her, longed to see this look in her eyes, longed to love her.

He pulled her to him and kissed her softly and she melted into him, the feel of her so familiar and so new at the same time. The kiss grew deeper and his hands moved over her, finding all the favorite places he remembered about her. Feverishly, he needed to touch every part of her, because he knew this wouldn't last. Knew she would be gone and knew he would go back to feeling lost and ruined again.

She clung to him hungrily and her hands clasped the back of his neck, fingers running through his hair like she always did and it drove him crazy.

Honking horns broke the trance and they looked at each other and laughed.

Something passed between them and no more words needed to be said.

He pulled into traffic and drove to his place where their clothes fell into a pile and she didn't even have a chance to say hello to Reverb.

Afterward, as he held her, the afternoon sun warming their skin, she said to him, "We're not going to let this happen to these kids. We're not."

He touched her face and she turned up to him. "No. We're not."

CHAPTER 39

Luke and Ellie had an epic day.

The best they'd had in weeks. Jimmy and John had come over and they had all abused the air hockey table in the basement, then watched a movie while his mother made them supper. Chili dogs and tater tots. Even his sisters and brother joined in the party. Ellie laughed more than he had seen her laugh in a long time. It was good.

He could tell there was a tension lying just beneath the surface of everything, but if he didn't think about it, he found he could ignore it. His dad stayed busy doing dad things, but even he joined in on a game of air hockey for a few minutes. He and Ellie beat him and his mom.

After Jimmy and John left, Ellie's mom came by with her things. She stayed for a few minutes and talked to Luke's parents, though Luke couldn't hear what was said. Her mom looked distraught, but thanked them for taking care of Ellie. When she left, Ellie hugged her tight and held on to her. Her mother asked her if she wanted to come home and she said no. She needed to stay here for a little while. Luke would protect her. Her mother didn't look so confident of that fact.

After she left, Ellie leaned her head against Luke's and said, "I don't think she wanted me to stay."

"She's your mom. She's just worried about you."

Ellie nodded against his forehead. "I miss her already."

He took her face in his hands. "You can go home any time you want. You know that right?"

"Yeah. I'm just being a baby."

"I want you to stay, too, but I know what it's like being homesick. I don't like being away."

"But you like me here, right?"

"Duh?"

She punched him in the arm.

"I remember when we were in third grade," Luke said, "and you spent the night at Sheila Everby's house."

She laughed. "You remember that?"

"Of course. You two snuck out and threw rocks at my window until I woke up."

"And then we giggled like the stupid girls we were and ran away."

"I knew it was you and called you back. You guys were in your underwear."

"We were not!" she said, shocked. "That was pajamas."

"Looked like underwear to me. I saw your pink panties."

She turned red.

"Anyway, you guys stayed under my window for a long time and Sheila kept saying she wanted to go home but you didn't."

She was smiling.

"You came down and she got mad and left," Ellie said.

"Then we got caught and put on restriction for two weeks. Your mother was so mad at you."

She laughed.

"So was Sheila's mom."

"I missed you those two weeks," he said.

"You did? I thought girls were 'ucky' back then."

"They still are," and he pulled away from her making a face.

She pulled him back to her and kissed him.

"Are you sure we're 'ucky'?"

"Totally."

They stayed close and quiet for a minute and then he said, "I wanted you to stay with me back then. I even asked my mom."

"I bet that went over well."

"She actually considered it for a minute and I thought she was going to let me ask you and then she said no, it wouldn't be appropriate."

"Well, I'm here now."

"Yeah, but you're even 'uckier' than before."

"But I'm better at air hockey."

"Ok—I'll give you that."

He reached up and brushed the hair behind her ear and let his hand linger at her neck. She leaned into it and closed her eyes.

"Why does that feel so good?"

"Because I'm not 'ucky'?" he said.

She smiled, but kept her eyes closed. "Guess again."

"Uh—because I'm good at air hockey?"

"Just say it," she whispered and opened her eyes, looking deep into his.

His whole being felt open to her as if she could see everything within him, feel everything he could feel, share everything he could share, everything that mattered. She was all around him, in him, part of him and the world faded away, her blue eyes the only thing he could see, the only thing he could feel, the only thing that was real. He couldn't look away.

He finally whispered, "Because I love you."

"Yes."

CHAPTER 40

Jaxon walked in to the station with Victoria following behind him.

The mood was still somber as the loss of one of their own was still fresh, like an open wound, but the appearance of an old friend, even one who had defected to the Feds, was an occasion to be happy. She reveled in their camaraderie and many of the old timers had stories to relive and jokes to tell. Stansfield came over and gave her a hug. Her old partner looked awkward around her, but Jaxon could tell he was glad to see her.

It felt surreal to be in this room, with these people, and her here with him. They stole glances at each other and for a moment, Jaxon felt the world tilt. Almost as if time had doubled back on itself, the old and the new merging. It lasted only a second, and then the real world came back, just as it always did. Victoria's cell rang, and it was Holt.

She took the call in a quiet corner and Jaxon kept looking her way. He didn't know what he expected, but whatever he was feeling, it left a bitter taste in his mouth. She laughed loudly at something Holt said, and Jaxon actually felt a pang of jealousy. Looking inward, which was something he hadn't done in years, it had been too painful, he chuckled to himself and realized he would have to fight for this woman if he wanted to have her back. Holt was now the enemy, in a sense, and that felt weird. She ended the call and came over to his desk. He must have had a funny look on his face.

"Ok?" she asked.

"Yeah—you?"

She nodded. "He was checking in. I hadn't called him since this morning. He was updating me on the hacker's computers we sent to Quantico."

"Anything?"

She shook her head. "The geeks are working on it, but the kid was good. They don't want to lose any of the data and are taking it slow."

He nodded, not expecting anything new from them.

"Something's bothering you?" she asked, sitting on the corner of his desk, the bruise on her forehead a little more prominent. The makeup she applied at his place had been rushed and she hadn't been able to fix herself up as well as before. He grinned knowing he had something to do with that. She saw him staring at her head and said, "What?"

"Nothing." He turned away. "I have this tingling going on in the back of my mind and I'm trying to figure it out."

"Spidey-senses kicking in?"

"Yeah. Right."

"Let's talk it through and see if it brings something to the surface."

"An FBI tactic?"

"Yes. It works. Just try it, all right?"

He sat back in his chair and spread his arms wide.

"Go for it."

She grabbed the chair from the desk next to them and pulled it up close to him.

"What did we learn today?"

"That I still got it?" He grinned.

"Will you stop it!" she whispered. "Seriously—come on."

"All right, all right." He sighed. "We now have four more dead bodies."

"Right. The Hacker and his family. Quentin Jenson. What did we see there?"

"Lots of flies."

"Are you going to even try?"

"Well, there were. Let's see—more animal decapitations with the heads missing and the boy's head which is also missing."

"But the adults he left intact."

"He did, didn't he? I wonder why?"

"He made it a point to keep the dogs' heads and some of the kids' as souvenirs, just like he's done in the past. With a few exceptions."

Jaxon saw it right away.

"Michael."

"Right. Why was Michael different?"

"I don't know."

"Did Michael mean something different to him? I can't make myself think like him. Michael keeps getting in the way. We're too close to this."

"I keep hearing his voice in my head, his real voice. He said Michael was nothing to him. I don't believe him."

"I don't either." She paused. "He also knew we had spent time with Luke and Ellie. He must have some way to see what they're up too. We need to check Luke's court and see if we can find any cameras." She stopped. "Shit, he may know she's there."

"Even if he does, we've got guys crawling all over the house and neighborhood. Luke's father owns a gun, too, and said he wasn't afraid to use it."

"I hope he won't have to."

He nodded.

"Ok," he said, "What else? He knows quite a bit about technology, yet he let himself be tracked by a bunch of kids."

"He's got to be arrogant," she said. "We know he likes to taunt us, so he underestimated these kids. He'll probably keep thinking he's smarter than they are and that may be a mistake. How did he know about the Hacker? That's what's bothering me."

"Right—no cameras or web-cams in the Jenson area. Do you think he's got a bug, or tap, on the Harrisons' phone? We never thought to check that."

"I wouldn't put it past him. Let's follow up on that."

He made some notes.

"Let's keep working backwards," she said. "Before the Hacker's house, we were at the Harrison house talking to the kids."

"We discussed the Hacker and talked them into giving him up. Ellie had also received a message from Smith saying he knew her father."

"Leonard Worthington, and her real name is Eliana Worthington. Or at least it used to be." He was typing into the computer and watched as information came up on one Leonard David Worthington. The last known address was Ellie's.

"Nothing on him since he lived there?" Victoria said. "I'm calling Holt and see if we have anything in the database."

She called him and while she was giving him the info, he scanned the rest of the file. Driver's License records were clean. No citations or DUI's. No arrests, either, but an old domestic disturbance call showed up. It was Ellie's address way back in 1997.

"He'll get back as soon as he has the info," Victoria said hanging up. She leaned in close as Jaxon continued to scan the report.

They both saw it at the same time.

"You were the responding officer," she said. "You made this report." She looked at him stunned.

"I don't remember," he said. "I wouldn't normally respond to a call like this. I must have been in the area and the patrol officers were tied up somewhere else." He thought for a second, then said, "No wonder she's been such a bitch to me. She probably remembers me from that call. Damn! Why can't I remember?"

"Is this what your Spidey-senses were tingling about?"

"Has to be."

He looked at the computer and scrolled down the screen. The report listed Madison Worthington as the caller. She had dialed 911 complaining that her husband was drunk and 'out of his head' breaking things and screaming at her. Apparently Jaxon had been able to convince the man to behave by 'informing him of his parental duties and the consequences of neglecting those duties.'

"What did you tell him?" Victoria asked.

"I don't know." He thought about it but came up with nothing.

"Did you threaten to have Social Services take his son away?"

"Sounds like something I would do."

"Yes, it does." She gave him a look and stood up. "Come on."

"Where are we going?"

"To see Madison Worthington—or Pemberton. Whatever her name is. Maybe she knows where he is."

They pulled up to the house to find the older brother messing with what looked like a model airplane. The engine was running and he was revving it up and down while he held on to it with one hand. White smoke was streaming from the exhaust. It sounded like a bunch of angry bees or even a miniature chain saw.

Jaxon and Victoria walked up and he shut the engine off, looking irritated.

"Patrick, right?" Jaxon said.

The kid nodded.

"Is your mother here?"

"Yeah. She's inside."

"Pretty cool toy," Jaxon said leaning down and looking at it. "Is it hard to fly?"

"I don't know. I haven't tried it yet. I just got it."

"I'll bet it was expensive."

"I don't know. It was a gift."

"Does it burn that alcohol fuel?"

"Yeah." Patrick reached down and grabbed a gallon jug of greenish fluid. It had some kind of pump attached to it. "This is what it uses."

"Be careful breathing those fumes," Jaxon said. "They contain a chemical that might knock you out. It's called Diethyl Ether."

The kid looked at him like he was crazy.

"Have fun," Jaxon said as he turned and walked up to the door.

When they were out of earshot Victoria said, "What was that all about?"

"Just passing on some knowledge I learned," he said, grinning.

"He probably thinks you're an ass."

"Maybe, but he'll still remember it."

"Doubt it."

He knocked on the door and Madison Pemberton answered looking tired and a little grayer. Her face registered annoyance and then worry.

"What happened," she said quickly.

"Everything's fine, Mrs. Pemberton," Jaxon said. "We didn't mean to worry you. We just wanted to ask you a few questions if you have a moment."

"Don't you think you should be out trying to catch the man who wants to hurt my daughter?"

"It's related to the case, ma'am," Victoria said.

"And you are…?" Madison said.

"Special Agent Elliot, FBI ma'am. The Detective and I are working on the case together."

"May we come in?" Jaxon said.

She hesitated, and then opened the door wider and stepped aside.

Jaxon let Victoria enter first. The layout was very similar to the Harrison house only flip-flopped so the stairway was to their right as they entered and the half bath was to the left. She led them into the living room and asked if they wanted anything to drink.

"No thank you, Mrs. Pemberton," Victoria said, sitting in a chair that looked horribly uncomfortable. Jaxon chose the couch.

"Mrs. Pemberton," Jaxon said, "we've met before all of this, haven't we?"

She nodded.

"I didn't think you remembered. 1997. I had to call the police on my husband and you were the responding officer."

"What happened?"

"You don't know?" she said, surprised.

"It's been a long time. Refresh my memory."

"My husband was not a pleasant man," she said. "He had been drinking and we got into a fight. I was pregnant at the time with Ellie and was not providing him with enough—uh—'entertainment' as he put it and he started slapping me. He was a hitter. I ran from him and called the police. Your delayed arrival allowed him to drink even more. As soon as you arrived he started in on you, and you had to—subdue him. Patrick was two at the time and was crying from all the shouting. My husband screamed at him to shut up and you then threatened to take the child away if my husband didn't settle down. He must have gotten the point, because he stopped struggling and shut his mouth. It was like a switch had been turned off."

Jaxon nodded, remembering now.

The man had been huge. Six-four, six-five, two hundred fifty pounds at least. The only reason Jaxon was able to get him on the ground was because he was staggering drunk.

"Leonard was very protective of his son," she continued. "He did not appreciate you threatening him and he told you…"

"That I would regret it."

"Right—so you do remember."

"It's coming back."

"I was surprised you didn't take him in," she said, looking directly at him.

"It usually only makes things worse. He seemed under control after that."

"He beat me with a belt."

Jaxon didn't know what to say.

"I almost lost the baby and had bruises that stayed for weeks."

"I'm sorry," he finally said.

She turned away from him and stared off into the distance as if it didn't matter.

"It's over and I'm free of him."

"Did he ever touch you again?" Victoria asked.

"No. My father took care of that since the police couldn't seem to."

She turned and looked him in the eye again. He had to look away.

"My father stayed with me for months and pointed a shotgun at him every time he came around. He finally got the point. My father even fired it at him, but if it hit him we never knew. He left and has never been back."

"I'm truly sorry, Mrs. Pemberton," Jaxon said. "The system failed you and I don't know what to say. I feel like I let you down."

"You did," she said bluntly. Then dismissed it. "It doesn't matter," she continued, waving her hand at him. "All that's in the past. What I want from you now is to not fail me again. You need to find this madman and stop him from hurting my daughter. Can you do that?"

"Yes, Mrs. Pemberton," Victoria said. "We can."

She looked Victoria up and down, and then nodded once.

"Where is he now?" Jaxon asked.

"My ex-husband? I don't know and I don't care."

"You have no idea where he might be?"

"Why do you care? What do you two want from me today?"

"Ellie didn't tell you about her father?" Victoria asked.

"What about her father?" Madison suddenly looked alarmed.

Victoria looked at Jaxon. Jaxon said, "Ellie got another message from the killer. He said he knows her father."

She looked shaken. She sat back in her chair, deflated, her hand rising to her face, then stopping where it fluttered for a second and then sank to her lap.

"We need to find your ex-husband, Mrs. Pemberton. We need to find Leonard Worthington."

"You can't," she whispered. She looked haunted and her eyes grew dark.

"We will," Victoria said. "Whether you help us or not."

"You can't," she said again. "You can't, because he's dead."

* * *

They spent the next half hour getting the full story from Madison Pemberton and then made some hard decisions about her future.

It only took a few minutes to decide. It was the right thing to do, and as Jaxon had learned in his years of police work, sometimes people just took things into their own hands and justice was served. Victoria felt the same way. She called Holt back and told him the Worthington thing was a dead lead and not to expend any more time and energy on it.

Jaxon could only hear one side of the conversation but Victoria told him what was said. Holt was curious as to what had happened but did not push it. She hinted it was something she would discuss with him later.

"Are you going to tell him?" Jaxon asked after she hung up.

"I think I'll have to."

"What will he do?"

"The same as we're doing—look the other way."

Jaxon wasn't so sure. Holt seemed like a by-the-book kind of guy.

After Madison Pemberton's revelation, they got her talking.

Apparently her father had been a better shot than she had originally stated. During one of Worthington's surprise visits, he became violent and would not leave. Her father broke the gun out and pointed it at him telling him to vacate the premises. Worthington refused and charged the man. He fired the weapon. It took two shots to bring him down.

The father took complete charge of the situation and disposed of the body in a location Madison didn't have knowledge of. No one missed him. His parents were dead and he had no brothers or sisters. Madison's father died a few years later and the secret of his burial place died with him. Madison never learned what her father did with Leonard David Worthington.

Jaxon and Victoria talked and told her they would keep the information confidential unless they discovered she had lied to them. She thanked them and swore what she had told them was the absolute truth. Jaxon saw something in her eyes that had changed. The burden of her secret lifted from her shoulders and for the briefest moment she appeared happy. Then, when they mentioned they were going over to check on Ellie, the world came crashing back in on her and the strain of everything weighed her down again. Jaxon suggested she have a stiff drink.

As they were leaving she said, "My father was a good man. Please don't tarnish his memory by glorifying my monster of a husband. My father was only protecting his daughter and grandchildren."

Jaxon and Victoria believed her.

They were now parked in front of the Harrison house about to go in and check on the kids.

"Should we tell the girl anything?"

Victoria looked at him and said, "We could lie and tell her we checked him out and there was no way William Smith could know her father."

"It's partially true," he said. "He could not know him if the man is dead."

"It might make her feel better."

He nodded. "All right, we'll be vague."

They stepped out of the car and walked over to the uniformed officer parked in front of the house and talked with him for a few minutes. Everything had been quiet he said. The other car was parked over in the court behind the house watching the entrance to the backyard from the pool complex. Quiet there too.

They knocked on the door and were greeted by Mr. Harrison who looked a little relieved to see them.

"Thanks for stopping by," he said, and opened the door for both to enter.

"How are the kids?" Victoria asked.

"Actually, pretty good. There's a little tension in the air, but they had some friends over and have been pretty busy goofing off. Don't challenge those two to an air hockey game," he said. "They kicked my butt."

Victoria smiled and looked relieved.

"I don't want to upset them but we have some news that might make her feel a little better. Can we talk to them?"

"Ok—I'll find them."

He left to search the kids out.

Jaxon and Victoria sat in the living room, and the kids walked in together a minute later. The girl looked much better and the boy beamed beside her. They sat on the couch next to each other, holding hands again, and waited expectantly.

"You guys look happy," Victoria said. "Have you had a good day today?"

They both smiled and nodded.

"Well, except for this morning," Luke said, looking a little somber now.

"Good," she said. "I'm glad. Ellie, we found some information that might make you feel a little better."

Jaxon watched the girl who looked at them warily. She didn't trust them yet, and Jaxon didn't blame her. She'd been through a lot and probably had doubts about life in general. Her perspective had grown up a lot in the last few months and she was getting an above average dose of adulthood tossed her way.

"What is it?" Ellie said.

"We tracked down information on your father and there is no way William Smith could know him."

"What kind of information," Ellie asked, and this surprised Jaxon. He expected her to just take their word for it. Victoria never faltered.

"He is nowhere near us and hasn't been for some time," Victoria said.

"Where is he?"

Victoria looked at Jaxon. He had nothing to offer. Maybe this had been a mistake.

"Can you just take our word for it right now?" Victoria offered. "I know it's confusing for you, but just trust us."

She seemed to accept this and nodded her head and sighed.

"Well, that's good," she said. "That does make me feel a little better. The killer's still out there though, right?"

"Unfortunately, yes," Jaxon said. "But we've got you well protected here, and I know he won't try anything. Besides, he doesn't know you're here."

"I hope not," Luke said.

"We will still pretend like he does and keep a couple of officers parked in front and back," Victoria said. "Does that make you feel safe?"

She nodded hesitantly.

"What is it, sweetheart?" Victoria asked.

"He's smart," she said. "He always seems to know what's happening."

"It appears that way at times, doesn't it?" Victoria said. "What if Detective Jennings and I stayed in the house with you tonight? Would that make you feel safer?"

Jaxon jerked his head toward her, but saw the girl smile and nod her head. Victoria looked at him and smiled, and he knew he'd be sleeping on a couch tonight.

Ellie said, "Great!"

CHAPTER 41

Jaxon sat in a recliner, his radio next to him on the table, volume turned low so it wouldn't wake any of the kids.

Victoria was on the couch, her laptop resting on her knees. She was going through some of the data Holt had e-mailed her. The lab at Quantico was still struggling with the Hacker's computer system, but the forensic guys in DC had gone through a lot of the evidence collected from the Jenson house. Most of it was nothing new.

After getting permission from each other's bosses, Jaxon and Victoria explained their intentions to the Harrisons and both seemed grateful for the added security. The father had actually taken a deep breath, as if he had been struggling to fill his lungs all day and finally found relief.

Jaxon ran Victoria by her house where she picked up a few things, and then they stopped by the Hoover building so she could grab some electronic eavesdropping detection equipment. Holt was there, and though it was a little awkward for Jaxon, he muddled through and Holt noticed nothing. One more stop at Jaxon's house to feed Reverb, and they arrived back at the Harrisons' at around 8:00 p.m.

Breaking out the eavesdropping equipment, Victoria scanned the house and phone lines, while Jaxon searched outside for cameras. The light was fading so Jaxon didn't have much time. Neither found anything.

"If he doesn't have any electronics around, how does he know so much about what is happening with these kids?" Jaxon asked.

"Could he be tracking their cell phones?"

"Possibly," Jaxon said, "but he would have to be able to listen in on their conversations to find out anything about the Hacker. How could he know Quentin Jenson provided Luke with software just from observing him visiting the house?"

"Yeah, that doesn't make sense."

They sat in silence for a moment.

Victoria finally said, "Could he have an accomplice? Someone watching the kids or even someone who knows them?"

Jaxon sat up.

"Or maybe he's bugged one of the friend's houses. What're their names?" He snapped his fingers a couple of times. "John and Jimmy. What if Luke's buddies are inadvertently supplying the guy with intel? They wouldn't have a clue if their phones or computers were bugged."

"We'll see if we can get permission to check the house tomorrow."

"Just wave that FBI badge and that should do the trick."

"It does seem to work most of the time."

They sat quiet for a few minutes. He listened to the noises of the strange house, trying to familiarize himself with its personality. The quiet squeaks of the floor, or the groans of the A/C system as it came on. Hopefully, he would recognize something strange if it happened while he slept. After a few minutes he looked over at Victoria and then got up and walked over to the couch. She was typing something into the laptop and he reached up and brushed the hair away from her forehead, looking at the healing bruise underneath.

She stopped and looked up at him.

"Not here," she said.

"I know," he said and let his hand fall to his lap. The bruising was looking better and he told her so.

"It feels better," she said, reaching up and touching it. "I don't notice it as much anymore."

He stared at it remembering the horrible panic he felt seeing her lying there after the house exploded. She must have read his mind because her eyes softened and she said, "I'll be ok."

He searched her face. Was this really going to happen? Could they give it another go?

They had been so busy today they barely had time to reflect on their little tryst this afternoon. They hadn't even talked about her relationship with Holt, and maybe that was on purpose. He was a little afraid to hear what she would say about him and maybe she was afraid to think about it.

He pushed it away and thought about the last few days.

It had seemed like months and realizing it had only been a few days, it made him think he hadn't even had time to grieve for his partner. Sally was like a distant memory and he hated himself for relegating her to some small compartment in his mind, to pull out later and look at.

Seeing her lying unmoving and lifeless in his mind immediately brought the image of Victoria up again, bleeding from the head, the sinking feeling in his soul, thinking she was dead. And then the relief he felt when she was ok.

"Back in Indiana," he said softly, "when I saw you lying there, I felt empty. In the split second before you woke, I thought you were dead and any hope of my life ever being whole again was sucked away like a vacuum. I could feel it. Physically feel it. The air turned stale and hot, and I couldn't breathe. I knew I would never get to tell you how I felt. That I would never get to feel your touch again. That I would never hear your voice again. The world had ended for the second time in my life, and I didn't want to go on. Then you spoke to me."

A single tear traced a line down her face, but she smiled. "I was glad it was you when I came to. I wasn't afraid with you there."

A comfortable silence settled between them. He knew this wasn't the best place to talk about it, but his mouth overrode his head.

"What happens now?"

He could see a small shadow move across her face and she looked away.

"I feel happy," she said and looked back at him. "I want to be with you, but…"

"But it's complicated," he finished for her.

"No," she said. "It's easy. I've always known in my heart that if you would take me back, I would go. I think Holt knows it too, but he's been able to look past it. I just have to do this in my own way. Ok?"

"What are you going to do?"

"I'm waiting for you to tell me you want me back."

"I want you back."

She smiled.

"Are we going to be able to get through all this?"

"I'm willing to try."

"That's all I need to hear," she said and touched his face. "Give me some time to deal with Holt. Just promise me you won't make it hard on him. He's a good man."

"I'll take it easy on him. A few rabbit punches and a Judo chop should do it."

"He'd probably shoot you."

"Bring it on."

More silence and then Jaxon said, "How can you leave him so easily?"

She sighed.

"It's not easy. But he's not you."

"Have you really been pining away for me?"

"You wish," but she smiled. "I know you've been blocking me out of your mind for a while, but I've thought about you almost every day. Whenever I thought of Michael, you were right there with him in my mind."

"Then why Holt? What made you want to be with him?"

"I was lonely. I needed something to fill the huge void that was left by the loss of Michael and then the loss of you. If he hadn't been there, I really believe I would have just dried up and blown away in the breeze."

Jaxon's radio squawked and he got up and answered it.

"Jaxon."

"Just letting you know of the shift change, sir. This is Michelson and it's midnight."

"Gotcha," Jaxon said. "Try to stay alert out there."

"Roger."

"Jeffries, out back," another voice said and Jaxon acknowledged him too.

"Boy, I'm glad I don't have to pull those shifts anymore. Has to be the worst."

"Depends on who you spend it with," Victoria said.

"I always got stuck with Wiesnewski. He smelled like cabbage."

"And garlic," she said, chuckling. "What the hell did that guy eat?"

"You mean what didn't he eat. What's an FBI stakeout like?" Jaxon asked.

"The same. Just add designer clothes."

"Somehow, I believe you."

She closed the laptop and yawned. "All right, I've had enough. I'm going to take a nap. You get first watch."

"Wanna' fool around?"

"Yes."

"Like that's gonna happen."

"You asked. I didn't say we would be able to," but she smiled, crossed over to his chair and gave him a soft kiss. "Later," she whispered.

"You're killing me."

"Don't die on me yet. We just found each other again."

CHAPTER 42

Jaxon woke stiff and tired.

Sleeping in a recliner was not one of his favorite things. Unless he'd had a twelve pack and some chicken wings. Victoria was missing and then he heard her voice coming softly from the kitchen. It sounded like she was talking to Mrs. Harrison.

He got up, stretched, and used the head by the front door and then followed the smell of coffee into the kitchen.

"Good morning, Detective," Mrs. Harrison said. "Did you sleep ok?"

"Yes ma'am," he lied and glanced at Victoria who looked perfect. She was grinning at him and he realized he must look rumpled. He reached up and felt his hair sticking up in clumps and smiled sheepishly.

"Here," Victoria said handing him a cup. "Looks like you could use this."

"Thanks." He glanced at the clock and saw it was 7:30. She had let him sleep.

"I'm glad it was quiet last night," Mrs. Harrison said. "I felt safer with you two down here."

"No problem, ma'am. It was the least we could do," he said.

"Will you be back tonight?"

"As long as it's ok with your family," Victoria said.

"Thank you," she said and hugged Victoria.

She looked surprised, but hugged her back after a second.

"I've been so afraid for Lucas and Ellie. I don't know what I would do if something happened to them."

"We won't let anything happen, Mrs. Harrison. Nobody will get within fifty feet of them," Jaxon said.

"Do you promise?"

"Yes," Victoria said.

Mrs. Harrison looked back and forth between the two and then said, "I believe you."

"How are your other children handling this, Mrs. Harrison?" Victoria asked.

"Please, call me Natalie," she said. "Do either of you have children?"

The temperature in the room dropped a couple of degrees and Jaxon saw Natalie's face register confusion. Of course, she had no idea what that simple question meant to Victoria and him. He was about to answer when Victoria did it for him.

"Our son was killed, Natalie. Murdered."

Natalie almost dropped her coffee and she looked back and forth between them.

"Both your sons?" she asked.

"Victoria and I were once married," Jaxon said. "We don't mean to shock you, but there's no nice way around the answer. The same bastard who is stalking these kids—your son—is the man who took our son from us." The venom in Jaxon's voice even surprised him. "You see, we thought the man responsible for our son's murder was rotting in a jail cell awaiting his turn to die. But, we were sorely mistaken."

Victoria interrupted, "This information has just come to our attention. We would be aggressively trying to apprehend this madman regardless, but the case has our undivided attention now, if you understand my meaning. We will find this man and put an end to his atrocities one way or another."

Natalie Harrison stood in shock. Her hand was raised to her open mouth and she looked like a deer caught in the headlights.

"Oh my God!" she said. "Oh my God. I'm so sorry."

Victoria went to her.

"It's all right, Natalie. You had no idea. I'm sorry if we upset you, but I want you to know we will stop at nothing to get this guy. Nothing."

"What's going on, Mom?" Luke asked from the doorway. "Did something happen?"

All of them stood looking at each other for a moment and then Jaxon cleared his throat.

"Everything's fine, Luke. Nothing's happened. Agent Elliot and I were just having a talk with your mother. Nothing to worry about," and he smiled, though it felt strained.

He seemed to buy it. "Is Ellie up?" The tension broke and they all smiled at the boy.

"No, sweetie," his mom said. "I haven't seen her yet. It's still early. Let her sleep, ok?"

"I'm awake," Ellie said from the doorway, appearing just as Luke had from thin air. Jaxon wondered how much of the conversation the two kids had eavesdropped on. Luke turned and smiled bigger than any kid he'd ever seen and if he was acting, then Jaxon was a drag queen. They hadn't heard a word and he was relieved. No sense in stressing out the kids any more than they already were.

"Hey," Luke said.

"Hey," Ellie said back. "Your hair is sticking up," and she giggled.

He turned red and then pointed at Jaxon.

"So's his."

Then they were all laughing and the dramatic conversation from a few minutes before was long forgotten. Kids had a tendency to do that.

* * *

Jaxon dropped Victoria off at her condo and went home to shower and eat.

They would be poring over all the files, new and old, trying to connect the dots. The information over the last few days had grown dramatically and they needed to devote some time to researching any leads that may surface from reviewing old cases. Maybe a piece of the puzzle would fall into place.

Jaxon knew that sometimes it was the smallest, seemingly trivial piece of evidence that could start an avalanche of discovery. There had to be something they were missing.

Later they would visit Jimmy and John Besner's house and check for bugs. He doubted they would find anything, but it was worth the effort.

Reverb was lying in the middle of the kitchen floor like he always did, lounging right in the path of Jaxon's sleepy feet, and as he tripped over the old mutt, catching himself on the counter, something caught his eye. He bent to the floor and looked at the baseboard of the cabinet. A small, yellow-orange colored, broken piece of corn chip was leaning against the shoe molding. He picked it up, turning it in his fingers. He sniffed. Bar-B-Que.

Jaxon hated Bar-B-Que anything.

Someone had been in his house.

CHAPTER 43

The doorbell rang and Luke went to answer it.

His dad beat him to it saying, "I got it!"

It ended up being Patrick, Ellie's brother. He stood there holding a suitcase and a box in his hands, a big stupid grin on his face.

"Hello, Patrick," Luke's dad said. "Is that for Ellie?"

"Yep," he said.

"All right, come on in."

Luke stepped back so Patrick could come in and as he passed, Luke said, "What's up?"

"Nothing," Patrick said and then just stood there.

Apparently, he was still acting somewhat cool to him. Nothing Luke could do about it so he went to find Ellie. She was in his brother's room, her hair wet from the shower.

"Patrick's here," Luke said. "He has some stuff for you."

"Probably some more clothes. My mom said she would send him over with it."

They went downstairs together and Patrick handed her the stuff.

"What's in the box?" Ellie asked.

He shrugged his shoulders.

"It was delivered today. I didn't open it. You'd kill me if I did, anyway." He turned and left.

Luke's dad said, "Talkative, isn't he?"

"He's a jerk," Ellie said. "He's probably mad because my mother made him bring this over."

She grabbed the box and Luke took the suitcase, and they went back upstairs. In the room she put the box on the floor and Luke set the suitcase on the bed.

"Did you order something?" Luke asked.

"No. I don't know what this is. Probably some swim team junk. Coach always sends me scholarship crap."

She tore open the top of the box and looked inside.

She started screaming. She didn't stop for ten minutes.

* * *

Jaxon's desk was piled high with documents and boxes.

The desk next to him, which Victoria was using, looked the same. They had been perusing the old files for three hours and had little to show for it.

He felt tired and edgy, and she must be feeling the same because they had talked very little this morning. It was good they were comfortable together, but her presence was somewhat of a distraction. She was dressed in a skirt again this morning and a blouse which, though professional, showed off her cleavage in just the right way. A lot of the guys were walking by repeatedly and Jaxon knew why.

He was currently looking at the old file on Stewart Littleton, reading through the interviews of the family and neighbors from the time of his missing person's report in 1984. Very dull. The investigator back then was one S. Holmes. He thought it was a joke, but the guy's real name was Samuel Holmes. Jaxon wondered if he ever considered changing it to Sherlock. He told Victoria this and she laughed.

"His partner wasn't a doctor was he?"

"Uh…" he leafed through the documents. "No—Jedediah Smith."

They both looked silently at each other and then burst out laughing.

"You're kidding, right?" She said.

He couldn't answer because he was laughing so hard so he just shook his head. He handed the paper over to her and she looked at it and started laughing even harder.

"The chief back then probably had no choice but to put them together," he laughed.

"Oh—right! How could you NOT team those two up?"

"The English investigator extraordinaire, and the brazen mountain man!"

They were laughing so hard that people were coming over and wondering what the hell was going on. They couldn't stop to tell them. Jaxon just waved them away and they wandered off looking back over their shoulders at the two overworked and exhausted crazy people.

Jaxon was still trying to control himself as he looked over the papers in his hand for other unusual names associated with the case. He found one he recognized and at first it didn't register anything other than being familiar. Then his laughter stopped suddenly and he sat up.

"Fuck me," he said, and she said, "Not here."

He looked up at her and she was still giggling. She saw his face and stopped. He handed her the piece of paper and said, "Third paragraph down, about midway through."

She found it quickly and looked up at him. "We need to talk to June Littleton."

* * *

As they were driving to June Littleton's, Jaxon's phone rang.

He answered on the third ring and one of the officers at the Harrison house told him he needed to get over there.

"What's going on?"

"The Pemberton girl got a package and it must be from the guy."

"What's in it?"

The officer told him.

"Shit. On our way."

He turned on his lights and made an illegal u-turn heading back to Annandale. He left the lights flashing but kept the siren silent.

"What's going on?" Victoria asked after recovering from his violent maneuver.

"Ellie got a package delivered."

"What?"

"From him."

"Is she ok?"

"She's hysterical. We're going there first. Call the Crime Scene Techs and get them over there."

She took her phone out and got things rolling. If the traffic held up, they would get there at the same time.

After she hung up, she said, "Do you know what was in the package?"

He nodded. He told her and she turned and stared out the window.

"Fucking bastard," she said under her breath.

"Yes."

They got there a few minutes before the Crime Scene guys and walked in to the house. Everyone was in the living room, crowded around Ellie who was still sobbing, holding on to Luke as if her life depended on it. It sounded like she was saying, "Get it out of here! Get it out of here!" over and over again.

The officer took them to an upstairs room and showed them the box.

Inside was the thawing head of a dog. The mouth was open with a grayish tongue lolling out and its eyes were open, but yellowed with the pupil's bottom edge showing from beneath the eyelid. The brown, matted fur still had dried blood on it and Jaxon could even see raw flesh where the head had been severed from the torso.

"Is this her dog, Bentley?" Victoria asked.

The officer nodded. "She kept saying that name over and over again after she stopped screaming. The boy said it was her dog. Poor girl's a wreck."

"Have you touched anything?" Jaxon asked.

"You know better than to ask me that, sir."

"Right. Sorry. How did it get here?"

"The brother brought it over along with a suitcase."

"Do we know how the brother got it?"

"Lucas Harrison said the brother told him it was delivered this morning. I haven't talked to the brother."

"Ok. We'll talk to him. Good job. I'm glad you called us."

Jaxon took out a pen and used it to flip over the lid of the box exposing the shipping label. It was addressed to Eliana Worthington, not Pemberton. He showed it to Victoria who frowned.

Just then the Crime Scene Techs stomped upstairs with their stuff. Jaxon and Victoria let them do their work.

Walking into the living room, Victoria went to Ellie and touched her shoulder. She was huddled against Luke with her face buried in his sleeve. Natalie Harrison was trying to soothe her, but she appeared inconsolable. Victoria's touch made her flinch.

"Ellie? It's Agent Elliot, honey. It's all right. Can you look at me?" Ellie turned to her and said, "Is it gone?"

"It will be soon. They have to go over it for evidence."

The girl's face fell and a noise escaped her that broke Jaxon's heart.

"Please, make them hurry!" Ellie said. "I can't stand to think it's in this house."

"Let's go outside," Victoria said, standing and extending her hand. Ellie looked from it to Luke, but didn't move.

"Luke can come with us. It'll make you feel better. Just until they're done, ok?"

Ellie nodded and reluctantly took her hand. Her other hand grabbed Luke's and Victoria walked them out back while Jaxon stayed in and talked to the parents. Ellie looked a little better already.

Ellie's mother came to the door looking distraught and Jaxon led her to her daughter. Ellie sagged into her mother's arms and cried even harder. At least her mother was here.

Back inside, Jaxon determined the Harrisons knew very little about the package and he knew his best bet would be to talk to the brother. They would stop by on the way out of the neighborhood after everything calmed down.

The Crime Scene guys finished up quickly at the urging of Jaxon and left with the dog's head and box within an hour. Ellie looked instantly relieved, but still would not go up to the room. They talked with her about staying at the Harrisons' and the importance of remaining hidden and she said she wanted to stay.

"Would it be ok if I slept in another room?" She asked.

"You can sleep in my room with me," Deana said, and smiled. "I can move some stuff around and put the blow-up mattress on the floor."

Ellie smiled and said, "That would be great."

"Are you sure you don't want to come home, Eliana?" her mother asked.

"I think she will be safer here," Victoria said. "He sent the package to your house in the belief she would get it there, so he must not know she's here. Plus, Jaxon and I will be here again tonight, all night, along with the officers out front and back, and the officer in front of your house for appearances."

Madison Pemberton nodded, but did not look happy. Jaxon was sure she missed her daughter and probably worried herself sick over her being here. Mrs. Harrison must have known it too.

"Madison? You can stay here with her if you like. We have room."

She hesitated, but then shook her head.

"I really appreciate it, Natalie, and I really want to, but that would mean leaving Patrick alone and I couldn't do that. He won't stay here even if you begged him."

"You're both welcome to stay if you change your mind," Natalie said, and smiled.

"Thank you," Madison said, then to her daughter. "Are you all right? If you need me, just call. I'll answer quick and come over right away."

Ellie nodded, a few tears showing, but she held it together. She gave her mom a hug and Madison left.

"We're going to follow your mom to your house so we can talk to Patrick about the package," Jaxon told Ellie. "The two officers are still here, so don't worry. If another package shows up, don't open it. Don't even bring it into the house. Call us right away and we'll be over immediately. That goes for everyone. Nobody opens any strange packages."

"Where are you going after my house?" Ellie asked.

"We have some leads to follow, sweetheart," Victoria said. "We still have to catch this guy and we're getting closer."

"What did you find?" Luke asked.

"Not right now," Jaxon said. "We've got a lot to do so we can get back here tonight. We'll fill you all in when we get back."

Luke looked discouraged, but nodded anyway.

"Keep the doors locked and call the officer out front on the radio immediately if something happens. Got it?"

Jeffrey Harrison said, "We'll be all right."

Jaxon opened the door and said, "I know you will."

Victoria touched Ellie's arm and smiled, then she walked out the door and Jaxon followed behind.

"We're getting too close to this," he said.

"I know. I don't care."

"I'm starting to care too much about those kids."

"So am I."

"We're gonna get burned on this."

"No way around it," she said. "I'm not giving this case to anyone else. I can't let anything happen to those kids. If Holt tries to pull me off, I'll physically hurt him."

She wasn't smiling.

"We need to be careful," he said.

She suddenly stopped and turned on him.

"Bullshit! I'm doing no such thing! I'm going to go after this guy like the crazed lunatic that he is! If you want to back off, be my guest, but I'm all in." He stood there stunned. She turned, walked away, and said, "I thought you would be too."

He caught up to her and grabbed her arm.

"Hey! I'm on your side. I want this guy just as bad as you do."

She wouldn't look at him.

"Look at me," he said. She moved her eyes to his. "I'm in. How could you think that I wouldn't be? I'm just worried about you."

"Well, don't be. I can take care of myself."

He smiled at her and said, "I know you can. I should know better than to be all protective around you. But we look out for each other, right? I've got your back. You can't keep me from looking out for you."

She finally smiled a little.

"You'd better."

They stood like that for a minute, the tension bleeding off.

"We done freakin' out now?" he said.

"Yeah."

"Let's go get the asshole then."

"I love it when you curse," she said, stepping to the car. "It gets me all worked up."

"In a good way?"

"You'll find out later."

"You said that last night."

She just smiled at him.

* * *

Patrick Pemberton didn't know squat.

Jaxon thought the kid was an asshole too, but that was just his opinion. Teenagers these days were all assholes most of the time.

Victoria had asked him nicely, "Did you happen to see who delivered the package?"

"No. Why?"

"It might help us solve the case, Patrick," Jaxon said.

"I didn't do anything."

"We know that," Victoria said. "We're not here to hassle you, we're just trying to find out some information. Do you know when the package was delivered?"

"No."

"When did you realize it was here?" Jaxon asked.

"When I left to take Ellie her stupid suitcase."

"Did you happen to see anyone around or a delivery truck? Anything like that?"

"No."

"All right, if you think of anything or remember anything else, call." Jaxon handed him a business card. He took it and stuffed it in his pocket and shut the door.

"That was a lot of help," Victoria said.

"No wonder Ellie called him a jerk."

"Because he is one," they both said at the same time and then laughed.

Next stop, June Littleton's.

Not only was she pissed because she expected them two hours ago, but apparently her husband was out drinking and hadn't shown up home yet. She kept looking at her watch and saying, "Son-of-a-bitch."

Victoria, ever the FBI agent, started the questioning.

"Mrs. Littleton, we were going over the interviews from the time of Stewart's abduction and we wanted to ask you a few questions about Stewart's friends."

"That was a long time ago," she said. "I hope I can remember things."

"By the way, Mrs. Littleton," Jaxon said, "When you re-married, why did you keep the name Littleton?"

"I wanted Stewart to be able to find me. If I had changed my name, he wouldn't know that, would he? He wouldn't be able to find his way home. Not that it mattered."

She looked at her hands in her lap and fiddled with the tie on her apron.

This is what Jaxon thought, but he wanted to hear it from her.

"That was smart," he said. "I'm so sorry about Stewart."

She nodded but said nothing.

"Do you remember one of Stewart's playmates back at that time?" Victoria asked. "His name was Leonard Worthington. He was mentioned a couple of times in the reports and was even interviewed."

Her face turned cold.

"Yes. I remember him."

"What can you tell us?" Victoria said.

She sighed. "He was a big boy. Six foot something and a lot of muscles for his age. He was older than Stewart, and at times he would let Stewart know this."

"How much older?"

"Three or four years. Stewart was twelve and the Worthington boy was fifteen or sixteen."

"At that age, that gap is huge," Jaxon said. "Why did they even hang out together? It surprises me Leonard would even give a twelve year old the time of day."

"I thought the same thing, but they got along most of the time."

"Most of the time?" Victoria asked.

"Every once in a while, Stewart would come home with a bruise, or a lump, or a bloody lip, and he would tell me he fell, or tripped, or ran into a tree. I think the Worthington kid was being rough on him."

"But Stewart would never admit this to you?"

"No." She sat thoughtfully for a moment and then said. "I saw the Worthington boy push my Stewart down once. Nothing too bad. It didn't hurt him or anything, it was just a shove that drove him to his knees, but Stewart got right back up and I let it pass without confronting the older boy. Sometimes as parents, you just have to let the kids work things out for themselves, because if the moms and dads get involved, it usually gets blown all out of proportion."

Jaxon knew she was right. He'd seen it all too often and had been to a number of calls when he was a rookie patrolman. Calls where the parents were in fistfights over something the twelve year olds did to each other. If they had left it alone, the kids probably would have been back playing with each other in half an hour.

"So, you could never prove the Worthington boy injured Stewart?"

"No."

"What else can you remember? Was there a reason a sixteen year old would hang out with your son?"

Victoria kept going back to this and Jaxon knew this is what bothered both of them the most.

"Stewart idolized him," Mrs. Littleton said. "In his eyes, he was the coolest kid on the block with the coolest things. He was fascinated with the Worthington boy's radio controlled airplane collection and this is what drove Stewart to him." She smiled. "Stewart loved airplanes."

"What did you just say?" Jaxon asked.

"Stewart loved airplanes?"

"No. About Leonard Worthington's collection? Did you say it was radio controlled airplanes?"

"Yes. He had lots of them. Big ones, little ones. The older boy was quite the pilot."

Victoria turned to Jaxon and they shared a look. June Littleton looked at her watch again and mumbled the same curse at her husband while Jaxon stared at Victoria in disbelief.

"Mrs. Littleton," Jaxon said. "Where did Leonard live?"

"Three doors down," she pointed out the window. "Right there. In the gray one."

Jaxon followed her finger and saw a gray, two-story house sitting back from the street in an overgrown, weed infested yard, the structure looking dilapidated in the late evening light. It looked deserted.

"His parents are dead, right?" Victoria asked.

"Oh, yes. They both died years ago. Car accident. It was a terrible tragedy."

"Who owns the house now?" Jaxon asked.

"Leonard."

"Mrs. Littleton, Leonard Worthington's dead."

"Oh, nonsense," she said waving her hand at them. "I saw him the other day. He's still the big man he always was."

Jaxon's draw dropped to his chest. Victoria sat up straighter.

"Are you sure you saw him, Mrs. Littleton?"

"Uh—yes. I'm pretty sure I did. He's hard to miss."

"Where did you see him?"

"Why, at the house," she pointed again to the gray two-story. "I hadn't seen him in so long, but I'm sure it was him. He was wearing an old…"

Jaxon was no longer listening to her. A tumbler in his head dropped into place. Radio controlled airplanes. Diethyl Ether in the fuel. Click! Leonard Worthington was a big man. Ellie and Luke, as well as Mr. Lolly, had said the killer was huge. Jaxon had seen him on surveillance. Six four, easy. Click! To Ellie: *"I know your father."* Click! To Jaxon: *"You'll regret this."* Click! *"These are not Malcom's. They are mine. I return them to you now."* Click! *"That's what I told Michael. But you never came."* Click!

Jaxon stood. He grabbed his radio and called dispatch to get the SWAT and bomb teams out here immediately.

"Mrs. Littleton, I want you to get to your basement and stay there until we say it's all right to come out."

She looked terrified. Jaxon's panicked actions had startled her and now this revelation he hurled at her, pushed her past the limit.

"What's happening?" she shrieked. "What's wrong?"

"Just do it!" he shouted at her and she moved quickly to the basement door and disappeared down the stairs.

Victoria had put it together by now, also, and was on her cell coordinating some Federal efforts to assist with whatever they needed here. Leonard Worthington was alive and had been in his parents' old house.

Jaxon stepped outside with Victoria and walked to the end of the driveway. The gray house stood quiet in the fading light and there were no windows on this side for anyone inside to look out. He looked skyward, trying to see light poles, lamp posts, trees, anywhere a hidden camera or web-cam could be mounted. Victoria joined him and after a moment, grabbed his arm and pointed.

Just inside the yard of a house directly across the street from the Worthington home, an old oak stood, its limbs reaching out into the street and over the yards. High up on the trunk, close to where the limbs branched out away from the tree, a small gray box with a black spot in its middle was mounted facing the Worthington house.

"Shit!" he said. "We can't risk going in there until the bomb guys check it out."

"Not only that," she said, "what about the neighbors!"

"Shit! I'll take this side and you take that! Go!"

Jaxon sprinted to the first house next to the Littleton house and pounded on the door.

"Open up! Police!" He pounded the door until a little old gray haired lady answered. He flashed his badge and instructed her to go into her basement and await further instructions. He told her he didn't have time to explain. He heard Victoria pounding on doors behind him. He ran to the next house.

Jaxon heard tires squeal in the distance and knew they were coming. Everybody ran silent in a situation like this. Jaxon had made it to four houses when the first squad car pulled up. He ran to it and told the officer to get the other houses' occupants to the basements. The officer ran off. Two more cars pulled up and then the SWAT team command vehicle rolled in followed by the bomb squad. FBI cars were now showing up too.

Victoria had joined Jaxon and they met the SWAT commander in front of the vehicle.

Dark had settled in and the flashing lights cast strange shadows across the trees and houses. If Worthington hadn't known they were here before, and he was in there, he definitely knew they were here now.

They were discussing the previous house in Indiana with the bomb squad chief when Jaxon's cell phone went off. It was Halson in the lab.

"There's a note in the box with the dog's head," Halson said. "It was stuck to the underside of the lid."

"What did it say?" Jaxon asked.

"'For Daddy's girl,'" Halson said.

Click! Another tumbler in place. This one was so obvious though that Jaxon wondered if he was being led again by the maniac. It was as if he was making it easy.

"Thanks, Billy. Gotta' go," and he hung up. His phone rang again almost immediately.

All zeroes on the caller I.D.

He showed it to Victoria who nodded once for him to answer. She had them all quiet down as best she could. He pressed the button.

"Hello Leonard."

Metallic chuckling came through the speaker and a bit of feedback with it. Jaxon pulled the cell phone away from his ear. "Bravo, Detective. Bravo. Unfortunately, you are a bit slow."

"We're coming for you, Leonard."

"Apparently, you aren't listening," Worthington said, turning off the voice distortion.

"Doesn't matter," Jaxon said. "You've got nowhere to go."

Jaxon heard what he thought was a whimper come over the speaker and then Worthington said, "Are you listening, now Detective?"

A whine and then a howl of pain as Jaxon recognized Reverb's cry. The line went dead.

He turned to Victoria.

"He's not here! He's at my place! Come on!"

They sprinted for his car and yelled for a couple more patrol cars to follow.

Victoria got on the phone with the SWAT commander enroute and discussed the options. They decided this team would stay in case Worthington was playing them and was actually here. The bomb squad would stay also and search the area for incendiaries and triggers. The FBI would send a team to Jaxon's place and they should all reach the apartment at about the same time.

Jaxon had the lights and siren on as they worked their way through the early evening traffic. Luckily it was light, but they had to travel all the way from Reston to Annandale. It was taking too long and Jaxon knew they would miss him. Victoria remained in constant contact with her team at the Bureau and kept Jaxon in the loop.

"We'll get there," she said.

Arriving at his place, the FBI group getting to his apartment just before them, Jaxon sprinted from the car, racing for the apartment. Victoria and the FBI team yelled for him to stop, but he was going in no matter what. He knew the killer was not here and he knew there was no bomb waiting for him. The only thing he was unsure of was Reverb.

Bursting into the apartment, he ran from room to room. He stopped short of the kitchen and slumped. Victoria came in behind with her gun drawn, the FBI following behind. She saw Reverb hanging from the light fixture in the small kitchen and moaned.

He had been skinned and eviscerated like game, the muscle and connective tissues still glistening in the fluorescent lights. Jaxon pounded the door frame with a fist and turned away. One of the FBI guys swept past and looked over the area.

Jaxon's eyes moved to Victoria's whose look of sadness was probably only matched by his own. She touched his sleeve.

"You guys need to see this," one of the FBI agents said.

Victoria looked past Jaxon and then moved into the kitchen. Jaxon stayed where he was. Victoria called to him and he finally turned and went into the kitchen. He avoided looking Reverb's way.

A piece of newspaper was ripped from the main page and scribbled in big black letters were the words, 'Too Late.' The asshole used a piece of trash to write on. It was like a slap in the face and Jaxon knew it was meant that way.

"Yeah," he said, under his breath. "We know we're too late, you prick."

Victoria suddenly grabbed his arm.

"Oh Shit! Maybe he means we're too late for the kids!"

Jaxon grabbed his phone and dialed the number.

Everyone was silent. Jackson had a sinking feeling as the phone rang and rang. He hung it up and pulled the radio off his belt.

"Guardian 1, this is Jaxon, over."

Silence.

"Guardian 1, this is Jaxon, do you copy!"

They ran for the cars.

CHAPTER 44

Leonard David Worthington drove calmly down the street, reminding himself what it was to be a survivor.

The scars he bore from the shotgun blasts were badges of honor he wore proudly.

That old fool had thought he took care of him, but he had been sorely mistaken. He had to admit to himself that he had almost succumbed to the injuries, but apparently, he was meant for greater things and somebody had been looking out for him. Too bad the person who had pulled him from the frozen lake hadn't been as lucky. The man had drowned saving him and there was nothing he could have done about it. Worthington had been too weak to do anything but help himself.

Smiling to himself at the memory, he pulled in behind the police vehicle. He could see the man look into his mirror as his own lights illuminated the interior of the patrol car. Worthington shut the engine off, extinguishing the headlights. He opened the door and stepped to the driver's window of the car. The officer was rolling down the window.

"Good evening, Officer," Worthington said. He was carrying a stuffed animal in his left arm. It was a purple unicorn with a bright pink bow wrapped around its neck. The officer looked at it and chuckled.

"That's not for me, I take it," the policeman said.

Worthington smiled. "No. It's for my daughter, Ellie."

The cop's smile faltered and Worthington could see some wheels turning in there.

The cop suddenly grabbed for the radio. Worthington's right arm shot up and the can of mace he was carrying fired directly into the officer's face. Worthington immediately reached in and grabbed the officer's neck, and with the purple unicorn soaked in model airplane fuel, he muffled the officer's cries with it by stuffing the unicorn into his face and holding it there until the officer succumbed to the fumes.

One down, he thought.

Walking into the backyard and through the hole in the fence, he approached the second squad car from the rear.

This time, he held the unicorn below the officer's line of sight and tapped on his window, startling the man. The officer rolled it down. Worthington maced him immediately, and then rendered him unconscious in the same fashion as the first.

Two down. Nobody had noticed a thing. His daughter waited inside. He wasted little time.

Striding to the basement sliding door, he shattered it with a swift kick, the noise loud in the night, but it didn't matter. He would be in and out within minutes. Commotion from upstairs could be heard as he strode briskly up the stairs.

Bursting through the door, he saw the mother directly in front of him, standing with her hands to her face, frozen. He took a step to her and grabbed the junction of the nerve bundle at the base of her neck adjoining the shoulder and applied pressure. She moaned and collapsed, unconscious within seconds, her head striking the floor with a sickening crunch.

The boy came around the corner and paused for a second, staring at him. Then Lucas Harrison charged at him and this surprised Worthington, but nonetheless, it was foolish.

As the boy came within range, he moved to his left and brought his knee up into his abdomen, bending him at the waist. His right fist struck the base of his exposed neck and he was down for the count. Worthington grinned and even admired the boy's foolish courage. Maybe he would re-evaluate the boy's destiny.

Hearing heavy footfalls above his head, Worthington moved into the hall and turned left into the living room.

And there she was.

The shock on her face only amused him. Of course she would not believe. He knew she had seen a picture of him, but the real recognition came when she saw his eyes. He watched as who he was registered in her mind and then was surprised when she said, "Hello, Daddy."

Then she ran.

It did no good. He was too quick for her and he cornered her easily. He talked to her soothingly as she struggled against the stuffed animal pressed to her face, but her struggles soon subsided. He lifted her, so small and so light, put her over his shoulder, and walked out the front door.

As he reached the bottom of the driveway, the father emerged from the house, shouting, pistol pointed toward him. Worthington did not hesitate. He drew the Glock from the small of his back and fired. The man went down without another sound.

Worthington walked to his car and lay his daughter carefully in the back seat. He opened his own door, glanced around the quiet neighborhood and then sat in the seat. He started the engine and drove away whistling.

His princess had finally come home.

Part 3

Richard C Hale

CHAPTER 45

Luke awoke not sure where he was.

His head throbbed and things kept swimming in and out of focus around him. Voices penetrated his fog and he could make out things like, 'bed 23' and 'I.V.' and 'hydrocodone,' but none of the voices he recognized. Then, Deana, his sister, spoke in his ear next to him.

"Luke? Luke? Can you hear me? Your eyes are open."

Luke turned his head toward her voice and the world spun crazily. It settled after a few seconds and Deana's face swam up from below. She smiled at him.

"There you are," she said. "Are you ok?"

He had no idea. He didn't feel much except for the throbbing in his head and the sickening spinning of the room. He tried his voice.

"Where?"

"Where are you?"

He started to nod, but stopped because the room started spinning again.

"You're in the hospital. Mom and Dad are here too."

"What happened?"

"You got knocked out," she said.

He couldn't remember. Were he and John doing something stupid, like the time he fell jumping over ramps with his bike? He thought hard, but nothing surfaced.

"Mom's on the third floor and is doing great," Deana went on. "Dad's still in I.C.U. but will be moved out today. He's doing a lot better."

Mom on the third floor? Dad in I.C.U.?

He crawled back through his memory and fought to sort things out.

It seemed like just yesterday, he and Ellie were playing Monopoly in the living room and she was beating the crap of him. Or was that last year? He remembered giving her cookies in a bag Mom had fixed up, but couldn't fit it into any time frame. Was it summer? Winter? Did he slip on the driveway and crack his head?

The Monopoly game kept swimming up to his consciousness and he saw his hand moving the racecar to Boardwalk over and over again. Every time there was a sound like water crashing or waves breaking over the sand whenever he landed on the spot.

"The police are right outside too, so don't you worry."

Police? What the hell happened? The racecar slid across the board and stopped on Boardwalk. 'Splash!' Ellie's face looking scared.

"Katy and Christopher are with Grandma and Grandpa, but they'll be back up here in about an hour. We sure were worried about you."

Racecar. Boardwalk. 'Splash!' Ellie scared. Racecar. Boardwalk. 'Crash!' Ellie terrified!

His eyes opened wide. Not a splash of water. A crash as glass broke. Ellie's face scared. Then the killer! In his house!

"Where's Ellie?" Luke tried to sit up. "Where's Ellie? Where's Ellie?"

The room started spinning again and he felt Deana's hands on him and her voice, soothing, trying to calm him down.

"Lay back, Luke. Lay back. Everything will be ok. Calm down."

Her voice was irritating to him. He didn't want to calm down. He wanted to know where Ellie was.

He stopped struggling and sat back in his bed and closed his eyes. The spinning seemed to slow. He kept his eyes closed but spoke.

"Deana. Tell me where Ellie is."

Nothing happened for a minute and he thought Deana left, but then he heard her sigh.

"They don't know."

"They?"

"The police. They haven't found her and they haven't heard from her father."

"Her father? What does he have to do with anything and where is she?"

"Her father took her. They thought he was dead, but he's not. He broke into the house and knocked you and Mom out, shot Dad, and left with Ellie. He's the killer, Luke. I'm sorry, but the pool dummy killer took Ellie and it's her dad."

CHAPTER 46

Jaxon was on his eighth shot of Crown and feeling no pain.

At least he kept telling himself that. He was probably in the most pain he'd been in since his son was killed. He was done. It didn't matter one way or the other. The killer had beaten him again and made it look easy.

Jaxon had turned his badge and gun in the night everything went bad and had been locked in his apartment for the past two days.

He hadn't been able to save the girl and the bastard had won. The phone was unplugged and his cell turned off. Someone had banged on the door once, but had left after he would not answer. He had been too drunk to remember who it was.

After the frantic drive to the Harrison home, Victoria working the phones trying desperately to get someone, anyone, to the house, they had arrived to find the officers from the Pemberton home at the scene, trying to get things under control. Three of the Harrison children were hysterical in the yard as they watched their father bleed from a wound in his chest. The ambulances arrived shortly after, and got Luke and his mother and father loaded up and stabilized. Ellie was nowhere to be found.

The two officers who had been rendered unconscious by Worthington, described the man as 'big.' They remembered little else. One said he had horrible dreams of a big purple unicorn trying to suffocate him.

The neighbors had seen very little. One man had witnessed a green Ford Fusion leaving the area after what sounded like a gunshot, but the man had only seen one person in the car. He didn't get the license plate.

Mrs. Pemberton and her son had shown up, hearing the commotion in the neighborhood and noticing their protectors missing. She had been frantic at the disappearance of her daughter and when she saw Jaxon, lashed out at him, screaming he was a murderer.

"You killed my baby!" she screamed, slapping at his chest as another officer held her back. "You killed my baby! You promised! You promised to keep her safe! You promised!"

By then the news crews had arrived and the whole scene went out live to all the local networks. Jaxon slumped under the weight of her accusations. What could he say? She was right. Victoria stood silently next to him, tears rolling down her cheeks. She had been as devastated as he.

Later, driving to the station, Victoria said two words.

"I'm sorry."

He didn't respond.

Arriving at the station, he left her sitting in the car and walked up to the chief's office. He looked the man in the eye and said, "I'm done."

Placing his shield and gun on his desk, he turned and walked out, leaving the chief's protestations fading behind him. When he got to his car, Victoria was gone. He drove home and got drunk.

Now, as he sat in his chair, the Crown Royal doing its job, he couldn't get the sound of Worthington's voice out of his head. *'That's what I told Michael, but you never came.'*

A pounding sound slowly brought him out of his stupor. Then a familiar voice followed the hammering.

For a moment he mistook it for his dead partner Sally, but then he realized it was Victoria. He didn't want to talk to her, so he poured another shot and slammed it down. The pounding went on for a bit longer and then it stopped. At least she had gotten the point.

Closing his eyes and leaning his head back, a vision of Michael and Victoria swam up from the depths.

They had been at Bethany Beach in Delaware. Michael was seven. Jaxon had rented some fishing poles for the day and was showing his son how to use them. The boy couldn't cast the big rigs on his own so Jaxon would wade into the surf, cast as far as he could, and then walk it back to the beach for Michael to hold. He had gotten a bite on the first cast. They laughed and howled as they reeled the fish in, but when he could see the fishing line drop off into the surf, Michael thought he had lost the fish. He looked so disappointed. Jaxon told him he'd catch another.

When Jaxon walked up to look at the leader and hook, he had been pleasantly surprised. He called Michael over and showed him the flat fish lying hidden in the surf. It was a flounder and Michael had jumped with joy. The fish had almost fooled them. Victoria had been so excited for Michael and she took a ton of pictures with him proudly holding up his catch. That had been a good day.

Somebody was shaking him. He slowly came back to reality and opened his eyes to find Victoria standing over him.

"How did you get in?" he slurred.

"I got the Super to open it," she said.

He nodded.

"I left Holt," she said matter-of-factly and sat on the couch across from him.

He didn't know how to take this.

He couldn't seem to make himself care one way or another. He was beyond numb and his aptitude for compassionate thought had left him hours ago. It still surprised him though.

"Why would you do that?"

She just stared at him, a look of such sorrow on her face a little twinge of compassion crept its way back into his mind. Just a sliver, but it was there.

"Don't do this," she said.

He waved a hand at her and then tried to stand up. He didn't make it.

Falling back into his chair, he kicked the bottle of Crown over and it spilled out onto the carpet. He tried to reach for it but couldn't get to it. She didn't move.

"Stop it," she said, but he continued to reach for the bottle. He felt like an infant trying to crawl across the floor for the first time.

She finally got up and grabbed the bottle from the floor. He smiled and reached his hand up for it. She turned and walked out of the room and when she returned she was holding a soda.

"Drink this," she said. "You need the caffeine."

"I want my Crown." he complained, but took the can of soda anyway. "You don't know everything," he said.

"I know you're going to drink yourself to death unless you get a grip on this."

He tried to focus on her face, but she kept swimming in and out of his line of site.

"I think I'm gonna blow."

"Good," she said. "That will help."

He must have looked green because she moved quickly and returned with a trash can. She made it just in time. When he was done, he could think a little clearer.

"Better?" she said.

He sipped the soda, but said, "No. I don't want to feel better. I don't want to feel anything at all."

"The girl is still alive."

He stopped mid-sip and tried to absorb what she had just said.

"Come again."

"Eliana Pemberton is still alive. He sent us a message a little while ago. Actually, he sent it to the whole country."

He was processing information a little slowly still and he didn't quite grasp what she told him.

"Ellie?"

She nodded, smiling now. She leaned closer to him and grabbed his hand.

"She's still alive. You need to get your shit together if we're going to help her."

He looked into her brown eyes and saw she was telling the truth. Something nudged back into place inside of him and he took a breath.

"What did it say?"

"The message?"

He nodded.

"Maybe you should wait 'till you're sober."

"No," he said firmly. "I need to hear it now."

She looked him in the eyes again and nodded.

"Let's go turn the TV on," and she stood, reaching for his hand to help him up.

"TV?"

"Yes."

He grabbed her hand and suddenly felt a little better. He was beginning to feel again and maybe that was a good thing. He stood slowly and leaned on her all the way into the kitchen where his little TV sat on the counter. She turned it on and tuned it to the local CBS affiliate. The story was still running.

CHAPTER 47

Ellie was bound to a chair in some kind of basement.

She could hear water dripping nearby just behind her and someone periodically moving around above her through the ceiling. She had no idea how long she had been down here, only that her wrists ached and she had to pee.

She was still groggy from whatever her father had used to knock her out, and her mouth tasted like rubber. It made her a little nauseous and she wished she could have a drink of water. Her mouth was so dry her tongue kept sticking to the roof of her mouth.

"Hello," she tried to shout, but her voice was just a hoarse squeak.

She tried to conjure up some saliva but nothing seemed to come.

"Hello!"

She managed a little louder this time and she heard what sounded like a chair slide across the floor above her and then footsteps as someone walked over her. A door opened and the footsteps made their way down a staircase getting closer to her. She started to squirm.

The man she now knew as her father came from behind her and stood towering in front of her. He was huge and she remembered trying to run into him that night in front of Mr. Lolly's house. It had been like hitting a brick wall.

He smiled at her and reached out a hand to touch her face. She flinched and turned away. When he did not touch her, she opened her eyes and saw he was now frowning. He moved behind her and worked on her wrists, untying the bindings. Her hands came free and she rubbed them trying to work some feeling back into them.

"Can I have a drink?" she asked.

He walked to a mini-fridge and pulled out a bottle of water. Handing it to her, he sat down in a chair in front of her. She gulped the cold water too fast and started coughing on it. She couldn't help it, it felt so good.

"Go easy," he said. "It will make you sick."

She was surprised at the deep voice. She expected some babbling psychotic fool, but he sounded normal.

"What are you going to do with me?" she asked.

"Keep you with me for a bit," he said.

"Why?"

"You have a purpose in this life and you and I are going to fulfill it."

She wasn't following him and her confusion must have shown on her face because he almost chuckled.

"You are destined for something special and I will help you reach it."

"What am I destined for?"

"Not now," he said standing. He pointed to the mini-fridge. "Drinks and snacks are in there." He pointed to another door. "Bathroom there. You cannot escape from here, so don't even try. You'll waste your energy and probably hurt yourself. There are no windows and only one door out which is metal and barred with a padlock and strong hasp."

He turned and walked for the steps.

"You are my father," she said.

He looked at her like she was accusing him of something, which in fact she was.

"Only in blood."

He climbed the stairs and she heard him locking the door behind him. She was alone.

She stood weakly and had to hold on to the back of the chair until the room stopped spinning. Maybe she should sit back down. Looking around the unremarkable space, she saw shelves behind her that held only a few old tin cans and a dilapidated cardboard box. Leaning up against the shelf was a mop inside of a bucket. The floor was bare concrete and the only other furnishings were the chair she had been tied to, the chair her father had sat on, the mini-fridge, and a small table.

She walked slowly around the space and stopped at the door for the bathroom. She opened it and groaned.

The bathroom was a closet with a toilet seat sitting on top of a five gallon bucket. A roll of toilet paper was sitting on the floor next to it. She didn't know if she could do this, but she had to go so bad her screaming bladder won.

It hadn't been too awful. At least she wouldn't have to pee her pants.

Feeling a little stronger, she walked over to the mini-fridge and opened it up. A few bottles of water and a single diet soda were on the top shelf. On the bottom sat a turkey sandwich from a vending machine, an orange, a package of peanut butter crackers, and a Ding Dong snack cake.

She grabbed the sandwich package and opened it. Taking a bite, she gagged and then spit it out. It was bad. Swigging some more water and rinsing her mouth out, she went into the bathroom and spit the water into the bucket. He was trying to poison her.

She decided she wasn't hungry, so she went over to the shelf and looked in the tin cans and the box. Nothing of any value in the cans, just some rusty bolts and screws, but the box was a surprise. It was filled with old pictures. Snapshots of her mother and him.

She took the box and pulled the chair over to the small table and started going through them. He must have put them in some kind of chronological order because they started off with pictures of the two very young. They looked so happy.

Wedding pictures followed along with pictures in front of what looked like a new car, then the house she now lived in with her mother. The trees in the yard were so small and new. Her mother and father (she couldn't get used to calling him that) were standing in front of the house smiling and holding what looked like a keychain up for the camera.

The next picture was of them both standing in the kitchen with tags still hanging from the appliances. She was looking at him, so happy and content. This couldn't be the same man who had killed all those kids and now held her captive.

There seemed to be a big jump in time, because the next picture was of her brother as an infant. He was chubby and pink, and holding on to a giant finger. Her father was smiling. The next picture showed the two of them together out front with him holding the baby. He was beaming, but her mother was not smiling. Ellie had no idea who the photographer was.

She flipped through more pictures of the growing family and a trend was beginning to show. Her father looked happy most of the time, though a few shots looked strained, but her mother rarely smiled and in a few, she wore huge, dark sunglasses that covered half of her face.

Her brother was growing and there were pics of him crawling, sitting in a high chair, standing and holding on to a table, and playing with some toys. Her mother was not in any of those.

There was one picture of a house she did not recognize. Neither her mother nor her father were in it.

The last ten or so were something else entirely and she held on to each one, feeling the anguish her mother must have been feeling. She was pregnant and standing alone, or a step or two away from her husband. He was glowering in most of them, and she never smiled. In one, her mother appeared to have a bruise on her cheek. She wasn't sure though, because all of these last ten or so had giant red 'X's' drawn over her mother's face. Added to the last picture in big red letters was the word, 'Bitch!'

Ellie sat there holding the pictures in her hand, trying to put herself in her mother's shoes. She shivered at the thought.

Her mother had suffered for a long time and this man had been the sole cause of it.

Ellie wondered when her mother realized she had married a psychopath. Was it the first year? Second? Or had she known all along, living in denial? Ellie hoped to be able to ask her one day. Somehow she felt her father had other plans.

Putting the box back on the shelf she returned to the chair and sat.

And sat.

And sat.

She had no sense of time. No clock, no windows, no outside noises to give her any clue.

She slept on the cold floor when she was tired and drank the water when she was thirsty. The crackers and orange hadn't lasted very long, and now she was down to one Ding Dong and one bottle of water. She had not seen or heard her father since that first visit. She wondered when he would return and yet hoped he wouldn't.

The hours and minutes dragged on and she longed to see daylight, or moonlight, or anything that would give her a sense of perspective.

She thought of Luke a lot, his face smiling at her and his tender hands holding her and stroking her hair. The last time she had seen him, he had been lying on the kitchen floor, either dead or unconscious. She hadn't had time to check as the madman chased her through the house. She felt sure he was alive, though, because she could sense him.

She thought of her mother too. Even her loser brother at times, but for the most part she thought of her father and what he was going to do with her. Her imagination ran wild with scenes of him torturing her, or beating her, or even killing her. She had no idea what he meant by her having a destiny and he would help her fulfill it. It drove her crazy and at the same time filled her with dread.

Some time had passed when she heard footfalls on the ceiling above her, then the jangle of keys and the door to her prison opened. The footsteps made their way down the stairs and then her father came in to view carrying a video camera, tripod, and some white poster board. She was terrified.

He set the things down on the floor and pointed to the chair and said, "Bring that over here and sit down in it."

She didn't move.

"Now!" he shouted and it made her jump.

She stood and went to the chair, sliding it over to the middle of the room and sitting as she was told. He went behind her and bound her hands together again.

"That's good," he said. "If you behave and do what I say, you'll only be hindered for a short time."

He bound her tightly, but not too uncomfortably. At least the circulation continued through her wrists.

"What is all that?" she asked.

"You're going to be a star," he said and smiled.

He set up the tri-pod directly in front of her and mounted the video camera to it, aligning it to her position. He turned the camera on and pressed a button. A red light appeared for a few seconds as he looked through the view finder and he said, "Say something."

"What do I say?"

"That's fine." He turned the camera off.

He disappeared behind her for a few minutes and then reappeared with the white poster board in his hands. He set that down and disappeared behind her again. She heard a scraping noise and a clunk and then he set something down behind her she could not see. She started to shake.

He spoke directly into her ear from close behind her and it made her jump.

"You're going to read what's printed on the cards when I hold them up. You'll read exactly what's on them and nothing more. You can read, correct?"

She nodded.

"Now, this isn't going to be too pleasant, but it's necessary for the effect."

She barely had time to process what he had just said when liquid was poured over her head from behind. The smell immediately assaulted her and she started gagging as soon as she realized what it was.

He had poured the bucket of urine over her and she was drenched in her own piss.

He stepped around her to the camera as she gasped for breath, the reeking ammonia smell making her eyes burn and tear up. He held up the first card and turned the camera on.

"Read," he said.

She couldn't see the letters and she couldn't catch her breath. She was sobbing now and struggling against the restraints as she tried to get away from the awful liquid soaking her clothes and skin.

"Read!" he shouted.

She concentrated on the card and a few words came into focus. Shaking and sobbing she read:

"I am Eliana..." she stopped.

"Read!"

"I am Eliana *Worthington*. I am alive...for now." She sobbed harder. "I am being held by a man who loves me." She looked quickly at him, but he shook the card at her to continue. "He will let me live if his demands are met."

He changed cards.

The urine and ammonia burned her eyes and now her skin was starting to sting. The words swam in and out of focus.

"Detective Jaxon Jennings is to locate me and attempt a rescue. If he does not..." she had to stop, she couldn't see for the burning in her eyes.

"Read, damn you!"

"I can't! My eyes burn and I can't see!"

She drooled as she spoke and felt bile rising in her throat. He turned the camera off and approached her with a towel. He wiped her eyes roughly and went back behind the camera. He pressed the record button again.

"Read."

She focused on the words and tried again.

"If he doesn't find me in three days, I will be killed." The card was swapped for another. "My father will only allow one clue and you have already seen it. You have three days." The card dropped and she pleaded with him. "Please! Don't do this! You're my father! Please!"

He turned the camera off and went upstairs leaving her tied to the chair.

He returned a few moments later and set something else down on the floor behind her. She braced for whatever else was coming, but instead she felt his hands as they untied her bindings and he told her to stand. He gathered the tri-pod and camera and carried them to the stairs. He turned before climbing them and said, "Clean yourself up. You stink."

He nodded at two buckets on the floor by her and she could see one was filled with soapy water and the other fresh. He tramped up the stairs and locked the door behind him. She sat back down and sobbed for a long time.

CHAPTER 48

Jaxon watched the video end and the local newscaster go on to say, "The disturbing video of Eliana Worthington was delivered to the station at seven o'clock this morning. The man she speaks of is her father, Leonard Worthington, who the police are seeking in the deaths of a number of teens in the DC Metro area. Dubbed the Swimming Pool Killer, he has led the authorities on a number of wild goose chases, and is believed responsible for the death of local Fairfax County Police detective, Sally Winston, along with a number of Indiana police officers, SWAT team members, and FBI agents who were lured into his supposed residence in Hobart, Indiana last month, and then killed in the subsequent explosion.

"The Fairfax County Police Department has remained unusually quiet and the FBI has refused comment. What this reporter wants to know is where is the detective who was so prominently mentioned in the video? Why has Detective Jaxon Jennings, the lead investigator on the case, disappeared? An exhaustive search performed by Mel Jacobs in our investigative department indicates that he is holed up in his apartment and refuses to acknowledge anyone on the outside. We go now live to Mel at the Oaktier Apartment complex for an update."

The picture segued into a shot of the outside of his apartment building and Jaxon groaned.

"Shut it off," he said.

Victoria stepped to the small set and flipped the switch.

"When did this first air?" he said.

"Four hours ago."

He rubbed his face and sat forward, bracing his elbows on his knees.

"I've got to sober up. Can you make coffee while I shower?"

She smiled and said, "Of course."

He stood slowly and went to step past her to the bathroom, but she grabbed his arm.

"We only have three days."

"He's calling me out. You know that, right?"

She nodded.

"I believe this has always been about you. He's using the girl to get to you."

"Yeah. Well, it's working."

She stared into his bloodshot eyes as if trying to find something he needed. He looked away.

"I've got your back," she said.

He turned to her and pressed his forehead against hers. "I know. Thanks."

"Now, go shower," she said, pushing him away. "And brush your teeth. You're killing me."

* * *

Luke watched the news from his hospital bed, sat up immediately and began dressing.

As he tied the laces on his shoes, Deana and his grandmother walked in with balloons and some comic books.

"Did they release you?" his grandmother asked.

"No."

"Then, what are you doing?"

"I'm leaving."

"Oh no you're not, young man. You had quite a bump on your head. You can't just get up and leave."

"You can't stop me," Luke said.

He grabbed his cell phone and headed for the door. Deana grabbed his arm.

"You can't help her," she said quietly. "You know that, right?"

"I can't if you don't let go of me."

He stared at her hand on his arm and then glared at his sister.

She let go. "What are you going to do?"

"Find her," he said as he strode out of his room. "Then, I'll kill that son-of-a-bitch."

His grandmother shouted after him, "Lucas Neal Harrison, you get back here this instant!"

Her voice faded as he turned in to a stairwell and descended to the ground floor. Luke's head still ached continuously, but the dizziness seemed to be in check. It didn't matter anyway, he'd ignore everything to get to her before it was too late.

Something had snapped inside him as he watched Ellie in front of that camera, soaked in some gross liquid he couldn't even guess at. She looked terrified and the fear she was feeling bore right into his heart, searing a place in it that could not be cooled until he knew she was safe.

He had to find her! The police were useless and Jaxon was nowhere to be found. She had no one to help her, and he knew that the terror she felt at being all alone was more than she could bear.

Exiting the front door of the hospital, he pulled out his cell phone and called Jimmy.

"Did you get your car yet?"

"Hey, man! Yeah. How are you? Are you home yet? Have you seen the news?"

"Just be quiet for a second," Luke snapped. "I need you to come get me at the hospital. Now."

"Uh—ok. What's wrong?"

"Ellie's what's wrong! You saw the news right? Now hurry and come pick me up. I'll be out front. Bring John too."

"All right—I'm on it! What're you gonna do?"

"You mean what are we gonna do? We'll talk when you get here. Hurry!"

He hung up and waited. For some reason, he was not afraid.

* * *

As Jaxon and Victoria exited his apartment, they were mobbed by reporters and bystanders shouting questions and accusations at them.

The throng encircled them, keeping them from getting to the car in the street and shoving microphones and camera lenses in their faces as they tried to get him to talk. The voices were like gunshots to his head and Victoria glanced at him, a little worried. He held up his hand for them to be silent and they slowly quieted, waiting for him to say something.

One reporter insisted on badgering him anyway.

"Detective! Why have you not responded to Eliana's pleas? How could you ignore that innocent child's request?"

The crowd was dead silent now, waiting breathlessly for his response. Jaxon saw the cameras and microphones jostling for the best position hoping to get the best shot or the best sound bite.

"I have only one thing to say to you people," he said through clenched teeth, "and I'm only going to say it once. Move out of the way or I will pull out my gun and shoot every one of you mother fuckers."

Any other day, the shock on their faces would have made him laugh, but he was dead serious and he had to make sure they knew that. Hell, he didn't have a job anyway.

Nobody moved or made a sound for about fifteen seconds, so Jaxon reached inside of his jacket as if reaching for his gun. The crowd shifted out of the way rapidly and he let his hand fall back to his side. Victoria led the way to the car, a small smile on her face and when they reached it a few of the reporters found their voices again despite the threat.

"What are you going to do?"

"You can't threaten us like that. We have the right!"

"Are you going to find her Detective?"

"Are you just going to let her die?"

He paused as he entered the car and then stood back up.

"No," he said and they drove away.

* * *

Jimmy picked Luke up in front of the hospital in a black, 2001 Isuzu Rodeo.

As he got in, his phone rang. It was a number he didn't recognize but he answered it anyway. It was his mother.

"Lucas. What are you doing?"

"Mom, I don't have time for this right now."

"You're going to have to make time for me. Where are you?"

"Heading home."

"You need to come back to the hospital right now! They have not ok'd you to leave. Besides, Deana tells me you're going to look for Ellie? What the hell is wrong with you?"

His mother had never cursed at him and as he thought through the situation, he really didn't blame her for being so upset.

"Mom, I know you won't understand…"

"Try me."

"The cops botched this and now Ellie is gone. Did you see her on TV? He's torturing her and then he's going to kill her. I can't let that happen."

"Nobody wants that to happen, Lucas. Especially not me, but you have no training, no back-up and no right to traipse off to who knows where hunting for your girlfriend. You could get yourself killed. This madman is not playing games and even if you were lucky enough to find her, you don't stand a chance against him. Come back to the hospital. If you won't do that, at least stay home while the police and FBI find Ellie and bring her back."

"They won't find her. They couldn't even find him before. Jaxon got his partner killed and then he let Smi…Worthington take Ellie from our house. Jaxon promised to keep us safe, and now he's been missing and nobody knows where he is."

"He was just on TV. He's going after Worthington as we speak. He and his ex-wife, the FBI lady. Please, Lucas. Please come back."

"I'm hanging up Mom."

"No! Dammit! As your mother, I'm ordering you to obey me! When your father is better, he's going to beat your hide harder than you've ever been beaten!"

"That doesn't scare me, Mom. Being without Ellie does." And he hung up.

Jimmy and John were staring at him.

"What? Let's go. To my house."

Jimmy put the Rodeo in drive and pulled out through the parking lot. He drove carefully, doing the speed limit, and in some cases just under it. Luke wanted to get to the house, but since Jimmy was a brand new driver, he let it go.

"What's the plan?" John asked, after a few moments of silence.

"We go after him."

"That's all well and good, Luke, but how do you think we're going to be able to do that?"

"I'll get my dad's gun and you guys have your hunting rifles. All three of us should be able to take him out."

"What the hell are you talking about!" John yelled and Luke just looked straight ahead. "We aren't cops. And we aren't killers, at least I'm not. And you're missing one other important point—we...don't...know...where...he...is!"

Luke turned slowly in his seat and glared at John.

"This is Ellie were talking about," he said. "Apparently she isn't worth it for you two to risk your lives. I for one cannot go on without her, so it's fine if you don't want to help. I'll do it on my own. I just thought I'd have a better chance if I had some friends backing me up, but I guess I don't really have the friends I thought I did."

"Calm down, Luke," Jimmy said.

"I won't! Dammit! He's going to kill her!"

"We'll help," Jimmy said. "Right, John?"

John looked back and forth between his brother and Luke, and Luke could see the fear in his eyes.

"I'm not scared, John," Luke said. "I feel pissed and I'm going to take my anger out on him. If you don't want to do this, I won't hold it against you. But I'm going after him."

John sighed.

"All right. I'm in. I can't let Ellie down and let you get yourself killed along with her."

"Thanks, my friend." Luke put a hand on his shoulder and squeezed. "I was hoping I wouldn't have to do this alone."

"How are we going to find him?" John asked.

"The same way as before," Luke said. "He may be smart, but he's got an ego bigger than all of DC and I bet we can trick him into making a mistake."

"We don't know his cell phone number anymore," John said. "He's not using the phone we know."

Luke nodded. "I know someone we can call."

* * *

Jaxon walked in to the station with Victoria next to him, officers staring at them and reporters keeping their distance.

Stansfield came up and said, "The chief wants to see you."

"I want to see him too," Jaxon said and walked past him to Benton's office.

A few of the officers gave him a thumbs up but most avoided eye contact. Jaxon was not very popular at the moment. He knocked on the door and Benton yelled, "Enter!"

Jaxon pushed the door open and strode in. Benton was on the phone, seated at his desk. He mumbled something into the handset and hung it up.

"Nice of you to show up," he said.

"I want back in."

"Too late for that," Benton said. "I've already processed your paperwork and Stansfield is running the case now."

"I don't care. Worthington is pointing directly at me and I need to point back. He isn't going to listen to anybody else."

"Too bad you didn't think of that the other day when you stormed in and threw your badge and gun on the desk. That stunt you just pulled with the reporters didn't help either. The mayor and the district attorney don't want you anywhere near this thing. You've fucked it up enough."

"Dammit! This is bullshit!" Jaxon shouted slamming his fist on the desk. "You and I both know this little girl is going to die unless I get involved!"

Benton stood and leaned over the desk into Jaxon's face.

"All I see is a drunk, washed up fool who may have already sealed the fate of a young girl! And you," Benton pointed at Victoria who had remained silent in the back of the office. "You need to call your boss immediately. Use the phone in the office next door."

Victoria remained where she was.

"That is not a request Special Agent Elliot. It's an order."

Victoria moved away from the wall and walked out the door without saying a word.

"Dammit, Jaxon! I was on your side until you disappeared for two days and then threatened the media with violence. You're a cop. You do know you could be brought up on assault?"

"I didn't draw a weapon."

"You don't have a weapon."

"It worked," Jaxon said and grinned.

Benton sighed and sat down.

"It did, didn't it? Still, my ass is in a sling because of you and the chief of the NBC affiliate was screaming at me on the phone before you got here."

"I needed to get moving and they were in my way."

Benton waved his hand at him dismissing it.

"I don't have anything for you. My hands are tied."

"I expected a little more from you, chief. A helping hand, you know…stand behind your man and all that stuff."

Jaxon watched Benton's face turn red and he knew he'd gone too far.

"You are to vacate these premises effective immediately," Benton said. "And if you return, I'll have you thrown in the tank without so much as a fuck you very much. Do I make myself clear?"

"Crystal," Jaxon said, turning to leave.

He stopped and turned back.

"This is on your head. I'll have my cell on when you change your mind."

Jaxon didn't wait for a response. He walked from Benton's office straight out the front door and to his car where he sat fuming, waiting for Victoria.

She followed a few minutes later, a scowl on her face as she strode up to the passenger door and sat in the car. They both stared straight ahead for a few minutes without saying a word and then she finally said, "Well—that was fun."

CHAPTER 49

Luke walked into the empty house with Jimmy and John.

He stood at the entrance and just listened to the silence for a moment. The last time he had been here everything had been almost perfect. Almost.

He walked upstairs and fired up his computer. Logging on to Facebook, he navigated to Quentin Jenson's page and clicked on his friends list. His uncle Bodey was number thirty two. He clicked on Bodey Jenson's face and it took him to his page. Clicking on the About button, he saw he had a website and e-mail listed and surprisingly, a phone number. Jackpot.

"Who's Bodey Jenson?" Jimmy asked.

"It's Q's uncle. He's the one who gave Q the program to decrypt the website that makes a cell phone number anonymous. That's how we got Worthington's cell phone number."

Luke dialed Bodey Jenson's number and it started to ring. It was answered on the sixth ring.

"I don't know you," the voice said, "You'd better not be selling something because I will make your life miserable. If you hang up now, we're good."

"Bodey Jenson?" Luke asked.

"You know me," Bodey said. "Who is this?"

"My name is Luke Harrison and I'm a friend of Q's"

Silence on the other line and then Bodey sighed.

"Q's dead."

"I know sir. It's probably my fault. I got him to help me and this maniac killed him for it. I'm sorry."

"My brother, Q's father, was into all kinds of bad shit," Bodey said. "I doubt you had anything to do with it. I tried to get Q away from him, but he wouldn't leave his family. It's not your fault."

"You don't know the whole story," Luke said.

"Enlighten me."

Luke spent the next ten minutes explaining everything to him and when he was done Bodey sat quietly for a moment.

"Are you still there?" Luke asked.

"Just in awe my brother. Just in awe. That kid was always willing to help anyone. I told him to be careful who he messed with, but he wouldn't listen. I can tell you have a lot of guilt over this, but Q was able to make decisions on his own. He made a bad one."

"He saved a kid's life that night," Luke said. "Because of him, we were able to scare Worthington off."

"I appreciate you telling me all this, Luke, but I don't think that's the whole reason you're calling. Am I right?"

"Yes sir. I need your help."

"Is it going to get me killed?"

"I don't think so."

"Not too convincing are you. What do you need and I'll decide if it's worth the risk."

Luke told him.

"So your woman, Ellie is it...?"

"Yes."

"Ellie has been kidnapped by this same guy who killed my brother and his family and you want me to help you find him? Do I have this right?"

"Yes."

"You're psycho, dude," and he chuckled. "Why aren't the police handling this?"

"Because they suck."

"Yes—I imagine they do in your eyes. What does this Ellie mean to you?"

"Everything."

"That epic, huh? You do know you could get yourself killed over this? I don't think I can live with that."

"He's after me anyway. If you want to look at it as self preservation, you can add that to the fact I'd rather be dead than live without Ellie."

"You're kind of young to be this into one girl."

"You don't know her."

"You're right," Bodey said. "I don't. You know, you sound a little older than your real age."

"I've had to grow up a lot in the past few days."

"True that," Bodey said. "Double true. Give me your e-mail and I'll walk you through it."

Luke sighed.

"Thank you, Mr. Jenson. You don't know what this means."

"It's Bodey, since we're so intimate now, and I think I know all too well what this means. Don't get yourself killed kid."

"I've got help."

"I think you're going to need it. E-mail?"

Luke gave it to him and a few minutes later he had the program installed on his computer. Bodey walked him through how to work it. It took a few minutes because it was not very user friendly, but he eventually got the hang of it.

"How are you going to get him to call you?" Bodey asked.

"I'll send him a message on Facebook he can't ignore. He has a huge ego and I'm going to bruise it. He'll respond."

"Got it. If you can't get it to work right, call me back. I give tech support."

Luke actually laughed.

"Thank you, sir—uh—Bodey. You're awesome!"

"Luke?"

"Yeah?"

"Be careful."

"I will."

He hung up.

CHAPTER 50

Ellie woke to find her father standing over her.

"Get up," he said. "Time to move."

She rose slowly, shakily.

She didn't know how much time had passed since the video incident and she hadn't had anything else to eat. She still stunk of urine despite washing herself off and dunking her clothes in the soapy water. She had put them back on wet and lay down on the concrete, shivering. She hadn't wanted him to see her naked. Even if he was her father.

She eventually fell asleep and now he was back.

"Where are we going?"

"Someplace new."

"I thought you wanted Jaxon to find me," she said.

"I don't want to make it easy for him," and he grinned. "He has to prove he's worthy."

"Worthy of what?"

Her father didn't answer.

He told her to turn around and he bound her wrists behind her and then he marched her up the stairs. They emerged into a dingy room with a cot, a chair, a small table, and a hot plate, but nothing else. It had one window and Ellie could see it was dark outside. She felt confused because in her mind she thought it was morning. Her internal clock was all off balance and she had no idea what time it was or even what day.

He pushed her down a hallway and out a door to what looked like a back yard. It was overgrown with weeds as high as her shoulder. Further back, in the dim moonlight, she could see what she thought looked like a small outhouse nestled against a tree. The light was so dim it was hard to tell. A black or brown car was parked by it and he nudged her along toward it.

"No noise, now," he whispered.

He went to the passenger side and pushed her in. Shutting the door he came around, sat in the driver's seat, and reached around behind him grabbing a small bottle and a rag. She knew what was going to happen.

"Please," she said. "I'll be good. You don't have to knock me out."

"Yes I do," he said, soaking the rag with the fluid. A strong astringent odor filled the car and he rolled down the window. "Just hold still and let it do its work. You'll be fine in no time."

She started to cry, but didn't fight him. The rag was pressed to her face and she held her breath.

"You'll have to breathe eventually," he said. "Might as well do it now."

She took a breath and then another and soon the world started spinning. His grinning face, lit only by the moonlight, was what followed her into the blackness. She dreamed for what seemed an eternity, her father's angry voice shouting a single word over and over again: 'Read!'

No matter what she tried, she could not find where the voice was coming from. His low, deep, booming cry seemed to come from everywhere and nowhere. In the dream, she was free to move around and she ran from the command, but she could never get away. It followed her into the darkness, where she finally slept deeply and awakened, stiff and cold on a concrete floor, a thin wool blanket covering her legs.

She sat up shakily and looked around.

She was in a basement again, but someplace new. Another chair was sitting in the middle of the room, pushed up close to a folding card table. A Styrofoam cooler sat against one wall next to a door which stood partially open. It was dark beyond the opening and she could not see into it. If she had to guess, she was pretty sure it was another 'bathroom.'

On her left, a wall of cubbies stood stark and empty against a wall that had a window high up near the ceiling. The glass was painted black but she could see light leaking around the sill. At least she could tell it was daylight.

It was too high for her to reach even if she stood on the table. Maybe if she put the chair up on the table and stood on it she thought it might be within reach. She'd have to try when she wasn't so weak.

Standing slowly, her legs shaking beneath her, she wobbled around the rest of the space finding nothing of interest or value. A set of creaky stairs led to a locked, solid door that echoed when she rapped on it. No one came to answer.

Holding the railing she slowly descended back down, but the room started to spin and she lost her footing. Falling the last couple of steps, she twisted her ankle and cried out in pain as she landed hard on the concrete floor.

She sat there holding it and crying, the despair she felt magnified by her weakened and now injured body. Nobody was going to find her here and no one was coming to save her.

After a few minutes she got herself under control and tried to stand. She limped and hopped over to the Styrofoam cooler and looked inside. There were a few bottles of water, some snacks, and a sandwich nestled in some ice. She grabbed a handful of the cubes and held them to her swelling ankle. Hopefully she'd be able to keep it from swelling too much and stiffening up.

Grabbing the sandwich, she opened it warily and smelled. This one seemed ok and checking the date on it did no good because she had no idea what day it was. She took a tentative bite and chewed slowly. It was glorious. She swallowed whole mouthfuls without even chewing and even though she knew she needed to slow down, she couldn't help herself. She was famished.

She chugged some water after devouring one half of the sandwich, but her stomach revolted and she threw everything back up all over the floor. She started sobbing again, angry at herself for being so foolish and loathing the man who put her in this position.

Sitting on the cold floor, vomit in front of her, her ankle on ice and continuing to swell, a complete feeling of hopelessness washed over her and she actually started to believe she might not live through this.

Her despair was a living thing crawling around inside her.

She moaned aloud in the quiet room, trying desperately to push everything but Luke from her mind. The ache she felt slowly subsided as she closed her eyes and envisioned him in front of her, reaching for her and taking her into his arms. The room grew warmer and the stench of her clothes and vomit faded into the background as she lost herself in the vision.

The tears dried up and she felt a little better. The strength she received from Luke amazed her and she clung to his image like an overboard passenger at sea, hanging on to a life preserver. He was her life preserver and she would never let go. Never let go. Never let go...

CHAPTER 51

Jaxon watched Victoria talk to Holt on the phone.

They had driven to the Hoover building and were now in her office expecting to look over the uncut version of the video Worthington had sent to the networks. Jaxon was rogue now, and they had to be careful. No one seemed to care at the moment who Victoria brought into the building, but if Benton or Holt knew he was here, they would probably arrest him and her too.

They had to be careful, but they had to have information too. They were walking a fine line between investigators and criminals.

"Yes. I know," Victoria said. "I won't let that happen. Dammit Emory! You know I'm the most informed of any one on this case besides Jaxon." A pause. "You can't!" She hung her head and then picked it up again, angrier. "I will not have what is between us endanger this little girl's life! Can you live with your decision to pull me off of this case? If she dies, I will blame you for the rest of my life!"

Silence for a few seconds as Jaxon tried in vain to hear Holt's side of the conversation, but all he heard was noise.

"Yes." She looked relieved. "I can live with that. Twenty four hours is plenty." She was about to hang up when he must have said something else. She nodded to herself and then said, "Thank you," and hung up.

"That didn't sound too good," Jaxon said.

"It didn't start very well, but I got what I need. He gave me twenty four hours to produce some results or he's pulling me off." She stood. "Come on. We've got work to do."

"Where too?"

"Quantico," she said. "They're analyzing the tape there and they have some footage we need to see."

"What is it?"

"Apparently there is a picture that flashes up briefly in the video. Invisible to the naked eye, but they were able to freeze it."

"Did they say what the picture is?"

She nodded.

"It's a house."

An hour later they were in a room at Quantico and the man talking to Victoria held a manila envelope in his hand as he chewed the fat with her. He didn't seem to feel the urgency that Jaxon was feeling and it was getting to him. His head throbbed from the drinking binge and though he had taken a handful of aspirin, it remained a distracting spot of pain just behind his eyes.

"Vick, we need to get moving," Jaxon said, finally.

The man stopped in mid-sentence and turned to Jaxon as if seeing him for the first time.

Victoria covered. "He's right, Tom. Sorry, we need to stay on top of the time. We only have…" she looked at her watch. "Twenty two hours."

"I thought you had three days," Tom said.

"Three days—twenty two hours—two minutes," Jaxon said. "What difference does it make? This little girl is in a horrible place and the quicker we get to her the quicker she'll be away from him. Now, show us the damn picture."

She glared at him but didn't say anything.

Tom said, "All right," and took the picture out and laid it on the table.

Victoria took a quick breath in and Jaxon felt a jolt run through him as if he had been hit by 110 volts.

"I take it, you two recognize this place?" Tom said.

Jaxon looked at her and she said, "Shit."

* * *

Luke was in his parents' room standing in front of the bureau next to the bathroom.

John and Jimmy had gone home for a bit while Luke rested. He needed to get moving, but his body wasn't cooperating. The headache was still going strong and now the dizziness had returned, though not quite as bad as in the hospital.

He had sent Worthington a message on Facebook, but the man had not responded. Luke was worried he may have calculated wrong. Maybe the asshole wasn't going to be tricked into giving his position away and if that was the case, Luke was hopelessly out of the loop. He didn't have the resources the police and FBI had. His only ace in the hole had been Bodey Jenson and his software.

Closing his eyes and picturing Ellie in his head only made things worse. He couldn't seem to think of her without seeing her tied to that chair, reading the message and sobbing uncontrollably.

He clenched his fists and opened his eyes. Looking into the mirror that was over the bureau, he stared at his face.

What he saw shocked him. He didn't recognize it at first. His eyes were sunk deep in their sockets and black smudges were visible under them as if he had bruised them. His hair was sticking up in large clumps and his clothes were wrinkled and stained. They were the clothes he had been wearing the night Ellie was taken.

His mouth was set in a thin line and his brow creased in a permanent scowl. He looked ten years older.

The world started to spin again and he grabbed on to the edge of the bureau and steadied himself. It passed in a few seconds and he took a deep breath. Opening his father's sock drawer, he pushed the black and brown and gray and white socks around until he found what he was looking for. The gun felt huge in his hands, but the weight, pleasantly solid; powerful.

He looked at himself in the mirror again as he held the weapon and didn't like the small grin on his face. He turned away and carried the weapon into his room.

Sitting on the edge of his bed, he popped the clip out and checked the ammo. It looked full.

His dad had said the Glock held fifteen rounds but he didn't know if his dad had fired it the other night. Deana had found it under a bush after the police had left and had placed it in its hiding place. Everybody in the family knew the gun was there.

He carefully popped out each round and held the small brass cache in his hand. Fifteen exactly. Dad had never gotten a shot off. He pressed the bullets back into the clip and then rammed the clip home. His dad had gone over the gun again with him the night before Worthington had shown up and Luke was glad he had insisted on it. The gun felt foreign in his hands, but not so alien he couldn't make it do what it was made to do. He just hoped he'd be able to hit something with it. Namely Worthington.

His phone rang and he looked at the caller ID. He answered Jimmy's call, turning the weapon over in his hands, feeling the weight of the metal. It made him feel powerful.

"Anything yet?" Jimmy asked.

"Nothing."

"What do you want to do?"

"Nothing we can do," Luke said. "We'll have to wait until he gets the message."

"Do you think he'll answer?"

"Yes."

"How can you be so sure?"

"He can't let a kid challenge him like that and not answer. His ego is too big."

"He's smart though. He may just keep quiet. You know, like radio silence in a battle."

"He'll call."

"If he doesn't?"

"He'll call."

"I know you called him out, but what did you say exactly?"

"I called him a pussy and said he couldn't hide from me. I would be coming for her and I wouldn't stop until he was lying on the ground bleeding and dying while I pissed in his face."

"Damn. Yeah, that'd piss me off."

"I'm counting on it."

CHAPTER 52

"It's our house," Victoria said.

"Your house?" Tom asked.

"Well, it was," Victoria said. "It was our first place. Michael was born there."

"You two are married?"

Victoria looked at Jaxon and said, "We were."

Tom turned to Jaxon and said, "You're Jaxon." A statement, not a question.

"Come on, Vick," Jaxon said. "We've got to move."

They both turned and started to walk out.

"I thought you wanted to see the video," Tom shouted after them.

"We've seen it already," Jaxon shouted back.

"If you find anything else in it," Victoria said, "Call my cell. Thanks!"

In the car, Jaxon jammed the accelerator to the floor and put the lights on. His car was still his and they couldn't stop him from using what he had. It took only thirty minutes to make the trip from Quantico to Herndon where the house sat. 90 to 110 MPH got you there fast.

"She's not going to be there," Victoria had said on the way.

"I know."

"We've got to try anyway."

Jaxon knew she was just affirming what they both already knew.

"He'll have left another clue," he said.

She nodded, knowing this to be true. She turned to look at him. "I hope we can figure it out."

"We will. We have to."

She spent a few minutes on the phone briefing Holt on the situation. When she hung up she said, "He offered to send back-up."

"We don't need it."

"That's what I said. I told him they would just be in the way."

"Good."

"He knows you're with me."

"You told him?"

"He guessed."

Jaxon nodded. It made sense. It would be stupid for her to be doing this on her own.

"Is he going to do anything about it?"

"No—not right now."

He stared straight ahead and dodged the traffic.

"He's giving you the same twenty four hours as me and then he's going to have you arrested."

"Screw him."

"No."

She smiled and he caught it out of the corner of his eye. He smiled too and a little of the tension drained out of them. Only a little.

Turning in to the old Herndon neighborhood of Oak Place, Jaxon was appalled at the state of disrepair. The houses that had once been cute and appealing, were now trashy and run down. Sad popped into Jaxon's head. The neighborhood had been his and Vick's first and Michael had been born here. They had moved shortly afterward, when Jaxon had been promoted to detective, his income taking a nice jump.

The streets were littered with garbage and abandoned cars, tires, refrigerators and window A/C units. It was bordering on a slum. As their old house came in to view on the right, he slowed and approached quietly, coasting to a stop one house over. They sat for a second, staring at the ruin of their past life. He felt embarrassed that he had once called this home.

The house sat back about fifty feet from the street, nestled in a yard of weeds and dirt that hadn't seen attention in probably two years. A small, faded, red wagon lay on its side in the middle of the yard, abandoned and apparently useless, one of its wheels missing. No children could be seen or heard anywhere near their immediate vicinity.

The siding hung off in places and the once dark brown paint had faded to what looked like old, dried blood. A few of the window screens were missing, with one hanging tilted in its frame, the screen ripped and torn. The front door was half open and moved slightly in the breeze. The driveway was empty. As a matter of fact, the whole neighborhood looked empty. Not a soul moved about or made a sound. It was like a ghost town.

Jaxon opened his door and stepped out scanning the area. Victoria did the same. Jaxon cleared his throat and the sound seemed horribly loud in the silence. They looked at each other but didn't speak as they walked up to the door and pushed it open.

The inside was a wreck.

Trash and leaves littered the entrance and a broken chair sat blocking the way in. Drywall hung off the studs in jagged tears and spray paint was the primary color on the parts that were left intact. Gang tags and lovers laments greeted the visitors all along the entrance hall. Jaxon kicked the chair out of the way and as they walked in to the main room, he saw the ceiling hadn't been missed either.

"How the hell did they get up there?" Victoria asked, her voice startling him.

"Beats the hell out of me. Come on, let's go to the basement. That's where she was in the video."

Walking into the kitchen, Jaxon was struck by the smell. They both looked at each other in shock.

"Oh no!" Victoria said and dashed through the house to the back where the basement door stood ajar.

The smell was stronger and they hurried down the steps into a dark cave of blackness, the stench of decay overpowering. Jaxon hit the light switch out of habit and was surprised when the basement lit up. Someone had paid for the electricity to be on.

The room was stark and bare except for two chairs, a table, some shelves and a mini fridge. The odor was strong and mixed with the stench of human waste. They went to the closet door and swung it open. The decapitated dog lay in a heap in the corner, flies swarming around it, the source of the smell revealed.

"Thank God," she said and turned away into the room. Jaxon saw the bucket with the toilet seat and put two and two together.

"He dumped her own urine over her," he said.

She turned and looked at him.

"That's why she was wet in the video. He soaked her in her own urine so she would be all freaked out."

Victoria turned away from him, a look of such sorrow on her face he wanted to go to her and hold her, but he knew she would not appreciate it at this moment. She was totally focused on finding the girl.

Scanning the room for any clue, he didn't see much in the way of evidence.

The walls were bare and the shelves mostly empty. The few tin cans on them held rusty nails and discarded screws, but little else. Victoria was squatting near the mini-fridge and he went over to her. She was looking at an old cardboard box full of pictures. She picked it up and carried it to the table.

Inside were pictures of the Worthingtons.

They looked to go back about fifteen years and when he saw the man they were now hunting, memories of the domestic disturbance call he went to at their house flooded back in.

He remembered it all now. The man had been belligerent and out of control. Jaxon had actually been afraid. The man had been huge and wildly drunk. Jaxon was no midget himself, but compared to Worthington he was small. The drunken state he had been in was the only reason Jaxon had been able to subdue him.

The pictures all contained Leonard, Madison and a baby. Jaxon grabbed a picture of the Worthingtons and stared at it closely. He recognized the people in the picture and the house where Ellie and her mother and brother still lived, but nothing else jumped out at him.

"There's nothing here," he said, throwing the picture on the table and looking around the room frustrated. "How the hell are we going to find her?"

"He must have left something. We're missing the obvious," she said. "He's probably put it in plain sight and we've walked right on by. Maybe we need to check the rest of the house."

Jaxon picked up the picture again and waved it at her. "This is the only thing we've seen that ties anything in this house to him. A bunch of shitty family shots that mean nothing!"

Victoria grabbed the hand holding the picture and reached for it. She pulled it from his fingers and worked her fingernail into the edge. A picture had been stuck to the back of the one he had been waving and when she saw it, she smiled. She showed it to him.

"Come on!" he yelled and they bolted toward the stairs.

CHAPTER 53

Luke's cell phone went off.

The music signaling he had a text message jarred him from his sleep and he sat up quickly, unsure of his surroundings. He had been dreaming and in it he and Ellie had been swimming in the pool with Jimmy and John. Nothing ominous or threatening in that simple act, yet the dream left him feeling disjointed and uncertain. It had been too happy considering all that was happening at the moment. His head still throbbed and he had a brief wave of dizziness as he reached for the phone on the nightstand.

The sender's number was all zeroes and his heart skipped a few beats.

"Gotcha' you bastard," he whispered as he opened the text. It read simply, '*Bring it, kid!*'

Luke called John and Jimmy immediately and told them to get their butts over to his house. Worthington had just sent him a message. They were over in less than two minutes.

Luke was plugging his phone into the computer with a USB cable and loading up the program Bodey had e-mailed him when they both bounded in out of breath.

"What did he say?" Jimmy asked.

"He told me to 'Bring it,'" Luke said.

"That's it?"

"That's all it takes," Luke said grinning. "I don't care if he texted me one letter. As long as I receive anything from him, we'll know his new number. Watch."

Luke hit a few keys like Bodey had instructed and the program went to work. A few seconds later a whole list of numbers filled the screen and John said, "Whoa! How do we know which is his?"

"Hold on," Luke said, and clicked a button on the screen. The page changed and more numbers popped up, but an offset area displayed what he needed. He pointed to it and smiled.

"There he is."

Jimmy and John moved in closer and just stared at the ten digits in awe.

Luke wrote the number down and closed the program out, opening the software they had used to track Worthington before. He inputted the cell phone number in the program and clicked 'next.' The screen that popped up was not what Luke expected and he felt deflated.

SEARCHING……..QUERY……A13244997……...EXECUTED ……..UNABLE TO LOCATE GEOSYNCHRONUS POSITION AT THIS TIME………RESCAN AUTOMATICALLY EVERY 30 SECONDS?

"Shit!" Luke said.

"What does that mean?" Jimmy asked.

"I think it means the program can't find the cell number. He must have the phone off. Dammit!"

John pointed to the screen. "It looks like it can keep scanning for it. See?"

Luke looked at the screen closer and saw it. He typed the letter 'Y' into the box and pressed enter and the screen changed.

AUTO SCAN ENABLED……….AUDIBLE NOTIFICATION WHEN FOUND?

Luke typed the letter 'Y' again and hit enter. The system would give some sound when it found the signal. Luke sat back and sighed.

"We wait?" Jimmy asked.

"All we can do," Luke said, and stood up. "I need a drink. Anybody want a soda?"

They stood with him and went downstairs to the kitchen.

CHAPTER 54

As Jaxon ran through the house, Victoria shouted to him, "Jaxon! Wait!"

He stopped and turned. She was just outside the door to the basement and when she saw him look her way, she pointed to something he could not see. He walked back into the room and followed her finger. He hadn't noticed it before.

High up on the wall, mounted near the ceiling, a little gray box aimed its black lens down on them, its blinking red light mocking them. Jaxon walked up to it slowly and then reached up his hand and gave it the finger.

He turned to her and said, "Let's go!"

As he slammed the front door open, Jaxon saw a group of teenagers huddled around his car. They were trying to pop the lock through the driver's window. He didn't even slow down.

They saw him coming and two of them stepped away, but the one working the slim jim never faltered. Jaxon slowed as he got closer, but strode up to the one at the window and, without hesitating, drew the weapon Victoria had given him and pressed the muzzle against the kid's temple.

"I appreciate you wanting to open the door for me, but I've got it."

The kid raised his hands and backed away. Jaxon thought he was going to piss his pants. The other two looked about to help their buddy, but Victoria had her FBI credentials out and her weapon pointed directly at them.

"Don't fucking move!" she said. They froze.

Jaxon shoved the kid out of the way, grabbed the slim jim from his window and threw it over the house as hard as he could. He beeped the locks with the remote and slipped into his seat at the same time as Victoria. He started the car and rolled down the window.

"Have a nice day," and floored the accelerator, laying down rubber for a hundred yards. "Fuckers," he said under his breath and Victoria chuckled.

"Their lucky day," she said.

He nodded.

The house they were speeding off to surprised them both, yet now that he knew Worthington's next move, maybe it wasn't such a surprise. The picture had been a shot of Jaxon and Victoria's second house. The one they were in when their marriage ended, the bank taking it in foreclosure. The one Michael was killed in. It was the only picture that didn't fit.

"He knows we're on to him," Victoria said, holding on tight as he took a sharp turn at high speed, the tires squealing in protest.

"He's going to move her again, I know. We have to find a way to predict his next move."

"He's guiding us to exactly where he wants us. Are we going to let him lead us right into a trap?"

"At this point, we don't have any other choice."

"He's always one step ahead. We have to find a way to cut him off."

"I'm racking my brain, Vick! I'm not coming up with anything. Are you?"

She looked away angrily, "No. But he's giving us easy stuff to use. Think about it. That picture was obvious."

"We wouldn't have seen it if you hadn't peeled it from the other one."

"But I don't think he meant that to happen. I think it was random. I'm sure he planted that picture in there for us to find easily, but we almost missed it because it was stuck to the back of another picture."

"What are you saying?"

"We've bitten on the easy bait. We've missed something that might give us an edge."

He thought about this but could not put anything together in his head that made any sense. The pictures in the box were the only things associated with Worthington and Ellie in the whole house.

"What were the other pictures of?" he asked, grabbing onto the only thing he felt was important.

"Worthington and the Mrs. Family shots. Kids and first houses, and toys and cars."

It made no sense. Who cares about Worthington's old family memories. His hate for his wife made the sentimental value of the shots unimportant, so why were they in the basement?

"Were the pictures for Ellie?" Jaxon asked. "To make her see he's not as bad a guy as she believes?"

"That doesn't make sense. There were pictures with her mother crossed out of them. A big red 'X' right across her face."

"We know he hates her. Does he want Ellie to hate her too?"

"They weren't meant for Ellie," she said. "They were meant for us."

"How can you be sure?"

"Ellie would never hate her mother. He knows that. And the picture of our house was in there too. Those pictures are ours."

He knew she was right.

They turned in to the neighborhood about fifteen minutes later as dusk was settling over the city and streetlights were starting to come on.

The neighborhood was still clean and very lived in. Manicured lawns were the norm and children played in the fading light, mothers calling to them to come home and fathers pulling in to driveways from a long day at work.

The house they used to live in sat back in a court off of the main road. As they pulled up, they were surprised to see an old for sale sign in the overgrown yard, the faded red letters announcing, 'Foreclosure' and 'Reduced.' Apparently it had not been lived in since they had abandoned it.

They parked in front of it and stepped out of the car into the muggy night.

Jaxon could hear a dog barking in the distance and the sound of a television turned up too loud in one of the houses. A man stood on his porch three doors down, smoking a cigarette and looking their way. He ignored him and strode up the driveway with Victoria beside him.

He tried the door, it was unlocked, and he drew his pistol as he pushed it open. The house was dark and quiet.

He looked at Victoria who nodded and then positioned herself behind the door, her gun out to cover him. He slipped inside and she followed. They went directly to the basement, both of them scanning the walls and ceiling for blinking red lights and remaining alert in case Worthington was somehow still here. He doubted it though.

They went through the kitchen and stepped to the basement door. A red light caught his eye and he pointed to it, the web cam just within reach. He knocked it off of the wall and crushed it beneath his shoe. He turned and looked at Victoria who shrugged.

He was reaching for the doorknob when his cell phone vibrated in his pocket. Even with the ringer off, the buzzing seemed extraordinarily loud in the silent house. He hesitated, raising his eyebrows to her but she shook her head, 'no.' He'd check it later.

The door swung open on quiet hinges and he reached into the dark. If anybody was down there, they were hiding in the blackness. The void below them remained eerily silent.

Jaxon went first and felt his way along the steps, the feel of them stirring up memories of the house when his life had been happy and full.

It was surreal stepping down into a hole of blackness, feeling nostalgic and terrified all at the same time. He pushed the memories from his mind and concentrated on keeping his footing in the dark.

Reaching the bottom landing he panned around the space, but the little bit of light leaking from the open door above provided nothing he could discern and the space felt empty. He didn't know how he knew this, just a cop's sixth sense and one he didn't analyze, so he lowered his gun and holstered it, moving to the light switch and flipping it up. Nothing happened.

"I guess the electricity was too expensive to turn on here," he said, his voice booming in the quiet dark. Something moved behind him and he spun, pulling his weapon out and crouching low. Victoria turned on the flashlight she brought from the car and shone the beam around, keeping her body hidden behind the stairwell wall in case somebody shot at the light source. Jaxon followed the light beam and then saw a rat the size of a small kitten skitter through the beam and disappear into a hole in the wall. He relaxed and lowered the gun.

The basement was empty.

CHAPTER 55

Ellie woke to a rag being pressed hard against her face and the familiar fumes invading her lungs.

The world spun, and then she was out again. She had dreams of being carried away by a cool stream, the raft she floated on bobbing easily in its gentle wake. The water faded and she dreamt of home. Her mother, brother, and even Bentley. The feel and smell of her house comforted her and cradled her in a feeling of peace and warmth, safety and familiarity. Then it shifted again and she dreamt of blood.

* * *

Jaxon and Victoria searched the basement with her flashlight for thirty minutes and found nothing. It was barren. A chair, table, and Styrofoam cooler were all that remained of the missing Ellie. Apparently, she had gotten sick on the floor and Jaxon worried she was being tortured.

The urgency he felt ramped up a notch and his nerve endings felt fried.

He was jittery and the headache that had followed him all day grew stronger, with white pinpoints of light invading the perimeter of his vision. He didn't need a migraine now and he downed four more aspirin, dry, his acid stomach protesting but letting him keep it down.

"Who called you?" Victoria finally asked as they made their way back up the stairs.

Jaxon had completely forgotten about his phone vibrating while they entered the basement. He pulled out the phone and looked at the caller ID. It was a number he didn't recognize and the icon for a voice mail blinked in the upper left corner.

"I got a voice mail," he said and let it play out through the speaker.

"Mr. Jennings?" a young female voice said. "This is Deana Harrison. Luke's sister. Can you please call me back? Luke has left the hospital and says he's going to find Ellie. I'm scared! My parents are still in the hospital and we need your help. Call me back as soon as you get this."

"Damn that kid!" Jaxon said. "This is all we need."

"Call her back," Victoria said. "Maybe he's come to his senses and returned to the hospital."

Jaxon called and the phone was answered almost immediately. Deana told him what had happened and what she thought Luke was going to do.

"When did he leave?" Jaxon asked her.

"About eight hours ago."

"And you're just telling me this now?"

"I'm sorry," she said and started to cry. "My mother tried to talk to him, but he wouldn't listen. We didn't know what to do."

"All right," he said. "It's all right. I'll find him. We won't let anything happen."

She cried a little more and he reassured her they would get to him before he did anything stupid. She seemed to relax a little and he was finally able to get her off the phone so he could try and call the Harrison boy.

"How long has he been out?" Victoria asked.

"Eight hours."

"Shit!"

"Yeah. Let me see if he'll answer the number I have for him."

He scrolled through his call log list and found the number, dialing it. It rang eight times and just when he was about to hang up, Luke answered it.

"Have you found her?" Luke said, the excitement in his voice palpable through the connection.

"No," Jaxon said. "And I don't need you keeping me from my job."

Luke was silent for a moment and then Jaxon could hear the disappointment and anger in his voice.

"From what I hear, you don't have a job."

"That won't keep me from finding her, but if you're out there blundering around in the dark, it only makes my job harder. What the hell do you think you're doing?"

"What you can't," Luke said and Jaxon winced.

"Don't do this. I don't have time to be protecting you while I hunt for her. Stay at home."

"You can't stop me. And I have the edge."

"What are you talking about?"

"You couldn't find him before," Luke said, "but we did. And we'll find him again."

"Don't be messing with this guy. You know what he's capable of. Just about your whole family is in the hospital because of him. If you're willing to risk your life and theirs, then by all means keep doing what you're doing, but this man will hunt you down and take everything that means anything from you."

"He already has."

"Dammit Harrison! I'm warning you! Stay out of it!"

"Too late."

"What are you talking about?"

"He's already contacted me. We can track him."

"Then give the information to me," Jaxon said quickly. "Victoria and I can stop him. We have the whole DC Metro area police force behind us. Tell me where he is."

Silence.

"Harrison?"

"I don't know where he is yet. But I will soon."

"Give me what you have then."

"No. You botched it before, you'll botch it again."

Jaxon turned to Victoria looking for help. He was losing and didn't know what to do. She signaled for the phone.

"Hold on," Jaxon said and handed the phone to Victoria. She put it on speaker.

"Luke, this is Victoria. You can't do this alone. You know that."

"I have help."

"Even if you do, you're putting your friends' lives at risk. Can you live with that? Think about what you're asking of them. Is it worth their lives for you to stumble around blindly, anger this man, and get them killed?"

"They know what's at stake. They're with me."

"I can tell you have your mind made up and I know what Ellie means to you. She means the world to me and I'm sorry we failed her. But we will not fail again. We will not let her die! Jaxon and I are willing to give up everything to save her. Let us do our job. If you won't listen to reason, then at least let us work together."

"You had your chance," Luke said. "She's where she is because of you two."

"I don't blame you for being angry, but don't risk her life because you blame us. You do know that's what you're doing, right? You're taking her life into your own hands. A kid from the suburbs of Virginia, putting his girlfriend's life in his untrained hands because he has something to prove. If you know something that can save her, tell us what it is and let us save her."

"You had your chance," is all that came out of the speaker. "You had your chance. You failed."

And the line went dead.

* * *

Luke held the cell phone in a hand that shook.

Jaxon and Victoria had gotten to him even if he had ultimately refused to help them. He was feeling unsure of his actions and his resolve felt weakened. He stared out the window into the dark night and talked to her.

"Ellie—I don't know what to do. I'm sorry! I miss you so much. Please—tell me what to do."

He slammed his fist into the wall and hot tears burst from his eyes. Of course, no answer came to him and he stood staring into the black void beyond the window and let his sorrow overtake him. He heard someone come into the room and he got himself under control. Just then a musical chime played from somewhere in the house. Luke had never heard it before.

"Luke!" Jimmy yelled. "His phone just turned on!"

CHAPTER 56

"This could help us," Jaxon said.

"How?" Victoria asked, the cell phone in her hand, silent after Luke Harrison hung up on them.

"We can use his own tool to help us."

She looked at him.

"What are you talking about?"

"We'll get the software that he gave us and track his own cell phone with it. When he goes after Worthington, we'll follow him to the spot and take it from there."

She smiled and then frowned.

"How will we keep Luke out of it?"

"He's made his own bed. Now he'll have to lie in it."

"That's not fair," she said. "We helped make that bed and now we're going to just abandon him to chance? We can't do that."

Jaxon knew she was right.

The kid was only acting this way because he and Vick had dropped the ball.

"What the hell do we do?" he asked. "We need him to lead us to Worthington."

She nodded, thinking.

"We need to beat him to Worthington."

"That would take being a mind reader. We wouldn't need Luke and his software if we knew where the asshole was."

"Maybe we'll be able to guess."

"Big risk."

"Any better ideas?"

He shook his head.

"Let's go to the Hoover building and get the laptop. We'll grab it and wait with it in Luke's neighborhood so we'll be right on his tail. Just in case."

She looked into his eyes and grabbed his arm.

"He's not going to win."

"You don't have to give me a pep talk, Vick."

"Maybe I need one," she said and smiled.

He squeezed her hand and smiled back.

"Come on."

CHAPTER 57

Worthington's phone was on, but he wasn't moving.

Luke, Jimmy, and John had all been watching the blip for the last hour. It sat stationary on I-495 near Tyson's Corner. It wasn't a house or hotel, just some random spot on the interstate.

"Maybe he parked the car and left the phone to lead us away." Jimmy said.

"Are you sure you have the right phone number?" John said.

"Yes," Luke said. "Bodey told me how to work the software and I watched Q use it too. The numbers that came up were just like when Q did it. He's waiting for something."

"Let's go to him," Jimmy said.

"Not yet," Luke said.

He wasn't convinced Worthington meant to stay there. He would wait until they watched him move to a house or some other place they could approach without him knowing it.

His cell phone rang and Luke picked it up. He looked at Jimmy and John and they knew what he knew. Worthington.

"Hello."

A deep voice, not the electronically altered irritation Luke had heard before, came over the speaker.

"Where are you?" he said, mockingly. "I've been waiting for you and you haven't shown up."

This voice, though normal, was somehow worse than the other one. This voice was human and Luke couldn't seem to link it to anything human at all. The man was a monster and it bothered Luke that the monster could sound so normal.

"Is she all right?" was all he managed to get out.

"Listen."

Luke heard rustling and then a moan. Then her voice, sleepy, as if he was trying to wake her and she didn't want to wake up.

"No. I don't want to eat," she mumbled. "You can't make me," and her voice trailed off. The relief he felt was so great, he almost started to cry. Worthington stopped that.

"She won't be alive much longer," he said. "You'd better hurry."

"Don't touch her! I swear I'll..."

"You'll what!" he shouted. It made Luke jump. "I don't see you here! I doubt you have it in you to even find me much less stop me. Bring it on, kid! Bring it on!"

The line went dead.

"He's moving," John said.

* * *

Jaxon and Victoria sat in his car two blocks from the Harrison house.

They were right by the pool complex with the laptop open and the tracking software running. So far, the Harrison boy was still in his house.

"You don't think he left his phone at home, do you?" Victoria asked.

"I doubt it. Kids don't go anywhere without them nowadays."

"Still, what if he did?"

"We're screwed."

She sat silent for a moment and he knew her wheels were spinning. They had been spinning since they left the Hoover building.

"What are you thinking?"

"About the pictures," she said.

"What about them?"

"They bother me."

"They bother me too, but we found his clue. He made it easy."

"We're missing something."

"We're missing a lot."

She gave him a look and he turned away. The Harrison kid was still there.

"Why all the family shots? Why show us how his life was when he was with them?"

"Maybe he liked them."

"Then why did he leave them for us?"

"He wanted to show me how I ruined his life."

"Could be," she said, but he could tell she didn't believe that. "Or, he wanted us to see his house."

"But we already know he lived there. That's common knowledge. I've been there before and hell, I almost removed him from it."

"But his house was in every picture," she said, turning to him.

He thought about this and a little tumbler fell into place. Click. He jerked back to her and she was smiling.

"Every picture," she said again.

"Shit!"

Just then he noticed Harrison's cell phone moving. He pointed to it and she said, "He's on the move! He must be on foot because he's not moving very fast."

"It has to be the house!"

"Let's go!"

CHAPTER 58

Ellie woke from the nightmare and shook herself awake.

She had been having a horrible dream, but when she saw where she was, relief washed over her. It was all just a nightmare. Her kidnapping at the hands of her father had all been a dream.

She looked around her basement and wondered why she had fallen asleep down here. The TV was off so her mother must have done it. She went to get up, but couldn't move.

She was tied to the chair.

Suddenly, she knew it had not been a dream. Her nightmare was real and she was still living it. She struggled in the chair, panicking, but it was useless.

Her hands were tied behind her and her feet bound to the legs of the chair. She stopped, hearing a noise and realizing someone was behind her. Twisting around, she could see blond hair in her peripheral vision, but nothing else. The person behind her was unmoving.

"Hey," she said. "Hey! Wake up!"

A moan escaped the person behind her and she recognized the timber of the voice.

Patrick!

"Patrick! Wake up! Come on! Patrick!"

He moaned again but did not wake. She heard voices coming from above now, and she recognized one as her mother's. She listened quietly, because she could tell the other was her father. Her mother's voice was high pitched and getting louder and then she heard a slap followed by her mother screaming. She panicked.

"Leave her alone! Leave her alone!"

She scooted in the chair, trying to move, but she must be tied to the chair her brother was in and he was a big kid. The chair barely moved.

"Come on Patrick! Wake up! Wake up!"

Tears were falling down her cheeks and she was rocking the chair front to back trying to get him to respond, but he was passed out. The shouting above her grew louder and then she heard a loud thump and her mother's voice suddenly cut off. Silence.

"Oh no!" she whispered. "You bastard! Leave her alone! Leave her alone! Bastard! Bastard!"

* * *

Luke went to the meter box and pulled the switch.

He watched the lights go out in the living room. John was out back in the woods and Jimmy was across the street in some bushes in case Worthington made a run for it. Luke was going in alone.

The fear he felt was a crushing force that threatened to suffocate him and render him useless. He kept telling himself Ellie was going through worse and had been for two days. She needed him to be strong. Needed him to rescue her. Needed him to be her savior. He took a few deep breaths and moved. If he kept moving, he wouldn't freeze up.

He crept to the basement sliding glass door and peered inside. What he saw surprised him. Patrick Pemberton was facing the glass, his head down, his feet tied to the chair he was in and his arms wrapped behind him. He was not moving. Then he saw movement just behind Patrick and Ellie's head came into view. He gasped and felt elated. She was alive!

He quickly moved to the door handle and pulled. It was unlocked and he slid the door open quietly and slipped inside. The basement was dark and the outer edges of the room in shadow since he had killed the electricity. He could see Ellie and her brother from the dim light through the sliding glass door.

"Ellie!" he whispered and he saw her head jerk up.

"Luke? No! Get out of here! He's in the…"

A huge blast sounded in Luke's head and he was flung back against the glass by an invisible truck.

He sank to the floor, the air sucked from his lungs and he looked around not understanding what had happened. Faintly, he heard Ellie's voice as if coming through a fog.

"No! No! No!"

He watched a big shadow emerge from the gloom, a pistol leading the way as the rest of the huge man followed, grinning behind it. Then the pain hit him and Luke realized he'd been shot.

* * *

Jaxon was standing at the front door, his pistol out and up.

He had sent Victoria around back and he waited the full minute they had agreed upon to enter the house. A gunshot sounded and Jaxon decided he couldn't wait any longer. He kicked the door in and burst through it, his gun leading the way, but he found nothing but darkness and silence.

Then he heard Ellie's voice from somewhere deep in the house wailing 'No!' over and over again and it broke his heart. He knew Luke was around here somewhere, but they had not been able to beat the kid to the house.

He ran to the kitchen and tripped over something in the doorway. Slamming his shin into a chair he cursed and sat up, feeling for his gun. He found Madison Pemberton instead. Leaning in close, he could just make out her open eyes and the dark mass of blood which surrounded her upper body. He realized he was kneeling in it. Her throat had been cut and she was dead.

More wailing from Ellie, and Jaxon felt around until his hand struck his pistol. He snatched it up and jumped to the basement door. As he opened it slowly, Ellie's sobs grew louder but no other sound could be heard. He knew Worthington was down there.

He crept down into the darkness and reached the bottom landing without feeling a bullet hit him. He pushed the thought out of his mind. Turning into the room, he tried to see into the gloom. His eyes adjusted just enough for him to make out Ellie tied to a chair and crying.

Another figure was bound behind her, though it did not move or make a sound. He saw another shape slumped against one half of an open sliding glass door and heard a wet rasping sound as if someone was breathing through a damp rag. He realized it was Luke Harrison.

Movement in front of Luke caused him to jerk as a huge silhouette emerged from the left, backlit by the moonlight shining in through the door. Someone was struggling in its arms.

"Drop it, Detective."

The voice was Worthington.

He moved away from the door and the light shone onto Victoria's face. He was holding a pistol to her head and she was struggling feebly against him. He jerked her in his arms and she stopped fighting. She must not have waited the full minute either.

"Let the kids go," Jaxon said. "This is about you and me."

"Now, why would I do that? I've finally gotten to know them."

Ellie cried softly now, and Luke's breathing was getting worse. The ragged sound grew louder by the second and Jaxon knew he didn't have much time.

"I'll put it down if you let them go," Jaxon said.

"No!" The voice boomed in the room. Ellie squealed and started sobbing harder. Victoria remained still.

"I'm not putting the weapon down," Jaxon said.

"Fine. Then die."

Worthington pointed the pistol at Jaxon and fired.

It was like being struck with a fire hydrant. His shoulder jerked back, the gun flying from his hand, and he was flung against the wall like a rag doll. The blast from Worthington's gun shook the air like a cannon going off in confined quarters.

There was no pain. Just a feeling of weakness, as if someone was letting the air out his body. He was deflating like a tire and could no longer stand. He slumped to a sitting position and watched as Worthington struck Victoria in the head with his gun, her body slumping to the ground and then he strode over to Jaxon, kicking his gun out of the way and picking him up like he weighed nothing. The man grinned into Jaxon's face.

"You took my family from me," he said through clenched teeth and Jaxon could smell his sour breath. "Now, I will finish taking yours and then take your life."

He turned and fired the gun into Victoria's prone body.

Jaxon moaned as he watched it jerk and then lay still. He had lost again. The bastard had beaten him and taken everything that mattered to him.

A pain flared in his shoulder. Ice and fire screaming into his back and neck, and he welcomed it. It was like a jolt of electricity, jumpstarting his heart. He embraced the pain, moving his shoulder and creating more, a molten hot spike striking the core of his body. It made him angry, and angry was good.

Worthington was leering at Victoria, watching his handy work drain the life from her.

Jaxon's pain grew to a growling, menacing thing and it made his body tremble from the power of it. Worthington felt Jaxon shake and turned back to him.

That's when he struck.

Thrusting his head back and then launching it forward, he struck Worthington in the face with his forehead, a loud crunching noise echoing through the room as his nose was crushed from the blow.

Jaxon brought his knee up into his groin and Worthington bent over double, the gun dropping from his hand and Jaxon breaking free.

As Worthington was going down, Jaxon brought both hands up, his shoulder screaming in protest, but it only spurred him on.

He brought both fists down on Worthington's neck. Once. Twice. Three times, but the slab of meat that he was refused to go down. On the fourth strike, Worthington moved his head, and Jaxon's locked fists struck his skull and he felt the bones in his hand shatter.

Worthington got to his feet and launched a blow to Jaxon's abdomen that lifted him off his feet. The world spun and he felt his energy leave him. He sagged to the ground, but Worthington picked him up and pinned him to the wall, striking blow after blow to his body, his face, his ribs. Jaxon was losing consciousness and he knew he couldn't hold on much longer.

A cannon went off in the room, and Jaxon's world blazed in pain again. He had been shot again and felt the searing pain in his arm, bringing him back around. He looked into Worthington's eyes and watched in amazement as the life leaked out of them. Worthington sank to the floor in front of him.

Jaxon looked up to see Ellie holding a gun pointed at him, her face a mask of pain and sorrow. She sobbed uncontrollably, then dropped the gun and ran to Luke. Jaxon sank to the floor as one of the Besner boys ran in through the door holding a rifle in his hands.

"Call 911!" Ellie screamed as Jaxon blacked out, her cries following him into the darkness.

"Don't die! Don't die! Come on Luke! Don't die!"

Epilogue

Jaxon's hands were slowly healing.

It hadn't been the shoulder or the arm causing him the most pain. Those two were nothing compared to the helplessness and pain he felt trying to do simple everyday tasks like picking up a piece of paper. The bones in his wrists had been shattered and he had two surgeries to get them back in shape. Physical therapy every day afterward had given him a new respect for the word pain. If he could have, he would have punched every one of the therapists directly in the face.

Victoria hobbled in from the kitchen and set down a glass of tea in front of him. The straw sticking out made him smile.

"You know I'm supposed to be practicing picking stuff up," he said.

"Take a break," she said and bent over, giving him a kiss on the top of his head.

"Besides," he said. "I'm supposed to be waiting on you."

She sat in the chair next to him.

"You can't even wipe your own ass."

"Yes I can. Just not the way you think."

"I don't even want to know."

She set the cane she was using down next to her and grabbed his swollen hand. It was sore, but he didn't care. Her touch was all that mattered.

"Benton called again," she said.

"I don't want to talk to him."

"That's what I told him." She paused. "He wanted to give you a new offer."

"Not interested."

"That's what I told him."

"What was it? Just curious."

She smiled and told him.

"Not good enough," he said.

"How long are you going to let him beg you?"

"Couple more weeks."

She nodded.

"You know he may just stop offering."

He turned to her and looked into her eyes. He couldn't seem to get the vision of her lying in that basement out of his head. She must have read his mind again and she smiled.

"I'm ok," she said.

"Yeah—I know."

"Call him back."

He thought about it a few seconds and then leaned forward and took a sip of his tea through the straw.

"Soon," he said.

But he doubted he would.

* * *

Ellie sat in the swing in her backyard and rocked slowly back and forth.

Her grandmother was inside, but was not coping well with the death of her daughter. Having her here only reminded Ellie of the loss she felt every day.

A single tear trickled down her cheek and she turned to the setting sun feeling the warmth on her face as the cool autumn air chilled the rest of her. She would never be the same.

A hand on her shoulder startled her out of her thoughts and she jumped.

Luke sat down next to her and said, "Sorry, El. I didn't mean to scare you."

She leaned against him and rested her head on his shoulder as he pulled her to him stroking her hair with his fingers like he always did. She relaxed in his arms and she felt a little better.

Her mother's death had been something she could not bear and no matter how many times she went through it in her mind, she could not stop feeling guilty about letting her die.

If only she had been able to get free just a little sooner, she would have been able to save her too. She had horrible nightmares about her father killing her mother, and she woke almost every night crying out in terror as she heard her die over and over again, the muffled cries and thumps of her death replayed in her dreams. She shivered.

"Let's go in," Luke said and she nodded.

They walked hand in hand to the back door and Luke struggled to slide it open for her. She joked about how his strength was coming back after his gunshot wound, and he laughed with her, telling her he wouldn't be a wimp for too much longer. She closed the door for him and they went to the couch and sat.

"I'm still freezing," she said. "I'm going to go and get a blanket."

He turned the TV on as she got up to go to her room. The blanket she wanted was not where it was supposed to be and she sighed knowing that Patrick had probably taken it. He took it out of her room as if he owned it.

She went to his room and sure enough, it was thrown over his chair in a heap. She grabbed the blanket and a metallic clunk hit the floor. She gasped. As she bent over, his computer caught her eye.

It was open to Facebook and she looked over his wall posts, glancing at his friends list. A name she saw caused her to take a quick breath. She clicked on it and stared in disbelief at the conversation that had gone on for months between him and William Smith. The world seemed to vibrate as she read the first post to her dead father's alias. It was in response to the picture of Bentley's head her father had sent him.

'What was it like?' Patrick had asked.

Her father had responded, 'Like being born.'

* * *

Luke wondered why Ellie was taking so long and he was just about to get up when Patrick stepped into the room and stood in front of the TV.

"Hey, Patrick," Luke said. "I didn't hear you, man. You're silent as a ghost."

Patrick didn't smile and Luke wondered if he had been doing any better. Patrick, though older, had seemed to take the death of his mother the hardest. He had barely spoken to him since that night and Ellie had said the therapy they were both receiving hadn't seemed to help him.

"Doing all right, buddy?" Luke asked.

"I'm not your buddy."

Luke frowned and wasn't quite sure how to respond to him. He gave it his best shot.

"Well, I consider you a friend," Luke said.

"You're the enemy," Patrick said and brought his arm up. It held a pistol and Luke froze as the eye of the barrel came level with his own eyes. It was like staring into a bottomless cavern.

"Whoa! Dude, what's the deal?"

"You killed my father."

"Patrick, your father was a whack job, you know…"

"Shut up! He was a great man!"

Luke actually flinched at Patrick's booming voice. It reminded him of Worthington's.

"Easy, dude. All right, he was a great man."

"Now, you're mocking him," Patrick said and thrust the gun closer emphasizing his words. "He lived like no one else. He was a god."

"Ok, I believe you. Whatever you say."

"He taught me to grow like him. To be a man. To live beyond this life and take life as my own."

"You're scaring me dude."

"You should be," Patrick said, smiling now. "You'll be *my* first."

Luke felt the world slip from his grasp.

He knew in his heart that he was going to die. The room seemed too bright, and the TV too loud, and he couldn't seem to make himself move. The eye of the gun hypnotized him and he waited for the blast, knowing it would be quick. When it came, he was surprised how little he felt.

Then he watched a bright red spot bloom on Patrick's chest and his eyes roll back into his head as he sagged to the floor. Turning, he saw Ellie standing at the bottom of the stairs, the gun wavering in her hand, tears streaming down her face as she slumped to the step, dropping the gun to the floor where it lay smoking in front of her.

He went to her and took her in his arms, rocking her there as she clung to him, sobbing.

ABOUT THE AUTHOR

Richard C Hale has worn many hats in his lifetime including Greens Keeper, Bartender, Musician, Respiratory Therapist, and veteran Air Traffic Controller. You can usually find him controlling Air Traffic over the skies of the Southeastern U.S. where he lives with his wife and children.

Drop by his website and give him a shout. He'd love to hear from you.

www.richardchaleauthor.com

Made in the USA
San Bernardino, CA
15 May 2017